Splinters of Truth

Splinters of Truth

Storm Constantine

NewCon Press
England

First edition, published in the UK April 2016
by NewCon Press

NCP89 (hardback)
NCP90 (paperback)

10 9 8 7 6 5 4 3 2 1

Contents

Introduction by Ian Whates 7

Author's Foreword 9

Return to Gehenna 11

Violet's House, or Songs the Martyrs Sang 31

Do As Thou Wilt 55

They Hunt 73

The Order of the Scales 75

Kiss Booties Night Night 97

Colin's Cough 115

Spirit of Place 133

The Fool's Path 141

Haven 155

The Farmer's Bride 173

Fireborn 197

Just His Type 213

A Tour of the House 233

When the Angels Came 261

About the Author 269

Splinters of Truth

An Introduction

In her introductory comments to "Return to Gehenna", the opening story in this collection, Storm says of herself: *"I've never lived a particularly ordinary life. While a sociable creature, I've also always felt myself to be an Outsider."* This comment offers insight into a recurring aspect of Storm's writing – perhaps not overt enough to merit being called a 'theme', but it's often there, bubbling just beneath the surface. In some of her stories the protagonist is quite clearly the 'Outsider', existing in a situation where they don't quite fit, struggling to fulfil a role defined by society or their contemporaries for which they are temperamentally unsuited. In others the alienation is more subtle. In either case this inability to conform, and the frustration that results, provide fertile ground for tension and drama, helping to propel the narrative forward.

One of Storm's greatest assets as a writer is her ability to draw rounded, believable characters that the reader instantly empathises with. As a consequence, she can conjure fantastical settings such as those we find in "Order of the Scales" and "Fireborn" and make them wholly believable, because we invest in the characters that populate them. Likewise she can depict a world that is comfortably familiar and inhabited by folk we recognise, people who might almost be our neighbours, and then subtly shift reality so that we find ourselves slipping sideways into the shadows without even realising, tipping into realms of mystery and magic. In "Colin's Cough" we are introduced to a relative that the family tolerates without ever making the effort to understand, in "Violet's House or Songs the Martyrs Sang" we experience the angst and hurt of shattered friendship and imagined betrayal as three adolescents progress into adulthood at differing rates. The awkwardness and the pain in these stories are powerful in their own right, but the author skilfully shades each sufficiently to add a whole new dimension. In "The Fool's Path", a cautionary tale set around the bar at a theatre, the shading is darker still.

If characterisation is one of Storm's fortes as a writer, it is a quality that springs from one of her greatest strengths as a person. I've been privileged enough to know Storm and work with her for many years, and something that never ceases to impress me is her generosity of spirit. Rarely have I encountered an individual more willing to invest their time and abilities to assist and support others. There is a warmth inherent in Storm as a person that manifests in her work, so that even in the darkest of shadows she might cast upon the page you will find a sense of optimism to guide you back towards the light. Rarely is this more apparent than in "A Tour of the House," a tale set in Storm's iconic and ground-breaking Wraeththu milieu, in which long-standing enmities are acknowledged so that all concerned might move forward and face the future with renewed optimism.

Storm Constantine is a writer of dark corners that harbour the spark of hope, and it is this, as much as anything, that makes reading her fiction such a joy. Long may such sparks be kindled.

Ian Whates
Cambridgeshire
November 2015

Author's Foreword

Authors are magpies. Whatever we see, hear, experience, feel, taste or smell is a glittery thing to be hoarded away – all of it stored in the vast bio-computer of our brains. Sometimes only small chips of these collectings find their way into stories, evanescent as dreams. Other times a tale is influenced strongly by one particular event, one particular person. As a writer, my instinct is to embellish, dramatize and enhance the sparkling story fragments I come across in life – to scramble the glittering jewels together and create an ever more shimmering artefact from the parts.

Any writer is often asked 'where do your ideas come from?' and I hope this collection goes some way to answering that. The truth is, the ideas come from everywhere – even you who asked the question! Inspiration can shiver in the slant of evening light across a landscape, in a fragment of overhead conversation, a feeling in a room, in an expression exchanged between two people who do not know they are being watched. A sound in the dark. Stories woven into music that are created anew in each listener. Ideas can be conjured by films, by the work of other writers, by an article in a newspaper or a magazine. Writers continually ask themselves: what if? And stories are our response to that perennially intriguing question.

A lot of my short stories derive from anecdotes my friends tell me – strange things that happened to them, or how their hearts were broken. No two heart-breaks are ever the same. These precious words often form the basis of a tale, but always only that. I take the treasures and get to work with the 'what if?' engine.

The stories in *Splinters of Truth* are just that – tales born from real life but transformed into dreams.

Storm Constantine
November 2015

Return to Gehenna

I've never lived a particularly ordinary life. While a sociable creature, I've also always felt myself to be an Outsider. Sleep-walkers and sheep, and their ridiculous notions, often grated on my nerves, especially when I was younger. After a truncated art school education, and an impatience with academia and its language of estrangement, I drifted into office jobs, simply to earn money and live the life I wanted outside this dreary nine-to-five existence. But sometimes, I'd daydream during working hours, scribbling drawings of supernatural creatures, writing poems and ideas for stories. No one else I worked with shared my interests or my view of the world, but I found myself wondering what it would be like if one of the sleepers woke up. I also wondered why I was so different to everyone with whom I worked, and why they were so blind to the wonder of life that blazed outside the office walls.

I didn't write this story until many years after I'd been fortunate enough to abandon the day jobs. But I remembered the feelings well.

She didn't know how she'd caught the awareness. Perhaps she'd walked through an infected area one night, when she'd been drunk, and hadn't felt its presence. Or, it could have been coughed onto her by someone. Maybe. Perhaps its spore had impregnated itself into a piece of paper she'd handled at work. She hated work. Wouldn't it have come for her there? Work was hell.

It was hard to pinpoint exactly when the awareness had started, and whether the incident that occurred on the dead-skied Tuesday had actually been the first or not, but it was the first that Lucy could remember.

'Hell is not a place, it is a state of mind.' So said Dolores, who occupied the desk opposite Lucy's.

Lucy had just kicked herself backwards across the floor on her swivel chair, having announced, 'This place is hell.' Her work bored her rigid; the company sold insurance.

Dolores, with her long pink nails, which Lucy suspected were false, liked work. She had double chins, and a strangely slow tongue that reminded Lucy of a parrot's. It was pointed and narrow, and peered out without speed to lick the sticky parts of envelopes like a questing blind worm. Dolores disapproved of what she saw as Lucy's lazy temperament and streak of rebellion. Everyone had to work, so why not do your best? To help fulfil this urge, Dolores made copious cups of tea for the boss – a mangy non-entity, who smelled salty – and grovelled before the boss's wife whenever she called into the office. The boss's wife was vague and always seemed slightly surprised, unnerved by the obsequious Dolores. Lucy could not imagine that all of these drab people had a life beyond the office walls.

Lucy hated Dolores' smug piety more than she hated the job, but if she didn't get on with the woman, life there would be unendurable, since there were only the two of them and the boss didn't count. She also suspected that Dolores was quite capable of losing her her job, if she felt riled enough, but fortunately the woman made an effort to excel at being kind. Dolores was just too good; perhaps it was why she looked so poisoned and bloated.

'You make life so hard for yourself,' Dolores said. She was filled to the brim with platitudes and sayings that advised on how to exist nicely and properly. Niceness and properness were concepts that filled Lucy with dread. She felt she had somehow been cut adrift from the life she was supposed to have had and become marooned here, eking out a living in a nine-to-five job that barely paid for her small apartment. It wasn't as if she could get a better job, with her lack of qualifications. Sometimes, she wished she'd done something with herself at school, or perhaps later, but in her early twenties all she'd wanted to do was party. Now, on the cusp of thirty, all her wild friends had turned suspiciously into people who wanted children and normality. Somehow, without Lucy noticing, they had acquired degrees or training that ended in certificates. They had deceived her; they were not the people she'd believed them to be. If they did come out for an evening, they talked about what their kids did, or joked about wall-paper. Lucy's horror had reached its height when she'd spotted a set of golf clubs in the boot of a car belonging to a man who had once sold drugs in the shadowed corner of the local student bar and whose hair had been long. Lucy's old friends were all sailing away from her and she could only wave sadly at their departure. Recently, she had half-heartedly made newer, younger friends, who were happy to go out whenever they could afford it, but they seemed shallow in comparison to the memories of her youth; they had no opinions and no fire. They were too interested in money.

'I've woken up in the wrong life,' Lucy told Dolores. 'But I can't remember when it happened.'

Dolores smiled in gentle disbelief and shook her head. 'Really, Lucy, I think you enjoy being miserable. You're an attractive girl. What's the matter with you?'

'I'm not a *girl*,' Lucy said, slouching backwards in her seat like a relaxing puppet, arms hanging down to either side. 'If I was, it might not be so bad. I'd have time to change things.' She could see from Dolores' quick, bright glance that the woman was longing to tell her to sit up straight.

'Have you done the filing?' she said instead.

It was dark at five o'clock when Lucy left the office, leaving Dolores to fuss around (unpaid) for an extra fifteen minutes before locking up. Outside, the air was cold and damp with invisible rain, and sound seemed muted. Soon, the nights would be drawing out; Lucy looked forward to spring. This year, the winter seemed to have been going on forever. In the mornings, she hated leaving for work in the dark and then having to come home in it again at night. Lucy preferred heat, raging heat and blistering light. Was it feasible to emigrate to a warmer country when she had no money and no training?

Lucy hurried to the bus stop, intent only on getting home, where she could shut out the night. Just as she was rounding the corner, she saw the bus coming toward her, having already drawn away from the stop.

'Damn!' She threw up her arms and waved frantically at the driver, but he ignored her. Greenish faces peered down at her in mild curiosity through the passengers' windows.

'Damn!' Lucy glanced at her watch. Since when had the bus been early? It was supposed to leave at ten past five, and she could see it was still only five past. Usually, she had to stand there waiting, getting progressively more annoyed. Living on the outskirts of town as she did, she wouldn't be able to catch another direct route bus for at least half an hour. Half an hour of standing in the depressing drizzle of a late January evening. She didn't have enough money for a cab; it was too near the end of the month when her bank account tended to dry up, or rather her overdraft did. She considered approaching a cash dispenser in the hope of invoking money, but knew her prospects of success were bleak, and it would take her at least five minutes to reach the machine in the square. She might as well walk home. If she walked briskly, it would take only twenty-five minutes.

Her shoes weren't made for walking; they leaked. Lucy cursed the fact she had forgotten about that before she'd started off. As she walked, it seemed the dreary town shimmered in a mist, but the effect was not beautiful. Cars and buses hissed along the main road, throwing up dirty spray. People hurried along with their heads down through the garish gouts of radiance thrown out by shop-fronts. The puddles of light on the floor seemed muzzy at the edges, as if Lucy's vision were blurring. She blinked, cleared her eyes. *Perhaps I am crying*, she thought, subsequently wondering why she felt so numb.

She turned into the narrow street, Victoria Terrace, which provided a short-cut back to Carlisle Avenue where she lived. Normally, she would take the long way round, as the terrace led to silent, dim-lit areas, where her heart would beat faster and her ears strain to detect threatening sounds. Tonight, she assured herself that at this time of day there could be little danger, and there wasn't. The danger came from inside her.

Lucy knew the area well. On the boss's birthday, she and Dolores would accompany him to one of the many, small Chinese restaurants that lined the street, where he would pay magnanimously for a very mediocre meal. Further down, was the sandwich shop where Lucy went to buy her lunch. Acknowledging the landmarks of restaurant and shop, Lucy considered that her life had become narrow and its horizons were contracting all the time. Atoms of herself must be left on this street that she traversed so regularly. When she died, her ghost might haunt it.

Reaching the end of the Victoria Terrace, Lucy turned left. The street-lights here were few and far between, and high, narrow three-storied terraced houses of grey stone huddled together on either side of the road.

Lucy hesitated at the corner. She had walked down this street hundreds of times before, yet this time, on this cold, dark Tuesday, it was not the same. Normally, Lucy would see a row of terraced cottages – once cream, now soot-drenched, on one side of the road – while on the other, a line of shops, most of which were boarded up and abandoned, with litter in their porches. This street of tall, grey houses she had never seen before.

I have been day-dreaming, she reasoned, *I have taken a wrong turn.* Looking back up Victoria Terrace, she realised the thought itself was folly. The only intersection was halfway up and she could see it from where she stood.

Lucy's first instinct was to retreat, take the long way home, even return to the main road and wait for a bus, because this couldn't be happening. She must have gone mad, but in a moment of total disorientation she found herself wondering if the street had always looked this way, and it was her memory that was faulty. Now that she thought about it, could she really swear the street had been lined with shops and dirty cream houses? Perhaps she was thinking of another street.

But I have never been here before...

The scene was utterly still; no lights burned in the tall, crowded buildings. At the far end of the road a massive edifice reared up, like an ancient factory or a prison. Its severe outline spoke of despair.

Without thinking, Lucy began to walk up the centre of the road. Looking up, she could see the sky was no more than a narrow, grey-orange band between the looming roofs. She did not feel afraid, only rather insubstantial, as if she too could blink out of existence at any time.

Her feet made a dull sound upon the tarmac, and the sounds of traffic seemed to fade away. *I should turn back*, Lucy thought. *Where am I going?* She thought she could hear faint music, lively and staccato, but when she strained to hear it properly, it died away. Perhaps the sound existed only in her mind.

The huge building at the end of street was growing larger before her. It might be a mental institution or a temple to a dark god. No, it was a factory. People toiled there.

A movement on the road ahead caught her attention. She saw what appeared to be a thin skein of smoke twisting in the air, close to the ground. As she approached, this perplexity resolved itself into a crumpled piece of paper, fretted by ground-level breezes. Closer still, and Lucy saw, with surprised disbelief, that the paper was in fact a fifty pound note. After looking around herself to check for owners of the note, and finding none, she picked it up.

Strangely enough, the note was dry. Someone must have dropped it very recently. Lucy looked up. Perhaps it had fallen from an open window, or even from an aircraft. She had heard of how human waste, and even dogs, had been known to plummet from the sky to splatter unsuspecting victims below. She did not object to being the victim of such a relatively large amount of money.

A noise now caught her attention, and she moved her perception from the magical note to the side of the road. Dim, crimson beams of light spilled from an open doorway, illuminating the wet sidewalk. The door apparently led into a bar of some kind; above its lintel a bottle shaped from pink neon tubes glowed and buzzed, two cocktail glasses winking in and out of existence beside it. Lucy was sure that moments earlier there had been no crimson light, no neon display and no bar. She smiled to herself as a foolish thought came to her: it was almost as if finding the money had somehow prompted the doorway to spring into being. Didn't she crave for excitement in her life? What further nudging did she need? Lucy approached the open doorway, the money still held in her hand.

Inside, the bar was very dark, its air filled with what sounded like live, jazzy piano music, although she could see no piano. Its decor was shabby but somehow alluring; shredding red plush and pink and red lamp-light. At first glance, she could perceive no patrons other than herself. There was a smell of stale beer and tobacco smoke, beneath which lurked an odour of hamburger and onions. Lucy approached the bar itself, although there did not appear to be anyone on duty there. A tall, oblong spill of yellow light, which interrupted the gleaming shelves and mirrors behind the bar, indicated an open doorway, which perhaps led to a kitchen. Lucy leaned on the polished counter. She could buy anything she fancied; the thought of a whole bottle of wine was attractive. Then she could sit at one of the shadowy tables, alone with a bottle and a glass, kick off her wet shoes and drink for an hour or so. Normally, Lucy would not feel comfortable doing any such thing, but she felt she had somehow stepped into an enchanted pocket of time and space, and the opportunity should not be wasted.

As a woman came through from the brightly lit area, it seemed a shadow had been conjured into being at the end of the bar. Lucy could see now that she was not the only patron, for a thin-faced man in a heavy, dark coat sat hunch-shouldered on a stool, half turned toward her. He did not look up, but stared into a tumbler of amber liquid around which he had cupped his hands, although his fingers did not touch the glass. The bar-tender, who wore a bright red blouse of shiny material came to stand in front of Lucy. Lucy looked up at her. The woman had a tired face, yet her eyes were unusually bright, almost as if a more vivacious creature were trapped within the listless flesh. 'A bottle of wine, house red will do,' said Lucy.

'We don't serve wine.' The woman's mouth barely moved, although her eyes darted quickly to left and right; it seemed to be a tic.

'Beer?'

'No beer.'

Lucy peered past the woman at the shelves behind her. They were filled with a startling array of weirdly-shaped bottles, which all looked as if they contained liqueurs. 'What do you recommend?' Lucy asked. She did not recognise the names on any of the bottles: Ogerond, Betwixtit, Tegammera.

The woman shrugged. 'What's your favourite colour?'

'Black,' Lucy responded, to be awkward.

Without changing expression, the woman reached behind herself and produced a tall, dark bottle. From this, she measured a small amount of what appeared to be black ink into a glass that resembled a miniature champagne flute. 'Two pounds.'

'I've only this. Sorry.' Lucy handed over the fifty pound note, eyeing the strange little glass before her with caution.

The woman took the note from her, but did not hold it up to the light for inspection as most people would. She sniffed it. Perhaps there were many ways to check for forgeries.

While she busied herself with sorting out change at the till, Lucy lifted the little glass and sniffed its contents 'What is this?' It smelled highly alcoholic and faintly of coffee, but also of molasses, and perhaps spoiled milk.

'A drop of black, as you asked for.' The woman handed her a bundle of notes and coins.

Lucy did not bother to check her change. She stuffed it all into her bag. 'But what's it called?'

'Axings,' replied the woman. She went back toward the oblong of yellow light, and was swallowed by it.

At this point, Lucy considered that she might actually be

dreaming, and would soon be awoken by her alarm clock, nagging her into another pointless day's boredom at the office. She knew it was possible to be aware that you were dreaming while you were doing so. If that was the case, she would enjoy it. Anything was possible, surely, in a dream? She took a sip from the tiny glass. It was difficult. She felt like Alice in Wonderland; a giant of a girl trying to drink from a doll's glass. Perhaps the liquid in it *was* ink. The liquor stung her tongue, but its taste was that of fear of the dark, of untraveled roads, of seduction. Astonished, Lucy put down the glass. How could such things have tastes? 'Surreal!' she said aloud.

'A distillation of feeling.' The voice came from further down the bar, from the mouth of the thin-faced man.

Lucy looked at him. He was handsome in a gaunt sort of way. 'What?'

He raised his glass to her. 'Curiosity or fear?' The words sounded like a toast.

Lucy suddenly became uneasy. She felt the bar had filled up behind her, for she could sense pressing bodies, but when she looked around, it was still empty. Nervously, she took another sip of the drink, braced herself against the strange sensations its taste conjured in her mind. She felt the thin-faced man's scrutiny, the oppression of invisible bodies behind her. Whatever she looked at appeared stretched, as if it might break apart at any time. She glanced down at the diminutive glass held between in the fingers of her left hand. It seemed she had made no impression on the contents. *I must not finish what I started...*

Not knowing why she thought that, Lucy found herself at the door. She could not remember having walked away from the bar. Looking back once as she stepped out into the night, she saw the bartender had come back into the room and was standing next to the thin-faced man. Both of them were looking at her with expressionless faces. Her glass stood where she had left it, only something small and scurrying seemed to be moving swiftly away from it. Lucy went out into the street.

She felt disorientated, not frightened but confused, and staggered down the street for a few yards. *Where am I going? I should go back the way I came.* Her head was swimming. As she looked up, the world spun before her eyes. *Can I be drunk from one sip of the black?* Her vision cleared and, when it did, she fell back against the wall of a house behind her.

The street appeared as it always had; drab little cottages, once clean, now soot-drenched; a row of worn-out shops. The sound of traffic murmured distantly from the main road hidden by a huddle of decaying buildings. She heard a siren and the hoot of an angry horn.

'No!' Nausea came suddenly, and she had to double-up to vomit onto the sidewalk. It looked like blood; black in the street-light, but immediately after the spasm had passed, she felt better, normal.

At home, Lucy turned on all the lights, and emptied the contents of her bag onto the tiny Formica-topped table in her kitchenette. A tide of paper scraps came out. Lucy pawed through them with shaking fingers. Receipts, faded with age and like felt to the touch for being kept in the bottom of a coat pocket; an extortionate electricity bill addressed to 'the occupier' at an address she didn't know; a letter from a bank advising of an abused overdraft facility, written to 'whomever it may concern'; an eviction order for non-payment of rent. A catalogue of tears and woe – financial distress in all its forms – but anonymous; evidence only of universal, urban misery. Lucy stared at this drift of cruelty for over a minute, the fingers of one hand pressed against her mouth. Then she began to laugh. *Fairy gold; of course...*

The following day, when Lucy arrived at work, Dolores remarked upon her appearance, which she said was 'peaky'. Lucy considered, for a minute, telling her colleague about what had happened last night on the way home, but then remembered she had enjoyed discomforting Dolores a few weeks previously by describing her eventful drug-taking experiments of some years back. It was easy to imagine Dolores' private inferences, if not her overt responses, to Lucy's story. Perhaps acid flashback *had* been the cause of the episode. It was comforting now to think that.

At lunchtime, Lucy slouched through a slicing rain to investigate the street of transformation. By day, it was its mundane self; a thin, lank-haired woman came out of one of the houses with a push-chair, one of the few active shops remaining had a stock of exotic vegetable produce displayed outside its window. Lucy went to stand in the road. For a few moments, she closed her eyes, willing some bizarre image to manifest before her. When she looked upon the world once more, it seemed the scene before her shimmered, as if another place existed there, waiting to be focused upon, brought into being. Lucy blinked. A headache was starting. She had tried too hard to recapture a dream. It hadn't happened.

Nothing too remarkable occurred for several days after that, although in retrospect Lucy did wonder whether she'd just missed the awareness when it crept across her. Then, one lunchtime, as she strolled along the main street looking into shop windows, she suddenly had the distinct impression she was walking through a movie set; nothing she saw was real, but a facade. It seemed she only had to half-close her eyes to become aware of something beneath the skin of the city; another place at once more exotic yet decayed. Her flesh shuddered in a thrill of anticipation, excitement and fear. There was something she wanted so badly, yet she had no name for it. Merely the thought of its existence filled her with an unexpected hope. A noise swooped towards her like a wind, a great whine, a buzzing, trailing a jet-stream of suffocating perfume, redolent of vanilla and ashes. Lucy gasped, threw back her head, trembling and vulnerable.

The feeling soon passed and, collecting herself, Lucy noticed that several passers-by were taking a wide detour around her and pointedly looking in a direction other than hers. She wondered whether she was starting to experience some mild form of epileptic seizure. Could there be a weird condition of the brain that caused sensory hallucinations? Thoughts of making an appointment with her doctor began to form in her mind, but before she could make any firm decision a man walked close by her, brushing her arm with his coat. Lucy opened her mouth to complain – he had plenty of room to pass without jostling her, after all – but when she saw him, no sound came out of her. It was the man she had seen in the red-lit bar several nights before.

Their eyes met.

He did not slow his pace, yet they seemed to be within close proximity for several seconds. He said. 'Curiosity or fear?' And then was gone, swallowed by the lunch-time crowds.

Something is happening to me, Lucy thought, and for a while she dared to hope that it was something that could show her the door to the life she had misplaced somehow, the life she was supposed to live.

Back at the office, the weird sensations pulsed in and out of her awareness. At one point, sitting opposite Dolores as they drank tea during their break, Lucy felt she possessed tunnel vision, and that only the area in her line of sight appeared normal. If she could but turn her head quickly enough, she would see the room that existed beneath, or alongside, the office that was so familiar to her. She sensed it was a darker place of crumbling decadence, its appointments baroque. Dolores herself, would be seen as she really was; a large, colourfully-plumed bird with limited intelligence but able to be trained to perform certain routines.

'Are you all right?' Dolores asked, her face creased in concern. 'Are you eating properly, Lucy? Do you sleep enough?' She laughed in mild censure. 'I'm sure you spend too much time burning the candle at both ends.'

'I burn my candles from the middle,' Lucy answered.

Dolores shook her head. 'You should look after yourself. None of us is getting any younger.'

Lucy was not disposed to thank Dolores for that reminder.

From then on, the awareness came upon Lucy more frequently. It could strike at any time, in any place, teasing her because it did not reveal any secrets, only hint that they were there. Sometimes, when she was out in the open, she thought she caught glimpses of the thin-faced man, although he did not speak to her again. Once, she tried to follow him, but without success. Several times, desperate for answers, or a conclusion, she walked home the short way, hoping that one evening she would come across the tall, grey buildings again, but the narrow street at the end of Victoria Terrace appeared as it always had. She got the impression that the special conditions that had allowed the 'other place' to materialise had moved on to somewhere else in the city, like a cloud. She would just have to find it.

During these weeks, Lucy confided in no one about what was happening to her. She stopped going out with friends, but spent her nights either sitting in her apartment willing the awareness to steal across her or else walking the streets, searching for an area of magic. She soon realised that concerted effort provided the least success. It seemed that only when she wasn't thinking of the awareness would it come upon her, and then, because she now hungered for it, with annoying brevity. She noticed, without experiencing any particular emotion, that none of her friends had bothered to call her to discover why she had dropped out of circulation. Obviously she meant little to them, but this did not surprise her. She felt little for them in return. No one was concerned about her, but for Dolores, whose concern she could well do without.

As March tried vainly to transform the dirty streets of the city, Lucy's boss and his wife celebrated their silver wedding anniversary. Wanting to share their happiness and provide a treat for their two employees, the couple offered to take Lucy and Dolores out for a meal on Friday night. In the office, Dolores agonised about a suitable present, which she felt she and Lucy should buy for the couple. Lucy, disinterested, donated ten pounds, which she could tell Dolores didn't think was enough. Neither could she be bothered to discuss what should be bought. 'I'll leave it up to you,' she told Dolores, who would probably top up the fund to at least forty pounds with her own cash.

'They're very good to us,' Dolores said, her voice full of hurt disappointment. No doubt she often wished she had a colleague more like herself.

Lucy experienced a pang, which began as a warm kind of feeling, but quickly hardened to resentment. 'They keep you comfortably on your perch,' she said, 'but you could be flying free.'

Dolores stared owlishly at Lucy, clearly attempting to decipher this cryptic statement. Lucy saw her *truly* then. She was not a bird, but certainly bird-like, dressed in disintegrating rags of red, yellow and blue, her hands scaled like the claws of an eagle, her face drooping with pendulous jowls that were very similar to the wattles on a chicken. Lucy stared at Dolores, who had now dropped her attention back to what lay on her desk. The desk itself was different: an ancient, carved table, covered in leather-bound ledgers and dusty, glass candlesticks, coated with thick wads of colourless stale wax. Long, yellow flames burned steadily up from the mess. Lucy lifted her eyes. Around her, the office had transformed from beige and cream tidiness to a high, cavernous room of grey and brown. It was enormous – Lucy could not see its nether end – and filled with huge, shadowy, metal machinery. She was sure these machines were the photocopier, computers, printers and coffee machine, all evolved from some kind of alternative technology, which was massive where modern technology was small. The scene before her was horrifying and beautiful, alien and endless. Tilting back her head, she could see that far above, cracked sky-lights provided a dim illumination, augmented only by the sputtering candle-light. The ancient panes were occluded by the dust and grime of centuries. Lucy became aware that beyond the office walls, there was a thumping sound, as of vast machinery churning and grinding.

The boss came out of his office, which was now a yellow-paned booth reached by a flight of wooden steps. He looked like a corpse, clad in a robe of rotting brown sacking, his hands bound with flaking bandages. Lucy stood up and walked slowly across the room. She saw a small window frame, covered by fraying brown fabric, which she lifted with one hand. Outside, a limitless horizon of unfamiliar buildings reared up in Gothic spires, or spread low in curling labyrinths. Dominating all was the huge dark factory she had seen near the phantom bar. Tiny figures moved in and out of it in regular lines and sometimes an orange glow would ignite behind its myriad windows. Steam issued from rusting conduits in the walls, while behind it roiled a yellow-black sky, punctuated by the reaching limbs of metal cranes, so gigantic they disappeared into dirty cloud. Lucy's eyes ached for the scene before her. She wanted to drink it all in.

Only when she had opened the window to let in the unsmelled odours of the true city, did she realise Dolores had her hand upon her arm and was repeating her name. Time and space jerked, with a feeling like a cricked neck, sudden and sharp. The awareness had gone.

'What were you doing?' Dolores sounded panicked.

Lucy shook her head. 'I saw something.'

'That was obvious!'

'Take the rest of the day off,' said her boss, clearly discomforted by what he perceived as women's strange behaviour, perhaps connected to hormones.

'No,' Lucy said. 'I'm fine.'

Friday evening, Lucy dressed with care, faintly depressed that this riskless gathering was going to be the high-light of her month. Her apartment, she felt, was a bubble of normality within a plasmic mass of uncertainty outside. Soon she would enter into it, step out into the dark and potential.

As she'd anticipated, her walk to the appointed restaurant was surreal. Sometimes, it seemed as if there were more than two realities pulsing in and out of her perception, but none of them gained a hold. Realities overlapped. Along the normal city street, a troupe of women dressed in black feathers stalked, wearing grimacing masks, their hands sheathed in scales of dull metal. A shining dark vehicle streaked by like an instrument of torture; barbed and sickled. Lucy saw an old woman, dressed in a sensible camel-hair coat and flat brown shoes, gazing into the window of a shop where a naked, shaved-headed boy pirouetted on a plinth. His limbs were oiled and gleaming in a ruddy light, his chest and arms laced with cuts that leaked dark liquid, which did not look exactly like blood. Lucy laughed out loud at this particular tableau, which caused the old woman to glance around in fear. The shop before her sold tasteless clothes, Lucy could see that now, and the window display was only of stiff, tired mannequins from an earlier age that gestured blindly at one another in the dark.

As she strolled, almost drunkenly, toward her destination, Lucy realised her life had become interesting again. She might be going mad, and this indeed seemed the most likely explanation, but, if so, she welcomed it. Anything was better than the non-life she had slipped into. Perhaps this acceptance was part of the madness, and soon she'd be found, mindless and drooling, lost to the 'other place' that tantalised her senses. She tried to imagine how Dolores and the boss would cope if this should happen at work. She'd be carted off to the funny farm. *And would that mean that, one day, she'd wake up, in a bare white room, cured of her delusions and thus sentenced to eternal tedium in a world she had grown to despise?* The thought of that frightened her more than anything her mind might be doing to her now. She must learn to control her episodes of awareness, or hide them. Incidents like that which had occurred in the office today must not be repeated. If the awareness came to her, no one must know it but herself.

The meal, surprisingly, took place entirely in the realm of the ordinary. Lucy, though deprived of weird sensations, felt utterly dislocated from her companions. Strangely, this made her feel unexpectedly warm towards them. Her boss and his wife were absurdly happy celebrating this anniversary of perpetual dullness. Their innocence and ignorance touched Lucy's soul. And sad Dolores, manless and childless, caring so much about others, when no-one was prepared to care about her.

After the meal, Dolores suggested that she and Lucy might share a cab home, even though they lived fairly widely apart. Lucy, however, liked to walk everywhere nowadays. The awareness never came to her in cabs or on buses. She could see the disappointment in Dolores' face as she refused the invitation; the woman did not want the evening to finish. For Lucy, it was yet to begin.

Out on the street, she somehow guessed that tonight something was scheduled to happen. Desperate for revelation, she forgot about going home, and ventured down any narrow, dark street that yawned before her. Instinctively, she sensed that these places were the most likely gateways to the 'other place', among the trash-cans, beneath fire escapes where desperate measures had been taken in lives devoid of all hope. Walking down unfamiliar alleys, where the buildings pressed close together in damp darkness, it would be difficult to tell when she crossed over. She must not strain for it. She must just walk.

She heard the music first: jangly piano. Then the red light spilled across her shoes, and she looked up. There was the bar almost directly beside her. Victory crashed through her body in a hot wave. She virtually ran into the building, determined to ensnare it in her senses before it vanished.

Inside, the bar was full of people, and Lucy realised it was not the same one she had stumbled across the first time. This place was more brightly lit, and less shabby. Huge fans turned slowly in the low ceiling, carving the smoky air into amorphous lumps that caught the light – red and green – and became twisting vaporous creatures, alive only for a minute. Bloody light glinted off crystal and gold; the carpet beneath her feet was like red velvet. The clientele all looked as if they were on their way to somewhere else. All wore coats, drank rapidly from glasses of every shape and size, talking animatedly, making sharp, thrusting gestures with their hands. Lucy was slightly disappointed that they all appeared so ordinary. She would have expected to see a collection of people like those you'd find in a fetish club; leather and straps and spikes. But then, she reasoned, such fads and fashions were the trimmings of her own, hated city. Here, it would have to be different. When she looked closer at the people around her, she realised they were not ordinary at all, but the difference was in their eyes and in their movements; a sense of danger and threat and promise.

I am home, Lucy thought, and then, *Am I home?*

She walked up to the bar and a thin, sallow-skinned girl in a black, halter-neck dress came to take her order.

'Do you have wine?' Lucy asked.

The girl shook her head, and behind her Lucy saw an array of ornate bottles come sharply into focus, dream bottles that had perhaps not existed a moment before.

'Give me something red,' she said.

The girl said nothing, but swung away to plunge her arms in among the sparkling bottles, delving for something too far back to be reached.

Lucy looked around herself. For a moment, she thought she saw Dolores sitting on a stool a short distance away from her, then realised it was only a very similar woman; large and fading, with her hair tumbling out of confinement around her neck and shoulders. Dolores' hair, Lucy realised, was created to tumble, but she always pinned it up severely, so that it had to strain to escape. Perhaps this stranger *was* Dolores, but a Dolores who had never allowed herself to exist. The woman sensed Lucy's attention and directed a smile at her. Something in the expression, which was not exactly predatory, but very akin to it, made Lucy shudder and turn away.

The bar-tender was putting a glass down before her – a small globe of crystal on a twisted stem, its bowl blistered with vitreous crusts of gold and green.

'How much?' Lucy asked.

The girl jerked her head. 'Paid for. By him.'

Lucy glanced down the bar and saw the thin-faced man raise his glass to her. Two coils of long, black hair framed his face. He was grinning. She knew then that she had to go to him. It was time, at least, for that.

'Thank you for the drink,' she said.

'Taste it.' His voice was low, and balanced on the edge of laughter.

Lucy was afraid it would taste of blood, but it didn't, not entirely.

This was a taste of ecstasy, of passion, of intense hatred, a road accident, a field of burning poppies. 'Different,' she said, and waited for him to respond with the words, 'Curiosity or fear?' but he didn't.

'You were waiting for the taste,' he said.

'Tell me,' Lucy said, 'I need to know where I am.' She felt he knew she was a stranger to this reality, a visitor.

The man shrugged. 'There are many junctions.'

'That is not an answer.' She sighed, fixed him with a stare. 'I wonder whether, one day, I'll be able to stay here, and not go back.'

Again, a shrug. 'That is your choice.'

'Who are you?'

He smiled more widely, showing very white teeth. 'A catcher of dreams. And you?'

'Perhaps a spinner of dreams.' She laughed uneasily. 'This is all so weird. I can't believe I'm accepting it.'

'*Are* you accepting it?'

Lucy looked into his face. It was like looking down a long tunnel. 'Yes. Anything is better than nothing.' She paused. 'Were you waiting for me?'

He put his head on one side. 'I have suspicions about you, that's all. A hunch. There's no pressure.'

'I want to see this world,' Lucy said. 'I don't want to hover on the edge. I want to be in it. I know that it exists.' She faltered. 'I don't want to go back.'

'Why not?'

'My life is hell back there. It is nothing. I might as well be dead.'

The man raised his brows. 'Oh!' He turned toward the bar, signalled the skinny girl, before glancing back at Lucy. 'Another drink?'

'I haven't finished this one yet,' Lucy said, and then realised that she had. 'Oh, all right.'

He put a glass into her hand, and this one was the size of a normal wine-glass and filled with a rich green liquid. When she tasted it, summer fields soared over her like a wave. It was an innocent drink and tinged only faintly with the fever heat of tortured jealousy.

The Dream-Catcher led her out of the bar, onto a terrace at the back of the building. Here, the city spread before them, an impossible jumble of tormented shapes and sounds and smells. Lucy breathed it all in, through every pore. It was ugly, yet entrancing; a fantasy world, where anything was possible. The people here would not be dull or obsessed with trivia. She sensed they all led dangerous lives, were tragic and fey, cruel and mysterious. Like the man beside her. She looked at him.

'Tell me I'm not mad,' she said.

'You're not mad.' He leaned upon the rusting railings, which were entwined with dead stalks of a plant that looked like the bodies of desiccated serpents. Fragile, withered blooms rustled like paper among the fibrous coils. 'One day, you became aware of the worlds beyond the narrow imagination of the ordinary, that's all.'

She sensed he could tell her much more, but perhaps she had to ask the right questions to invoke the information. 'But why me? I'm not that imaginative. Does this happen to many people?'

The Dream-Catcher looked at her askance. 'Only the hungry,' he answered, 'the *very* hungry.'

Lucy turned round and leaned back against the railings, her arms spread out to either side. 'I feel like I'm being given a second chance.' She shook her head. 'I really don't think I could bear to go back. That is... only if I can't come here again.'

'You come here often,' the Dream-Catcher said. 'You see this world all the time.'

Lucy shook her head. 'I see *glimpses* of it. That's not enough. I want more. I want to meet people, talk to them. I want to explore every corner. Just an evening a week would do. I could put up with my ordinary life then, I'm sure.' She didn't know whether the Dream-Catcher was a powerful figure in this world, but she suspected he had the ability to grant her request if he wanted to. What must she do to convince him? She asked him this.

'You do not have to convince me of anything,' he replied, 'but you do have to be sure, for once you decide there is no going back. You cannot exist wholly in two worlds. You have become aware of this one, and the gate is open, but you are just sampling the place at the moment.'

Lucy uttered a scornful laugh. 'I have nothing to go back for. My life is empty. Here...' She gestured widely to encompass her surroundings. 'Here, there is life and adventure and purpose.'

'How do you know that?'

Shrugging, she turned away, feeling embarrassed. 'Okay, I got carried away. But you just have no idea what my life has become.' She glanced at him. 'Then maybe you do.'

He shook his head. 'I do not know you,' he said. 'There are far too many people to know.'

'Are you happy here?' Lucy asked him sharply.

He smiled. 'There is a colour for happiness, and it resides in a pearly bottle. It may be drunk. There are an infinite number of colours.'

'I think I want to go back now,' Lucy said.

'So much for exploring.'

She gave him an arch glance. 'I only need to think.'

Everyone had moved on; the bar was empty, but for the skinny girl, who was wiping the counter with a rag in lazy, circular movements. She did not look up as Lucy passed her. A clock was ticking loudly and the music was silenced. *Do I want to leave?* Lucy wondered. When she stepped outside, it was probable she'd walk back into her mundane life. What if she couldn't find the gateway again? Did she really need to think? There was no fear inside her. She wasn't really sure why she was hesitating over the decision. Tomorrow, being Saturday, she'd have to go to the supermarket and stock up on her meagre supplies. Then, she'd spend the evening walking around again, perhaps without success, looking for a way into this other world, a place where she could hold onto it. What was the point in that?

She walked back out onto the terrace, half expecting the Dream-Catcher to have vanished, but he hadn't. He was still leaning against the rail, staring out over the city.

'I've made up my mind,' Lucy said. 'What do I do?'

He turned round slowly. 'Are you sure?'

She walked toward him, and rested her forearms upon the rail. Out there, she heard the echoes of screaming, and a gout of flame spurted up, followed by muffled thunder. There were gun-shots, and the crack of leather against flesh. There was hysterical music and crazy laughter. Below, on the street, a young, pale girl danced by in the arms of a tall, dark man. They were followed by a grotesque child, banging a tambourine, and a monkey in a waist-coat, strewing petals from a little basket. Behind them, soaring high, stood the great dark building Lucy had thought was a factory. She could see now that it was a palace. Enormous black statues of winged men flanked its yawning, dark entrance. Fire burned within, flickering behind panes of crystal.

Lucy surveyed this scene for a few moments, then said, 'I am sure.'

The Dream-Catcher nodded. Now, he wasn't smiling, and appeared tense. Was he afraid she'd change her mind again? 'Then take off your coat, for you are home.'

It was only a light overcoat, insubstantial against the winter chill of the streets she knew and wanted to forget; a garment bought cheap in a sale because she could afford nothing better. Lucy undid the buttons and, with a feeling of abhorrence, wriggled out of the coat, letting it fall to the ground. As she did so, it seemed something larger than a mere garment fell from her shoulders. She felt taller, and already the tide of memory was turning, reeling in the life of Lucy, going back and back, to the time she had entered the grey world of the mundane. The Dream-Catcher handed her a glass. This was filled with a purple liquid. When she tasted, it was the essence of kings.

'Well?' said the Dream-Catcher.

Slowly, Lucy felt herself settling into a persona who had been sleeping. It felt slightly uncomfortable and unused, but familiar. Not all of what she had experienced was clear yet, but she knew what the Dream-Catcher wanted to hear. 'I was right,' she said. 'But I had to see for myself. They claim to avoid the unspeakable, yet in their greed and ignorance, they have created all the worst possible forms of what they perceive as hell.' She shook her head, smiled quizzically. 'Famine, slaughter – they are some of the faces – but there are others too, the grey faces of conformity and dead minds and hearts. It is bizarre, but the process must work in reverse now. Hell's torments are torments no longer. In that grey world I have seen people attempting to emulate the extremes of the inferno in an attempt to escape the horror of their predicament, which is nullity. They have created a void for themselves. It is terrible.' She reached out for the Dream-Catcher with one long, sinuous, bronze-skinned arm. How beautiful her flesh felt to her soul. He nestled to her side, and she kissed him. 'Dark angel, I have missed you!' she said.

'Welcome home,' said the Dream-Catcher.

Violet's House
or Songs the Martyrs Sang

This story isn't based upon anyone's particular anecdote or history. The characters aren't drawn – however remotely – from life. But what is real about this piece is mourning for lost youth, something I've discussed with writer friends, especially in respect of the otherworldly and mysterious. This mourning is not for the younger physical body but for the younger mind – the way we experienced things: what we saw, what we felt, what we believed. In early years, all children are story-spinners, imaginative and full of curiosity. Only the lucky few retain those precious faculties intact into adulthood. My tale concerns the moment when the magical world of the child shifts into the harsh mundane world of the adult, when wonder begins to die, and the ghosts of lost innocence haunt the high summer landscape – that most magical time of all.

I will always remember Aunt Violet, standing there in the drawing room of Herons, with evening sunlight pouring in like treacle at the tall narrow windows, saying, 'But my dears, forget your Halloweens and dark nights of winter, the truth is the ghostliest time of year is high summer. If you don't know that yet, you will find it out, because this house is a haven for ghosts.'

Violet was tall, given to shawls and draperies. She was something of an anachronism, in her late 40s, smoking cigarettes in a tortoiseshell holder, speaking in the tones of a vanished era, rather like a ghost herself, I suppose. And her beautiful house, the oaken chest of my dearest childhood memories, was in its very bricks extraordinary.

It was the custom of that time for children to be farmed out for the convenience of parents whenever possible – children, that is, of fairly well-to-do families. As Aunt Violet possessed Herons, a crumbling family inheritance that nobody else wanted, 'out in the middle of nowhere' – as my own parents were fond of saying – with spacious rooms and sprawling gardens, it was an ideal summertime venue where Violet's siblings could deposit their offspring. Violet did not mind. She said she liked young people around – although for the two months we stayed at Heron's, her own rather louche crowd of bright young things were kept at bay. She had a moralistic thread within her that considered children must be protected from certain aspects of life. I doubt we ever saw the 'real her' and I do wonder what that was like.

Sometimes there were four of us, but usually only three: Felicity and Nancy, daughters of my father's sister, and occasionally Beatrice, who was the child of my father's brother, and then me – Katherine, or Kitty as I'm known. Felicity and Nancy were always called Fliss and Nan. Bea wasn't quite like the rest of us – we found her rather dull – and we were always glad when it was just the three of us. Generally, Bea would appear for weekends, while Fliss, Nan and I would gorge ourselves on freedom for the two whole months of July and August. I was the youngest at fourteen, Fliss was fifteen and Nan, regarded as a mysterious beauty, was teetering on the brink of womanhood at sixteen, her toes still curled about the cliff edge of childhood, but her arms outflung, her head thrown back, waiting to fall into life.

Summers were hot back then, or my memories of them are, but I can remember only few rainy days and even then I wonder if I changed the weather to fit my memories because grey light is more apt for sadder times. We knew little sadness at Violet's house.

That one Sunday, only two days after we'd arrived at Herons, I remember Fliss hanging tiny bells in the rowan tree near the fish pond. They were Christmas decorations, I believe, and as this was in the days before wind chimes were popular and easy to find, the bells were the nearest we could get to the air playing music to us.

We lay on our backs on the grass in a row, sinewy blonde Fliss, black-haired Nan and me with my red curls and annoyingly-freckled pale skin, listening to the almost inaudible tinkle.

'This is the start of our summer,' said Fliss, stretching contentedly, flexing her bare toes in the grass, 'and that is the sound of it.'

The house was built halfway up Mere Hill and the gardens gave a spectacular view of the landscape – soft ancient hills and blurry forests. The mere lay at the bottom of the hill and extended a large way round it, surrounded by spindly trees. Beyond that, a strange backbone of rock stuck up from The Climb, one of the nearby hills, and crawled across a valley to Stag's Top; we imagined this crag as the petrified body of a dinosaur. If you narrowed your eyes and stared for long enough, you could see curious shapes within it. Sometimes, I imagined it as a huge saurian, which had died upon its knees, its great head lying sideways on the earth. That day, squinting across the valleys, I fancied a bent and crooked castle was built into the side of the crag, where the dinosaur's hips would be. Its towers looked down over a great drop and I pictured at once the unfortunates who might have been thrown to their deaths from there. 'There's a castle in Rookstone Ridge this year,' I said.

Fliss and Nan half-closed their eyes, followed my gaze. 'So there is,' said Nan.

'That's where the bells are,' said Fliss softly, 'can you hear them ringing?'

'Why would a castle have bells?' Nan asked, although in a dreamy tone.

Fliss was silent for a moment. 'It's... I think it's a kind of monastery, or used to be.'

'Yes, it was... It's not now, though.'

'No.'

'But the bells still ring,' I said.

We listened. Small bells nearby or the distant clamour of far-off chimes? To us, the choice was obvious.

'Girls! Girls!' came a cry and a clapping of hands from the house, which was Aunt Violet calling us like cats to our tea. We leapt eagerly to our feet and ran, hair flying behind us.

I always think of Herons as a purple house, because this was the colour that dominated it in various shades, and of course the name of its mistress occupied that band of the spectrum. Wanton swags of wisteria clung to its old grey walls, obscuring several of the upper windows. Within, lilac drapes framed the windows and in the drawing-room there was always a bowl of wilting violets, petals on the table around it. There was a library with half empty shelves and old leather chairs, where the walls were a dusty imperial purple, which complemented beautifully the faded gilt of picture frames between the book shelves. The pictures were of dim landscapes like dreams. There was a bay window in this room, where an old round dining-table had rooted; late afternoon light always fell over its tired yet satiny surface. Here we would consume our tea because we liked the room so much, and Violet let us eat where we pleased. She approved of even the slightest hint of eccentricity.

We ate salty egg and cress sandwiches and slabs of creamy Madeira cake, sipping strong and very sweet tea from enormous china cups, patterned with purple irises and sitting on plate-sized saucers. As I chewed, in utter sensual contentment, I fancied I could still hear the bells blown on the breeze. This sounded almost like many people singing, a long distance away. I sat with my back to the window and opposite me was Fliss, ethereal in the golden light, the edges of her hair transparent and glowing like a waist-length halo. She was always thinking of 'other things' and in fact became quite a famous novelist later on. Fliss started the dreams and adventures for us, but I'd caught some of that imagination from her; it was remarkably infectious when we were at Herons. 'Can you still hear it?' I asked her, waiting somewhat breathlessly for her reply and thus her confirmation of my fancies. She would never deny an idea, but she might embellish the details a little.

She nodded, took a dainty nibble of cake. 'Yes – I told you: it's the sound for this year.'

And there always was, every year, or rather it was more than sounds, also scents and tastes, and an overall ambience or emotion that was beyond human capacity to describe.

'Something is waiting to happen,' Nan said. She rested her elbows on the table, her chin in her cupped hands. This made me think of praying for some strange reason. 'It's shimmering all around us.'

'This year feels really good,' I said.

Nan half closed her eyes and smiled at me warmly.

Fliss said, 'yes,' her head bent towards her plate, since crumbs were spilling from the last bite of her cake.

That evening, as I took my bath before bed-time, submerged in lilac-scented foam, I could still hear the soft tinkle of bells from the garden, through the open window. I slithered down beneath the water, imagining myself as some river creature, with weed for hair. And down there, in visualised depths of green shadows and hidden currents, I fancied the bells became voices singing again, but so far away I could barely hear them. I could make out neither words nor tune, just the susurrating rise and fall of tones. There was a sadness to the song, though. In my mind I swam towards it, undulating like a fish, but could draw no closer. I pressed my cheek against the smooth enamel of the bath and it seemed the voices were louder then – almost too strident and too near. Unnerved, I rose up from the water, flinging my arms high, as I imagined a Nereid might when she emerged from her element. In the dry air there were no sounds at all.

While I was an imaginative child, who adored mysteries and make-believe, I was also a very practical creature. As I towelled myself dry, I thought that the sounds must have been caused by the plumbing in this aged domain; all the wheezing and coughing of furred-up pipes. Knowing this, I would be happy to *imagine* what I'd heard was a ghostly choir, chanting at the boundaries of hearing.

I was so tired that night that I fell asleep almost instantly, cocooned in the most comfortable of beds, and slept the whole night through.

At breakfast the following morning, Nan seemed a little distracted – her raven hair wilder than usual. 'They were singing all night,' she said, '*all night!*'

I glanced at Fliss to see what her reaction would be. 'Your room faces the ridge,' she said, as if this was obvious.

'Who was singing?' I asked.

Nan waved a hand in the air. 'Oh, the people in the castle, whoever they are. We must see.'

'I heard singing when I was in the bath,' I said, 'if I put my head underwater.' I didn't think I should mention my theory concerning the pipes. 'And even when we were eating tea, as if the bells had changed to voices.'

'They sing when the bells call them,' Fliss said, buttering a piece of toast. 'They're not monks or nuns, though. They sing for a different reason.'

I waited for Fliss to elaborate, but she did not, thoughtfully munching her toast. Perhaps she didn't have the right idea yet.

'We should go to Rookstone,' Nan said.

My first instinctive reaction was to say 'no!', but I didn't voice it. I was surprised at the sudden frisson of fear that gripped my mind. We didn't travel that far alone when we were at Herons. The grounds, the mere and the surrounding woodlands were large enough to accommodate our adventures and, even after visiting the house annually for around seven years now, there were still places we hadn't fully explored or claimed for our own. I wasn't sure Aunt Violet would want us going so far, especially when the danger of injury – or worse – was a possibility. There would be many places where we might fall on that sheer bone of rock. And yet I didn't want to be the one to spoil the game, to voice such practical thoughts. I pleaded silently for Fliss to say something similar, but in keeping with the game. She said nothing, but had a determined look on her face. Pushing her chair away from the table, she got to her feet and sauntered to the nearest library shelf, running her hands over the faded spines of the books. And then it was in her hands *Follies of the County*, with a worn colour cover showing three pictures of broken stones – a tumbled arch, a roofless summerhouse and the ridge.

Nearly a hundred years before, a rich man named Benjamin Caldwell had lived in a house below the ridge. He had not inherited it; he had bought it. The house was gone now, lost in a fire when no one was at home. Not a creepy, meaningful fire; just an accident. No one had died or even been harmed. The damage had been considered too great for the place to be resurrected, so the remains were dismantled. Rookstone Ridge was part of the estate and Caldwell had found it inspiring; upon its wide flat backbone he'd built follies – three towers, a tumble down chapel, two pagan temples dedicated to vague idols such as 'the winds' and 'the seasons'. He'd even created the foundations of a small Roman town, which pretended to be genuine remains, and above them, jutting out from a cliff – the dinosaur's hips – the ruins of a castle.

While Fliss read these details to us, and showed us cloudy old photographs from the book, I felt light-headed. We invented dreams all the time, but not once had any of them proved real. They were our imaginings, safely untrue. I'd said there was a castle and now there was – and, more than that, it had been there all the time.

Neither Fliss nor Nan appeared to find this astounding or unusual – to them it seemed only fitting my observation had been based on fact. It was at this point I realised they believed in our games more than I did.

'Let's go today,' Nan said, the book open on the table, her fingers resting on one of the photographs.

'We should ask Aunt Violet,' I said, blushing immediately. My cousins gave me catlike stares. 'Well, it's quite far. Won't we need to take a picnic? And we should tell someone where we're going... really... shouldn't we?'

Nan nodded and closed the book. 'You're right.'

'It's less of an adventure that way,' Fliss argued. 'We could smuggle food out if we wanted to. It's not as if anyone would notice.'

True, Violet's staff were all as wafty and dreamy as she was. The housekeeper, Mrs Barr, seemed hardly worthy of the title and spent much of her day sitting in the kitchen, talking with Violet. The two girls who helped Mrs Barr with the house appeared half asleep most of the time.

'We *should* tell her,' Nan insisted and glanced out of the window, a peculiar half-smile on her face. I saw Mitch, the gardener, strolling away from the house. He was new to us that summer, although he'd been taken on by Violet at the end of the season the previous year. A flurry of irritation went through me. At the time, I didn't know why.

As one, we went to our aunt, who always took her breakfast alone in a small airy room near the kitchens. She had told us on our very first visit she was a bear first thing in the mornings and not fit to be in company, but we considered our mission worth the risk of confronting this perhaps fearsome animal. Violet was wrapped in a fringed shawl of purple silk, reading a newspaper. She didn't appear to be angry when we knocked on the door and walked in on her.

'Well, what's this?' she asked, smiling, perhaps sensing an adventure.

We told her, not about the bells or the singing, or any of our imaginings, but just an interest in visiting Rookstone.

Aunt Violet pursed her lips. 'Well, it's private land,' she said, 'but I'm sure Alex Caldwell – who owns the land – wouldn't mind you girls going over there. He's a friend of mine.' She paused. 'It *could* be dangerous, though, all sorts of drops hidden among the shrubs, and those towers... a lad once broke his back climbing out at the top of one. The wind blew him down.'

'We'd be careful,' Nan said, in her most sensible tone.

'We wouldn't climb the towers,' Fliss said.

Violet hesitated. 'Well, I don't know. The place has run wild since Alex's grandfather landscaped it – half the hazards must be hidden now. I think someone should go with you, at least.'

'You?' I asked, hopefully.

She laughed. 'Oh, I've never been much of a hiker. I'll ask Mitch to take you over. It's going to be a glorious day.'

'Can we take a picnic?' I asked.

Violet reached out to muss my hair. 'A day out is not a day out without a picnic! Go and talk to Mrs Barr. I'll have a word with Mitch.'

Arrangements were made, and before noon we were ready to depart. Fliss and I weren't happy we were to be escorted by the gardener, although Nan didn't seem to mind. Fliss rolled her eyes at me, grimaced. 'Don't be dopey,' she told her sister as we put on our shoes in the dim hallway.

'It was supposed to be just us,' I complained, in a tone whiney even to my own ears. 'How can it be the same if he's there, getting in the way?'

Nan shrugged. 'He seems nice,' she said. 'It's better than not going at all, isn't it?'

I was the last to leave the house because I'd forgotten my hat. Violet was insistent our heads were covered or we'd faint from the heat. As I ran down the drive, to where the others were waiting by the lion-guarded gateway, I was compelled to pause and look back at the house. There was someone in Nan's bedroom, looking down at me. In fact, I realised, it was Nan herself. Had she changed her mind about the trip? She looked strangely young and childlike and rather sad. I waved at her. She raised a single hand, pressed the palm against the glass, then turned away. How odd. Perhaps womanly afflictions were upon her – I had yet to be visited by The Curse – and she'd been forced to stay indoors. No wonder she looked sad, I thought.

And then I turned a curve in the drive and could see them ahead of me: Fliss, Mitch – and Nan. I stopped, looked back – there was no one at the window. The girl had looked so much like Nan, and yet it must've been one of Violet's droopy house staff.

'What is it?' Fliss asked, when I reached them.

'I saw Nan at the window,' I said, pointing back, 'or thought I did.'

'No, I'm here, *marvellously*,' said Nan and stretched out her arms.

Looking back, I can see easily that Mitch was a dangerous sort, a certain archetype of a man. He was handsome in an indolent, boneless sort of way, with dark hair falling over his eyes. His lips were sensual and rarely out of a smile. He was watchful, particularly in respect of Nan. As for her, that day she burst open like a bud into a spreading exotic flower. She pranced around, she flung her hair about, she flirted. Mitch smiled at it all, but he was, as she had suggested 'nice'. He joked with us, treated us as if we were younger male friends of his, and didn't expect us to flounder over stiles or be helped up steep hills with treacherous stones underfoot. Grudgingly, I liked that about him.

We walked across fields spiky with the first mowing and Rookstone became larger before us. There was majesty to it, a feeling of great age. In those days no fence surrounded it and we passed simply from the sunlight of a hay meadow into the shadow of ancient rhododendrons that had grown so huge and wild they were like prehistoric trees. The blossoms had gone from them by July and, as we clambered up a narrow trail through them, I wondered what they would look like in full bloom – a blaze of colour on the cragside.

We had quite a walk to reach the place where the castle folly stood, or what remained of it. Once we'd negotiated the steep slope to a more level area, we found a patch of sunshine on a lawn among the trees, and here decided to eat our lunch. Nan opened the hamper, which Mitch had carried and had now laid on the ground. She spread out the blue checkered tablecloth within, began extracting sandwiches.

'What're you wanting to come up here for?' Mitch asked us. 'Thought girls like you would want the town, shopping and that.'

Fliss directed the most scornful glance she could muster upon him. 'We're interested in local history,' she said primly. 'There are follies up here, castles and temples.'

'Not much to see now,' Mitch said. 'Caldwell's let it go.'

'You know about this place?' Nan said in a bright voice.

He shrugged. 'A bit. Used to play up here as a lad.'

'Not that long ago, then,' said Fliss sharply.

He eyed her guardedly. 'No, not really, but it feels as if it was.' He lit a cigarette and the smell of tobacco enfolded us. 'You'll feel the same one day, look back to this afternoon and think it was a century ago, yet it'll only be five years at most.'

I could see Nan approved of this thoughtfulness, perhaps an indication of him having depth and character.

'Do you know about the castle?' she asked.

'We thought it was real when we were kids.' He said nothing more on the subject – then.

After we'd eaten most of the sandwiches and slaked our thirst with the lemonade Mrs Barr had provided for us, we pressed on. Mitch picked up the hamper again, slung its strap over his shoulder. He handed his cigarette to Nan. 'Want some?'

'No, thank you,' she said. 'I don't.'

He shrugged. 'Suit yourself.'

We didn't talk much on the final steep climb to the castle, concentrating more on not slipping and sliding back down the slope. The sun, where it pierced the tree canopy of ancient oaks and beeches, was hot on my head, despite the hat. I could hear the bells now, and the singing; faint tidelike swells in my mind. Nan began to hum tunelessly beneath her breath.

We came to the shadow of the castle wall and here we could see it was constructed of large stones, but also some parts of it were common brick, weathered and crumbling, powdered with moss and lichen. A broken metal railing poked threateningly from a walkway overhead, its bars twisted and cruel.

'There's more to see from the other side,' Mitch told us. 'In its day, old Caldwell used to stay here overnight – he had proper rooms built and a hall where there were parties.'

'Did anyone ever die?' I asked. 'Did they fall?'

'There are always stories like that,' Mitch said, 'kids like to make things up.' He shaded his eyes and smiled up at the dark walls. 'When you play in a place like this, you can't help thinking of scary things that might've happened, ghosts that might've walked.'

Again, I noticed Nan's wide and increasingly adoring smile of approval, as Mitch proved himself to be imaginative as well as thoughtful. He led us round the side of the building until we came to a ramp partially obstructed by fallen masonry that led into a courtyard. Half-fallen towers surrounded this space and below them a colonnade ran round the inner wall, draped in shadow. Proprietorial rooks complained about our intrusion, filling our ears with a more hectic kind of music. I couldn't hear the bells here, nor any singing.

'How wild it is,' Nan said in a voice hardly more than a sigh. She took off her wide-brimmed hat, shook out her mane of rook-feather hair. The wind caught this in its fingerless grip, pulled it over her face, so she had to hold it back with both hands. I half expected the birds to come wheeling around her head, to pluck strands of her hair for their nests.

Mitch showed us to some narrow damp steps that led to the back of the castle, where the original owner had had his recreational rooms constructed. To reach this area, we'd have to negotiate the walkway that girdled the folly. It was dangerous on the sheer side, and here the wind felt malicious, but the safety railing was still intact and Mitch said that if we kept close to the wall on our left then we'd not be in danger of falling. If we'd leaned upon those railings, they probably would not have been as solid as they appeared. I felt strangely light-headed and a little sick as we negotiated that narrow trail. I couldn't help thinking of leaning upon the railings, for the iron to be rusted and rotted through at the base, for one or all of us to be flung out into the air, uttering thin screams before our bodies shattered upon the rocks below. All I could hear was the wind and screeching rooks, as if we'd emerged from the quiet summer element into a realm more fierce and dangerous. The thought occurred to me: were the castle and its guardians angry that we were here? Presumably, the folly had been molested by children for generations, some of whom had no doubt contributed towards its physical decline, yet I had the feeling few visited it now. The air was desolate.

Mitch led us round to the ruinous main hall, which was in shadow. The roof was still there in places – spiky broken beams, and in one quarter a number of roof tiles. I could hear pigeons now, their soft croo croo. Bright green weeds grew between the bricks and among the remaining tiles.

'This is a brooding place,' Nan said.

'It feels as if people died here,' Fliss added with relish. She rubbed her arms. 'Dark and damp, yet full of ashes.'

'If you want to believe the castle is real, perhaps that's possible,' Mitch said.

A light came into Fliss's eyes and I saw her estimation of Mitch rise instantly; he was prepared to share the game. 'Were there not ruins Caldwell built on?'

Mitch shrugged. 'It would've been a good spot to build a castle.' He grinned. 'And perhaps there was a siege, or it was set on fire. The house in the valley below burned, you know, a long time ago.'

'Perhaps this too came alight at exactly the same moment,' Fliss said.

As I peered at the walls, I thought they did look blackened, as if by a fire.

'This way,' said Mitch.

We followed him into a short, lightless stone tunnel that led to an unpainted wooden door. He glanced back at us, grinned, then knocked upon the door. He put his ear to the wood, raised his eyebrows, then pushed on the door so it opened. 'My lady's chamber,' he said.

Nan was the first into the room. The windows were still whole, miraculously, and light and heat streamed in through them. The air at first smelled musty but also faintly sweet, as if of flowers or incense.

'Marvellous!' Nan breathed.

Fliss entered the room behind her. 'It's intact,' she said. 'Perhaps someone still cares for it.'

I stood at the threshold, frozen. I couldn't enter that room. The smell in there had turned repugnant, still sweet yet also somehow bloody. I couldn't describe it, but I felt close to gagging. This was a dreadful room. Without saying anything, I backed away. The others didn't appear to notice I'd not followed them.

Stumbling – dizzy and nauseous – I found my way back to the dank, gutted hall, where the pigeons still made their soft song. I felt I'd emerged into a different place to where we'd been before. The hall now smelled strongly of excrement and rot and I saw the lower walls were slimy. *No one ever came here to do any good*, I thought. Desperate for clean air, for light, I inched back along the walkway and down into the sunny courtyard, where the rooks still wheeled and squawked. This was not how the day had been supposed to proceed. Somehow, I had been cast out of the adventure, perhaps didn't exist anymore for those still wrapped within it. I couldn't even hear their voices now. Then a susurrus of song came to me, the same as I'd heard beneath my bath water, faint on the breeze, hardly there at all. It came from everywhere at once and yet nowhere. For a moment it swelled loudly and I felt that if I gazed up at the high walkway I'd see the singers, ranged in a line, chanting into the wild air. But when I did turn, there were no figures outlined against the sky, and further concentration on the song transformed it simply into the wind whispering through old stones, mingling with the croak of the rooks and the more distant murmur of pigeons. These components had always made the song, I thought. There were no ghostly choirs around. Nature herself was the ghost.

After some minutes, while I calmed down and unpleasant sensations subsided, I became angry my cousins hadn't come after me or asked what was wrong. So, I'd just go home without them, then. Eventually, they'd have to worry.

Tense with resentment, my head aching with it, I retraced our steps to the outside of the castle. The place seemed tawdry to me now; no enchanted realm, but a folly of disintegrating bricks stuck onto a crude skeleton of corroded iron. There was nothing to be scared of, but equally nothing to be awed by. The forest below it was more beautiful, the fields beyond more fragrant.

By the time I reached Herons, I was beginning to feel guilty for storming home on my own. I felt Aunt Violet would be disappointed in me, so didn't go into the house. Instead, I wandered to a favourite spot by the mere, where the willows rinsed their lush tresses in the still, mosquito-kissed waters. I sat down on the prickly grass, my heart thumping. The place didn't feel the same without Nan and Fliss beside me. Usually, to our imaginations, this was the haunt of lissom water maidens, of whom we yearned in vain to catch sight. Now it was simply a forlorn and empty place, where the stagnant waters reeked foully in the heat of the day. Miserably, I put my face against my raised knees and curled my arms over my head. When would it be safe to go back to Herons? I wanted to run there now, to hear Violet's warm voice, to be embraced by the colours, the scents of home. How could I explain my behaviour? The answer came to me, and in a flood of relief, I jumped to my feet and ran up the hill to the house.

Later that day, in the early evening, Fliss and Nan came to my room, where I lay in bed, attempting to appear delicate and worthy of sympathy. 'Why didn't you *say*, you silly thing?' Nan said in concern, sitting down on the coverlet.

'You were having fun,' I answered awkwardly. 'I didn't want to spoil it.'

'This illness came on very quickly,' Fliss said, a note of suspicion in her voice. It was – and still is – very difficult to deceive Fliss.

I shrugged, wouldn't meet her eyes. 'I just had to get out because I needed to be sick. I didn't want Mitch to see that.'

My excuses were all plausible; there was no reason to disbelieve them. The truth was I actually *did* feel ill now, slightly feverish.

That night, I had a dream, of which even to this day I can remember every detail. I was walking round the garden of Herons in moonlight, barefoot. The grass beneath my feet was slightly damp, yet warm, and where I trod the shorn blades released a green scent. I came to a place where usually there was a stone fountain fashioned of grey, lichened urns. Now, this spot was occupied by a rhododendron bush in full bloom. Even in the moonlight, I could see its flowers were a deep violet colour, with pink hearts that emitted a rosy glow. Around the bush, motes of muted light floated and spun, like down or feathers, almost grey in colour but occasionally lighting up in pin-pricks of brilliance. I had never seen anything so beautiful and went towards the bush, which was twice my height at least. As I drew close to it, I could smell that the blooms were scented, which was unusual for a rhododendron. I wanted to bury my face in those magical, fragrant blooms and reached out to touch them. But the merest contact of my fingers made the whole bush shudder. In horror, I watched every single flower fall down simultaneously to pile upon the stones beneath my feet. The strange motes of light swarmed up and flew away. Then it was over. I didn't wake up, but moved to some other dream that I don't remember.

The following day, Aunt Violet told me to keep to my bed. I had a temperature. Despite this, I no longer felt ill and was restless. I couldn't hear my cousins and imagined darkly they'd gone off with that Mitch again, on some other adventure. All day, I either read or dozed, simmering with jealousy but also disappointment I was being excluded from the day's activities. The only person who came to see me was Anne, one of Violet's staff, who brought me lemon barley water and some biscuits, since I didn't feel like eating anything more filling.

Around tea-time Violet put her head round the door to see how I was. I insisted I felt much better and was hungry. She allowed me to dress and go downstairs. The thought of food still made me feel slightly bilious, but I was determined to hide this, to think myself well. The illness wasn't real after all, so it would just have to accept that and go away.

Downstairs, I found Fliss in the library, curled up with the book we'd been looking at the day before. She glanced up when she heard me enter the room. 'Hello, feeling better now?'

'A bit,' I said. 'Have you been out?'

Fliss shook her head. 'No. I've been helping Mrs Barr with the baking.'

'Why didn't you come to see me?'

'Violet said to let you rest.' She smiled. 'Anyway, you're up now.'

'Where's Nan?' I demanded.

Fliss shrugged. 'I don't know. She didn't want to do any baking and went off by herself.'

These activities were so far removed from our usual habits, I felt unnerved. If we did ever go to the kitchen, it was all together and only to beg for left over cake mix or lumps of icing, rather than actually involve ourselves in culinary tasks. None of us ever went 'off alone' either.

'Something's wrong,' I blurted.

Fliss raised her eyebrows at me. 'What do you mean?'

'It started yesterday in that awful place,' I began, then lost confidence to continue. I could see that Fliss and I were in different fields, an ocean of grass between us. There was no immediate empathy as there usually was between us.

'Awful place?' Fliss put down her book. 'Kitty, what's the matter with you?'

I turned away from her. She'd not felt a thing. My eyes grew hot with tears that could not fall. 'Nothing,' I said. 'I think the heat got to me yesterday, or there was something in the sandwiches disagreed with me.'

'Poor you,' she said. 'You do look a bit odd.'

'You didn't come after me,' I said plaintively, still unable to look at her.

'We thought you were behind us,' Fliss said. 'And when we were ready to leave, you'd just gone. I'm *sorry* we're not psychic. You should've said something.' Her voice now was sharp.

At that moment, a stranger walked in through the French windows – a stranger wearing the body of my cousin Nan. She had on her wide-brimmed hat as before, but also a more formal blue polka dot dress with a full skirt. When she took off her hat and laid it on the table by the window, I saw her lips were crimson with lipstick that had clearly been recently applied. She also appeared to have aged around ten years overnight. I could only stare at this apparition in dismay.

She laughed at me. 'Seen a ghost, Kit?'

'Where've you been?' I asked.

She touched her hair – which was neatly brushed, and ribboned into a ponytail – in a grotesquely adult way. 'Oh, just the village.'

'What were you doing *there*?'

She shrugged, laughed. 'You're so *nosy*, aren't you? I went to the tea rooms, actually.'

I knew then she'd been with Mitch.

Saying nothing more, I went out into the garden. What was the point now? To me, our summer world had simply... gone.

I went to where we'd strung our bells in the rowan tree; the air was achingly still so they didn't chime. Here I lay on the grass in the shadow of the branches, almost witless with a grief I couldn't explain or understand. Somehow, we'd *made* this terribly estrangement between us happen. I pawed back through my memories. Had I started it with that talk of the castle on the ridge? Maybe the ruin hadn't been real at all before I'd dreamed it up. Now it was a monster, warped and disgusting and stinking. The ethereal voices had been silenced.

No, I told myself sternly, *no. You can't invent a building of bricks and stone. That's just stupid. It* was *in that book, after all.*

What had been in that room? I wondered. That was the moment, surely? Until then, the day had been fine – more or less – but for Nan and Mitch, with their absurd mutual attraction waiting to happen. I wished he didn't exist, that he could in fact be wished away. If only we could get back to normal, but how could I make this happen?

When dinner was ready, Nan came out into the garden to find me. She put an arm around my shoulders and said quietly, 'Everything's all right, Kit. You *do* know that, don't you?'

Looking at her, I saw she'd wiped off her lipstick and had changed into shorts and shirt: *our* Nan, not that other one. I shook my head. 'I felt ill. I'm fine now.'

Nan kissed my hair. 'There, then. We'll do our usual things tomorrow, I promise.'

Looking back, I can see that Nan did try to keep things together as they'd always been, but it was like trying to shore up a building where the foundations had gone. Perhaps Herons, like me, was suspicious, even frightened, of change. Or perhaps I became more sensitive. I can't be sure. But I remember how I heard the house creaking all the time, as if stretching its bones in discomfort. When I mentioned this to Fliss and Nan they immediately thought up some far-fetched reason for this – something to do with a walled up girl and clanking chains. Even our make believe had changed somehow, become a parody of itself. I joined in as I'd always done, but it was as if part of me now was simply an observer looking on from a distance. Also, we had to share Nan with Mitch, who became to me obnoxious. I felt he was sly and feckless, with a satyr's face, and a satyr's disregard for people's feelings. Nan was careful to divide her time between us all, and Fliss didn't seem to mind. In fact, they now had whispered conversations apart from me that involved a lot of high-pitched shrieks and giggling.

Consequently, I spent time alone, but I wasn't unhappy. In just a week or so I became used to my own company and began to prefer it to that mockery of intimacy that waited for me in Fliss and Nan's presence. With Violet's encouragement I started painting in water colours – scenes of the mere and house, but always peopled with supernatural creatures – secret faces looking out here and there. Violet praised my work. I knew she was aware I was hurt by the change in my relationship with my cousins, but she didn't talk to me about it, perhaps waiting for me to bring the subject up myself. Sometimes, I saw her look at me in a certain way and felt she knew everything about me.

Once I heard Violet speaking to Nan in the sitting room, while I was rummaging around outside in the shrubbery near the house. The long windows were open. I remained very silent and still so they wouldn't realise I was near. All I caught of the conversation was Violet saying, 'You will be *careful*, sweetie, won't you? I'm sure you know what I mean.'

I didn't, but I intuited it must involve the vile Mitch.

'Violet!' Nan squealed, laughing in what could have been embarrassment or delight. 'You're terrible!'

'Not at all,' Violet replied smoothly. 'I know well enough that prohibitions and rules don't work in the hearts and minds of young people, who are naturally wilful. Best to give them advice on how to sail the dangerous waters than try and keep them to shore, since even if you tied up all the boats, or scuppered them, the young would simply swim away regardless.'

'I can sail *and* I can swim,' Nan said proudly.

'I hope so,' Violet said. 'Come, I have some dresses I think you might like.'

They moved away from me then, Nan talking swiftly but quietly. I heard Violet's low, comforting voice responding to her.

After we'd been at Herons for nearly three weeks, Beatrice came to stay for a week. I was surprised to find I was glad to see her. She seemed a solid piece of dependability, standing legs apart in the hallway, booming, 'Hello, everyone.'

Bea too had grown and changed since I'd last seen her. I realised she was becoming attractive. She was somewhat masculine, so I suppose the word to describe her is handsome rather than pretty. There was an open honesty to Bea that I felt no longer existed in Fliss and Nan, if it had even been there in the first place.

I offered to help carry her two suitcases to her bedroom. Here, she said bluntly, 'What's up with the ballerinas?'

I realised she must be referring to Fliss and Nan. 'Why? What do you mean?' Before this summer, I would have been outraged if Bea had referred to my cousins in a sarcastic way, and would at the very least have snubbed her. Now, I felt slightly satisfied. This, I knew, was a contemptible reaction, but it still felt cosy.

'You three were always thick as thieves. Not so now, is it?' That Bea could have picked this up from the scant ten minutes she'd been with us all in the hall was astounding, if not a little frightening to me. 'Had a barney?' Bea enquired relentlessly.

'Well…' I wondered then if I could tell Bea everything, but decided against it. 'There's this boy,' I said.

'Oh, is *that* it?' Bea said. 'Let them get on with it, then. Nothing you can do about that.'

That evening, I saw Nan sitting in the garden beneath the rowan tree. There was something about her posture that impelled me to go to her; I felt she was sad. She had her back to me, gazing down at the mere where the shadows were clustering thickly, preparing for night. Was she remembering previous summers? Did she mourn for them as I did? I felt that now was the time to talk frankly with her, try and reclaim our friendship. But as I drew closer, I realised it wasn't Nan at all. In fact, there was no one there beneath the rowan, just the shadow of gently-moving boughs.

I dreamed again of the violet rhododendron in the place where a fountain should be. This time, I was crying as I stood before the naked tree. I was scooping up the fallen petals, which I could see were already turning brown. I was attempting to attach them once more their branches. I woke from the dream to my moonlit bedroom, and I knew then that the rhododendron was the past and that I couldn't make it come back.

From that time, I often caught sight of Nan-who-wasn't-there around the house and gardens, always a distance from me. I'd see her walk past the sitting-room windows, or spot her disappearing round a corner in the corridors of the house. I wasn't sure if what I glimpsed so fleetingly was a ghost or a figment of my imagination. I'd wanted so desperately for ghosts to be real, for the supernatural to be real, but faced with a situation that might possibly *be* supernatural, I didn't feel the level of excitement I was sure I *should* feel. I couldn't discuss it with anyone because Nan and Fliss felt so apart from me now, even though we maintained an act of close camaraderie. I believed they'd think I was making it up to get attention.

While Bea was with us, we all played tennis and badminton, and if bad weather confined us to the house we played cards and Monopoly. Once I saw the non-Nan standing by the door of the library while we sat round the table, laughing and chattering. She was there for only a moment, and I thought she'd been looking at herself – wanly, sadly. This was a younger version of Nan, so it couldn't possibly be a ghost. Nan was very much alive, more present in the world than any of us.

Later that day, as Bea and I had moments alone together before dinner, Bea said, 'what spooked you earlier?'

I took more notice of her now and had learned she was an observant person, who could interpret the words and actions of others quite accurately. There was no point denying it, because clearly she'd seen me stare at the doorway for some moments, no doubt with mouth open or a blanched face, or other typical symptoms of seeing something odd. I looked at Bea for a moment, then said, 'you wouldn't believe me if I told you.'

'If you believe it, that's good enough for me,' Bea said. 'Doesn't mean I have to believe it myself, of course, but that doesn't matter. Tell me.'

And so I did. I didn't mention that I thought I'd somehow *created* the castle. I emphasised Nan's flirtation with Mitch, and then somewhat more reluctantly told Bea of the phantom I saw so often. 'Our visit to Rookstone changed everything,' I said miserably. 'I wish I could take back what I said. I wish I'd never seen that castle in the stone.'

Bea drew in a breath. 'Kitty… you can't stop Nan growing up, and that's what you're describing. I've seen it at school. People seem to change overnight sometimes, even people you care about, who you think you know.' Her face was sad, and I knew she'd lost someone to adulthood too.

However, this rather dampening explanation did not satisfy me. 'But the ghost…'

'You know what I think?' Bea announced, brightening, stamping her memories down. 'You need to go back to that place. I'll go with you.'

'Why? Why go back?'

'Face your ghost,' she said.

'But I didn't see it there… It was here.'

'Things turned the moment you entered that room in the castle,' Bea said. 'You said the smell changed and then you had to escape.'

'Bea… do you believe there's something *unnatural* about what's happening?' I was actually aghast she might think that.

'I really don't know,' she replied, 'but I think that's what you should do.'

I considered. Perhaps I shouldn't have run away that day. Perhaps returning *was* appropriate. 'Do we go with the others?'

Bea shook her head. 'No, let's just go together.'

It was not difficult to escape Fliss and Nan. While Nan gave us her time most days of the week, on the remaining days she'd be off in the village, presumably with Mitch and his friends. She sometimes smelled of cigarettes, and I believed she'd taken up smoking herself. When Nan was absent, Fliss spent much more time with Mrs Barr and her assistants. Bea remarked rather scathingly that while Nan had taken a shine to boys, Fliss had turned to the skills of home-making. 'She'll be a wife not a lover,' Bea said. Sometimes, she could come out with what seemed to me extraordinarily adult statements. I wondered where she heard such things.

Thursday gave us our opportunity. We didn't bother taking food with us, or attempt to make the visit to Rookstone anything but an essential task. We'd go there, see what happened, come home. No one would know.

As we left Herons, I turned to glance back at the house, see if the ghost-Nan was in the window again. She wasn't.

The day was dappled – mostly fine but sometimes clouds muffled up the sun. Bea did not dawdle, so it took far less time to reach the shade of the rhododendron forest than it had on my first visit.

I felt no trepidation as I led the way to the hall and the room beyond it. Disgust for the place had left me; it was just a ruin. I wondered in fact why I'd even bothered to come. What had happened was within Nan, Fliss and me, not something external. Bea was right – time alone was changing us all. We couldn't remain children for ever. That in itself was a shock, but of course for everyone there comes that moment when we realise this. The moment had in fact passed for me.

At the entrance to the hall, with its dank, dirty smell, I turned to Bea behind me and said, 'Is there any point to this?'

'Don't you want to go on?'

'I'm not bothered. Do you want to see it?'

'Yes.'

We stepped into the green shadow of the hall. As before, pigeons hummed above us, but the smell was not as bad as I remembered. Still, it was an unwelcoming place. As we made our way to what I now called 'the hidden chamber', I heard a noise that halted my steps. 'What's that?' I murmured.

It was a series of noises, a song perhaps, but nothing like the ethereal choir I'd once imagined I'd heard. Grunts, cries, rhythmic – almost tribal. The sounds appeared to be coming from the room ahead of us; its door was closed.

'Kitty…' Bea said in an uncertain tone, 'I don't think…'

No, I had to find out. If there *was* something supernatural here, I was compelled to open the door on it. I had Bea with me, who was strong and fearless, so I wasn't afraid either.

I put my hand upon the round knob of the door, which was warm, as if someone had recently held it for a long time.

I thought he was killing her – the sounds were dreadful. She was lying on the floor, her skirt up around her waist, her legs spread wide. He was lying on top of her with his trousers round his knees, bouncing up and down on her. Disgusting!

'Nan!' I yelled and hurtled into the room, throwing myself on top of that vile youth, beating at him with my fists. 'Get off her, you beast!'

'Kitty, no!' Bea cried behind me, then I felt her hands on my shoulders, pulling me back. I struggled, but she was stronger than I was.

I saw Nan's face, horrified, staring madly at me over Mitch's shoulder. Her mouth was open, lipstick smeared over her lower face. She didn't seem to recognise me.

Mitch's head was turned to me, his face furious. 'Fuck off you, stupid brats,' he spat. 'Just fuck off.'

Bea dragged me protesting to the door. She closed it, leaned upon it, held me close. I'd begun to cry. 'Come on,' Bea said, 'let's go.'

She led me, arm around my shoulders back to the hall. I felt dazed, as if I'd fallen and hit my head. What had I seen? Once we'd made our way to the courtyard, Bea produced a handkerchief, which she held out to me. I took it and wiped my eyes, blew my nose. 'What was he *doing* to her?' I asked. 'We should stop it. We can't just...'

'She doesn't want us to stop it,' Bea said.

That night, I awoke from a dream I couldn't recall. My room was lit faintly by moonlight. I was compelled to get out of bed and go to the window, which I opened wide to let in the scent of the dark. I saw the phantom Nan standing under the rowan tree. She was gazing up at me, and from that distance I couldn't see her expression. She was a true ghost, though; white, almost transparent, very beautiful. I didn't have to shout, because I knew that she'd hear me. 'Go away,' I whispered. 'You must go away now. You're dead.'

I realised some years later how lucky Nan had been to avoid a teenage pregnancy, which would have been a far more traumatic situation then than it is today. I'm quite sure now that all she'd had to protect her was

Violet's mild warning. Our summers inevitably changed. Nan in fact did not come to Violet's house again for the holidays, and Fliss only for one more year. That last summer when we'd been together, after the incident in the castle, and Bea's rather embarrassed explanation to me back home, Nan underwent another change. Perhaps Mitch had been spooked by being caught, or he'd had what he'd been after and wanted nothing more, but he turned cold on her. He gave up the job as Violet's gardener. Nan no longer went to the village or put on her lipstick. She cried a lot, and didn't sleep very well, becoming a lot like the little ghost I'd seen of her. First love – a tsunami of pain we have to survive. She didn't share any of it with me. She blamed me, I think, for Mitch dumping her. I never told on her, didn't even tell Fliss, although I believe Nan confided in her sister, because Fliss too withdrew from me. The rest of the summer passed uneasily, although Bea wrote to her parents and asked to stay for longer. I was grateful to her for that.

Once we were all women, engrossed in new lives, my cousins and I became close again – in a different way to how we had been before. We never talked of that summer. It left a scar on Nan. She became a brittle, sharp creature, and the years only honed the blade of her. She was always very witty, but had a series of disastrous relationships with unsuitable men, including three marriages, which culminated with her early death at the age of 35. At the funeral, Fliss said to me, 'She'll be happier now.' I wanted to believe the potential for what she became had been in her all the time, and it hadn't been Mitch who'd turned her that way. Because, if it had been, we might've helped her, stopped it. But if any of us were remotely responsible, it was Violet. She should have sent Nan away the moment she realised what was happening.

Bea and I continued to visit Violet in the summer times, through the remainder of our childhood, through our college years, through relationships – in my case, marriage – break ups, career moves and house purchases. We kept on visiting right up until her death, and that was a good many years, for she was ninety-six when she died. During her final illness I stayed with her a lot, taking my work with me, since I was freelance and could work where I liked. The modern age had come. I could work on my computer in the old library, surrounded by childhood memories. One evening, as we sat drinking gin cocktails in the dusk of a perfect summer day, I told Violet all about that *other* summer, even up to stumbling upon Nan and Mitch at Rookstone, and how I'd foolishly believed I'd conjured up the castle and made it all happen.

Violet had smiled at that. 'You know,' she said, 'there might be something in it.'

I grinned. 'Oh, come on! What do you mean?'

'That castle you describe – I never saw it as a girl, and I went to Rookstone quite regularly. And that book you found in the library – I can't recall ever seeing that either, and I *did* know the books in there quite well.'

Violet was very old by then. Her memories often became confused with dreams. It's likely she was mistaken.

Do As Thou Wilt...

This story was inspired by an incident in the life of a woman, following a rather messy romantic yet platonic affair, who was a member of a pagan magical group. Details have been changed radically to protect the identities of those involved. In any case, it was the essence of the drama that interested me, specifically how this woman – the Leah of the invented tale – lost her faith in magic. 90% of this tale is 'made up'.

We hear often of Christians losing their faith, and also those involved in other religions, but paganism is not exempt from this either, even if it follows no strict dogma. Losing faith in oneself is perhaps the truth of it here.

I think it is also true that some people we meet in life are vampiric, not in the literal sense, or even a psychic sense, but in that they gorge themselves on the emotions of others and revel in creating dramas. These creatures may walk away from collisions intact, leaving others severely injured in their wake. In this story, I wanted the injured to get even.

Following the strange affair with Brett Lyle it took Leah Metcalfe almost five years to realise the level of his scorn merited action. She might never have done anything, simply allowed the pain to heal and fade, get on with life, as you're supposed to do after a bereavement. She read stories in the media of men who conned gullible women out of all their money – she had always thought them rather careless women – but in her case of conning, Lyle, she felt, had cleaned out her soul rather than her bank account. Or at least he had murdered a little bit of it. She grieved for this sundered part, long after it was polite or sane still to be noticeably doing so. After the vanishing years of moping and longing, which had felt like some nightmarish enchanted sleep, she had eventually become utterly disgusted with the emotions and had put them away, at last awake and aghast at herself for wasting so much time on what had ultimately proved to be nonsense. Only when her friend Sophie (in whom she had confided during the two years of her involvement with Lyle) brought his name up in conversation during one of their fortnightly lunch meetings did Leah think about him again.

The two women still met each other with an embrace and the greeting, 'Blessed be,' even though Leah had not been part of Sophie's magical group for several years. She and Sophie rarely spoke of such matters nowadays; their friendship was confined to the mundane. It had been Sophie who'd put considerable effort into maintaining their relationship; Leah was fully aware of this. Perhaps Sophie considered it a charitable act.

A few minutes after they sat down to their lunch, Sophie eyed Leah carefully. 'Brett Lyle,' she said. 'I don't know if this is still a "no go" area for you, but I thought you should know. It's just burning a hole in me. You weren't the only one, you know. He was still at it after you. Still is.'

Leah shifted awkwardly on her seat. The cafe was hot, felt steamy. Cold rain hammered the shopping precinct outside, where women marched about their business. Some had bare legs. Rather unwise, Leah thought, in February. 'I'm hardly shocked,' Leah said, although just the sound of his name had shocked her.

'Well, of course. I realise that. But... Not everyone is as *aware* as you. Not everyone can get over *things* so easily.'

Leah did not really think squandering years of precious life on mourning the loss of a man like Lyle could be described as being aware or getting over it easily, but decided to let this pass. Perhaps Sophie meant it as a compliment. 'Why do you mention it? Have you heard something?' Leah realised she was in fact eager to know. She wanted to hear details of another woman's emotional car crash. *Inside, we are all ghouls*, she thought.

'This one is a lot younger than you,' Sophie said, sipping her latte, 'thought it was for real.'

Leah coughed up a laugh. 'And I didn't?'

Sophie screwed up her eyes briefly, shook her head. 'Sorry, you know what I mean. She doesn't have your *experience*, you know? At least you *did* get over it. I saw the way you were. You did... *incredibly*.' She grimaced. 'Ack, whatever I say sounds crass.'

'Don't worry about it, tell me what you know.'

'It's this girl I work with. You've probably heard me mention her: Cassy.'

'The one who got burned on a sunbed?'

Sophie smirked. 'Yes, *that* one. Complete airhead, but a kind girl. I didn't even know about this *circumstance* until it was too late. We don't talk that intimately, you know. I just noticed something was wrong with her. She was... listless. Totally not like her. So I asked her. And this look she gave me... I recognised it, Leah. Made me shiver.' Sophie shivered theatrically to emphasise her words, and Leah found herself freckled by a shiver too.

'She was haunted, *lost...*' Sophie continued. 'For a moment she was *you*, and that was even before she told me his name.'

Leah, chilled, said evenly, 'What a chilling coincidence.'

'You seem to be taking this very calmly.'

'I don't know what I'm taking yet, go on.'

'Well naturally, she didn't spill her guts to me immediately. As I said, we're not that close, but she wanted to talk, I suppose, and simply told me "this guy, he's doing my head in". I just said something soothing like "Oh men, bane of our lives, aren't they? Can't live with or without, as they say". Cassy answered, "yes, it's just like that", then walked away from me, right as I was saying something else. At the time I thought it was rather rude.'

Leah didn't interrupt or make any noises or gestures of encouragement. She found, in fact, that she was becoming increasingly frozen and was aware of a soft whistling noise in her head.

'Cassy didn't get any better, and it started to affect her work. As her supervisor, I was eventually obliged to get her into the office and have a little talk.' Sophie paused, clearly waiting for a signal Leah was listening or interested. 'Are you okay with this?'

'Of course. Merely waiting to hear.'

'You're not completely okay with it, are you? You just can't resist knowing.'

'Then just tell me.'

'The merest comment on Cassy's recent behaviour had her in tears. She told me she had a disease, and at first I took that at face value and thought she'd got herself into some embarrassing trouble, but even little airhead Cassy can speak in metaphor. I told her to tell me about it, and she did, then. What she described, the mind games, the hot and cold episodes, the yearning to escape, only to be reeled back in, it was familiar. I think I knew even before she found the courage to say his name.'

'Lots of people behave like that, men and women alike,' Leah said. 'That kind of behaviour isn't confined to one man, or even one gender.'

'It goes further than that with him, you know it does.'

Vampire, Leah thought. 'I'm not sure. My views on the man are hardly unbiased.'

'Take it from me, it *does*,' Sophie continued. 'Cassy told me how she'd met him, how he'd seemed like a brother at first. He brought light to her, she said. She fell into love, like someone falling into a vat of acid; to be eaten away, slowly and painfully. They met almost every day – to *talk*. Sometimes, he'd lightly touch her... his eyes would hold her with promises he never said aloud. She wanted more and expected it, even dared to make subtle moves.'

'And then the shutters came down.'

Sophie nodded. 'But of course not entirely, because that's not part of the game, is it? He knows how to drive someone crazy, so cracked his knuckles and got on with it.'

'Poor girl.'

'When she revealed his name, I had to... I hope you don't mind, I didn't mention yours... but I told her I'd heard of him and that someone I knew had gone through the same thing. I told her she had to break contact immediately, because it could go on for years, him feeding off her; it would get worse, and never better.'

'Did she listen to you?'

'Did she, hell! Did you?'

'And does she know about the wife?'

'Yes. She got the same story as you did, too pathetic and clichéd to be real, but utterly gobbled up.'

Leah grimaced. 'His problem is he's bored and wants affairs, but lacks the balls to do anything physical about it. He's more conventional than he likes to think he is. It's no more than that, and some of us are stupid enough to think we can change people.'

Sophie raised her brows. 'Is that how you've cleaned it up in your head?'

'I believe it to be the truth. I'm just as at fault as he is, and so is Cassy. Neediness, insecurity, the garbage we carry around.' Leah made a casual gesture. 'Tell her that.'

'You don't believe a word of that,' Sophie said. 'He has magic. He might not be aware of the fact but he has, and he uses it. Perhaps the time's come for others who have it to take him to task.'

'It's none of our business. Everyone is responsible for...'

'Leah, stop it, you've not heard me out. I spoke with Matty about this.'

Matty was a mutual friend, who was also a friend of Lyle's. Leah still met him once a month for dinner. Lyle was never mentioned, probably because Matty felt guilty for introducing Leah to Lyle in the first place. 'What did he say?'

'He told me there had been two others, who he knew of, after you. Cassy would be the third. Apparently, the second one got out quick, although the first one was beaten up pretty badly by it. Matty only knew about them because they were part of his and Lyle's social circle and he saw it happening. He didn't know about Cassy. And gods know how many more there are! Lyle sucks the living energy out of people, Leah. It's food to him. Do you honestly think it's okay to know predators like that are hunting vulnerable people and not do something about it? Don't you want to help Cassy? She's helpless, she's... *bewitched.*'

'What do you propose to do?'

'Turn a mirror on him,' Sophie said grimly. 'Throw that leech energy back at him. Make him taste his own self. If that doesn't choke him, nothing will.'

'Pointless,' Leah said. 'He's impervious to magic, believe me.'

'You sure about that?'

'Yes, because I threw the book at him. I tried everything to bring harmony into our sick situation, communication, honesty, all that bullshit...'

'Bullshit?'

Leah shook her head. 'It was a waste of time. He's impervious.'

'And *that's* what killed your faith in yourself,' Sophie said, folding her arms and leaning back in her chair. Her expression had become flinty. 'You lost your faith in magic, which is why you left the group. That's the truth, isn't it? The real bullshit was the excuse you gave us about how you'd suddenly become too busy to be spiritual.'

Leah gestured helplessly. 'I don't want to argue about this, we should drop it. I don't want any further... contamination... by even thinking about Lyle, never mind doing some ritual to try and bring him into line, which wouldn't work anyway.'

Sophie wiped her hands over her face, sighed. 'I remember a woman who believed we were capable of anything. I remember the amazing times we had, the energy we raised, the good we did. That woman was an inspiration. I can't – and don't want to – believe a shit like Brett Lyle could destroy that woman for good.'

'I let him happen to me,' Leah said. 'If you must look at it in terms of magic, let's just say he was a test I failed. And much as I would like to see him gunned down in cold blood, never mind be given a civilised, chastening lesson in self-awareness and responsibility, it's unethical to try and influence another's will. You know that, Soph. We've always abided by that.'

'But what about the will of those he targets?'

Leah shrugged. 'As I said, a test. We don't have to fall for it, but some do. And you mentioned the "second one" who got away quick. She passed the test. There are no doubt others.'

'I don't want to believe Brett Lyle is on this Earth as a life lesson for vulnerable women,' Sophie said. 'That's too cruel to contemplate.'

'Yes it is. It's bloody cruel. And however many rituals you do, or believe that the universe loves you and wants the best for you, the cruelty is still there. I'm sorry, Sophie. We should have talked about this before. Yes, I lost my faith. Magic is a comforting illusion, like the religions we so scorned, and there's nothing wrong in that, or the aim of groups like ours who want to make a difference. But in the end, most of the positive results must be down to luck, or coincidence. I think focused will *can* move mountains, yes, but perhaps not to order, and not all the time. One thing I learned is that we are truly alone. There is no greater power looking out for us.'

Sophie stared at Leah unwaveringly. 'He should be tried for murder,' she said.

Leah was unhappy at the way she and Sophie parted. She was unhappy that the truth was out, because she didn't want to hurt her erstwhile group mates. She knew she had been a kind of figurehead to them, so for that reason had tried to bow out subtly and slowly. She hadn't wanted them to know she simply couldn't believe in what they did any more. Just thinking about them sitting in a circle, with linked hands, believing they could change the world for the better, made her heart contract with love. It was better to be like them than like she was now.

Unlike Sophie, Leah was self-employed and worked from home. She ran a successful catering business that, aside from weddings and other such big events, offered themed evenings for groups of female friends. In the past, this had included Arabian Nights, Egyptian Magic, Celtic Dream, to name a few. This had been Leah's favourite part of her job. The food and drink, especially tailored to the events, had a superficially witchy gleam. A friend from her magical group, Ellie, used to come along with merchandise – trinkets, glittering scarves, perfume and jewellery – which the women would browse through and then purchase as they nibbled their exotic treats. As part of the evening's activities, out would come the Tarot cards, and the women would pay a little extra for that. Most evenings, another friend, Sarah, would be there to offer healing or massage. And with repeat clients, once they realised the three women they invited into their homes to pamper them were *witches*, rather different commissions appeared in Leah's in box. Word spread. She and her friends had been asked to help with sickness, with broken hearts, with money troubles. And to the best of their ability, they did. This was so successful it got to the point where Leah had been obliged to turn commissions down.

When Brett Lyle plunged the final knife into her by abruptly exiting her life without chance for discussion or even a decent farewell, the shock of it, never mind the pain, had diminished Leah considerably, and she had taken a break from her work. In fact, she had been unable to concentrate on preparing the food for *any* events, never mind the special ones where she was required to sit and read the cards, or try to help people magically when their lives had taken a turn for the worse. All she wanted to say to them was, 'You shouldn't be paying me for this. Life is either crap, great or bearable, and Fate takes a swing at us when it likes. If things are good, enjoy them, if they're bearable, count your luck, if they're bad, poor you. Find a lawyer, a doctor or a psychiatrist. Nothing I can do will change a thing.' She had this little speech off by heart, practiced as she lay on her couch in the dim afternoons.

Eventually the emails and calls seeking to hire her died off. At this time, she began to drift away from her magical group also.

After a couple of months, realising that life inevitably continues, as do bills, Leah started looking for work again, and also reinvented the special part of the business, which she regarded as her personal indulgence. Now she offered parties having the theme of a genteel life gone by; afternoon tea on delicate china, such as would have been enjoyed by 'ladies' in earlier decades. She scoured second hand and charity shops for appropriate crockery and cutlery, eventually building up an impressive collection. She experimented with baking recipes she found in old cooking books, and after some careful promotion and free teas in strategic places, the new business shone like the old. Emulating the 'extra services' offered by the previous parties, Leah employed two girls to accompany her and provide facials and manicures. Women of all kinds liked the parties, which proved more successful than Leah had envisaged. But then, she had a gift with preparing food that some would call magical; she *invested* into her business on more than one level, and paid great attention to detail. It might have been a nice touch if, as part of the events, she'd read the tea leaves for her clients, but Leah firmly refused to let herself offer that.

And yet, despite her scepticism and denial, didn't magic still *nibble* at her? When she baked her cakes, working good feeling into the mixture, and sought out the exact special kinds of teas she felt were right, wasn't she still indulging in ritual?

After lunch with Sophie, Leah entered her house and, in the hallway, faced the mirror that hung on the wall opposite the door. The glass was faintly smoked, giving a reflection that had always looked to Leah like a scene from a spooky film with a blue filter over it.

'Really, Leah,' she said to herself. 'When *are* you going to forget what happened? You don't kid *me*, you know.'

Shaking her head, she turned to her answerphone on the table beneath the mirror to listen to messages from clients wanting to hire her. She wrote down the details on the pad by the phone. Then came the last one, the third, the fateful knocking upon the door.

'Hello, this is Carol Lyle. I'd like to book a tea party, please, for my birthday in three weeks' time, the 7th. I hope this isn't too short notice, but a friend recommended you. My address is number 8, The Ashes and if you'd like to return my call, my number is...'

At first, Leah didn't realise who it was; she merely wrote down the address and phone number, thinking she might not be able to fit this woman in. And then, as if her reflection was still displayed in the smoky mirror and calling to her, she thought, *Wait... wait a minute!*

She went quickly to her office in what was supposed to be the dining room and looked at her cloth-bound appointment book, which lay on the desk. In this she wrote down her appointments in a neat curling script. 7th March. She flicked to the relevant page. As she thought, someone had already booked her for that day; one of her regulars.

Looking at the page, she picked up the phone on the desk, stabbed in a number. 'Hello, is that Shannon? Hi, it's Leah Metcalfe here, I'm really sorry but I'm going to have to cancel our appointment for the 7th. Something unavoidable and rather serious has cropped up.... I'm more than happy to give you a free party on another date if you'd like one....'

Leah ended the call, punched in another number. 'Hello, is this Carol Lyle? This is Leah Metcalfe from 'Tea Cakes'. You called me earlier about a party...'

Leah had no idea what was urging her on, but decided simply to go with the flow. It was a coincidence beyond all fathomable coincidences that Brett Lyle's wife had called her on the very day that Sophie had told her about Cassy. *You don't believe, but just go with it... If you're being thrown a bone by Fate, snatch it up...*

Leah had never met Carol Lyle, and only knew what she looked like from when she had once investigated Lyle's Facebook page where he displayed 'jolly' photos of family get togethers. Leah had seen a rather plump, short but attractive brunette, with a wide and innocent smile. She had been smiling in every photo. On the phone, Carol sounded chatty and rather nervous. She laughed a lot.

'I know it is rather short notice,' she said.

'That's no problem,' Leah replied in her smoothest, most comforting tone. 'As luck would have it, there's been a cancellation for the 7th. You must be sure to have all men folk out of the way!' Leah added one of her smokiest laughs. 'My parties are girls only.'

'Of course, of course,' said Carol Lyle. 'I wouldn't be getting anything for my birthday if I wasn't doing this myself. Just some girlfriends and my mum and sister.'

'Great,' said Leah. 'Shall we discuss the menu?'

Leah considered not taking her assistants along, but then decided she should not alter her habitual ritual. (*There it was again.*) The party was set for 6.00 pm – an odd time, really. Clients usually opted for an afternoon event or an evening one; not this in between time when people normally ate dinner and then did something else.

Leah prepared the food with especial care. As she conjured her mixtures, she found she had much sympathetic feeling for Carol Lyle.

That nervous laugh, that trusting smile. It seemed particularly cruel for the vampire Brett Lyle to be married to someone like that. *But I suppose she's malleable*, Leah thought. *She won't make a fuss, even when she suspects...she was chosen precisely.*

As she was standing at the door to number 8, The Ashes, (new housing estate, pricey), on a fairly mild March evening, with her assistants behind her, Leah knew why she was doing this. She had to *see*. And when she had seen, she might act.

While they waited for Carol to answer the door, Leah remembered Brett Lyle taking her in his arms, enfolding her as if with wings. 'This is how we are,' he had murmured. She had felt like a mortal woman seduced by a dark angel. But their kisses had always been chaste. His gaze, however, had never been that.

Leah dismissed the memory, pulled herself together. The door was opening, light spilling out.

Carol Lyle bounced onto the front step. 'Hi, hi. Do you need any help with your stuff?'

'No, we'll carry everything,' Leah said. 'Can you just show us to the kitchen? Amber and Rachel will need somewhere to set up, too, if that's all right.'

'Come in, come in...'

Leah stepped over the threshold. This was Brett Lyle's front, this middle class life on an ordinary if upmarket housing estate. This was his lair, to which he always returned; his coffin full of native soil.

It was a comfortable home, although everything was new as if it had only just arrived from a furnishing warehouse. Anyone would have thought the Lyles had recently moved in, except Leah had known 8 The Ashes as Lyle's address when she'd been seeing him. It hadn't been that difficult to discover.

A group of women were sitting in the front room, drinking wine. Leah nodded and smiled at them as she followed Carol Lyle through to the kitchen. Here Carol thrust a huge glass of Shiraz at Leah, even before Leah had set down her crates. 'I have white too if you prefer,' she said. 'Or... juice or something?'

Leah took the glass and swigged. 'This is great, thanks.'

She set the glass down on the counter and began to remove her cakes and sandwiches reverently from their packaging. Carol, meanwhile directed Amber and Rachel to two of the spare bedrooms where they could work. Then she returned to the kitchen as Leah was arranging an array of heavily iced, liqueur-laced cupcakes on a tiered stand.

'They look *so* beautiful,' said Carol Lyle. 'I love the decorations.'

Leah removed her *piece de résistance* from the crate at her feet. 'This is a present for you,' she said. 'A birthday cake.' It was immense, robed in dark chocolate butter icing, fortified with Tia Maria and a lavish pinch of chilli. A mass of black and white fondant roses spilled across its surface in a tangled trail. On each stem, the dark green leaves and thorns had been carefully formed. And the tips of the thorns were red. Half hidden among the petals and foliage was a silvered plaque – again edible – with the words *'For Carol, her birthday'* engraved upon it.

Carol's eyes misted up. 'Oh, that's... oh, I really won't want to eat it and spoil it.'

Leah laughed. 'Take some photos, then eat it. That way you'll have the appearance *and* the taste. Trust me, it's scrumptious.'

'Later, then,' Carole said. 'Thank you, Leah. I didn't expect that.'

'My pleasure.'

As well as the array of teas, the cakes, the exquisite sandwiches, wine continued to flow. Leah later blamed this for what happened. When the birthday cake was carried ceremonially from the kitchen, now lit with tiny green candles, the women in the room gasped. One of them said, perhaps the mother, 'it's amazing, Carol, but rather like a funeral cake! That thing in the middle looks like a gravestone. And whatever made you choose those colours?'

Carol cast an embarrassed glance at Leah. 'I... I didn't. The cake was a present.'

The other woman laughed. 'Really? I hope nobody wants you dead, love!'

'That was a horrible thing to say!' Carol snapped. 'No one wants me dead. How could you say that?'

'It was just a joke,' the woman said.

'I made the cake,' Leah said smoothly, 'and my taste veers towards the Gothic. I assure you there's no bad intention in it.'

'It's beautiful, and I love it, Leah,' Carol said hotly. 'Now I'm going to eat a massive piece of it.' She brandished the cake knife with a humorous evil leer.

65

Everyone laughed and Carol cut the cake. Its innards were a dark treacly brown, plump with dates, spiced with cinnamon. Carol quickly dispensed portions round the room, even handed one to Leah. Then, after a moment's silence, all the guests bit into their slice of cake. Leah left hers untouched.

'Oh my god, it's amazing!' Carol cried. 'What's *in* it, Leah?'

One of the other women laughed, wiping crumbs from her lips. 'Ah, she's not going to reveal her secret ingredients!'

'On the contrary,' Leah said, smiling. 'I can tell you that the main ingredients are strength and love.'

Everyone laughed again, clearly thinking she was joking.

Perhaps it was mention of the Gothic, the appearance of the cake, or the woman's clumsy joke that instigated it, but somehow the conversation in the room veered towards the occult. Someone started talking about a friend of a friend who'd visited a fortune teller. 'She was accurate to a tee,' the woman said. 'Knew stuff she couldn't possibly know.'

Another woman had just come back into the room, holding her hands out in front of her, since Amber had painted her nails. 'I went to one,' she said. 'Had the cards read. She told me about how I'd have Harry, although I'd no intention of having kids at that point. Was taking every precaution too!'

'I'd love to have my cards read,' Carol said wistfully. 'I never have.'

'Hoping they'll say kids for you too, Carol?' someone asked, giggling.

Carol pulled a sour face. 'Fat chance of that.'

There was a moment's silence.

'I can read the cards,' Leah said. She could have bitten off her tongue, but the words simply came out. Nothing could have prevented them. 'I have a deck in my bag.' She had never removed them, since the days she'd carried them with her always on purpose.

'Ooh, do me!' someone said.

'And me!' cried another.

Leah glanced at Carol. 'The hostess first, I think. Yes?'

Carol nodded. She wasn't smiling now. 'In the kitchen?'

'If you like.'

Don't think about it, just do it, Leah told herself as she seated herself opposite Carol Lyle at the breakfast bar. She took the dog-eared cards out of their silk wrap and began to shuffle them. They felt familiar, like old friends. A musty scent of the rose oil with which she'd once perfumed the silk drifted around both women. Even though faintly spoiled, the smell wasn't unpleasant.

Carol was leaning on her crossed forearms on the bar. 'They look really old,' she said.

'They are getting on a bit,' Leah said, 'seen a lot of use. Here, will you shuffle them too? Just empty your mind of everyday thoughts while you do. Do you have a particular question you'd like to ask the cards?'

'Yes,' Carol replied.

'You don't have to tell me of it, just think about it.'

'I will.' Carol took the cards and closed her eyes. The cards slipped through her fingers obediently.

After a minute or so of silence, Carol opened her eyes and handed the cards back to Leah, who began to lay them out in a simple spread.

'Will you say if it's bad?' Carol asked. 'I mean, it must be awkward for you if what they say is bad.'

'I'll tell what I see,' Leah said, 'but the cards are only a snapshot of now, really. Nothing they say is written in stone. If you like, they are sign posts on the road of life. *You* have the power to change your destiny, but sometimes the cards can help you clarify things in your head, make decisions.'

'That sounds like a get out clause to me!' Carol said, laughing. 'What if I get the Death one?'

'That card means change,' Leah said. 'Quite radical change, yes, a rebirth perhaps, but it does not mean you're going to get run over tomorrow.'

The cards were laid out, face down. Now Leah was nervous of turning over the first one. Her hand hovered over it.

'Let me,' Carol said, and turned the card face up. 'The Moon. What does that mean?'

As the cards revealed their story, one by one, Leah wondered whether she was impartial enough to read them accurately. Was she seeing what she wanted to see? A woman deluded, occluded, befuddled? A faithless man? She struggled to voice her interpretation. 'You feel you are lacking facts...'

Leah was conscious of Carol staring at her. She knew she wasn't reading very well; it was stilted.

Then Carol announced. 'You must know why I hired you?'

'What?'

Carol rolled her eyes, took a swig of the wine by her left elbow. 'Come *on*. I do *know*, Leah. At least... My question was, and is, what happened between you and my husband?'

Leah felt her face colour up. This was the last thing she'd expected. 'I...'

'And why did you take the job, Leah? You knew it was me too.'

Leah made a helpless gesture.

Carol reached out and touched one of Leah's hands. 'It'sokay, I'm not mad at you. I just want to know.'

Leah sighed deeply. 'I honestly don't know. Curiosity... A compulsion...' She paused. 'Why contact me now, after all these years?'

Carol shrugged. 'I just always wondered, that's all. I saw you, this glamorous older woman, and he told me you were just a friend. I always wondered. It didn't seem likely.'

An uncomfortable prickle coursed down Leah's spine. '*How* did you see me?'

Carol laughed, rather bleakly. 'It's not that difficult nowadays, is it? Your web site, social media. Didn't have to be a private detective lurking round corners. So tell me.'

'There isn't much to tell, Carol. I was a fool, that's all. Nothing physical happened between us that you'd call him being grossly unfaithful to you. It was a silly crush that got out of hand.'

Carol took another mouthful of wine. 'I don't believe you.'

'It's true. I never slept with him.'

'I don't mean that. I mean it wasn't just a silly crush, was it?'

Leah met Carol's gaze. 'No. No it wasn't.' She shook her head. 'There's no point saying I'm sorry, because I was so *enraptured* I didn't care about you.'

'Well, of course. I'm never in the way.' Carol frowned. 'The problem is, Leah, I still love the bastard. I know he has this thing with women. It's happened many times. But somehow... recently... I don't feel I can hide behind the fancy curtains of this house any more. I feel I'm married to a ghost, who's not really here. He's never been bad to me, always generous, always pleasant. That's what's made it so hard. There was nothing for me to put my finger on, except for my hunches, and the women he befriended. He never hides that, you know. He always tells me about them, his *friends*. It's almost like he makes it easy for me to look them up, as if he even *wants* me to. But I never get to meet them, as you'd expect with friends, if they really *are* just that.'

Leah nodded. 'You're right,' she said simply. 'They're not just friends, but neither are they lovers. I would call them... victims... prey.' She grimaced. 'No, let's keep this sensible. He likes the attention. No doubt there's some reason for that, buried in his past. He's stayed with you, Carol. He hasn't exactly strayed. I think to him it's all just a game.'

Carol sighed, stared at the counter. 'I wasn't sure whether I'd fess up like this to you. I had this urge to meet you, that's all. Someone told me about you, your party thing, and it seemed the right time. Strange, really.'

Leah found she didn't want to tell Carol Lyle about the destruction her husband tended to leave in his wake, the tarnished lives. 'You want it to stop, of course,' she said. 'You don't want to leave him, do you?'

Carol looked up. 'I want my husband to want *me*,' she said. 'I wish he didn't need all these... *dalliances*. I suppose I'm scared that one day he'll meet someone who somehow tips him over and then he'll be gone. He can't be happy, can he, if he has to have this *attention*, as you called it?'

Leah paused. 'Was there another reason why you wanted to speak to me particularly?'

'I think you know the answer to that. I know quite a lot about you.'

'You want it to stop.'

'Yes. I think you have a responsibility.'

Leah closed her eyes briefly. 'Okay.'

'You didn't eat your cake,' Carol said. 'Why not? What did you put into it?'

'Strength and love, like I said,' Leah replied. 'They were for you, not me.'

Carol lifted her wine glass, gestured with it. '*In vino veritas*,' she said. 'It can be a git, can't it?'

'Definitely,' Leah said. She lifted her own glass, clinked it with Carol's.

As Leah was driving home, having dropped off her assistants, she noticed that the moon, so clear in the sky, had lost her first slice; the dark was on its way. Leah's mind was empty of busy thoughts, or even analysis. She felt only a pure conviction. Carol Lyle might say she felt haunted by a husband who was barely there, but Leah felt she had seen the true ghost in that relationship. It lived in Carol's eyes, in her nervous gestures, the joking yet bitter reference to having no chance of children. Meanwhile her husband was no doubt off somewhere, telling some woman, perhaps the unfortunate Cassy, how their friendship was special, how it sustained him. His piercing gaze would be holding hers; full of unspoken longings. Words and a gaze that were a trail of delicious crumbs leading only to a spiked pit. Brett Lyle made ghosts of his victims without a single killing. He'd had it all his own way for far too long.

In her house, Leah acted decisively, as if guided by an outer force. In her workroom, she sat down to meditate and fashioned a bullet purely from thought and intention. Into it, as into the most careful of her baking mixtures, she poured a purpose. The bullet was as silver-white as the moon; a lunar dart. Leah did not feel a magical mirror was the answer for Lyle; his armour needed to be pierced. So she fashioned the bullet and gave it to a dark angel with a gun.

Carol Lyle had tried not to think about Leah all the time, but it had proved difficult. On that birthday evening, Carol had taken action for the first time, been someone different. Just that moment of saying to Leah 'you must know why I hired you' had been empowering. And then the pivotal moment when Leah had closed her eyes for a second, her murmured word 'Okay'. Carol knew that Leah had meant it. She just didn't know *how* she meant it.

One week following the party, Brett was home for the evening. He was camped in the front room, shorn of the mask he wore for his female 'friends', playing a video game. In the kitchen, preparing dinner, Carol could hear the blast of machine gun fire and the cries of computer men as they died. These sounds annoyed her; they always did. There was no good reason for him to have the volume turned up so loud. Carol threw a half peeled carrot into the sink, dried her hands and marched towards the living room. She saw Brett sitting cross-legged on the carpet, looking like a boy. He did not glance up at her, hunched as he was over the game pad he was holding. On the screen, men exploded in red gouts amid loud explosions that shook the walls. Carol's mouth opened to complain.

And then *he* folded out of the corner of the room. Dressed in black leather, immensely tall, a face pale like moonlight. And he held a gun. Carol saw the blue-black sheen of the weapon as he raised it; almost organic in appearance.

The shot was white, like a sky full of fireworks; it was a sound that had an image. And then her husband's head had exploded; red splashes and gobbets over the TV screen, up the walls, all over her. Carol heard herself screaming, the kind that will never stop, saw the pale-faced assassin glance at her once. He bowed to her, walked backwards through the wall.

'What the hell is wrong with you?' Brett was holding her, shaking her, perhaps seconds away from slapping her face.

Carol was utterly disorientated for a moment, then reality somehow see-sawed back into focus. She saw her husband in front of her, unmarked, and clearly not sure whether to be angry with her or amused. 'You were shot!' Carol cried. 'You were dead!'

Brett Lyle laughed, let her go. 'Idiot,' he said amiably. 'What are you talking about? It's only a game.'

Carol stared into her husband's face. She saw a red fleck amid the blue in his left eye. Had that always been there? 'It's not always a game,' she said in a low voice, 'not to everyone.'

He pantomimed a double-take. 'What's that supposed to mean?'

'You know,' she said and headed back towards the kitchen.

'Well, no I don't actually,' he said, in a stiffly offended tone.

Carol wheeled on him, spoke harshly but evenly. 'Yes. You do. I'll always be there now, Brett. Remember that. You'll never be alone.'

She didn't need to say any more than that, and wouldn't, no matter how hard he pressed her, even when the crazy dreams started happening, when uncertainty seeped into his mind. *Remember what ghosts do*, she would whisper into his sleep. *They haunt you.*

They Hunt

This short piece appeared in The Drabble Project, edited by Rob Meades & David B Wake, in 1988. A drabble is a novel of one hundred words. The image derived from a scene in my head, conjured by the poem 'India' by W J Turner, which I loved as a child. The poem begins: 'They hunt, the velvet tigers in the jungle...' It's a beautiful poem and even now, reading it again, it makes me shiver deliciously.

Night in the forest. Twinkling points of light, but mostly darkness. Rustling. We are hungry. Combing our hair with claws and teeth; night-time fellowship. Our leader hisses her craving and we echo her.

Undergrowth-burrowing; belly to soil. We search. Slickly slithering. Noses raw. Pushing forward. Then, it's upon us; heat smell. Red-steaming, visceral, *summoning*. (And they're alone! Stupid, stupid! Alone!) Here in leaf-shadows, we're up on our haunches; silent. Stiff limbs, straining, quivering...

HOWLING! HOWLING!

Crashing! Tearing! Spraying! Kicking! Shrieking!

Tumbling... Sighing... Whimpering...

Trees tremble to silence. Red drips from a single leaf; pointed, shiny. Muzzle to gut; we feed...

The Order of the Scales

When Allen Ashley, the editor who accepted this for his 'Astrologica' collection, wrote to me about my story, he thought it was based on the competitiveness of football clubs, and although in one respect he'd got this right, the sport was not football. Rather, the tale was inspired by an e-sport, if it can be called that. Based on events that took place in my World of Warcraft guild, it's a story of betrayal. For those who don't know – and I'll assume there are some – WoW is an MMO, a massive multi-player online role-playing game. Guilds form in this game so people can play together, but the group activities can be cut-throat, and players can be poached by other guilds, or get frustrated with their teams. Some can actually betray their guilds, throw hissy fits, subject their friends to loot drama, and perform many other delectable demonstrations of human pettiness. Our guild once nearly collapsed because of underhand behaviour by one of our members.

In this story, I filed off all the serial numbers that connected its world to the fantasy realm of Azeroth in WoW, and opted for a medieval ambience of 'noble' knights and orders. But the events follow fairly closely what happened. The personalities, however, have been changed, although it's unlikely anyone could be recognised from their in game character.

The theme of the 'Astrologica' collection was signs of the zodiac, hence the connection with Libra, the scales.

Castle Mersita had stood for over five hundred years upon one of the seven sacred hills of Carabelt, island home of the sacred military orders of High King Marinux XX. Mersita was the stronghold of the order known as My Lady of the Scales. In ages past, the orders had been founded by noble families who had come together to fight a greater ill under High King Marinus I. Now, while some of the old families were still represented within the organisations, and in some cases held high ranks, the orders mainly comprised knights who had come to seek their fortunes in Carabelt and had stayed, or had been recruited from the courts of foreign kings.

Conflicts abroad were rare nowadays, as the politics of the great empire of Sadaphora had moved towards territorial battles of a different kind that involved far more trade and much less bloodshed. The orders, while all holding land of some magnitude or another and not without means to make a wedge of silver when needed, were now more involved in sport. Since the days of bloody battles had waned, war was remembered in the arena, the jousting court and the fighting ring. Successful knights were celebrities of the land, made rich and powerful and much sought-after by the largest of the orders. My Lady of the Scales had her fair share of accomplished knights, while lacking the resources to attract the greatest. Still, her income was steady, her reputation strong, and if occasionally the High King had need of warriors to teach an upstart lordling a lesson or two, or to help out an ally in a far land, he and his advisors were more likely to turn their eyes to an order like The Scales than one whose heart had been given unreservedly to the audiences of the Hastiludes, the tournaments and contests held throughout the empire.

The grand mistress of My Lady of the Scales was Lady Fae Rachapelle and she had held her seat for ten years. It was common for orders to be named in a quasi-mystical manner, and terms derived from the occult study of the stars were popular. The duchess Liadora Capanne, who had founded The Scales generations before, had felt that qualities of balance and equal-mindedness were essential to those of a chivalric disposition and she had named her order for the constellation of Astraea, she who held the scales of Venala, the goddess of love, in which the hearts of men and women were weighed. The order was regarded as being of a stable nature, if given to occasional dramatic tippages of one basin or the other, if only to remind her members of the origin of her name.

Movement of knights between the orders was common, and there was much vying to attract the most accomplished. Some orders strove to remain apart from such shenanigans, while others – generally the least successful – embraced it whole-heartedly and poached where they pleased. As with all the orders, the commanders of The Scales occasionally sought to augment her ranks with those who were open to transfers, or who were lone knights attached to no order at all, little more than mercenaries. Still, worthwhile types could sometimes be found among them, and often those who rode without the shelter of a castle behind them might have had good reason to leave an order they had once supported.

Such was the case when Sir Modesto Clowers was introduced to The Scales by Lady Shara Calabro, a knight who was ailing, past her fighting days and soon to retire inland to the retreat owned by The Scales for its older members. Modesto, she assured Lady Fae, would be an asset to any Order. An old friend of hers, he had been alone for some years, following the dissolution of one of the greatest fighting orders known to Carabelt, The Most Excellent Fellowship. This preeminent order had succumbed to terrible inner turmoil three years before, resulting in a legendary outburst of conflict on mid-summer's eve, the outcome of which meant many survivors had made a solemn vow never to enter an order again. Some, in fact, went down on their knees before the current king, Marinus XX, pledging their fealty but begging to be released from the fraternity of other knights. Solitary towers were set up for some of them, hung with melancholy emblems. Modesto had been coaxed out of such retirement by Shara, who said she wished to make a final gift to the Order that had been her beloved home for many years.

Lady Fae, and her two commanders, Lord Porfirio Rickel and Lord Anibal Roquemore, were surprised Modesto had remained unordered for so long. A man of early middle years, of middle stature and a presentable if unstriking appearance, he proved to be affable and pleasant, and quickly made friends among his fellows. In fact, he soon became something of a stalwart of The Scales, and was a reliable participant in its activities. Lady Fae could not help but be a little bemused by this august presence among her ranks. Modesto's tongue had licked the golden fame of one of the greatest orders of all time. It seemed odd he'd be satisfied with The Scales' less than giddy accomplishments. Yet, when subtly questioned, he claimed his days of great knighthood were past. For years, he had shunned the company of his fellows and now wanted only to bask in the comfort of a stable order and the camaraderie of like-minded beings. He complained that the greatest orders had become the stamping grounds of hot-headed youngsters with whom he had no patience. They had no idea of what the glory days of the mighty orders had been like.

It was a good year before the commanding officers of The Scales encountered anything other than utter compliance from Sir Modesto Clowers. During this time he ingratiated himself fully with the rank and file, always ready with a wry witticism and, more often than not, good advice when it was needed. There were certain challenges of the

Hastiludes that attracted him, the behourd and the tupinaire particularly, but as The Scales regularly participated in these Sir Clowers had nothing to complain about. His quarters were comfortable, he was the recipient of a generous stipend and owned modest fame, augmented by his past glories.

Then, one day, Lord Roquemore requested a meeting between not only himself, Lord Rickel and Lady Fae, but also the lesser commanding officers of the order, all of whom comprised its ruling assembly.

Gathered around the white marble table known as Ferigadi, at the top of the Swan Tower in the west wing of Mersita, the officers sat in a ring to hear what Roquemore might have to say.

'I'll get straight to the point,' he said. 'The tupinaire known as the Challenge of Flames is no longer profitable and is in fact causing us a loss.'

Several officers shifted uncomfortably upon their seats, aware at once of the implication in Roquemore's words. Within each mind, a bell rang clear: the Challenge of Flames was the favoured activity of Sir Modesto Clowers, and several of his closest friends. The tupinaires were theatrical in nature, some of them extremely complex and taking place in multiple locations, including set pieces created for the event. The Challenge of Flames took place partly underground, a decision many orders had questioned when the King's Chamber of the Hastilude, the body directed to invent and organise the games, had announced the idea. While the challenges were great, owing to the fact knights would be fighting skilled opponents in very difficult conditions – a labyrinth of tunnels where occasional jets of fire would make quick escapes impossible – spectators couldn't see much of it. There were viewing areas built into the tunnels, but these were cramped and didn't give a decent view. Seeing one horse on fire streak past in smoky conditions didn't really match up to watching magnificent combatants in conflict out in the open air. The Challenge proved popular among young knights, but audiences quickly lost interest, however dangerous it might be. As far as The Scales was concerned, the tupinaire required the participation of more than Sir Clowers' immediate clique. If the assembly decided to drop the event, there would be no way Clowers and his cohorts could continue with it.

'The people have become tired of it,' Roquemore continued, 'as have most of the knights involved, outside of Sir Clowers' little cabal. As you know, the Chamber did seek to bring part of the tournament to the surface to make it more entertaining for crowds, but even so, on rest days the stands are no more than a third full. I don't need to remind you that our revenue relies on sturdier attendance than that. In my opinion, the Flames' day is done for us, and the time has come to move on to more fashionable ventures. If we don't, we risk falling behind other orders, who at present are nowhere near our ranking in fame and popularity.'

'Modesto has an especial interest in that tupinaire,' Lady Fae said carefully, voicing the thought upon everyone's mind.

'I will speak to him,' Roquemore replied briskly. 'He cannot expect the order to pour funds endlessly into an event from which we gain scant revenue. He is a sensible man and will see this for himself.'

Lady Fae shrugged, surprised that she felt such a frisson of anxiety about this situation. 'As you wish, Lord Roquemore. I'm sure most of our young bravos will be eager to unleash themselves against new challenges. I'm happy to leave this in your hands. May we vote upon it, brothers and sisters?'

There was not a vote against.

Lord Roquemore did indeed speak to Sir Clowers about the Challenge of Flames, in the colonnade surrounding Mersita's fabled rock garden, two mornings following the assembly meeting. The reaction his soft words provoked quite shocked him. Sir Clowers took personally the assembly's decision to end visits to the tupinaire and voiced his displeasure in the strongest terms. Listening, Lord Roquemore decided that what he was hearing were thinly-veiled threats rather than simple complaints or objections.

Were The Scales not aware of the damage it could inflict upon itself by disgruntling such a large portion of its membership? Clowers demanded. Were the wishes of the order's major crowd-pullers of such little consequence to its officers?

Roquemore listened patiently, for he felt he owed Sir Clowers that, but when the outraged knight ran out of words, Roquemore said daintily, 'If you were to fund the event from your own purse, we would of course provide knights to assist you there. Otherwise, I'm afraid we can't afford to run it any longer, and that is my final word upon the matter. I have the backing of the assembly.'

Modesto Clowers glared at the commander. 'I am not happy about this at all,' he said. 'I have served The Scales well, and I alone am enough to command a crowd at the Flames. I fail to see how you can't indulge me in this matter. It can't be causing the order that much of a loss.'

'I give you freedom to inspect the accounts,' Roquemore said, inclining his head respectfully. 'Also, the losses involve more than simple finances. Several of the knights presently attending the Flames are starting to complain about it. They will not continue to attend under pressure, so it seems your visits there are numbered in any case.'

Uttering a wordless gibber, and with an impressive swirl of his cloak, Clowers turned and marched off along the colonnade.

Roquemore gazed after the knight thoughtfully, wondering if he had just cast a stone into a still pool and how far the ripples would reach.

For a time it seemed the ripples had been few and not enough to disturb the waters. Another year passed and Sir Clowers appeared to get over his disappointment concerning the Challenge of Flames. He remained affable and popular, although by this time Lady Fae and her commanders had begun to perceive the steel wrapped within the velvet of this estimable knight. If denied his own way, he was most adept at appearing compliant while actually causing difficulty for the assembly. Following his confrontation with Lord Roquemore, he never raised his voice again. Even when dissenting and causing trouble, his tone remained calm and sweet, and other members of the order tended to take his side, simply because he *was* so genial about whatever he wished to discuss. After some debate, given Clowers' standing within the order, and hoping to appease what they perceived to be a potentially damaging force, the assembly offered him the position of Officer at Table. This was refused. It was not in his nature, Sir Clowers avowed, to take on a mantle of power. He had seen first-hand how it had corrupted others, speaking purely of his experiences within The Most Excellent Fellowship that had foundered. All he wanted now was a quiet life, free from such responsibility.

The Assembly of the Scales was somewhat relieved by his decision, although none voiced this sentiment aloud. But at least the offer had been made, and Clowers had been given the no doubt pleasurable opportunity to refuse it.

The Scales did find her fortunes rising following Lord Roquemore's suggestion they move on to newer and more fashionable events, which inevitably were greater crowd pleasers than the Challenge of Flames. People flocked to attend, not least because there were regular casualties, and nothing warmed the hearts of spectators more than the sight of a little honest blood. What did become clear as the months progressed was that in order to take the greatest advantage of its fortunes The Scales needed to expand. It would be in her best interests, and most lucrative, if she could field two professional-level teams of knights instead of one. This would serve not only to fatten the order's purse but to increase her renown. However, unlike other orders who, finding themselves in this position, would recruit recklessly from whatever livestock responded positively to advertisements, the Assembly of the Scales preferred to rely upon tried and tested methods; careful vetting of recruits or else accepting those recommended by others whom they trusted. To the assembly, this was vital, since it ensured the equilibrium of the order remained intact and her legendary scales tipped neither one way nor the other too dramatically.

Now Modesto Clowers swept in to assist. He knew of many accomplished knights, some presently unordered. There were others too, who could easily be swayed to change loyalties since they had found themselves in orders little to their liking. Sir Clowers was invited to speak to the assembly, which he did at the first opportunity. Lady Fae noticed how at home Sir Clowers appeared in that high room of the Swan Tower, how his hands rested so comfortably upon the table Ferigadi, as if they had lain there regularly for many years.

'Yes, yes,' Clowers enthused, holding up his hands and beginning to count off the names he listed upon his fingers, 'Sir Titus Purpura, Sir Kraig Lamanten, Sir Claudio Trivette, Sir Eusobio Tragre... these are but a few. There are others. At my recommendation, they will pledge their loyalties to The Scales. We will have more than enough fighters to double our attendance at events.' He appeared excited.

'This is wonderful news,' murmured Lady Mara Greenstone, 'but, if I might ask, who is to lead our second team of worthy knights?'

For a moment, everyone present glanced at each other around the table. Currently, it was down to Lord Roquemore to organise the events, since he had the most expertise, never mind the most patience, to do so. Yet surely it was beyond any human being's capabilities to manage around forty fighting men and women, plus reserves. The self-worth of some knights was of no small consideration and more difficult to control than prides of enraged lions. These gigantic egos inevitably collided heavily with others, and it was down to the officer in charge to defuse disruptive situations and attend to the casualties. It required a man or woman of mettle, and perhaps saintly tendencies.

Lady Fae turned her attention to Sir Clowers. 'Modesto, might we prevail upon *you* to lead the second team?'

Modesto preened his whiskers. 'My lady, I have not changed my stance upon taking a position of responsibility within the order. I regret I can't comply.'

At this moment, Lord Porphirio Rickel, as if presented with a vision of future doom he was powerless to prevent, uttered a great sigh that reverberated around the chamber in a chilling fashion. '*I* will lead this team,' he said.

'You?' Lady Fae and Lord Roquemore uttered as one.

The rest of the assembly fell to muttering. Lord Rickel, while not an organiser as such, was a leading force of the current fighting ensemble. His presence at an event raised morale. If anything he was regarded as the luck of the order. No wonder his offer was greeted with a dire shudder of foreboding.

'You all know as well as I do that no one else will embrace the task,' Lord Rickel said.

All the other officers were now unable to meet his eye. It was clear that not one of them had the heart to fill the thankless vacancy.

'It will make sense,' Lord Rickel said. 'You'll see. We have knights coming up the ranks and one of those can take my place.'

'Perhaps so,' said Lady Fae, 'but the events for this season's Hastiludes are soon to be unveiled. For new trials, it is best to have our most experienced knights together.'

'I think you will find,' Lord Rickel said, 'that if we are to pursue a larger itinerary, there will be no other way.'

And of course he was absolutely right.

Over the next few weeks, it seemed a day didn't go by when someone celebrated wasn't trotting beneath the grand archway into Castle Mersita. Over a dozen of them rode in, wreathed in smiles. The castle staff flung garlands of flowers to them to wear about their necks, and females were hurled into a tizzy at the sight of some of lither and younger specimens passing beneath the shadow of the arch.

From their vantage point at the western window of the Swan Tower, Lady Fae and her commanders watched some of the newcomers arrive. 'Well, it can't be denied they look impressive,' said Lady Fae.

'No one is impressive until they have been tried in combat,' Lord Roquemore reminded them.

Lord Rickel shook his head. 'If they can follow an order, and not fall to squabbling over the slightest matter, that will be fine by me.' He sighed dismally.

Above the arch, her eyes cast towards the mountains, the order's immense gilded statue of My Lady of the Scales held her emblem aloft, the afternoon sun conjuring fire in her golden basins.

For a short while, the new knights were required to train together, to establish a rapport between them. Lord Rickel, reporting regularly to the Swan Tower, spoke with surprising enthusiasm of his recruits. His nebulous fears, it seemed, had been unfounded. 'We might sit each of our teams in the Lady's golden basins,' he said. 'We have truly found balance.'

It was decided that each team should be given a name rather than be known by number, so neither team felt less than the other. The originals took on the name The Fine Destriers while the newer members adopted the name The Dancing Nymphs. The latter name, of course, was something of a joke, because there wasn't anything nymphlike about the team's members. Lady Fae decided she disliked a couple of them intensely. While never actually saying so aloud, these individuals made it plain they considered the other knights of The Scales somewhat beneath them. They had fought for the greatest noble orders; to them The Scales comprised mere amateurs. They were not openly rude about this, but it was an atmosphere that began to infect every corner of Castle Mersita and soured the air. A few of the new recruits had taken to *strutting*, it was noticed. Lord Roquemore, never one to take a slight lightly, was most offended by the newcomers' haughty behaviour. Lord Rickel, while not disagreeing, reminded his fellow officers of the assembly that the idea of securing these new members was to advance the order; it wasn't necessary to *like* them. On the other hand, two of the recruits – Sir Claudio Trivette and Sir Eusobio Tragre – were pleasant and likeable individuals. Sir Tragre was the quieter of the two, but neither caused any trouble and in fact went out of their way to befriend their fellows at order, the long-standing members of The Scales. Both were exceptional fighters.

And yet there was also Sir Titus Purpura, an especial, long-standing comrade of Sir Clowers, who proved to be rather unstable. Lady Fae confessed to the assembly she found him unhinged. His manner was peculiar and he seemed to need attention from others every minute of the day. Even during rest times, when most of the castle occupants were inclined to avoid the training yard in favour of less onerous pursuits, Sir Purpura would rail against his fellows, demanding that people should spar with him or even visit some of the event sites for practice runs. The words 'please give this matter a rest, Titus' only inflamed him to greater demands for participation. Many of the order admitted to finding this behaviour wearing at best.

The Dancing Nymphs were first to demonstrate their prowess in the new season. Trotting forth splendidly into the jousting court known as Seven Helms, just off the Great Northern Way, the Nymphs opened this particular hastilude of the season. Their lances adorned in a wafting cloud of scarves donated by starstruck ladies, the Nymphs effortlessly reduced all their opponents to unhorsed crumples. Commanded by Lord Rickel, but indisputably led by the outstanding and showy Sir Trivette, the team romped to success. Spectators cheered, and some wept openly at the knights' fine prowess. It would be a hard act to follow.

On the evening of the Fine Destriers' first event, Lady Fae, who was a member of that team, happened to glance at the statue of the Lady as she made her way to the stables. Was it a trick of the sunset light, or were the golden basins somewhat out of balance? The weather occasionally affected the delicate balance of the bowls, and a couple of times in the past particularly virulent storms had required some adjustments to be made. But there had been no storms recently. The weather had been tranquil. Somewhat unnerved, Lady Fae, strove to ignore the uncomfortable itch in her flesh. It was not an omen; she must not think of it as that.

But nevertheless, the Destriers did not do well on their first hastilude, a behourd entitled the Lily Palace. The Destriers were first to defend this mock castle against an opposing team, which was the kind of event the knights could generally complete with closed eyes. However, on this evening, nothing went well for the team. Knights made silly mistakes, communication between them seemed unaccountably muffled, and the opposing team triumphantly cut through their ranks and claimed the Lily. When it was the Destriers' turn to attack, their opponents jeered and whistled from the battlements of the Lily, which inevitably further rattled the attackers' confidence. They were defeated.

Back at Castle Mersita, the Nymphs were consoling to the Destriers. All teams have bad runs, of course, and this was just one of them. But even so, Lady Fae sensed there was a gloating edge to all the kind words offered by the Nymphs. To them, this simply proved they were of better calibre than the members of the Destriers.

The following day, Lord Roquemore held a meeting for his team and sought to raise morale. 'We must not make the mistake of comparing ourselves to the Nymphs,' he said, 'nor to resent their successes. We must simply apply ourselves to our own challenges and ignore what the other team might or might not achieve.'

The Destriers solemnly agreed, but Lady Fae felt as if they were a fruit that had been entered by a worm. Something just wasn't right.

As the weeks passed, the Nymphs rode to ever more golden heights, while the Destriers remained slumped in shadow. Their performance became worse and worse, while the Nymphs excelled in all that they attempted.

During one meeting in the Swan Tower, Lady Fae blurted out, 'See to the statue of our Lady!'

All eyes turned to the window through which the statue was visible.

'Yes, my lady?' said Lord Roquemore gently.

'The basins are out of balance,' Lady Fae said.

There was a silence.

Lady Fae did not need to turn her head to know that the statue and its basins were perfectly in order.

Inevitably, this state of affairs had a dramatic effect on the well-being of the Destriers. It seemed impossible for them to lift themselves from the slump they now occupied and each sparkling success of the Nymphs seemed only like an iron boot to stamp further into the dirt. Most of the Nymphs, including their reserves, were now openly smug about their achievements. The Destriers were, as the Nymphs had thought, ill-educated amateurs. They should confine themselves to less challenging events, at which they might succeed. As it stood, their failures only tarnished the reputation of the order.

One evening, as she walked in the castle gardens with Lord Roquemore, Lady Fae said, 'They took our luck. They took Porphirio.'

'He offered himself,' Lord Roquemore said, though bitterly. 'He was right; no one else would have stepped forward to lead them.'

'But in order for them to exist and thrive, we crippled ourselves,' Lady Fae said. 'Now look at where we are. Superstition aside, I think we know now how important Porphirio was within our team. Without him, we are without a heart, and we are falling into the endless hole that he has left.' She brushed away a tear she could not contain.

Lord Roquemore hesitated, and from this Lady Fae deduced he was unsure whether to speak. 'Porphirio is not happy in the Nymphs.'

'He has told you this?'

Roquemore nodded. 'In confidence, yes. He wishes to return to us, but is tied. The Nymphs know only too well how important a role he plays. If he were to leave the team, it would cause uproar.'

'I'm tempted to say I do not care,' snapped Lady Fae, then sighed. 'But of course the Nymphs have done well for the order. Our coffers are enriched.'

Roquemore nodded. 'But gold is not the only form of riches.'

Matters came to a head on May Eve, when the order held its annual meeting of all members. Lord Roquemore was first at the pulpit in the Soaring Chapel, and here gave an address, paraphrasing the accomplishments of the order over the past year. He expressed regret over the fortunes of the Destriers, but invited its members to look upon this time as a new beginning and to go forward with renewed purpose. He also proposed, very carefully, that in order to maintain equilibrium within the order, members of the Destriers and the Nymphs should perhaps exchange between the teams.

In response to Lord Roquemore's words, Sir Titus Purpura leapt at once to his feet with a bray, and began to upbraid the Destriers. 'You people are weaklings,' he declared. 'You don't bother to prepare yourselves. You are lazy, unworthy of the term knight. You should be ashamed of your disgraceful performance. No, the Nymphs will not consent to mingling with you people. We are testament to our own success as you are to your failure. Do not attempt to taint our blood with yours.'

At this, Sir Marne, one of the Destriers, leapt up also. 'Confound you, sir!' he cried. 'We made a sacrifice that your team might live, and this is the thanks you give us for it? Without Porphirio you would be nothing.'

'Without *us*,' said Purpura smugly, 'The Scales would be nowhere in the ratings this season. I think that says it all. You might make the excuse of Porphirio to put a balm over your wounded feelings, but the fact remains that your team is amateur.

'Titus!' Sir Trivette snapped. 'Do not presume to speak for all of us.'

Purpura pointed a finger at Roquemore without glancing at him, staring keenly instead at Sir Trivette. 'And you are content to mollycoddle these people? What of your reputation? You are a worthy knight, not a nurse maid nor a teacher. That was not the purpose of you joining this order. You joined to win, to fight alongside the rest of us Modesto recruited. And win you have. We all have.'

'*That* is quite enough,' said Lord Roquemore mildly, although his voice carried far, as if he had shouted the words.

Lady Fae, seated on the officer pew behind the pulpit, could see the entire congregation. She saw Modesto Clowers, sitting on the front row, his legs crossed carelessly, his head tilted to one side, gazing at his toes. He was preening his whiskers and smiling. He had not said a word.

'I regret to say this,' Lord Roquemore continued, 'but your behaviour, Sir Purpura, conflicts with our code of conduct. As such, I must discipline you. You may not take part in any events until the solstice.'

'Preposterous!' yelled Sir Purpura, his face inflamed. 'You have no right to do that. Porphirio, tell him! Exert your authority like a man.'

Lord Rickel shifted uncomfortably upon his seat. 'The code of conduct must not be broken,' he said. 'And broken it you have with your intemperate words. This was neither the time nor place to vent your feelings in such a manner. I cannot disagree with Lord Roquemore's resolve.'

Uttering a wordless growl, Sir Purpura flounced from the chapel. After a few moments, several of his team members followed him. Sir Trivette was not among them, nor Sir Eusobio Tragre. Both wore expressions of stone and clearly did not condone Sir Purpura's actions. In the silence, Sir Clowers cleared his throat, got to his feet and bowed briskly to Lord Roquemore, before sauntering out of the chapel after his fellows. He paused at the open door, the moonlight glinting off his ceremonial sword, and gazed right at Lady Fae. She could tell the knight felt he had scored a victory this evening and wanted her to know it.

The following day, Sir Modesto Clowers presented himself at Lady Fae's office. He bowed to her, his expression set into that of wry humour. 'It saddens me,' he said, 'but may I speak honestly to you?'

'Only if it will not distress me or cause any further unpleasantness,' Lady Fae responded stiffly. 'What is it, Modesto? Are you here to apologise for your protégé?'

Sir Clowers uttered a soft laugh. 'Apologise? No. And what I have to say *may* distress you. I will get to the point. I left my last order because of a conflict very similar to what we witnessed last night. I will tell you now this situation will only get worse. You have brought it upon yourself with your gross mismanagement of your order. I have no desire to witness the carnage, so regret I must hand in my seal to you now.' With precise movements, he laid the symbol of The Scales on the desk before her. 'I wish you the very best in surviving the coming storm.'

Lady Fae stared at the seal. In her mind, she could only visualise a complex castle built of cards, and the first one was tumbling. 'You must do as you think fit,' she said.

'I hope you understand,' Sir Clowers continued. 'I have had enough of this kind of overwrought melodrama to last me several lifetimes. I have seen its like and its outcome before. Although for my own well-being I must leave The Scales, I hope we can remain friends.'

Lady Fae raised her eyes to meet the smile in Clowers' gaze. 'It is a shame you feel this way, and are prepared to leave all your friends behind, not least the ones you brought to us.' She could not keep the venom from her voice. 'I confess to being confused as to why you can't help us resolve this situation rather than run from it.'

Clowers laughed again. 'I am *not* running, merely avoiding. As I said, I've been through all this before and have no desire to participate, even as a spectator, in anything similar again.'

Lady Fae announced the news later that day, after summoning the entire order to the Soaring Chapel. Members of the Nymphs had their eyes upon Lord Rickel rather than her; most appeared anxious. Sir Purpura felt compelled to leap to his feet and deliver a series of complaints in a loud voice. Lady Fae silenced him by having him escorted from the chapel by two of his fellows. She rubbed a hand over her face, knowing this meeting was far from the end of the matter.

She resolved to keep an eye on Sir Purpura particularly, and entrusted her squire to assist her. He reported to her later that day that Sir Purpura was moving his belongings out of the castle in a clandestine manner, to all appearances in advance of absconding himself.

'Right!' said Lady Fae. If she *was* a representative of The Lady's golden basins she felt she had just cracked right down the middle. She marched to Sir Purpura's quarters. He was sitting outside in the evening sunlight, enjoying the company of several of the Nymphs.

'Sir Purpura,' Lady Fae said silkily. 'Hand me your seal and leave the premises.'

Purpura glanced at his fellows and laughed. 'What?'

'You heard. Get out. Go like the minion you are to Modesto Clowers. I wish you both the best of it.'

Purpura immediately began to protest, but Lady Fae had foreseen this. She raised a hand and two of her personal guard appeared from the shadow of nearby trees. Silently, and with emphatic gestures, they escorted Purpura into his dwelling. Lady Fae walked away without another word and could hear Purpura's plaintive complaints all the way back to her own apartments.

The assembly was amused, more than anything else, by Lady Fae's impulsive action. None of them had liked Titus Purpura, who was regarded at best as an irritant. 'He is not that great a knight,' Lady Greenstone said. 'Without Sir Trivette to hold his hand, he will be nothing.'

'What will they do?' Sir Marne enquired. 'Will Clowers and Purpura seek another order? I thought they'd given them up.'

'Many would take them in,' Lord Rickel said crisply. 'They won't be without friends.'

'I don't care about their social calendar,' Lord Roquemore declared. 'I'm just glad they're gone.'

'What of the Nymphs, Porphirio?' Lady Greenstone asked. 'How will this affect your team?'

'We can manage with the personnel we have from both teams,' Rickel replied. 'Purpura was the loudest noise causing dissent within the castle. I trust that now he's gone, things will improve.'

Two days later, Lady Fae's squire came hurriedly to her office at noon. He was breathless and had to pause for some minutes before he could speak. 'I ran directly from the Circus of Declarations,' he said. 'A new order has been created and its manifesto has been posted on the public announcements panel. Sir Modesto Clowers is its leader, its deputy Sir Titus Purpura.'

Lady Fae drew in her breath. 'Summon the assembly!' she snapped. 'Do it now.'

By the time the assembly was sitting down around Ferigardi, the resignations in the lower parts of the castle had begun. Lord Rickel reported solemnly that already five of the latest recruits had handed in their seals to him. He had no doubt more would follow.

'Even Sir Trivette and Sir Tragre?' Lady Greenstone asked querulously.

'I trust not,' Lord Rickel replied. 'They are happy with us, but... They are also old friends of many who are now deserting us.'

'So much for Clowers' talk of not wanting power,' Lady Fae said bitterly.

'Let them go!' Lord Roquemore said. 'These people have brought discord and imbalance to our sanctuary. We are better off without.'

'Reverting to original size?' Sir Marne enquired.

'We will be no worse off than we were before,' Lord Roquemore replied. 'We must simply weather the storm.'

Over the next few days, the resignations came steadily. To no one's surprise, all of the new members departed to join Clowers' new order, but what was more unsettling was that some of The Scales' longer-standing members, who had been cultivated by Clowers, also handed in their seals.

Lady Fae could not bear to watch the relentless departures. She felt by the end of the week the castle would be empty but for the assembly and its staff. She was aghast Clowers could do this. He had professed so strongly, on so many occasions, he wanted no responsibility. Now he had stepped from the shadows, wielding steely organisational skills, and appeared dedicated to ruining The Order of the Scales, by divesting her of as many members as he could. His soft and silky tongue had been busy. Many of the assembly freely admitted they had been approached by him and invited to positions of prominence within the new order. All of them had refused. Clowers had even propositioned Lord Rickel. Significantly, he had kept his distance from Lord Roquemore.

Eventually, it seemed all who were prepared to desert The Scales had done so. The assembly took appraisal of what was left to them, and once the dust had settled this seemed not so bad a situation as they'd feared. Trivette and Tragre were still with them, and the trimmed down roster in fact presented a far stronger and more focused fighting team than they'd ever had. Perhaps everything had happened for the best.

But before this could be put properly to the test, Sir Trivette requested to meet with the assembly in the Hall of Audience. Not for him a clandestine melting-away. As with all actions he undertook, Sir Trivette's resignation was conducted with a certain amount of showmanship, albeit tastefully. He told with regret of his intention to leave the Scales, and that he would be taking Sir Tragre with him, but begged permission to explain why.

For Lady Fae, this was too much. Without waiting to hear more, she strode from the Hall and made for the stables. She was blinded either by fury or tears; it was difficult for her at that point to discern which, but whatever the case, her vision was red. She saddled her palfrey and rode from the castle, out into the wild mountains. She could not bear to watch Trivette and Tragre lay down their arms and hand in their seals to the assembly. They were happy with The Scales. Yet even so, this was not enough for them to resist whatever seductive poison Clowers had fed them. At the very least, he would have told them their employment would be under threat since The Scales could no longer field two competent teams. Lady Fae felt in her waters that Clowers would have offered a shining alternative, a team of professionals, a brand new order untainted by history or regret.

She returned to Mersita in the evening. There was a quiet and desolate air hanging above the gardens. All seemed quiet. Lord Roquemore was waiting for her in the stables.

'They are gone?' she asked.

He nodded.

'And the excuse?'

Lord Roquemore shrugged. 'Trivette said it was an inevitable parting of the ways. He would not feel comfortable remaining with us when all his friends had joined Clowers' order. I believe him when he said he was unhappy to do this, but that for the sake of old loyalties he could not be torn. Especially so when he might be competing against some of these people in the Hastiludes.'

Lady Fae sighed glumly. 'Clowers has won.'

Roquemore put an arm around her shoulders. 'No. Never that. Do we not believe in balance and fairness in all things? Let him work his schemes. I don't feel any good will come of it for him. The only treachery he can work now is against himself.'

'What of *our* balance?' Lady Fae asked bitterly.

Roquemore steered her outside, where the statue of The Lady was limned against the stars. 'There it is,' he said.

The Lady stood strong, starlight captured in her basins, which were perfectly aligned.

The Scales' capacity for survival was evident in the fact she had existed solidly for so long while hundreds of other orders had failed. Her foundations had been strong and still were. The officers of the assembly knew they could weather the setbacks of their diminished membership and took no desperate action to augment their ranks again at once. Let matters take their course. For now, they were content to concentrate upon their original team. The name of The Fine Destriers was dropped. They were simply The Scales again, as they'd always been.

Both amusement and outrage were caused by the fact that Clowers had seen fit to plagiarise almost in entirety the charter of The Scales for his new order. While he had scorned The Scales' management, he now saw fit to emulate their principles and rules. He was riding a veritable foam of success and advancement, it seemed.

Lady Fae tried to ignore this. These things happened within the orders. The Scales themselves had suffered events in the past when unscrupulous individuals had attempted coups of various kinds to topple the assembly and claim the order for themselves. All had failed. But then, none of these scuffles had involved people thought to be trustworthy, to be friends.

Lady Fae went to the temple of Astraea and there spoke to a priestess of all that had occurred. She was troubled, she said, and did not enjoy the imbalance in her heart. She did not want this anger and disappointment inside her like a canker.

'What would be your desired outcome?' the priestess asked.

Lady Fae did not hesitate. 'Disgrace for Clowers,' she said. 'Not even ruin. Just disgrace.'

The priestess nodded. 'Think on this,' she said. 'Many knights of the noble orders are little more than thick-wits. They follow blindly. They are the rank and file who pad out the rosters and help win tournaments. The orders need them. But the brightest stars... Ah! These are the men and women with brains. They live on their wits, and it would be lost on none of them that a man who could betray his fellows in one organisation is quite capable of doing so in another. I call it the way of the sheep-killing dog. Some individuals, I regret to say, once having tasted that kind of blood cannot live without it. In the case of Modesto Clowers, that blood is crisis and discord. Yes, he played you well, Lady Fae; you were the subject of his latest performance. However, I suggest you ask around concerning the demise of The Most Excellent Fellowship. You might find it enlightening.'

Lady Fae smiled at the priestess. 'Thank you, madam. You have given me much to think upon.'

The priestess inclined her head. 'You cannot disgrace a man who is already in disgrace,' she said. 'And why worry? Your luck is returned to you.'

'Porphirio?'

'There is nothing more I can tell you. Burn some incense for the Lady before you depart. Make your wishes known to her. She does not tolerate imbalance, nor treachery, for long.'

Her heart full of noble sentiments, and a determination to cast aside unworthy feelings of resentment and anger, Lady Fae returned to Mersita. When her palfrey trotted beneath the arch she discerned a feeling of excitement in the air. Or was it that? A sense of activity, certainly. She went at once to the Swan Tower, sensing her fellows of the assembly would be there, and they were.

'Lady Fae!' Lady Greenstone cried, 'Thank the stars you've returned. There is momentous news.'

Lady Fae took her appointed seat. 'What news? Has Modesto Clowers been eaten by dogs?' She laughed, but none of her companions smiled back. They seemed a little nervous. 'What, then?'

'Everyone plays a long game,' Lord Roquemore said. 'Remember The Most Excellent Fellowship?'

Lady Fae nodded, placing her gloves on the table. 'Of course.'

'That night when the order disintegrated and all fell to combat... evidently it wasn't such a drunken skirmish as it appeared at the time. Last night, during a behourd dramatising the betrayal of kings, Sir Trivette, instead of attacking the enemy rogue, turned upon his team mate, Sir Modesto Clowers, unhorsed him, and wounded him grievously. Before he was arrested by the King's guard, he declared this was in revenge for the fate of Lord Severly, erstwhile leader of the Fellowship, whose demise – Trivette declared – was at Modesto's own hand, but arranged to appear as something entirely different. Lord Trivette, incidentally, cut off that hand.'

Lady Fae touched her throat, trying hard to keep her face straight. 'This is... astounding,' she said. 'Will Sir Trivette be tried?'

'Inevitably,' Roquemore replied. 'To attack the leader of your order is regarded as the worst treachery. Trivette should have taken his suspicions to the Council of Hastiludes, or the King's Chamber, rather than take the law into his own hands. The best he can hope for is exile.'

Lady Fae shook her head. 'Why did he not say... confide in us?'

'I think it's quite clear he had his reasons,' Lord Rickel said.

Lady Greenstone snorted. 'A hand is one thing,' she said. 'Trivette should have cut out that forked tongue, if you ask me!'

'The Fellowship was not the first to be damaged by Clowers' machinations and I expect The Scales will not be the last,' Rickel said. 'Men like Clowers persist. Lady Mara is right, it would have been better if the tongue had been cut for Clowers will surely use it to slither out of this situation now. Trivette will be the one to pay.'

'Clowers will no longer be able to fight, though,' Lady Fae said.

'True,' Rickel said, 'and he'll be more dangerous for it.'

'Somehow,' Lady Fae said, glancing out of the window at the statue of the Lady, 'I doubt that.'

Lord Rickel sighed. 'I hope you're right, Fae, but in any case, glad was the day Clowers walked beneath our arch and left us.'

When the trial of Sir Trivette began, The Assembly of the Scales felt obliged to speak up on his behalf. Sending Lord Rickel as representative to the court, they revealed what had occurred within the order and that, in their opinion, Sir Trivette was a noble and honest man driven to extremity. Whether their calm yet honest plea had any bearing on Trivette's fate cannot be known for sure, but he kept his head and was instead banished from the kingdom.

Modesto Clowers, who was still recovering from his injury and therefore not present at the trial, seemed to drop from sight. Little was heard again of his order, and it passed from the public's attention. The Scales resumed her modest position within the rankings, and maintained her perennial reasonable success.

Seven years later, Lord Roquemore and Lady Fae were walking through a colourful market that had been set up about the annual summer carnival of Carabelt. As usual, beggars and ne'er-do-wells thronged the entrance arch. Lady Fae set her gaze straight ahead and ignored these creatures, but then Lord Roquemore caught her arm. 'Fae,' he murmured. 'Look.'

She turned her eyes to where Roquemore was discreetly indicating. An unkempt, aged wastrel sat beside the arch in rags, holding out a bowl for money. He had only one hand.

'By the golden basins,' breathed Lady Fae. 'It can't be.'

'It is,' Roquemore said.

He moved towards the man, and Lady Fae could not stop him. She felt he'd be wrong to spit upon this wretch, because whatever he had done, he had once been a knight, but Roquemore was deaf to her words, and shrugged off her restraining hand.

He stood over Modesto Clowers, staring down. Then he reached into his purse and withdrew a coin, a single copper, which he tossed into the beggar's bowl.

Clowers looked up at him with filmed eyes. Perhaps he did not recognise his erstwhile commanding officer.

Then Roquemore turned away, took Lady Fae's arm. 'A neat and tidy end to an old affair,' he said. 'Shall we?' He gestured towards the lights of the carnival, which were just beginning to blaze, as the sun went down behind the mountains, its ember rays reflecting from the golden basins of Astraea, visible even from this distance upon Mersita's hill.

Kiss Booties Night-Night

The inspiration for this story came from a friend of mine who was in a Goth band in the 80s and 90s. They performed in many countries and at different venues and events. One time, they were engaged to play at a fetish club. My friend was a great raconteur, who had a gift for mimicking voices, and I ended up with my stomach aching from laughter after hearing his tales of this particular gig and the people he came across there. His partner, a beautiful and immensely Gothic woman, was accosted some time during the evening by a man on a lead, being dragged about by some kind of dominatrix type. He was entranced by my friend's thigh high PVC spiky boots and uttered the phrase 'kiss booties night night' while attempting to lick them. When I heard this, the seed of a story took root, and here it is.

The sun, a fevered blister, hung low in a pagan sky of ceremonial colours; purple, red, deepest orange. She stood among the rattling sticks of petrified reeds, on the edge of the slow-moving slick they called the river. Behind her, the manse was dark, but for the winking violet lights of the security systems at eaves and porch. The garden was so beautiful. She never grew tired of it: the rank weeds; the blackened ivy over the walls of the ice-house; last year's lilies not cleared away, fainting at the feet of this year's forced growth that had been brought in from the hothouses of the city centre, soon to die out here in the air.

She put a tarless cigarette between her ink-lacquered lips and drew in a stream of chemical fume. Her boots caught the light of a security beam far across the river. Otherwise she was non-reflecting, her skin pale and flat like bleached ashes, her dark clothes a void against the descending night.

Maradissa Ferone, heiress. She played at having a career – buying and selling the more intriguing artefacts from the past that had escaped destruction into the present. She loved the past. Sometimes, she designed parties, which she sold to the sons and daughters of her dead parents' friends; Creatures of the Contemporary – as they styled themselves – who lived further up-river, where the ugly old factories had been turned into apartments and the river strained and treated to become something sterile, which it was safe to touch, if not to drink.

Maradissa lived alone, although she was not reclusive. She was often sighted in the more expensive night-haunts of the Industrial Park, west of the river. Several times a year, she would throw a themed party at the manse. Many people thought the decay was contrived, but it was not. Maradissa took pleasure in watching the slow dissolution of all that her mother had worked to achieve; the manse, a rotting heritage. This was not a rebellion against her mother, or her mother's success, but simply a statement that everything was running *her* way now. Unlike her peers, Maradissa shunned cosmetic surgery, but for the decorative scarring on her breasts and stomach. She was always the same sex.

Tonight, a hurrying air, a sense of imminence, volted through her as she stood beside the river. Her skin prickled as she watched the roiling surface of the water. When this feeling came, she savoured it. It was fear. Excitement. Life still held promise in the throes of apprehension. She was dressed, ready to drive to the Park, in period Gothic of the late twentieth century: tight, matte black, and spikes. Her hair was a frothing black halo, teased and stiff and lightless. Smoking the cigarette, she stoked her excitement. Sometimes she had to make it come like this; take in the chemicals, watch the poisonous sunset, psych herself up.

She threw the remains of her cigarette into the river, smoothed her taut black thighs, enjoying the feel of herself. There was power in the fume she had taken, power in the lowering night, the colours on the oily surface of the water. There were no seasons here and the smells of the land were confections. She turned away from the river.

Feeling watched.

She paused, knowing how the smoke could warp her senses. It could kindle a feeling of agitation, of being an actress for an invisible audience. It could bring with it a fleeting understanding of gods.

For a few sanctified moments, the silence of the garden was absolute, then the lilies rustled their thorns. Maradissa walked purposefully towards them. She was not afraid, and still young enough to believe in her own immortality. As she approached, something scrambled away from her; the foliage of life and death rattled loudly. Maradissa did not challenge, made no sound, although it was clear to her that whatever hid among the lilies was too large to be animal. Instead, she plucked an ivy cane from the ice-house wall and struck the place where the rustling had started.

Silence. Something crouched, something feared.

For a moment, Maradissa considered entering into the gripping shadows of the hanging plants. She even put one pointed boot upon the soil, then retreated. She would speak to her butler about it; the sniffers could inspect the grounds. She had no time to deal with intruders, certainly not those that ran from her.

He did not think she was beautiful, for to him she was beyond beauty, a goddess. She was remote and perfect, apparently unaware that her grounds were full of unseen gardening graduates, working to maintain the graveyard disarray that she loved. Michael had worked in her gardens now for nearly a month, and only during the last week had he realised, or become aware of, the strong feelings she kindled within him. At first, he had seen her only briefly, whenever she left the house to climb into her car. He'd been fascinated by her appearance, the bizarre clothes. Other gardeners joked cruelly about her eccentricity. They were scornful, resentful, jealous of her wealth and luxuries. They liked to make lascivious comments, speculate about how well she'd perform in bed. Most were scathing. Their bitter envy made them want to debase her. Michael did not feel like that. His fantasies of her did not involve sex. He wanted to speak to her, worship at her feet. Those feet, clad in shiny black, forced into the pointed shape. It must hurt her.

Every evening before sundown, a bus came to pick up the gardeners and take them back to their apartments in the Colonies, but for the last two days Michael had lingered behind when his colleagues went off-duty. He'd worked out that as the mistress of the house never entered the gardens during the day, she must do so after dark. And he was right. Hidden among the ragged foliage, he could watch her undisturbed for a glorious half-hour or so, before the security systems were activated. She was regal, mistress of her domain as she stalked around its boundaries.

His trespassing had terrified him at first, for he knew the very least penalty for discovery would be dismissal, but he could not resist this private pleasure. If he was careful, she need never know. But then, he wanted her to know. One day, he might even dare to make his presence known to her, an abject slave to her power. In part, he wanted to invoke her outrage. He had never felt this way before.

Now, he knew that she had sensed him in his hiding place. He'd watched her lean body become tense: so much shiny gloss in the ragged crepe of the dried leaves around her. He'd scuttled backwards into the comfortless arms of an ancient rhododendron, and here he had crouched down, peering through the thick leaves. She had walked towards him. He had smelled her perfume, the scent of her cigarette and the reek of the lacquer with which she styled her hair. He had never been able to study her so closely: a black and white ghost in the twilight. Her mouth, he realised, was small, its lack of generosity further emphasised by the severe black lipstick. This slight fault only made her more alluring. She'd stood, poised, a lithe cat ready to pounce, and he'd been frozen before her; terrified and longing for her predator eyes to fix upon him. Then, relaxing her muscles, she appeared to dismiss whatever sound had alerted her and wandered back towards the house.

Michael fell to his knees upon the damp earth. His heart pounded madly. She had known he was there, but she had not chased him off. Neither had she shown fear, but he'd not expected that, in any case. She had become a conspirator in his fantasy.

In the hallway of the house, Maradissa drew on her long black gloves and spoke to her magic mirror. In it, no reflection, but an image of her butler, Leony, who lived some distance away in an apartment that Maradissa owned.

'Something in the gardens tonight,' Maradissa said, admiring her long fingers in their velvet. 'Not invited. Check it for me?'

Already Leony was reaching for the pads that would activate the sniffers. Late. They should have come on before sundown, but Maradissa's loitering by the river had probably deferred them.

'Nothing unsanctified,' Leony said, looking at a display Maradissa could not see. 'Staff working late?'

Maradissa pulled a face at the mirror. 'They watched me.'

Leony laughed. She was allowed certain privileges. 'What do you expect?'

Maradissa smiled back, thinly. 'No one stays here after sundown unless I request it. See to it, Lee.' She made a pass across the mirror with her gloved hands.

'Your word, oh mistress, is my command,' said Leony, a diminishing genie in the mirror as it clouded and darkened and veiled its magic.

Before the sniffers were released to patrol the grounds, Michael had slipped like a shadow over the wall. It took a long time to walk back his apartment, and once there he felt too unnerved to eat his evening meal. As it lay cooling in its delivery slot, he lay on his bed, his stomach churning, and prayed to his goddess. She must hear him. He was her soul's servant.

Maradissa met her friends, Crickforth and Evalie, in the bar called The Bat Cavern on Eldritch Boulevard, at the edge of the park. It was a haunt favoured by all those whose espoused Maradissa's chosen fashion period; a lot of black was seen around. Crickforth and Evalie were drinking bright green cocktails from triangular glasses.

'Babba, you just have to see!' Evalie announced as Maradissa slid onto the fishnet-covered seat beside her.

'See what?' Maradissa peeled off one of her gloves and put it beside her drink, lifted her glass with the ungloved hand.

'The most divine freaks!'

Maradissa looked at Crickforth. He had suffered a mild stroke recently, which had frozen the left side of his face. His parents had cut his allowance, owing to the fact that a new fashion drug had been responsible for the stroke, and were punishing him further by making him wait for corrective surgery. Crickforth, always an optimist, was using his deformity as a fashion accessory at present. He limped a bit and wore one black leather glove, a patch over his drooping eyelid. 'She means the fetzers,' he explained with half his mouth. 'There's a Fetzer Nite on.'

Maradissa sipped her drink. 'Oh? So what?' She delivered an admonishing glance to Evalie.

Evalie poked Maradissa's arm. 'Oh, where's your sense of adventure? The fetzers represent *your* time, my bab, your time. Of course you're interested.'

Maradissa shook her head. 'They most certainly *do not* represent my time, as you put it. What are you implying?'

Evalie would not be deterred. 'But it was all the thing back then. 'Eighties and 'nineties chic! Fetish nights, glamour-wear.'

'A little more than that,' Maradissa said, quietly.

Her remark was ignored. 'Mara, we *must* go and see them.'

'We wouldn't get in.'

'With your contacts?' Evalie chided. 'Don't be ridiculous.'

Maradissa shrugged. For outrageous sights, they could visit any number of bars in the Park; there was always something to look at. The fetzers were something else. They thrived on debasement; or on debasing. Nowadays, there were therapies to see to that. Sexual and social neuroses could be worked out in group VR; safely. Maradissa had studied thoroughly the periods that interested her, but she was selective in what she adopted, or adapted, from the past. It was only a matter of time before the fetzers were persuaded to abandon their obsessions. Already, complaints had appeared on the bulletin boards. Whatever the fetzers had chosen to drag into the present, they had embellished and exaggerated. Maradissa was aware of the rumours. It was unhealthy, and no protest about how this was all a kind of harmless fancy dress could convince those who saw it as a crack in the social seam. 'I don't think we should risk corrupting Crickforth,' Maradissa said, with a smile.

Crickforth grimaced. 'It wasn't my idea!'

'Mara, don't be tiresome,' Evalie said. 'Have you no curiosity? It's bizarre the fetzers got a licence for tonight's meeting. Strings were tweaked, obviously!'

'Not really,' Crickforth argued, wiping spittle from the dead corner of his mouth. 'It's best to keep these things regulated.'

'Well, whatever,' Evalie said with a careless wave of her hand. 'We could at least watch them going into the club.'

Maradissa considered this suggestion. The mere thought of the fetzers made her feel annoyed, or angry – she wasn't sure which. Her father had once said to her, "You risk becoming what you resist"; to have a strong aversion to a thing somehow gave it power. 'Where's it being held?'

'Key-mart's multi-storey,' Evalie answered lightly, sensing compliance.

The night club had once been a car park, in the days when there had been a plague of cars. Below, the converted aisles of the supermarket housed counsellors' booths, the tables and machines of sex yogis, and the darkened cells of light-therapists. Sometimes Maradissa and her friends took enlightenment drugs there or discussed non-existent dilemmas with earnest thin people. Naturally, the therapists and counsellors and self-appointed gurus had taken exception to the fetzer meeting taking place above their shrines, and had staged a non-violent protest outside, which everyone was ignoring.

The sidewalk was packed with neo-goths, zippers, body art flappers and haute couture junkies of every stripe. Chemical spliffs were passed freely among the cheerful throng that watched the fetzers walk up the ramp to the doors of the club. Most of the fetzers were in normal dress, clutching carryalls with a change of costume inside. They hurried past the on-lookers with set expressions. Others, mainly middle-aged male transvestites, who were into it for laughs rather than illicit pleasure, paraded and minced and made lewd gestures at the crowd, which was catcalled appreciatively.

Maradissa despised them all. To her it was an embarrassing display.

'We *must* go in,' said Evalie.

Maradissa glanced at Crickforth, who shrugged. 'Could be fun.'

Maradissa shook her head, exhaled a tolerant sigh and then pushed through the crowd.

With her Ferone Corporation credit cards, Maradissa sailed past the door-keepers, Crickforth and Evalie in tow. People in the crowd who knew them shrieked out amused and gentle obscenities, at which Evalie, bringing up the rear, made dismissive signals.

Inside, it was cold, with localised areas of intense heat. Maradissa shivered. The air was red. 'Changing room?' asked a uniformed receptionist.

Maradissa afforded him a scornful glance. 'Bar.'

In the event, Maradissa found it hard to be disgusted. The fetzers were playing at it. The occasion was no worse than a Gothic Renaissance night at the Pit Vault, only the costumes were sillier, and the music rather more vapid. Two men crawled past her on all-fours, leashed to a tall woman in badly-applied makeup, who was possibly a man. One sniffed Maradissa's feet. 'Now puppies!' said the leash-woman, and tapped her charges affectionately with a whip that appeared to be made of embroidery silk. The puppies looked at one another and giggled; such a fun game. Maradissa eyed them condescendingly, while Evalie hooted in pleasurable distaste.

After a while, the plethora of exposed genitals, naked breasts framed in straps and metal, bare tattooed buttocks and costumes of extreme brevity lost their shock value. Maradissa sat at the bar and gossiped with Evalie about people they knew. Crickforth was discussing the benefits of a new amenities centre in the Tech Park up-river, with a man who was encased in black leather from crown to toe, but for an open zip which exposed his mouth, and a hole at groin from which a flaccid penis hung.

'We could be anywhere, in any bar,' Maradissa said, interrupting Evalie mid-sentence. 'This is just another theme club. Only the clothes, or lack of them, make it different.'

Evalie nodded. 'Still, I wanted to come. I wanted to see.'

Maradissa slid off her stool. 'Can't help wondering what I'll find in the wash-room, though!'

'Want me to come with you?'

Maradissa rolled her eyes. 'Ev, *please!*' She pushed her way into the crowd.

The fetzers were friendlier than members of other cult-groups Maradissa had met. Her own neo-Gothic culture tended towards cliquishness and aloofness. Here, everyone she passed smiled and greeted her as if she had known them for years. It seemed foolish to maintain a frosty attitude.

In the ladies' wash-room, both men and women clustered around the mirrors, squealing with laughter as they refreshed their face paint. A thin middle-aged man, clad only in leather straps and rather heavy make-up, grinned in Maradissa's face. 'Great night, isn't it!'

Maradissa adopted a quizzical expression. 'Mmm.'

'Voyeuse!' The response was good-natured, rather than critical.

'No,' Maradissa responded, and then restrained herself from explaining why she was there. 'It's interesting here, but rather tamer than I thought.'

The man gave her a sly look. 'There are levels of experience,' he said. 'You just have to look for them. Visit the Chamber, and then say tame.'

'There is more?'

The man laughed. 'There is always more. For those who want it.'

But I don't want it, she thought. Still, there was no point in visiting this place without examining every option on the menu. She might discover something worth reporting to Evalie and Crickforth.

It took her some time to find the Chamber, because no one seemed willing to give explicit instructions concerning its location, but eventually, deep in the centre of the club, she found the entrance to the shrine of forbidden pleasures. There were curtains of shiny PVC across the doorway. As she lifted them and passed through, she noticed with amusement the health scanner that monitored her heart, before a mechanised voice breathed out an approving welcome.

Beyond, the light was redder, the air steamy. Figures were just moving shadows within the crimson fog. Maradissa heard the sounds; retching, laughter, groans, the slap of something yielding on flesh, something brittle shattering. Tribal music throbbed beneath this symphony of indulgence. On the floor, there was blood.

She felt both revolted and dazed. The light drew her in: through the sounds, through the steam peopled with indistinct forms. Occasionally, a seeking hand might reach out to stroke her, but she avoided their anonymous touch.

Crossing a slick-floored chamber, Maradissa entered a corridor of flesh – dampened latex fabric looped across the walls and ceiling, hanging down in writhing tatters. Here, there were sighs in the air and soft squeals of pleasure. Purple-pink light pulsed at the corridor's end, and Maradissa advanced towards it – cautiously, slightly in fear, slightly in anticipation. The flesh tunnel opened out into a vast chamber, where ribbons of incense curled around the cupreous scent of blood and the sharper, chemical reek of leisure anaesthetics.

Fascination and horror surged through Maradissa where she stood at the threshold. The smoky air purled in upon itself like a veil drawing aside. *Come, sweet flesh. Enter in...*

The pleasure of machines. They were part biological, like alien robots, towering, spreading and curious. Metal black. Manikins of subjection were mere bound scraps between the elegant pincers, the intestine coils of slinking alloy, the investigating probes, the scalpel-clawed prehensile digits. Their movement was hypnotic. Maradissa saw a swatch of hair hanging down from within an iron helmet. An arm shuddered pale within a tangle of dark cables. Above her, screens the size of hoardings advertised the forbidden sensuality. She understood that within the minds of these willing victims, the slow excoriation of flesh was twisted into dream-like virtual imagery that bloomed with mythic fantasy. Their pain was regulated to peaks they found acceptable. All was silent but for the slither of metal coils, the occasional mechanical hum. Every human mouth was plugged with rubber.

An undulating limb lifted up like the neck of a serpent from the tangled mass of flesh and machine. It turned an unwinking, glowing eye upon Maradissa, then snaked towards her slowly. A non-human voice breathed, 'Welcome...' and in its echoless cadence Maradissa heard the secret message of pleasures exquisite and undreamed of.

For one brief moment, she almost fell, mesmerised and willing, into the embrace of the fleshless arm. Then her stomach roiled involuntarily, and she had to turn away quickly, a hand to her mouth.

A woman had come into the Chamber behind her, blocking an easy exit. She was tall and fairly attractive, naked to the waist, clad in rubber leggings. Her torso was laced with bloody scars, and she held a thin blade in one hand. 'Don't run, my pretty.' The woman held out her hands to Maradissa. 'You want to be here. I am the Priestess of Perversity. Come, I will lead you to a nest.' She gestured at the machines.

Maradissa shook her head and tried to push past the woman, but the priestess grabbed hold of her arm. 'Don't be afraid. It's your first time, isn't it?' Her voice was soft with reassurance.

'Let me past,' Maradissa said, roughly pulling her arm from the priestess's hold. 'I'm not meant to be here.'

The priestess' expression changed slightly, hardened. She pulled back her lips into a sneering laugh and pressed the blade she held to her stomach. 'Open up!' The scalpel-thin knife sliced into her flesh.

'You're sick!' Maradissa hissed, and made to push past her. She averted her head, not wanting to look at the fresh wound, afraid there would be no blood.

The woman blocked her way again and laughed. 'Sick, huh? What are you doing here, little girl?'

Maradissa glanced up at her, could not help noticing the thin wet stream on the woman's upper belly. 'I just... got lost.'

The priestess shook her head. 'Oh, really? I don't think so. You came here to see, didn't you? You're curious. Want to see how the big girls and boys play. That's Okay. If you want to look, I can show you around.'

Maradissa was momentarily paralysed by fear, unsure of whether the woman was right in her assumptions. Then, firmly, she shook her head. 'No. Thank you.'

'It's all right.' The priestess smiled warmly. 'Everyone has a first time.'

Maradissa swallowed, tasted bile. 'I'm not like you. Let me past.'

The priestess gestured at her. 'Oh no? Look at you in your pretty, kinky gear, your little painted face! You're not that different from us.'

Maradissa recovered her composure, raised her hands like a barrier. 'You've got it wrong, she said. 'Excuse me, please. Or is assault part of your repertoire?'

The woman narrowed her eyes. 'Only if you want it.'

Maradissa uttered a short, dry laugh, rolled her eyes. 'No, thank you. I'm not into pain.'

The woman put her head on one side. 'Aren't you?' She reached out and slid her hand down Maradissa's side. 'I think everyone is, if they're honest. We're honest. This is reality. We are healthier because of it. Come on, loosen up. Enjoy yourself. Don't waste your visit. You wouldn't be here if you didn't really want to be.'

Maradissa backed away, affected her most haughty tone. 'I'm not interested, actually. Please, excuse me. I have friends waiting and they'll come looking for me soon.'

The woman folded her arms, the knife blade pointing into the air. She gave Maradissa's clothes and jewellery an assessing glance. 'Oh, I see. It's a little rich kid come to gawp at the freaks, is it?'

'Yes, I'm rich,' Maradissa agreed, unable to resist admitting it. 'So what? You're no healthier than I am. You must hate yourself to cut your body like that. I happen to like my body, and I respect other people's'

The woman sneered. 'Oh yeah? And that perfect nose is your own, is it? That faultless figure? You're into knives, girly, everyone's into knives!' She uttered a chilling screech of laughter, then pushed Maradissa back into the flesh tunnel, with the retort, 'Go home to Mummy and Daddy. Your kind isn't wanted here.'

Maradissa was burning with nausea and humiliated anger by the time she found Evalie at the bar. The injustice of being judged a surgery-junkie was almost as bad as what the Chamber had concealed in its bloody mists. She was not like them. It wasn't true. They were freaks.

She was not. 'I'm going,' she snapped at Evalie. Crickforth had disappeared. 'Stay if you want!'

'You've been ages,' Evalie said, getting off her stool. 'What happened? Are you Okay?'

'No,' Maradissa said. 'I want to go home.' For the first time in two years, she felt conscious of her age, and realised she was missing her mother.

On the way home, Evalie sympathised with Maradissa's revulsion, but was too eager for details, seemingly unaware that by describing what had happened Maradissa felt she was somehow legitimising it. The words should not be spoken. She dropped Evalie off at her parent's estate. 'Stay here tonight,' Evalie offered. 'Don't go home alone.'

Maradissa shook her head. 'No. I'll be fine.'

'Then I'll come and stay with you, if you like.'

'Ev, I'll be fine. Honestly. I was just taken by surprise back there, that's all. It'll soon be forgotten.' Maradissa didn't want anyone to know how upset she was. She smiled and waved and drove away.

At home, Maradissa sat in her salon and drank some brandy, which she rarely touched. She was aware of feeling soiled. The house seemed cold and empty. She played some music disks, but the lyrics seemed too pertinent. Images filled her mind; the laughing, painted faces, the exposed bodies, then the hidden pleasures of the inner chamber and the Priestess of Perversity's grin as she opened up her flesh with a blade. Disgusting! How could people be like that? What was there in human nature that made it manifest? Something primitive. And yet, when Maradissa dreamed that night, she was held in the embrace of a metal lover without a face, who invaded her hungering body with devices too large for her to accommodate. She felt her flesh tear, but the pain was translated into a different sensation, like smelling the most exquisite perfume, tonguing the most exotic liqueur. Then she was screaming against the invasion, gathering an occult strength. She transformed herself into the metal lover and what shivered pale beneath her precise force filled her with an aching tenderness of feeling. She awoke disorientated, her body tensing to the receding pulse of erotic thrill.

Once she had dressed, Maradissa called Leony. 'I'm not feeling too good,' she said, keeping the mirror shadowed. 'Make sure I'm not bothered, will you?'

'Do you need anything?'

'No. Just privacy for a while. I'm tired'

'Overdoing it, huh?' Leony laughed. Sometimes Maradissa went into retreat after lengthy, non-stop parties. 'Listen, that intruder you spoke about last night. I've looked into it. A new staff member. Didn't understand the sundown regulation. It's all fixed now. I briefed his supervisor.'

'Fine, fine. I just don't want to be pestered.'

'Feed and medicate yourself properly.'

'I will.'

Michael had been horrified when his supervisor had confronted him about why he'd stayed behind at the manse the previous evening. Red-faced, he'd blurted an excuse about wanting to get a particular job finished. 'We have set work schedules,' the supervisor said, her eyes hard. 'You don't get paid for over-time.'

If she'd guessed Michael's true reason for lingering in the garden, she did not press the matter. Michael felt bereft, cheated. The supervisor didn't understand that Ms Ferone wanted him in her garden, and because their potential relationship had to be secret, the mistress could not reveal the truth.

All day he worked near the house, peering through the windows at every opportunity. He saw his idol drifting from room to room, a glass in her hand. She seemed distracted – obviously agonising over her decision to report his presence to the supervisor. She had made a mistake and would have to rectify it herself. Michael was powerless, her pawn. Sometimes, it seemed as if she was aware of his eyes, hidden in foliage beyond the windows, for she would start as if at a sudden sound, and glance through the panes. He longed to stand up, show himself, but knew that was not part of the ritual. He knew he would have to engineer a way to remain in the gardens after sundown again, but not yet. There would be a sign when it was time.

That evening, Michael had to go home with all his colleagues. He found he was glad to get back to his apartment, because he could lie on his bed and think about Maradissa. He imagined the click of spike heels upon the hard floor beyond his door, the tap that might come upon the laminated wood from sharp, lacquered nails. He imagined her coming in across the threshold, standing over him, saying, 'You are mine.'

For the next three days Maradissa refused to go the Park with any of her friends. She needed solitude, and spent a lot of time meditating, trying to face up to the demons spawned from the episode at the fetzer nite. She dressed herself in a loose purple robe, kept her hair clean and straight down her back, wore no make-up. She found she wanted to bathe frequently, as if there was something to wash away. It was as if she'd witnessed a terrible atrocity, and had to exorcise the trauma of it. Her mind was drawn to reinvent images of what the Chamber had contained, her thoughts colouring in more detail. Her meditations of calming scenes would mutate without her noticing it into hideous fantasies that left her feeling soiled and ashamed. Self-disgust prevented her from seeking outside therapy. The experiences exhausted her, numbed her with an unfamiliar weakness. She was used to feeling strong and in control.

Hiding in her manse, Maradissa ignored the calls piling up behind her mirror's surface. Let Leony deal with them, offer excuses for Maradissa's silence. She had more important things to attend to. She fought with her demons alone. The fetzers haunted her dreams, the secret fetzers of the inner Chamber. She dreamed that the Priestess of Perversity came looking for her. She scratched the windows of Maradissa's manse with sharp, metal claws, murmuring, 'You want me to come. You want what I can give, what I can teach you.'

There were dreams, too, of tying faceless bodies down upon weird contraptions of wood and leather, anticipating with dread and desire an unknown torture that soon she would possess the knowledge to inflict. And the priestess was there to tell her, 'You see. You *do* belong with us. You just didn't realise in what capacity.'

During the day, she battled constantly with a feeling of being watched, sure there was an invisible presence beyond her windows staring in at her, compelling her to become aware of it. She chided herself for thinking it might be the Priestess, or some psychic emanation of the woman. Fleetingly, she remembered the incident in the garden before the fetzer experience. That must be it. A gardener looking in at her. Perhaps she should call Leony, but she felt too lethargic to bother. There was no sense of threat from the scrutiny, only an air of intense interest. Then, the night would come again, and Maradissa could not convince herself that it wasn't the fetzers who were watching her, bodilessly observing some weird kind of transformation taking place within her mind. The Priestess had cast a spell over her in the Chamber and now waited for her magic to take full effect. In the dark, contorted fetzer spirits surrounded the house.

One morning, Maradissa woke up angry. She would not be driven mad by what she'd witnessed in the Chamber. All the nightmares since were no more than phantoms of the mind. She leapt up from her bed and threw out her arms at the wan morning light beyond the windows. Enough! With this inner shout, it felt as if something inside her shattered and emerged in a wave of emotion. She felt light-headed, as if there was more space around her. There were parts of other people's realities that were ugly, but they were not part of hers. She had fought the spell of the Chamber and won, defeated the demons of dark desire.

She called Evalie on the magic mirror.

'How are you?' Evalie asked. 'I've tried to call for days, but all I got was the butler. Everyone's been worried about you.'

'A virus. I've beaten it!' Maradissa said cheerfully. 'Now, I need some entertainment. Out tonight?'

'Yes! Yes! Pick me up?'

'Okay. Usual time.'

Michael knew that tonight had to be the night. It was impossible for him to linger behind after work, so at lunchtime he pretended to be ill and took the rest of the day off. His goddess had seemed so miserable for days. His heart had ached to see her pale, forlorn face peering from the windows of the house. But that morning, he'd caught a glimpse of her and had seen that her spirits had lifted. She'd been smiling again, that cool, aloof smile, and had no doubt made a decision.

As the gardeners' bus rolled off towards the Colonies, Michael was hiding near the gates to the Ferone manse. He waited until the bus was out of sight round a corner and then slipped between the metal portals as they ground ponderously shut. He knew that security systems would soon be in operation, but trusted that Maradissa would be aware of his presence and delay their activation. As her devotee, he was ready. He'd been alert for signs and now would act.

In the garden, Maradissa was dressed for the night. Spike-heeled boots, a catsuit of glistening black. She smoked beside the river. In her heart, a new feeling. The familiar kindling of excitement, the potential of the future, but tempered by serenity, a sense of separateness. Nothing could touch her now. She'd been reborn, stronger and more aware.

Then, the feeling of being watched sneaked up on her senses. She froze for a moment, a brief image of the Priestess of Perversity padding across her mind. Ridiculous. It was the gardener again. Immediately, she realised that the first time she had sensed him had not been because he'd been unaware of the regulations. It was so clear. He had been watching her, and watched her still. Slowly, she turned around, and saw him, hiding in the lilies. A pale face through the dead and living leaves. She felt irritated, a little flattered perhaps, but resented the intrusion into her private time. The fume had empowered her. She was not afraid, and could defend herself against anything.

'Come out here!'

The man did not move. She could see the round holes of his eyes; he looked transfixed. An unfamiliar sensation shivered through her. When she walked towards him, she saw he was young. She had expected an older man.

'What are you doing here?'

He cowered down among the dead lilies, his hands steepled, trembling, before his face, as if in some kind of religious obeisance.

Maradissa laughed. 'Why are you frightened? Don't be absurd. Explain yourself!'

He seemed to find his courage then, and made to scrabble backwards through the leafage. Maradissa grabbed his arm, and it was as if his flesh turned to fluid in her hold. He did not resist her, but hung there limply, leaning against her legs. Maradissa pushed him away. 'Get off my premises. You'll lose your job for this!' She expected him to give her an appealing glance, say something. Instead, he lay there in the crackling foliage, beautiful and vulnerable. She saw, in his eyes, his feelings. How long had he watched her before he'd gathered the courage to stay after hours? He'd been reprimanded, but now risked dismissal, if not prosecution. What was he waiting for? What did he want from her?

Maradissa paused. It seemed that time condensed into a single moment, of which she was queen. She was conscious of her long limbs clad in shiny fabric, the slavering, fanged maw of her sex.

She straddled his fallen body, the heels of her boots digging into the soft soil. He lay still, waiting, his hair spread out over the crackling leaves. She imagined tearing the thin fabric of his shirt away, exposing his breast, like an empty canvas awaiting the marks of her nails.

Maradissa laughed uneasily, took a step to the side, stood over him. She felt dizzy. Time to go. She must dismiss him, go back to the house, call Leony, report the trespass. Evalie was expecting her and life must go on – it must!

The boy curled onto his side, still looking up at her with strange beseechment. He made no sound.

Maradissa extended one foot, placed it upon his face, so that her heel pressed against his trembling mouth. He reached up with grimed fingers, and the scent of leaf-mould was released, primal, almost anaesthetic.

He took hold of her foot, licked the leather. 'Kiss booties night night,' he said. And her heel drove into the soft flesh of his mouth.

Colin's Cough

I knew someone who was in the situation of having a relative they found very difficult to be around, and who felt really bad about this, because the relative concerned had 'problems'. Being repelled by such a person seemed a horribly cruel and selfish reaction, but they just couldn't help themselves. While stories of their encounters with the unfortunate relative were often quite funny, there was an underlying pathos to them. In writing this tale, again with all serial numbers rubbed off that connects it to real people and situations, I wanted to portray that – to conjure the occasional smile as well as sympathy.

The characters of Annie, James and Heather came to me all of a piece, as it were. As soon as I began writing, I felt as if I knew them, even though they are entirely fictional. They are people who might once have been termed 'yuppies', somewhat ill-equipped to deal with the situation when the supernatural creeps in.

How quickly short stories become period pieces! When I wrote this a couple of years ago, Top Gear was still on the BBC. I haven't changed any details like that to keep the tale current. It's a snapshot of its time.

The worst part of having Cousin Colin to stay was that he was repulsive. Annie could barely stand to look at him – not because his features were ugly particularly, or even in the slightest deformed, but just somehow creepy, discomforting. He was thirty-eight, going on fifteen – a child in a grown-up body; small of stature, thin, somewhat bent of spine and while he had a good set of teeth in his small face, seemed toothless. Even his name – to her – sounded like a cough filled up with mucus. He talked to himself obsessively – along with manifesting a host of other OCDs – and whenever he caught sight of her cats went into a frenzy of conversation that frightened the poor creatures into the deepest, darkest corners of the house.

"Here darlin', here, oooh lovely darlin', aren't you looovely, ooh sweeties, c'mere. You're all right, all right, lovely, aren't you darlin'. Oooh…'

And so on, to the accompaniment of skittering paws, bellies close to floor as they ran. This in fact made Annie feel rather sad. If he'd had some cruel streak that made it possible he might harm an animal, fair enough, but he merely wanted to be liked, by human and beast both, and unfortunately nature had cursed him to be utterly repellent.

So, Easter time, with the month of April in a good mood, flowers billowing forth, blue skies kissed with perfect little clouds. And Cousin Colin for the weekend. It was her turn. They all had turns – her brother James, her cousin Heather and Annie. The parents had all done their bit years ago and it was clear they felt this responsibility should now be passed on. They never said so; it was simply known among the family. So, while it would have been bliss to have a weekend alone for once, to lie on her very comfortable recliner on the lawn, to read lazily, drink wine, eat sumptuous foods, surrounded by her cats, instead Annie would have Colin, with his incessant chatter, his vampiric drain on the life force of any living creature. Wasn't his fault, of course – he'd been born that way, and left orphaned in his twenties. The family looked out for him, admired his ability to maintain a household and hold down a menial job, despite his disabilities. He was kind-hearted, loved people, and she knew it was really very bad of her to feel so sickened by the thought of having him around. *It's not his fault.* They all had to remind themselves of that, even when they were growing up and summers had been spent together, sun-drenched beaches, buckets and spades, escapades – and Colin. Then it was the parents saying, 'Now, take Colin with you, children', even though, for Annie at least, the prospect was filled with dread. The unpleasantness in him wasn't the fact he was 'a bit simple', as people would say in those days, but something else. She couldn't say what then and still couldn't now. It was as if he was an affront to all the senses.

Colin's first words when he arrived, before Annie had even opened the door to him, were 'Oooh, hello Annie, how are you? Did you sleep well? How are the cats? I've got some presents...' His thin silhouette bobbed about behind the pastel stained-glass of the door. Sighing, she opened it. There he was, despite the balmy weather, trussed up in a beige anorak.

'Hello, Colin. I'm fine thanks, and you?'

She ushered him into the kitchen where he unloaded all his gifts from a series of supermarket bags. A pang went through her – he bought her things she liked; special French cheeses, sticky liqueurs, expensive chocolate and a bottle of very fine single malt. 'That's thoughtful of you, Colin, thank you,' she said. She should smother the irritation he conjured in her, be a *better* person. 'But really, you shouldn't. You always spend so much!'

'Well if I can't spoil my favourite cousin, who can I spoil?' He grinned at her, and she could see in his eyes the weekend spread before him – the comfort of her old but airy house, its carefully furnished guest bedroom, her immense TV and Blu Ray player, her cats, her company. She knew that for him these prospects were as wonderful as an ocean cruise on the most luxurious liner in the world.

'I'll make you a nice cup of tea,' he said, making a determined bee-line to the kettle.

'Well, okay...' She had wine out already but as he *did* make a good cup of tea – her cousin Heather had taught him carefully many years ago – she might as well drink it.

As he bustled about her kitchen, the air was filled with the cheap, flowery women's perfume he always wore, which perhaps on an elderly lady would have been fine, but not on him. It smelled musty, weirdly ancient, dead, and tended to fill the house like a creeping mist during his visits. Annie knew he would soon decamp to the bathroom, where he'd arrange his toiletries for the weekend – equally grandmotherly in nature – scented talc that she was sure you could no longer buy in the metal tins he somehow managed to find, a plastic vanity bag with various creams inside, toothbrush and toothpaste, a pink plastic hair brush, and his one concession to masculinity – a disposable razor. It didn't add to his appeal that he was so inordinately *hairy*, having to shave at least twice a day, and usually ending up bloodied from it, which he never bothered to wash off, despite apparent fastidiousness in other aspects of his toilet. She remembered that one time on a previous visit he'd surprised her in her small office, his face looming over her shoulder as she worked at her computer. She'd turned and had been faced at close quarters with the thick smears of dried blood and patches of unshaved whiskers on his gnomelike face. She had cried at him, 'For God's sake, Colin, go and wash yourself, wash all that blood off!' The image had been hideous and she'd never forgotten it. He was effeminate in a strangely asexual way and yet thick black hair covered him, spurting from the neck of his shirt, mossing the backs of his hands. She shuddered to think what his clothes concealed. If he fell over from a heart attack, or started choking, Annie wondered if she could bear to touch him. Perhaps that was why she always felt a little tingle of relief when she learned her neighbours would be at home on the weekends Colin came to stay. They were only a garden away.

'I've got some films for later,' she told him as he menaced the teapot. 'Two new horrors.'

This was a love they shared, both adoring of haunted houses and terror conjured through atmosphere and sound rather than gouts of red or spilling innards. When they talked about films he was almost normal; she could forget about the rest. This was perhaps the only thing that made the visits bearable.

While they sat watching the first of the films in the flickering light of the TV screen, the garden quiet and dark beyond the long windows, Annie noticed Colin was still coughing badly – a smoker's cough. In February, after phone consultations with Heather, Annie had bought Colin an electronic cigarette starter kit for his birthday – a rather expensive one. None of the family approved of Colin's chain-smoking habit, nor the fact that the cheap cigarettes he smoked seemed inordinately pungent and stale-smelling. Despite the fact they put up with nearly all of Colin's quirks, the family had to put their foot down about the smoking in their houses. Weirdly, even if he went outside to smoke in a porch, conservatory or garden, the smell fingered its way inside. It was Colin's business what he did at home, but all of them – Annie particularly – detested the rank stench his cigarette smoke had left behind in their rooms.

Colin had appeared to adjust to the electronic cigarette quite quickly. Annie taught him how to maintain it, and he now brought it with him on the weekends he came to stay, smoking continuously whenever they sat to watch films. And yet... he still had that smoker's cough. As an ex-smoker herself, who had used e-cigarettes to overcome the habit, Annie knew the cough should be gone by now.

'Still getting on okay with the e-cig?' she asked, after the first film was finished.

'Oooh yes, can't thank you enough for getting me into them,' Colin said, waving said artefact before his face. 'Saving me so much money as well. Real bargain.'

She sensed then, with a tired sinking feeling, he was still smoking as much as before in his own home. That was another thing about him that wound her up – his lying. He would say what people wanted to hear, always. You could never be sure any of his anecdotes, however minor, were authentic.

That night, when she got into bed, she lay in the darkness listening to Colin coughing two rooms away, accompanied by his doglike snuffling. This was going to be a long weekend.

A week later, before Colin arrived for the weekend, Heather had to pick up Henry from his karate class and collect Winona from ballet. God, she could do without Colin this weekend! So much going on. She had half a dozen cakes to bake for various customers, including a large decorative one, Rob needed help with his invoices, and they'd promised to pop over to see his mother on Sunday. Taking Colin along was always a trial, because Mary – Rob's mother – was not blood family so wasn't as forgiving of Colin's traits as she might be. She was too polite to say anything direct, but her lips would disappear for the afternoon, and whenever Colin passed close by she seemed to draw up her limbs like a spider feigning death.

Driving with unsafe speed, Heather threw her car around town, yanking offspring into it with barely a pause, careering back home with minutes to spare. They had a large old town house in the centre of the city, three stories high. Heather adored her home. She and Rob had restored it lovingly and it *was* a home, not a sterile show piece. You could tell a family lived there – untidy yet comfortable rooms, clutter on every surface, the delicious smell of cooking lingering like incense in the air, boots and shoes thrown around in the hall. Heather knew the house was haunted, but felt the unseen ghost's personality was that of a loving mother; it too was not terribly fond of Colin, though.

'Winnie, I'm super busy at the mo,' Heather called over her shoulder as she ran to the kitchen. 'When Colin comes could you make him some tea and take him in to watch telly for a bit?'

Winona rolled her limpid fourteen-year-old eyes, and taking the pins from her bunned hair, tossed back her glorious blonde mane. 'God, Mum, do I have to?'

'Winnie!'

'Why is it always me? Let the boy share some of the "fun"!' She pantomimed drawing commas round the word 'fun'.

'He's a *boy*, Win. 'Nough said. You know he can't cope with Colin.'

'Like *I* can!' Winona grumbled, prancing off to the living room to turn on the TV.

She could, though. Henry was simply terrified of Colin, as were their two collies – the three of them, boy and dogs alike, were usually romping bundles of energy, yet hid whining behind furniture when Colin was here. She really *had* heard her son utter a soft whine once, cuddling the shivering dogs.

Heather heard the doorbell ring and Winona's haunting sigh echo loudly round the hall, her dragging steps. Before the door was open, having spied the girl through the frosted glass, Colin was crying, 'Ooooh, hello Winnie. Did you sleep well? How are the dogs? I've brought some presents.'

'Great. Let's watch some TV while Mum gets dinner,' Winona said in the voice of a girl being led to the scaffold.

It was the snuffling that got to Heather the most. Colin breathed in and out through his nose very loudly and made this odd, doglike sound with it. He always drew in an even bigger breath after just having uttered one of his 'witticisms', pursing his lips in a proud smile at the same time, waiting for laughter. They always laughed, no matter how unfunny the words. Heather had trained her family well. When both children were old enough to understand, she had explained Colin's 'difference' and that they had to be patient with him. 'Just think, that could be you,' she said. 'Imagine being in his shoes for a day.'

Never had a bogey-man so dire been conjured. The thought made the more sensitive Henry cry, but then he had only been seven at the time. Winona, at nine and a half was twice as worldly as her mother had been at that age. 'He's not *my* cousin,' she'd complained.

'No,' Heather said briskly, 'he's your second cousin, and believe me, when the time comes you'll be having your turn with him too.'

'I *so* won't!'

Heather had left it at that. Her daughter *so* would!

Colin's noises and smells grated on Heather's nerves like a fairy chainsaw – invisible to the naked eye yet deathly sharp. Thank god, she and Annie had stopped the smoking between them, but that godawful perfume he wore – ack! It turned her stomach. She'd once bought him some decent aftershave as a birthday present, but if he had ever worn it, had never done so in her presence. She suspected it was still in its box, somewhere deep in the ragged squalor of his home.

After Colin's parents had died, within eighteen months of each other from mercifully swift-acting diseases, the parents of Heather, Annie and her brother James, had gutted Colin's house. Two skipfuls of rubbish and tat – curtains, carpets and beds that had to be burned, so sinister was their condition. But even so, despite what they'd tried to accomplish, the old bungalow was still dank and dark, fraying at the seams. And Colin ever since had been committed to filling the place with junk again. His parents, Ken and Fiona, (the mother being the blood relation), had been somewhat 'different' themselves, outsiders from the mainstream family, hoarders, who lived in a twilight world of curtains closed and slowly-crumbling lives. No wonder Colin was as he was. When she thought about it, Heather experienced brief spasms of anger against the ineffectual humans who had created and raised Colin. They had cursed him from the start. Cruel, terrible. She swallowed her disgust at him because he had been dealt such a rotten hand by life.

After dinner, a small argument broke out around the table. Heather, exhausted and feeling that because she had to deal with Colin deserved to get her own way tonight, wanted to watch several episodes of her favourite soaps she'd been saving up on the Tivo. Winona wanted to watch a new horror film because it had one of her favourite actors in it. She'd bought the DVD earlier that day. 'Mum! You know how long I've been waiting for this to be released.'

'Colin doesn't like ghost films, Win,' Heather said firmly.

'Oooh no, give me the willies,' Colin confirmed. 'Can't be doing with ghost films. Nice soaps, that's what I like.'

Heather gave her daughter a triumphant stare over the rim of her wine glass.

'Most of my friends have their own Blu Ray players, *in their rooms*!' Winona announced, before flouncing out of the door.

At the head of the table, Rob sighed. He would soon retreat to his workshop and build a cabinet or something, holing up there for most of the weekend, no doubt with Henry and the dogs huddled somewhere near him, behind some lumber.

As if the misery of her children, husband and pets wasn't bad enough, the house had also begun to act up. Since Colin had arrived two hours earlier, tap washers had given up the ghost in unison, light bulbs had blown in three rooms, two items of crockery had fallen from the dresser for no apparent reason, and the stairs creaked twice as loudly and on *every step*, as opposed to the three or four steps that usually liked to groan. Doors refused to remain shut or open, depending on how a human had last left them. Clearing up after dinner, Heather put her hands into her hair and mimed a silent scream. 'Don't you start too!' she told the house. 'It's not like I *want* to inflict this on you all.'

As if in grim reminder, the house allowed a whiff of Colin's perfume to sidle across the kitchen.

'For fuck's sake!' Heather growled and poured herself half a pint of red wine into a very large glass.

Annie was set to have a wonderful weekend. The last vestiges of Colin's perfume had faded from her rooms and the atmosphere within them was serene. Planning to see her lover tomorrow night, Friday had been allocated for feminine pastimes – washing her hair, painting her nails, some TV, then reading the new ghost story collection she'd downloaded onto her Kindle. There had been a jarring moment in the bathroom when she'd discovered the plug-hole in the sink was matted with a clump of thick, black hair – from which part of Colin's body this had derived she dared not think, and was not prepared to prod and unravel it to discover its nature. Could he possibly shave his armpits? She wouldn't put it past him. But how had she not noticed this during the week? Using toilet paper, she gouged out the hair and then flushed it down the loo.

Later, before going to bed, Annie found more remains of Colin in the bathroom – a wanton dusting of his sickly rose-scented talcum powder over the grey slate floor tiles. Of course, it *must* have been there earlier, she'd just not noticed it, so preoccupied had she been with disposing of the hair. But how had she missed it *all* week? Admittedly she had used the downstairs loo and shower a lot, because they were close to her office and she'd been working so hard, but surely she'd been up here at least once? Why couldn't she remember? Unnerved, she mopped up the powder with the sponge she reserved for cleaning the sink and bath, and then felt compelled to throw the sponge into the waste basket. She washed her hands thoroughly, as if she'd touched something poisonous. As a final flourish, she sprayed some air freshener into the room, then gagged; it smelled just like Colin's awful perfume and she could *taste* it in the back of her throat, chemical yet cloying. She opened the window swiftly, batting the air frantically with her hands, then scooped a couple of handfuls of water from the sink cold tap to rid herself of the taste. She went to her bed feeling somewhat anxious.

The following Friday, Colin was due to visit James, who lived alone in a relentlessly modern bachelor apartment.

'Hello, chap!' James greeted Colin at the door to his flat. Of he, Annie and Heather, James was the least affected by Colin's visits, simply because he refused to acknowledge oddness in anyone. He didn't have pets to be traumatised, or a current partner to be irritated, so he treated Colin as he'd treat any other male friend. As Colin dithered in the hallway, chattering about presents and had James slept well, James simply thrust a can of beer into Colin's hairy hand, saying loudly, 'Come on in, mate. Take your coat off. Just watching *Top Gear* on iPlayer.'

For the entire weekend, Colin would be carted around the venues of James' pleasures. He would watch James play paintball on Saturday and football on Sunday, an eerie spectre at the sidelines, among jovial, ordinary men. He would be taken to the pub. To offset any curiosity in his friends, James had explained to them that Colin was 'a bit special', making a twirling gesture at the side of his head with the fingers of one hand. Female friends took care of Colin for him, mostly because they recognised the fact James was entirely unsuitable to look after anyone. If given the job in rotation, James had found the women were less inclined to become annoyed or despairing. Most felt sorry for Colin and this emotion could last years if they were exposed to him in small doses.

James did not notice unpleasant smells or noises emanating from Colin and was oblivious to his aesthetic deficiencies. Colin's chatter passed over James's head like white noise. He could say 'Yeah, mate, yeah,' or 'what a bummer', or laugh at appropriate points, without really listening at all. This was partly why he tended not to retain romantic partners for very long. But despite James's laddishness, he didn't find Colin's visits a trial – they were just something he did, once every couple of months or so, a small blip in his social calendar when he had to cart 'someone a bit special' around with him. He didn't resent this at all. After all, Colin was happy to sit with the wives and girlfriends, spinning them a load of bullshit – James was not ignorant of the fact Colin spoke mainly in fiction – so there was no skin off anyone's nose.

And yet, following Colin's visit, something didn't feel right to James – a bit as if there was still someone else in the flat, but always in another room. Yet it was more than that... As James lacked the vocabulary to describe his uneasiness, he put it down to 'bad prawns' from the Chinese takeaway he and Colin had eaten on the Sunday night. He felt grumpy at work all day Tuesday, and when he went to bed that night heard the sounds of coughing and snuffling, seeming to emanate from the guest room. That was impossible, of course. It must be some bloke out in the street below. His excuse for not going to investigate was that he was too comfortable in bed and couldn't be bothered.

Next morning, his mug of coffee tasted weird – it reminded him of Colin's perfume, a smell that had become a taste, filling his throat and nose. Must be the milk. But the milk, when he sniffed it, was perfectly fresh. When he went to the bathroom to finish getting ready for work, he found that Colin had left his cheap pink toothbrush – almost child-size, balding and caked with old toothpaste – next to James's own, in the stylish stone pot he kept on the rim of his pristine basin. Also, a nasty little turquoise plastic razor – rimed with old soap – lay in a seeding of minute whisker fragments and scummy grey liquid next to the stone pot. James actually gagged, and realised for perhaps the first time that part of him was actually nauseated by Colin. 'Man, this blows,' he said to himself, somewhat reluctant to pick up the toothbrush and razor to dispose of them. It occurred to him he'd not noticed these items on the Tuesday morning, or indeed as he'd brushed his teeth before bed the previous night.

While he might be unimaginative, when James was faced with the inexplicable he simply accepted it and was actually curious. At work, the first thing he did was phone his sister, Annie. He realised it might be a bit early for her, since she worked at home, so rose later than those condemned to nine to five existences, but she answered quickly enough, even if she sounded a little sleepy. 'Hey Jimbo,' she said to him affectionately.

'Annie, there's something weird about Colin.'

She laughed. 'You don't say!'

'No, I mean it. I've found things of his in the flat that have just well... to be honest, they've just *appeared.*'

'What do you mean?'

'Stuff of his that deffo wasn't there when he left Monday morning. A fucking horrible toothbrush, and a razor.'

Annie paused for a moment. 'Any... um... *smells?*'

'No, but I tasted his perfume in my coffee this morning and last night... Well I heard that coughing and snuffling he does. Thought it was outside but now... not so sure. Is this possible? What the fuck does it mean?'

'I've found stuff too,' Annie said. 'He was with me a couple of weeks ago, and the first week after I found the most putrid lump of black hair in my sink, and then his talc all over my bathroom floor. Like you, I didn't see these things straight away. They seemed to appear *after* Colin had gone. And I've heard the cough.'

'Bloody hell!' said James. 'It's like he's a fucking ghost, haunting us! This is just crazy. What can we do? Will it go away? And why now, after all these years?'

'Good point,' Annie said. She hesitated, then said, 'James, we have to look at the most obvious explanation first: i.e. he's actually creeping back into our homes and putting these things there.'

'Aww, come on, do I have to look for a recording of a cough in my spare room? He's not capable of stuff like that, Annie. I really don't believe he is.'

'We need to look at that before a supernatural alternative,' Annie said. She laughed. 'This is weird. I feel it should be *you* saying that to *me*. I'm the artist, you're the... Well, you're the least likely to be spooked.'

'Call Heather today,' James said. 'See if anything's happened to her.'

Annie waited until she thought Heather's kids would be at school, then phoned her. Heather answered quickly, and there was a dreadful row in the background, as if builders were tearing the house apart. 'Just stop it!' Heather yelled angrily, away from the receiver. 'I'm on the bloody phone!' The row abated.

'My god,' said Annie, 'what the hell was that noise?'

Heather sighed down the phone. 'Don't ask. Really... don't.'

'I think I might have to,' Annie said. 'James and I have had some weird things happen... to do with Colin. It's why I'm calling you.'

'What kind of weird things?'

'In a nutshell, it's as if he's not leaving us, or he's leaving bits of himself behind when he goes.'

Heather uttered a mournful laugh. 'Don't tell me – his smells. Cigarette smoke, disgusting perfume...'

'Not so much smells with me, but *hair*... in my sink... and the cough. James heard the cough too, and he tasted Colin's perfume in his coffee. You've had things too, haven't you?'

Heather sighed. 'You could say that. You know we live in a haunted house, right?'

'Er...'

'We *do*, and the house is more upset than any of the rest of us. Colin's perfume will fill a room, then the house goes crazy.'

'That was the noise just then, the house?'

'Yes, the bathroom got invaded by smell a few minutes ago, so she made her displeasure known by doing a Can-Can with the plumbing.'

Annie laughed shakily. 'Well, this is new. A haunting being haunted.' She'd always known that Heather liked to believe she lived in a haunted house, but Annie herself had never felt anything unusual there, only a beautiful, homely atmosphere. And Annie had always longed to see a real ghost. 'Heather, I do wonder – and this isn't a nice thought – if Colin is creeping around, doing these things himself. Let's be honest, he loves coming to stay with us all. Perhaps he doesn't want to leave.'

'I don't think the house would get so cranky if it was that,' Heather said. 'She's like an animal, and senses things in the same way. The dogs are terrified of Colin. What about your cats?'

'Same.'

'Have they been acting strangely?'

'Not that I've noticed, but they're out a lot now the weather is nicer. I'll keep an eye on them.'

'We need a meeting,' Heather said firmly. 'Can you manage tomorrow evening? Would you ask James?'

'At yours? Wouldn't it be easier to meet at mine, since I'm sort of in the middle of you and James?'

'Well, I think the house should be in on the meeting.'

'I'll get back to you,' Annie said.

126

'The thing I don't understand,' James said, sitting in Heather's capacious sitting-room the following evening, 'is why this shit is starting to happen now? Or have we just been blind and not noticed before?'

'There could have been a trigger,' Annie said. She shook her head. 'Oh, I don't know. It *is* strange, though. What do you think, Heather?'

Heather sighed. 'I did consider what you said, Annie – perhaps that Colin is planting things in our homes – but that explanation doesn't feel right to me. I just can't see him scaling the sides of buildings and squeezing in through windows. Unless, of course, he's had copies made of our keys.'

There was a moment of horrified silence.

'I can't see that, though,' Heather added hurriedly. 'He's just not capable of planning in that way.

The conversation continued in circles, with no conclusion being reached. The three swapped stories of what it was like for them to host a Colin visit and decided it was abnormal, the strong effect he had on human and animal alike. And house. Apparently.

'He's not evil,' Annie said, 'quite the opposite and yet... all I can say is that I have a physical reaction to him, as if he floods my senses in a horrible way. Offensive to eye, ear, nose, hand and... I won't say tongue, but you know what I mean.'

'And you feel twice as bad for thinking that because he's the way he is,' Heather said.

Annie nodded.

'He's what... *backward*, right?' James said.

'I don't think we're supposed to call it that, nowadays,' Heather said, 'but essentially yes.' She raked her hands through her hair. 'I sometimes think our parents could have done more for Colin. There was a problem way back, but no one ever did anything. Fiona and Ken were not fit parents. Colin was neglected, which must have compounded his condition.'

'And now it's too late,' Annie said. 'But that aside, what's going on? Is there a message here for us? Or is it simply Colin gets creepier as he gets older?'

'I think,' said Heather, 'that in two weeks' time, when it's your turn again, Annie, we're going to have to eliminate the most obvious answer – that Colin's doing everything himself. We need to be alert for clues.

Perhaps James and I can visit you. We never see Colin when we're together.'

'Okay.'

'Other than that...' Heather began, but never finished her sentence. At that moment, the whole building shook to what afterwards the cousins could only describe as a tremendous sigh of exasperation.

'Jesus!' James exclaimed, a mild expletive for him.

'What the...?' Annie glanced around fearfully.

Heather got to her feet. 'What?' she said, her head raised as if to gaze through the ceiling. 'Tell us.'

There was a profound silence, as if all the normal sounds of the house, even human breathing, were suppressed. And then, from overhead, as if from a distant attic, the cousins heard an unmistakeable sound: a baby laughing, the free and innocent expression of happiness that rarely survives childhood.

'What?' Heather asked again, softly.

James and Annie were silent, staring at their cousin, holding hands.

There was another sound, as of fingers being dragged down a damp window pane. Heather turned and walked to the front of the room, peered at the condensation in the glass. 'Ask him,' she murmured.

'What?' Annie and James got to their feet.

'That's what it says,' Heather replied, pointing at the window.

They were like marks a child would make and yet, if you stared at them, the words were there: ask him.

After the regulation respite gap of two weeks, Colin's visits were set to start once more, beginning with Annie. Heather and James would call round on the Friday evening: the three of them had resolved to have a little talk with Colin. Heather's house seemed to think the solution was clear, although Heather had perhaps embellished the communication her haunting had offered. 'It's to do with his childhood,' she'd said. 'Obvious now. And we ask him about it.'

'If we can get the truth from him,' Annie had said.

'We got a message,' Heather had insisted, somewhat smugly. 'We have to act on it.'

Even James had refrained from mentioning mundane explanations such as faulty plumbing after the bizarre experience at Heather's house.

Annie felt slightly nervous as she waited for her doorbell to ring, and Colin's inevitable babble beyond the glass. She was still awed that a supernatural communication had apparently occurred and that Heather's haunting had had something to impart about Colin. That seemed to imply the supernatural was at work in Colin too.

He arrived early as usual, bringing a chugging steam of chatter and perfume into her home. The cats scuttled off. While he asked her senseless questions about her work – about which he knew little and could have no real interest in knowing – Annie mustered her courage.

'Colin!' she said firmly, stemming the flow of words.

He froze at the kettle, appeared momentarily frightened.

'Colin,' she said in a softer tone. 'When you use the bathroom can you clean it properly, please? I found talc all over the place after the last time you visited, and the plughole up there was full of your hair.'

'I *did* clean it,' Colin said. He had a cornered look about him Annie had not seen before and uttered a couple of forlorn snuffles.

'Well, that's odd then, isn't it?' she said. 'Come on, let's go into the garden. James and Heather are popping over later. We can get a pizza first, my treat.'

She felt the ground had been prepared.

The jollity felt rather forced when Heather and James arrived – together, as James had given Heather a lift. Annie and Colin had eaten outdoors, but now Annie ushered everyone inside since the air had begun to cool. Annie wondered if Colin considered it odd – the four of them getting together like this. It hadn't happened since childhood or the occasional big family gatherings. Still, he didn't appear perturbed in any way, and the brief episode earlier seemed forgotten.

Heather curled up on the sofa, sipping from the large glass of wine Annie had given her. She was plainly in charge, and Annie was happy to let her be. She had no doubt James felt the same. Heather began by reminiscing about their childhood holidays, recounting amusing little tales. Colin had a remarkable memory and could remember things the others had forgotten; a particular lady who'd lodged nearby to them two years on the trot, the proprietor of the newsagents, where one of their grandfathers had always bought his paper every morning, accompanied by Colin. His childhood recollections were caught in amber, glowing beautifully. You could see it in his face. All those happy times spent with the extended family, over summers that had seemed endless. Even back then he'd been farmed out to relatives – mostly to grandparents in those days.

Ken and Fiona were but murky shadows, never part of mainstream family life. Fiona had succumbed early in years to mental illness and had met her future husband while in hospital. Colin did not speak of them, only his other relatives. And while he was speaking of the past he didn't cough, he didn't snuffle, nor – most bizarrely – could Annie smell his perfume as strongly. He was still that boy, she felt, had never grown up, and yet the world had expected him to.

'It must've been hard for you,' Heather said gently, interrupting one of Colin's anecdotes about a neighbour. 'What with your mum and dad being the way they were.'

Colin hesitated, but not for long. 'Yes, they could be a bother,' he said, 'but I didn't take much notice. And the old lady used to care for me, even when I was a baby.'

'Which old lady was this?' Heather asked. 'A neighbour?'

Again, a slight hesitation. 'No, it used to be her house... Where we lived. She sang to me at night when I was in my cot.'

'You can remember that?'

'Yes. I never forget things. Sometimes, I was hungry and she'd sing to me then. Jessie, who lives next door, she remembers her: Ada Jones. But Jessie's very old.'

'Tell us about Ada,' Heather said.

Colin laughed. 'She said, "Young man, I'll help you through life," and she did...'

'Does?' suggested Heather.

Colin pursed his lips and a small snuffle emerged. 'I... don't *see* her now. That was only when I was little. She said when I was sad I should have a ciggy and everything would be all right.' He smiled wistfully. 'That was how I knew she was there – or was coming – the smell of her cigarettes and her perfume.'

'Jesus,' James murmured softly, leaning forward in his chair. 'Was she a ghost, mate?'

Colin nodded. 'Yes. That's why I never talked about her. People wouldn't believe, although Mum heard her over the baby monitor sometimes. I heard them talking, but Dad put it down to her hearing things.'

'So Ada isn't around anymore?' Heather asked.

'She'll always be around,' Colin answered, 'just in a different way now. I can remember when she faded out – when I couldn't see her. It happened bit by bit. And then her voice disappeared too. The smells lasted for much longer, then they were gone as well. But I know she's never left me.'

'No,' said Heather, 'I don't think she has.'

'I can feel things,' Colin said. He cast a guilty glance at Annie. 'She didn't like me not smoking. She missed it. The e-cig's not in her world, you see. She can't smoke that.'

'So you let her have a cigarette at home,' Annie said.

'Now and again. I can't really afford it now.'

'Is she cross with us, Colin?' Heather asked.

'She was cross about the smoking,' Colin said, 'but I told her she'd have to put up with it, because you've got to respect people's houses.'

'Were you cross about it too? Annie asked.

He shrugged. 'Not really. I know you didn't like the smell. People don't anymore.'

'Does she come to our houses with you?' Heather said.

'A bit of her does, I s'pose, because she's looking after me. But it's not like she's sitting here now.'

'Glad to hear that!' James exclaimed with feeling, earning stern glances from the women.

'You wear her perfume, use her toiletries,' Annie said. 'Is that to keep her around you?'

'I just like them,' Colin said.

'You'd live in the past, if you could, wouldn't you?' said Heather.

Colin's face lit up. 'Yes. I'd live in the summer times,' he said.

A tiny boy who'd needed help had reached out, Heather realised, perhaps through desperate screams in a darkened room, and someone had found him, come to his aid. While Colin's relatives ignored his plight, considered him as odd as his parents, the shade of Ada Jones had nurtured him, listened to him, given him advice on how to survive. And Colin *was* a survivor, existing in a world he found alien, trying to blend in, to be like others, but mostly lacking the tools to do so. Perhaps Ada, realising her power was diminishing in the modern world, had been trying to attract attention for a long time, make people *really* listen, smell and see, especially those who were able to take action. This is what Heather, James and Annie concluded. Whether Ada was real or had somehow been conjured by a desperate little boy hardly mattered. It had taken a haunted house to hear the message, to make a supreme effort to communicate in a manner dense humans would understand.

Things would never change dramatically. No matter how much practical help she and the others gave him now, particularly in respect of renovating his home, Colin would still be himself, full of annoying quirks and habits. And if he was once again allowed to smoke the occasional real cigarette outdoors, and the smell might drift inside, if his perfume lingered cloyingly on the air, and his cough reverberated through guest room walls, it was a small price to pay. Cats and dogs might still run spooked, but Heather's house was peaceful. That was perhaps the strongest message of all – beyond human senses.

·

Spirit of Place

This tale began life as the start of a novel. A friend of mine told me stories of her grandparents' house, where she'd spent a lot of time as a child. She remembered apparently supernatural events in the house, including the chimney incident described here. Her memories were hazy as to what happened after that, but I saw it as a good place to start a supernatural novel. Nothing happened to my friend that was anywhere near as traumatic as what the girl in this tale has to endure. She just remembered strange phenomena, which she didn't like particularly but which never threatened her, and eventually, I suppose, she grew up and such episodes no longer happened. She was happy for me to write about it and – of course, as it's a fictional tale – embellish greatly upon her experiences. The family, incidentally, are entirely made up, as are the dreams and the climax to the story. The garage and garden are based upon my paternal grandparents' home, where I used to spend weekends as a child – although I was never scared there. Unfortunately, the book never got to be written, as other projects took precedence, and its opening scenes languished in the backwaters of my computer for many years. Then recently, when I was browsing my half-finished works, I felt I wanted to finish this piece. I chopped it down considerably and added some new paragraphs. It's no longer a first chapter but just its terrible self.

The house went on and on and on.

Mia could not remember the first time she went there, because she'd been a baby when her mother had carried her over the threshold. Neither could Mia recall when the house *became* for her and assumed an identity of its own. Even when she began to get scared was impossible to determine: to Mia the frightening times had always happened. No-one listened to her, of course, although her grandmother now allowed her a night-light when she came to stay – a small concession to a child's fears. Sitting up in bed, dry-sobbing after having screamed for her Grandma to come to her, lights ablaze everywhere, Grandma in the bathroom running palliative water into a tumbler, she once heard an aunt's voice in the corridor outside, saying, 'She's such an *imaginative* girl!'

The house was very long and dark, an end terrace in the city that was so big its original owners must've had servants. To Mia, it seemed all the corridors were endless and disproportionately high. So dark. In some rooms, lights were turned on even in the daytime, even in summer. No light from outside could find its way in. And the darkness resounded with the ticking of her grandfather's clocks – one in every room. At night, they ticked louder, echoing down the stretching corridors.

There were numerous bedrooms on two floors above the ground storey. Not all of them were used, but those that weren't were ready stiffly to receive guests, distant relatives who might appear at Christmas or other family social occasions. Some of these rooms were more frightening than others. A few were so dark and still the air in them was almost unbreathable. The bedroom Mia had to occupy wasn't the worst one. She was glad of that.

Downstairs, there were three large reception rooms leading from a wide, tiled hall. Then, there was the big kitchen, where the family often shared their meals, followed by the smaller kitchen, where the sinister mangle stood. Beyond stretched the conservatory, a brief realm of light, although its panes were covered by mats of basking ivy, making that light green and watery. Here, Mia's grandparents, along with any of their children who happened to be at home, would sit on Sunday evenings in the summer to read the papers. Mia would spread out her crayons and paper on the floor, and lie on her stomach drawing pictures, waiting to be picked up and taken home by her parents. Sunday evenings were the best times in the house. Whatever watched her in the tall rooms and passages of the main building lingered in the small kitchen, avoiding the slanted rays of late sunlight. It could not cross the threshold of the green conservatory: at least, not on summer days. In winter, in darker times, it extended its territory, and Mia would have to recite her small ritual of protection as she crossed the bare flagstones beneath the glass roof. 'Mammy, Gammy, Gammio. I'm in-vizzy-billy-oh!' She kept her fingers crossed during this rite.

Beyond the conservatory, a short corridor with windows down one side led to the garage, giving access also to a small sliver of a room, which was the second toilet. Mia particularly hated that room, and would not use it. She felt the place had its own occupant, a separate thing entirely from what scared her in the main house. This thing lived in the pipework, and for obvious reasons use of the toilet was unthinkable.

Just before the narrow door to the garage was another little room, where her grandmother kept bottles of pickles, home-made jams and old mops. Perhaps it was supposed to be a coal house. The garage itself was shadowy, and pungent with oil and metal and weed killer. Tools covered the walls and there was oiled sawdust on the floor. A high wooden bench stood at the end, old and scarred, where Mia's grandfather did his mysterious 'jobs'. Mia never knew what these were but accepted they were 'men's things', involving metal, wood, hammers and nails. She liked the grinding wheel attached to the table and would spend hours turning the handle to make it go faster and faster. Above the bench was a fly-blown window that looked out over the small patch of concrete beside the high double gates that led onto an alley, which allowed Mia's grandfather to manoeuvre and park his slow, stately car in the garage.

Beyond the concrete lay the garden. This too was long, and in two halves, with the first half, nearest the house, lawned and bordered with flowers and shrubs. An overgrown fishpond sat in one corner, where black tench lurked, once caught by one of Mia's uncles. The top garden was walled by privet hedges, neatly trimmed, and a path through the tight leaves led to the orchard, and the gooseberry bushes, and the thick, fleshy rhubarb. There was a stream at the bottom of the path, which actually bubbled up through the earth – from an ancient grate – at the right hand corner of the garden. Sometimes, it was mysteriously dry. The first half of the garden was innocent, empty. Playing there, Mia would feel light, so light, as if she could just float away. Only the presence of the brooding house, which she would not face, kept her anchored to the earth.

There were watchers in the second half of the garden, and in the stream-bed, but to Mia these creatures were less threatening than what walked in the house. Not friendly, certainly, but distant, disinterested in tormenting her. She often thought they liked her being there, although she was never unwary. When she ventured into the thick, rooty-smelling patch of rhubarb, which she felt was a place of power, her ritual words for the watchers were, 'The garden is lovely, jubbly, zubbly, ubbly!' This she felt appeased the unseen occupants, although in her heart she wished she had stronger words, and that if she had, there would be something to gain. She could not think what, though.

Whatever might live in the lower garden, Mia loved to play there, enfolded by the greeny-black shadows and the high grass. She would run around pretending to be a horse or a lion, or she'd imagine herself a princess or a witch. 'Never, never, shall you see the sun again!' she would cry, entombing her enemies in lightless dungeons or magical caves. She swept, her eyes flashing, among the palace towers that were the trees, and beside the great river where majestic ships plied, which was the tiny stream.

Then, in the midst of her happy daydreams, a call would come. Her Grandma. Time for tea. And the day would close behind her like a fist.

At home, Mia was often alone in the front room, the kitchen, the bathroom, or her bedroom, but she was never frightened there. At her grandparents' house, there always seemed to be a lot of people around, but their presence did nothing to dispel the aura of gloom and threat. Mia's mother had three brothers and two sisters, all of whom were younger than her, and four of which still lived at home when Mia was very young. The uncles and aunts were mostly young and carefree, slamming in and out of the house with loud voices and groups of friends, but sometimes it seemed as if they lived in a completely different world to Mia. They used the house, but in some peculiar way they were not part of it. Neither did they seem a part of Mia. The house ignored them and they, for the most part, ignored Mia. Occasionally, one of them, in a moment of boredom, might be moved to play with her, but this was rare, and happened mainly at Christmas, when they'd been drinking. Mia often wondered whether her uncles and aunts could actually see her. The house saw her though, and it watched her continuously.

Mia is five years old, staying with her grandparents for the weekend. It is autumn-time and Mia has been sent to bed in the dark. The night-light is on, and Mia's Grandma has just finished reading her a story. It was about a little girl and her kitten; happy and shadowless. All Mia's bedtime stories are carefully chosen. Mia's Grandma does not want to have to get out of bed in the middle of the night to attend to the screams of the child. Mia has been drinking a hot, malted-milk drink, and her Grandma wipes her mouth with a tissue. 'There now! Sleepy-byes!'

Mia feels tired. The story has soothed her. Her Grandma is good at mimicking funny voices, and Mia liked the voice of the cat. It has been a good day. All the uncles and aunts are away for the weekend, and their absence has brought a strange peace, almost as if the house doesn't feel so mean when they're not there. Mia hasn't been frightened today, and the clocks have ticked evenly in the still rooms of the house. The sheets are crisp and fragrant beneath her chin. Her toes wiggle comfortably in the cosy depths of the bed. Tomorrow is Sunday, and her Grandpa has promised a day out in the car. Away from the house.

Grandma kisses Mia on the forehead. 'Night, night, sleepy-head.' Her voice is kind and calm. It always is. Mia knows her Grandma has never been frightened in this house, but tonight she does not think about it.

The door clicks shut.

Mia lies on her side and stares at the night-light on the table beside her bed until her eyes water. She holds her breath waiting for some fear to come, but it doesn't. Sometimes, she can go for weeks without being scared, and can even forget about the bad feelings, but just as she's nearly forgotten them completely, they come back. They pounce. Almost as if they have been waiting deliberately until she feels safe. Nobody else in the family believes in her fears, because none of them have ever been frightened here. Mia's mother has told her that she simply frightens herself by thinking too much. Her favourite picture book, a very old one handed down from her father's side of the family called *Myths from Other Lands*, has been consigned to the attic in a box until she's grown out of her childish terrors. Mia's family believe that books like that encourage her silly ideas, with their tales of deadly wild woods, cruel witches and creatures partial to child flesh.

Mia can hear a clock ticking. It sounds as if it's just outside her bedroom door, but she knows it's echoing down the corridor from the top of the stairs, where there is a spindly-legged table on which resides an aspidistra plant and a carriage clock. If Mia listens too hard to the ticking, it sounds as if it's actually in the room with her. Angry with herself, she pulls the blankets over her ears and hums softly beneath her breath to shut out the sound. It's been a good day. She mustn't spoil it.

Gradually, the child's breathing becomes soft and slow as she is carried into sleep. She dreams of playing in the garden, dancing with a black kitten who sings in a funny voice. The kitten is the same size as she is and capers about on its hind legs.

'Round and round and round and round, we run, run, run!' it sings.

Mia laughs, holding its front paws. She has a taste of lemonade in her mouth and her feet are bare. The grass is warm and moist beneath her toes. There are women in bright, flower-patterned summer dresses sitting on seats round the edge of the lawn. These are her relatives, although they are wearing different faces to the ones she knows. They smile and clap at the antics of the kitten and the girl.

Then a noise comes from the dark bulk of the house. A rustle and a crack. All the women turn their faces quickly towards it. Their hands freeze in mid-air. In her dream, Mia feels the dark bricks leaning over her, but refuses to stop dancing, refuses to look.

'Oh no!' says the kitten. Dropping onto all fours, it shrinks in size and scampers off towards the bottom garden.

'Don't leave me!' Mia calls after it.

Then she wakes. Breathless and hot. For a moment, the dream is still with her; she feels confused, and then she realises she is afraid. 'Oh no!' Her whisper echoes the last words of the dream-kitten.

The night-light is behaving queerly, flickering. Mia feels a cry building up within her. When she releases it, her Grandma will come, as she always does. She must let the sound go. And yet, it feels trapped somewhere, as if she's grown a kink in her chest. The cry can't get out. The walls of the room seem very far away, lost in a brown shadow. Mia can't even move to hide beneath the bed-clothes again. She wants to go to the toilet. She feels sick. Then the sound comes again. This was the sound that woke her, that pushed into her happy dream.

A rustle, a crack, a tumble of stones. It's coming from the fireplace.

Mia has never actually *seen* anything frightening in the house, yet even so wishes she could stop herself looking at the high, slate mantle, the dark hole beneath. There is smoke coming out, as if dust has been dislodged. Birds in the chimney; she's heard of that. A bird. Dust falls again, and stones clatter onto the empty fire-basket. There *is* something there, and it must be something real. She gets ready to call for her Grandma, sure the sound will come out now, because whatever is happening is a real thing. Then she sees a flash of movement.

In a moment of absolute stillness, before feeling or reaction can seize her, she sees the red boots coming down the chimney, sees them hanging there above the grate. One foot kicks spasmodically, as if whoever is wearing the boots is stuck. Mia is frozen by utter incredulity at what she sees. They are women's boots, high-heeled and laced. Then they begin to shudder, to vibrate, and the first scream seeps out of her in a thin trail. She can almost see it winding from her mouth and into the room; a bright, silvery colour. The boots kick and thrash. More stones come. The fireplace shakes. Whatever it is, it's coming in! The scream comes on like a train, like a steam-train shooting out of her. She can smell smoke, hear the high whistle, the rumble of wheels on metal. The house shakes. She will scream for ever.

Lights on. Voices murmuring. The slap of slippered feet on carpet. The door to Mia's bedroom is flung open and both Grandma and Grandpa hurry into the room.

'What a racket!' says Grandpa gruffly, and then Grandma sucks in her breath sharply, cries, 'Mia!'

Even when they slap her, the child will not stop screaming, her eyes bulging from her head, staring at the fireplace. Her face is brick-red, and she is surrounded by the ammonia reek of urine. Grandpa carries her rigid body from the bed. They take her downstairs. 'It's a convulsion,' says Grandma, and phone calls are made.

The doctor comes in the middle of the night. Parents are summoned. 'A fever, a juvenile fever,' says the doctor, shaking his thermometer. He has silenced the child with an injection, but her little body is still rigid and trembling, wrapped in blankets on the sofa, her eyes unfocused, but staring. They are waiting for the parents to come, to take the child away.

'It must have been a terrible nightmare!' says Grandma, glancing fearfully at her grand-daughter.

'Delirium,' corrects the doctor. 'Not as uncommon as you'd think.'

A couple of days later, at home, recovering from her fever, Mia listens to her mother telling her she had horrible dream, which had been caused by her illness. She tells her mother what she saw in the fireplace. 'Do I have to go back there?' she dares to ask.

Her mother laughs and ruffles Mia's hair. 'Don't be silly, darling! It was only a dream. You were poorly, but you're better now. You must be a good, grown-up girl for your Mummy.' She and Mia's father have a full social life that takes up all their time at the weekends. Boating trips, parties, the races. Mia's father's parents are often with them. It is more convenient to have the child stay with the mother's parents at the weekend.

'I don't like that house, Mum,' Mia says.

'I grew up there, darling,' Mia's mother replies in a gentle voice, trying to soothe her. 'I was never frightened. There's nothing there to be frightened of.'

They will never believe her.

They will send her back there.

And they do.

The Fool's Path

Many of my stories are inspired by the anecdotes and recollections of friends. I've found you can ask anyone 'what's the weirdest thing that ever happened to you', and nearly all of them can remember something strange and inexplicable. Wonderful for writers of the weird!

This story sticks fairly close to the reality as it was told to me, with of course many details invented to make it a rounded story. The character Carlotta's experiences are based upon something that happened to a woman known to a friend of mine. When writing from real life inspirations, I'm always careful to embellish the story heavily, change it, and generally hide any connections that might be recognised. After all, we always have that disclaimer on the copyright pages of our books – all persons and events are fictional and any resemblance to reality is coincidental. But the accident that happens in this story is fairly faithful to the truth as my informant knew it, including how the victim was found. The character herself is nothing like the original person, as she wasn't known to me, and my friend didn't know her that well either. So the personality had to be made-up. The narrator is entirely imaginary, as are the minor characters, but the magician – well, it was him who told me the tale!

The night Carlotta challenged the Fool began with laughter. There she was, mock sober, one foot up on the table in the spilled wine, bangles clanking, looking for all the world as if she'd been invented solely to fit her gypsy name.

'I'm not afraid of anything,' she said.

I remember the heat of the night and the way the slow-moving river below the theatre bar gave off a summer smell that was half of flowers and half of rot. The wall of windows over the river was open to the air and it was like being on a high boat, drifting through the season. Looking out, you could see all the lights burning on the theatre roof reflected like fireflies in the water. We were all too hot, fanning ourselves with anything that would lend itself to the job. And the heat had lured the magician out of his cave, or whatever place he lived in.

He came to the theatre bar often, although it was impossible to predict his movements, but we all knew that was the way he wanted it. Older than all of us, he'd come in and do card tricks at the round corner table, drinking beer because he said spirits or wine made him see things he'd rather not see. He told us about phantom drinkers, the ghosts who'd stand behind the living as they drank, make-believing they could still do it too. Apparently, the theatre bar had quite a few of those. It was impossible to put an age on the magician – he could have been anywhere between thirty-five and sixty. He was the sort of man who hardly ever changed and had probably looked mature, in a freakish kind of way, when he'd still been a child. Handsome? Yes, in a bizarre manner. He took girls away with him when he wanted to, at the end of the night, through the smoke and the fruity smell of stale beer. They went to hotels, never to his home, and nobody ever complained, even if they didn't say much about what happened. I think he told them to be secretive, just to wind people up. He probably taught them the smug smile too.

The magician would always come in late, and then the theatre staff, when they'd finished work, would drift into the bar and sit down to let him entertain them. Sometimes, a few of the minor actors would join them. Carlotta, the other bar staff, and me would flit about all night, waiting and yearning to join the raucous party in the corner.

I'd worked in the bar for five seasons, but Carlotta was new. Most people liked her, even though she made no secret of knowing she was gorgeous and could be a bit full of herself. She was a dare-devil with a loud, almost masculine laugh. She could rake her hands through her thick black hair and flutter her eyes, and a thousand empires might fall. I'm not sure why she ended up working in a bar – even a bar with high kudos like the theatre's – but I guessed she'd had a rough time of one kind or another and was down on her luck.

So, on this night, the devil was in Carlotta. She was hot and high, full of mischief. She'd told me earlier that she had her eye on one of the actors, and that she was sure he had his eye on her. The actor in question was my friend, Jack. He was not destined to be a leading man, but took fairly prominent parts in the productions on a regular basis. He was too lazy ever to be a huge success in life, but, while his looks lasted, he intended to make the most of it. I had no doubt his eye had noticed Carlotta, as it noticed any attractive female. During my five seasons, I had counselled over half a dozen Jack-broken hearts and now wondered whether I was due for another or whether Jack had met his match.

The magician came in at just before eleven and Jack was one of the first to join his party. Weirdly enough, given what happened, Jack was playing the Fool in the play – a court jester in actual fact. The following night would be the last performance of the current production.

When the last of the customers had been shooed from the premises, Hugh, the bar manager locked up and gestured for Carlotta and I refill the empty glasses at the corner table. It was Friday. We could tell Hugh was looking forward to a long night.

The magician already had his cards out and a young, pretty actress called Mel was in debate with him. She'd come in with Jack, and none of us really knew her. I'd heard what she had to say before, from other sceptical mouths.

'It's just sleight of hand, tricks,' she said. 'That's all it is.'

'Did I say otherwise?' said the magician.

'It *is* otherwise,' Jack said sternly. 'You've taught us that.'

The actress pulled a face. 'Oh, come on! Magic doesn't exist, not real magic. If it did, the world would be a different place.'

'It's the Cosmic Joker,' Jack said. 'The Fool. He governs it all.'

'What?' The actress laughed in the most convincing manner of her profession.

Carlotta and I sat down, and I sensed Carlotta's engine begin to rev beside me. I wondered if we were heading into dangerous territory. The magician hardly ever talked about the Fool – his obsession – unless it was with people he had known for a long time.

Jack leaned forward earnestly. 'The Fool exists. We've heard him.'

'Heard him?' said Carlotta.

Jack nodded. 'Yes. He's spoken through this guy here,' (indicating the magician). 'It's a different voice. Isn't that so, Haze?'

This last demand was addressed to me. I looked into the magician's eyes. He was squinting, drawing on a cigarette. I wasn't sure what to say. He might have been a trickster, but I respected the man. He blinked at me slowly, as a cat might, to signify approval.

'Yes,' I said. 'Some nights we've done séances and he's come through.'

Both Carlotta and the actress laughed, but not together. Neither noticed they were the only two laughing. 'Séances!' exclaimed Carlotta. 'It's like being at school!'

Now these women were attacking one of our traditions. I'm not sure how many of us actually believed in the séances or the card tricks, but in a way they belonged to us and were part of our culture. We moved in the magical world of theatre, the world of illusion, lights and glamour, and the magician was part of it, a character, a fixture. He had become the shaman of our tribe.

'Don't mock,' Hugh said. 'You don't tangle with the Fool. Treat him with extreme caution.'

'Huh!' Mel said. 'And what is he exactly? Mr Punch?'

I noticed she and Carlotta actually exchanged a conspiratorial glance and grinned together. Wonders will never cease.

'I'm not afraid of anything,' Carlotta said.

'Mr Punch is one of his masks,' said the magician.

'Right, I'm really scared now!' cawed Mel. 'A big scary kid's puppet. Has he got your hand up his ass?'

Carlotta snorted loudly.

'I would say,' said the magician, fastidiously knocking ash from his cigarette, 'that the Fool's hand is firmly up mine!'

Again, whoops of laughter.

The magician was quiet, serious, but I couldn't believe he was offended. No, there was another reason for it. He was playing to the house.

'The Fool,' said the magician, 'is one of the oldest archetypes. His is the path between Chokmah and Kether, from the realm of ideas to the divine and vice versa. It is the raw energy of creativity, without rules, without boundaries.'

Mel shook her head. 'Well, that makes a lot of sense.'

'That is a remark the Fool would make,' said the magician, 'seeing as you mean exactly the opposite.'

There was a sting in his voice that hooked right into Mel. 'I just don't believe in this hocus pocus crap,' she said.

'You should,' said Jack.

'Make him come through then,' Carlotta said, clearly having been waiting for this perfect cue. 'Do it now.'

The magician smiled to himself. 'Oh, I don't think you would like that.'

'Prove it to us,' Carlotta said. 'Come on. Prove he exists.'

I didn't like it one little bit and I could tell not many of the others did either, but Jack was fired up with wanting to convert the sceptics into believers, especially two attractive women, who he no doubt believed were his for the taking. Well, they probably were. 'We could,' he said.

'I want you to,' said Carlotta, with one of her best artillery fire glances.

Perhaps Mel sensed Jack was drifting away from her, and became more acutely aware of Carlotta's exotic, heady charm, because she said, 'Yeah, let's. I want it to be proved. I want to believe!'

She laughed alone that time, even though she'd made an effort to make the laugh sound pretty rather than cruel.

'Well?' said Jack to the magician.

He sucked a long draw off his cigarette and took some time carefully stubbing it out. Then he frowned. 'Perhaps,' he said.

'A séance!' Carlotta exclaimed. 'Dim the lights!'

We shouldn't have done it, not with Carlotta and Mel there, for the simple reason we should have known that the Fool would relish the situation. People thought of jesters' hats, goggling eyes and stupid antics, but the Cosmic Joker was a far darker character than that. The greatest darkness being that he hid behind this pantomime façade. The magician had taught us tricks, but he had also spoken long into the night of the secrets of the universe. Not to all of us, but a select few: Jack, Hugh and myself among them. In the strange hours before dawn, anything seems possible and anything can happen. We had seen things happen that, later, in the light of day had seemed ridiculous. With his quiet, whimsical voice, the magician had led us – willing apprentices – along the paths of magic. In the cold twilight before the sun rises, he had made us psychic. After many hours of fortune-telling play and guessing games with the dog-eared old bridge cards, when coincidence seemed to be aligning in our favour, the cards would be put aside and the magician's Tarot pack would come out. He'd unwrap it with reverence from a grey silk handkerchief. 'Chokmah's colour,' he'd tell us, 'silvery mist.'

Without the magician even touching the deck, we could pull any card we named from it. It had started as fun and ended up serious. We had gambled our lives and our happiness on it.

'This game exists,' we would say ponderously, our palms upon the cards, and then, 'If the Priestess comes to me, I'll get all that I want. I will cross the abyss of Da'ath to the source of creation. I will become my own god. If she turns her face away from me, I lose everything.'

And with that we made our pact with the universe. We meant it. Then came that moment, when the hand is on the cards and anything is possible, even though the top card of the shuffled deck has already been chosen by random chance. It's already lying there, face down. Or is it? That is what the magician taught us to question.

'That is the secret of magic,' he told us. '*You* must become the randomiser.'

And how many times had I taken that card in my hand, sweating all over, only to turn it face up and see the one I had named, be it the Priestess, the Empress or the Devil, gazing back at me from the picture. I never believed I could do it. Never. And yet, when the magician fired us up and prepared us over a long night, we *could* do it. If we didn't win, we'd play again, until we did, until we'd promised our very souls to the Fool. Séances were an intrinsic part of the proceedings. We'd talk to the Fool time and again throughout the night. Dangerous games. Occult Russian roulette. But at least we knew the rules.

Hugh looked at me and I shrugged. We could have stopped it perhaps. The magician himself was in two minds, I could tell, perhaps because he already knew the outcome. But he was the avatar of the Fool, his greatest detractor and his most faithful servant. We had already invoked him. The circumstances and dynamics of the evening were his. The dice had been rolled, the cards dealt.

Someone went to dim the lights, while someone else fetched the candles stuck in old wine bottles. We kept a plank of Formica behind the bar that, years ago, someone had inscribed with the letters of the alphabet and the words 'yes' and 'no' – our Ouija board. Not exactly decorative, but it did the job.

'Will the Fool speak through you?' Carlotta asked the magician as we arranged the table.

The magician glanced at Jack. 'Well, seeing as our young friend here is playing the court jester at present, I think it should be him.'

'Me?' said Jack.

No one but the magician had ever tried to channel the Fool before.

'Why not?' said the magician. He had some more tricks up his sleeve.

An upturned wine glass went onto the board, and in the flickering light, we all put a finger on it.

'Is there any presence here that wishes to communicate?' said the magician, his finger lightly on the glass. With his free hand, he lit another cigarette.

The glass began to move almost at once.

'Someone's pushing it!' cried Mel.

The magician ignored the remark and exhaled silvery smoke. 'Is there someone here who wishes to communicate?'

The glass sped towards the word 'yes' on the left of the board.

'No!' said Carlotta.

The magician withdrew his hand, folded his arms, hunched forward.

'Will you tell us your name?' he asked.

The glass sped crazily around the board, jabbing at random letters.

'Are you the Fool?' the magician asked.

The glass shot towards 'yes' again.

'Someone's definitely pushing it,' Mel said and removed her finger from the glass. 'This is stupid.'

The glass skidded towards the letter 'C', then 'V'. 'Me,' said Carlotta. 'It's talking to me. Those are my initials.'

The magician leaned back and delved into the pocket of his jacket. The Tarot cards came out, wrapped in their silk. We all took our fingers from the glass and watched the magician shuffle his cards. He then handed them to Carlotta. 'Shuffle and cut them,' he said.

Carlotta raised an eyebrow but did as he asked. She set the cards down on the table and cut them into two piles. 'Turn over the top card,' said the magician, 'the one from the middle of the deck.'

She did so. It was the Two of Swords.

'Demon of Chokmah,' said the magician. 'Turn over the other half of the deck.'

Carlotta did so and uttered a delighted squeak. The card revealed was the Fool.

'You did that,' said Mel to the magician. 'You fixed it.' She was so annoyed at no longer being the centre of attention; she was definitely not playing any more.

The magician shrugged. He didn't care.

'Put your fingers back,' Jack said. 'Come on. We're on to

something.'

'No, wait,' Carlotta said. 'The Fool came to me, so I want to ask him something. I challenge him now to prove he exists.' She turned to the magician. 'Can he grant wishes?'

'Anything is within his power,' said the magician. 'That is the game. Gamble with him.'

'What if she loses?' Mel asked sourly.

The magician gestured elegantly. 'Then she can win back whatever she loses.'

'I don't intend to lose,' Carlotta said. 'There's no deal and this isn't a game. If he's so powerful, I don't have to gamble.' She put her finger on the glass. 'Fool, if you're real, then make me beautiful for ever. Grant me eternal beauty.'

'What a strange request,' drawled Mel, arms folded defensively. 'Worried about your looks, honey?' It was as if she wasn't there.

The glass began to move slowly around the board, again towards letters that made no sense. Then Jack said, in a strange high-pitched, Mr Punch voice, 'I'll make you as beautiful as I am!'

'Jack!' Carlotta exclaimed. 'Cut it out!'

'Cut what out?' Jack said.

'That voice. Come on. We're supposed to be doing this for real.'

'I didn't say anything,' Jack said.

'Yeah, that's right.' Carlotta took her hand from the glass. She looked slightly unnerved. 'This is weird. I don't know why I'm doing it.'

'You just did,' said Jack.

No one wanted to continue that night. The working had been accomplished, although we didn't know it.

The following evening, the cast of the play planned a party after the show, in the apartment reserved for their use at the top of the theatre. I was feeling lousy, and in no mood for celebration, having drunk too much the night before, but Carlotta was determined to go. 'Oh come on,' she said to me in the afternoon as we began work. 'Come with me. We can share a cab home afterwards.'

'You go,' I said. 'I'm not in the mood.'

'Well, see how you feel later,' Carlotta said, disgruntled.

I realised she wanted support because Mel would be there.

Before the audience moved over from the hotel gardens along the river, Carlotta took some refreshments to the actors backstage. She was gone for ages, and I was starting to get annoyed by the time she bounced – or rather floated – back into the bar. 'For God's sake,' I said. 'Where have you been? There's going to be a riot in here soon.'

She took hold of my hands and waltzed me round the limited space behind the bar. 'Guess what? Guess what?' she sang.

'Something to do with Jack,' I said, dead pan.

'He said something really – *intriguing*,' Mel said.

I sighed. 'I bet.'

'He said, "There's something on the cards for you tonight, my lady".'

'How eminently flattering.'

'It was. He was all in costume and did the Fool voice and everything.'

'A game, that's all.'

'You weren't there. You didn't see his eyes.'

I could imagine them vividly. 'He's a flirt, Carly. You must know that.'

'So am I,' she said.

The night, as I'd predicted, was busy. It was even hotter than the previous evening if that was possible, and all I could think of was the balcony of my apartment and the bottle of Chardonnay chilling in the fridge. I yearned for it. I yearned for solitude and no babbling voices, my favourite CDs and communion with the stars above the city. Carlotta tried in many different ways to persuade me to go to the actors' party: threats, wheedling, flattery, you name it. I realised she was actually nervous of going alone, mainly because few of the bar staff, or theatre crew she knew fairly well, were going. Could it be possible that brazen Carlotta had a shy streak? I felt really mean saying 'no', but I just wasn't up to it. Sometimes, I enjoy the company of actors, with their fervid, peacock insecurities, but I knew that tonight they would have the same effect on my equilibrium as fingernails down a blackboard. 'Just go,' I said. 'They'll all be drunk. You can talk to anyone.'

'Fuck you!' Carlotta hissed. 'Just fuck you, Hazel.'

'Don't fall out with me over this,' I said. 'I'm not here just to accommodate you.'

'I thought we were friends.'

Were we? I realised I didn't really look upon Carlotta as a friend.

She was a work acquaintance. None of my friends were going to the party, not even the magician, who was visiting friends out of town. Jack didn't count, because I knew what he was like when he was on the prowl with women.

'Look,' I said. 'If it's Jack you're after, he'll be in the thick of things tonight. You might not get near him. If it's so important, I'll call him and we'll go out for lunch or dinner tomorrow. Just the three of us. Okay?'

'He likes you well enough to do that?' Her tone was slightly acid.

I sighed. 'We're friends, Carly, old time friends. Yes, he'll do lunch if I ask him.'

That mollified her. 'I'll share your cab home, then,' she said. 'Do you think you should ask him before we leave in case – like – he makes alternative arrangements?'

'Sundays, to Jack, are sacred,' I said. 'Trust me. I'll call him late tomorrow morning.'

The fact I had to ask for her phone number shows just how big friends Carlotta and I really were.

We didn't finish clearing up until nearly midnight and the last drinkers were forcibly ejected from the premises. I locked up because it was Hugh's night off. The cab was purring outside as Carlotta and I went down the steps to the street. Behind us the theatre was in darkness, but for the yellow lights on the high top floor. We could hear their music, their laughter. Now, I felt even meaner. Should we just go up for a while? Perhaps I could introduce her to some folk, then leave.

But Carlotta took my arm and opened the cab door. She didn't seem to care now, so I said nothing.

It was quite a ride out to where I lived, and some distance on from that for Carlotta. We talked in the cab about Jack, and I felt mellow enough to offer Carlotta a few crumbs from the table. He was probably quite lonely, really. Probably needed a woman he respected.

We were near to my street, when Carlotta started to get restless. 'I think I'll go back,' she said.

'What? But we're almost home.'

'I know, but I keep thinking about it, and Jack might think I'm not bothered if I don't turn up.'

Too many crumbs, clearly. I should have kept my mouth shut. 'Carly...'

'No, it's Okay, really. I have to do this. I have to do it alone. A test, maybe.'

The cab came to a halt by my door. 'Well, if you're sure.'

'Absolutely. Still call me tomorrow, though.' She laughed. 'If I'm at home, of course.'

It was only once the cab had driven away that I realised I hadn't given her the code to open the fire exit door or the actors' apartment phone number. There's no way they'd hear her at the front of the building. Oh well. Too late now. If her liaison with Jack was meant to be, she'd find a way in.

I waited until nearly midday to call Jack, but he sounded fairly spritely when he answered the phone. Perhaps a good sign. 'How was last night?' I asked, injecting a slightly lascivious tone into my voice.

He yawned down the line. 'Actually, quite dull,' he said. 'I went home at two.'

'Oh dear,' I said. 'What about your fan club?'

'Meaning?'

'Carlotta and Mel. Any cat fights?'

'Mel was busy networking with more incandescent guys than me, and Carlotta wasn't there,' he said.

'Oh damn, my fault! She went back to the party after we left the theatre, but I forgot to give her the door code.'

'Now that's a shame.'

'Yeah. Sorry. Look, I'll call her and perhaps we can all go out for lunch.'

'Okay. Give me an hour and I'll pick you up.'

He sounded really keen, I thought.

I rang and rang, but there was no answer from Carlotta's phone. The stupid creature obviously hadn't turned on her answerphone either. If she missed this, she'd kick herself. Perhaps she was a heavy sleeper. Fortunately, I knew where she lived, because it was in one of the apartment blocks that a lot of the theatre staff lived in. It was recommended to new employees who came from out of town. When Jack arrived, I suggested we went there and tried to wake her up. He only crossed one red light on the way there, which was good, considering his clear enthusiasm to reach our destination.

But Carlotta was not at home. Her apartment intercom at the main door was clearly marked with her name, but we could get no response.

I eventually roused someone else I knew in the building and got them to knock on her door. 'She's not in,' they said. 'Go away. I was sleeping.'

'Now I'm worried,' I said. 'Where the hell did she go last night?'

'I should have arranged something with her,' Jack said. 'I did think about it, but didn't get the chance.'

'Then what was that flirty remark all about?'

He frowned. 'What?'

I told him what Carlotta had said.

'I didn't say that,' he said. 'I'm sure I didn't.'

'In costume,' I said. 'The Fool.' We stared at each other for a moment, and were in complete and utter empathy. We had shared strange evenings with the magician. We had a link. We knew.

'Fuck,' I said.

'Come on.' Jack took my arm and dragged me back to his car.

He drove like a maniac to the theatre. I don't know what we thought we'd find, or why we even went there, but we did. The back of theatre faced a small yard, and was approached by a couple of alleys. We parked the car out front, and I half expected to see a forlorn Carlotta curled up before the theatre doors. No chance.

We went round the back. Nothing.

'Why are we here?' I asked.

Jack went over to a pile of rubbish sacks. I watched him paw through them, feeling sick to my stomach. He went to the fire escape, looked up, towards the door on the top floor. No one was there. 'Perhaps she's inside,' I said. 'We should look. You might not have noticed her.'

'I would,' he said. He turned away from the steps and stared at the ground.

'Haze,' he said.

I went over. 'What is it?'

'Blood,' he said, pointing at the ground. 'I think it is. What do you think?'

'It looks like blood,' I said, swallowing hard. 'Someone could have had a fight.'

Jack hunkered down and picked something up, then another: small things, white like pearls. I watched him turn his head to the side jerkily, press the back of one hand against his mouth.

'What is it?' I asked. 'Bone?'

'No,' he answered. 'Teeth.'

I looked up the alley ahead of us, and could see, in the shadows, the vague trail of blood that led to it. I felt faint but I walked towards it.

It was me who found her. I recognised her by her clothes. She must have crawled there, seeking help. At the time, I thanked God she wasn't dead. But that was more for me than for her.

The official report said that Carlotta Visconti, aged twenty-two, had fallen from the fire escape of the theatre and smashed her face on the ground below. She had escaped life threatening injury through sheer luck, although would require extensive reconstructive surgery on her face. It was assumed the effects of alcohol had caused her to fall while banging on the top floor apartment door. What the report didn't account for was the fact that the railings around the fire escape platform were intact and Carlotta wasn't drunk. But Carlotta herself, when she was able to give a statement, said that was what had happened.

I steeled myself to go and visit her in hospital, long before Jack did. I hadn't realised he was so squeamish. As I saw her lying there in the bed, unrecognisable but for her hair, one thought looped through my mind: you got your wish. You got your wish. Nose bashed in, cheekbones shattered, jaw ruined, a hideous caricature like Mr Punch. I will make you as beautiful as I am. The worst thing was she realised it herself.

That first time I visited, she took my hand and tried to weep, which was difficult because it hurt her so much. She wanted to thank me for coming, for facing her, I know, and I just squeezed her hand and said, 'hey, no problem. That's what friends are for.' It broke my heart to see the way that dreadful cliché comforted her.

Perhaps the best that can be said is that the whole experience made her a better person, because whenever I visited her, I sensed a deeper, more contemplative being within the skin. But who wants to get better that way, when your beauty was so important to you and no matter what the surgeons did, or how well they did it, some precious essence was lost forever? Lesson one: do not challenge the Fool. Lesson two: magic takes the path of least resistance.

Jack and I had dinner with the magician a couple of weeks after it happened. I said to him, 'You knew, didn't you?'

'Not exactly,' the magician answered. 'What kind of monster would that make me? They invoked it. I had no control over it. She was warned.'

'Not enough,' I said. 'Not nearly enough. By any of us.'

'She didn't say, "This game exists",' Jack said. 'If you don't say that, then you're not really playing. What happened could just be coincidence.'

'You don't believe that,' I said.

Carlotta herself was strangely sanguine about the whole affair. I'd expected suicidal grief, bitterness, anger or resentment, but it just wasn't there. I admired her strength, her ability to have faith that all would be well. But then, there was yesterday.

I visited her in the evening and she brought the subject of the séance up for the first time. 'It's real, Haze, isn't it,' she said. 'People have no idea.' The only tone in her voice was a kind of wonder.

I took Jack's stance. 'We have no proof of that. Life just is. Believing in all that stuff is fine for late at night, but we can't live by it, Carly. It would all get too insane. You had an accident, that's all.'

'It's real, Hazel,' Carlotta repeated. 'It's me who was the Fool.'

'Just clumsy,' I said with a hopeful smile.

'No.' She was emphatic. 'I didn't play properly. I mocked. I tried to trick him.'

'You shouldn't think like that…'

She fixed me with a stare. 'Bring him here, Haze.'

'Bring who? Jack?'

She shook her head. 'No, the magician. I want to see him.'

I cocked my head to one side. 'Er… Why?'

Her smile, in her ruined face, was scary. 'Because I have to play him at his own game,' she said. 'I have to win it all back.'

The Fool's path. Once trodden, it is difficult to find the way back. Riches pour from the trickster's sleeves and not all of them are fairy gold. I'm standing at my own cross-roads. To join her game or not. In Carlotta's place, would I risk the same? This game exists.

Haven

I've always loved the music of fairy tales, the particular rhythm and syntax they have, and I've written quite a few stories in this vein. Haven was inspired by the experiences of a friend, who fell in love with the wrong person. There was a gulf of difference between her and the object of her adoration – socially, culturally and spiritually. Being of a magical persuasion, her presence in this man's life was almost an irritant because he professed he had no interest in the subject and did not believe in anything he couldn't behold with his own senses. I wonder whether he was secretly scared by the unseen, the weird. For my friend, venturing into this man's world was a culture shock – she'd always had a very Bohemian and unconventional life, and the way ordinary people lived was baffling to her. Suffice to say, things did not end well. As a kind of consolation, I wrote my friend this fairy tale.

There was once a city that lay close to the ocean, at the edge of a vast delta land. Diamond-bright water and verdant isles glistened beneath the light of a mellow sun, and silver clarions sounded from the high towers of the city, proclaiming across the lands of this world and beyond that all was right in the kingdom. Banners the colour of saffron unfurled upon the lofty poles that rose above the towers. They moved slowly in the balmy breeze, which was scented with the aromas of the mellow flowers that grew upon the islands of the delta and in the tiered gardens of the city itself. Did this city have a name? Yes it did. Its name was Haven.

There were no thieves in the city, no dark alleyways, no terrible areas of mystery, no dragons, no ghosts. Only light and the dreamy smiles of those who were truly content in that gilded world.

The prince of this city, Garland, was loved by all whose gaze fell upon him. He was the beloved only son of the king and queen, and wherever he walked in the courts and echoing chambers, so petals of the rose were strewn at his feet. His words were recorded by a retinue of scribes, his witticisms and words of wisdom distributed throughout the kingdom so that all might share in his bright spirit. He towered over all, both in presence and in height and there were none in the kingdom more loved or more celebrated than he.

The king had ordered his artists, at the moment of the prince's birth, to paint the scenes of his son's life as it would be, and these pictures adorned the walls of a long gallery within the palace. Prince Garland would move among these pictures, secure in the knowledge that all was as it should be, and all would proceed as it was ordained, the path from birth to death. He could see his own passing, far in the future; he lying as an old man, pale upon his last bed, surrounded by his wife, children and grand-children, adored and safe in those final moments. And in the meantime life was good, pictures of bliss; those around him caught in poses of attention upon his words. He would not ride into battles, because the kingdom was peaceful. He would not take for himself an exotic and mysterious foreign wife, because it was already decided whom he would wed – a genteel lady of the court, of suitable pedigree. He would not have adventures, because it was dangerous to wander beyond the kingdom. He would make no changes to, nor leave true mark upon the world, because no one within the kingdom desired it to change. Haven would continue as it always had, beneath the light of that mellow sun.

But where would be the story in this bland, contented life devoid of storms and uprisings? You are right – there is nothing exciting to tell. But only if Haven's dull existence remained unchanged. And it is the nature of the world to alter.

Occasionally, the prince and his friends would ride out from the city and gallop through the marshy pools to the forest at the other side of the delta. Birds would fly up in a clatter as they passed, and silver water spray out from beneath the horses' hooves. Some of the young men would carry the banners of Haven, which streamed behind them, and some would blow upon silver trumpets so that no one could be in any doubt about who rode across the land. They were a beautiful company, full of laughter. They rode to hunt the white harts that roamed the forest, slinking like ghosts through the trees. There were no ghosts in Haven.

And, as is the way with tales of this nature, upon one of these excursions the prince became separated from his friends. How this happened no one afterwards could truly say. Perhaps a wind came up that blew the branches of the trees against his horse's eyes so that it frighted and veered off along a different path. Perhaps a strange magic twisted the paths between the mossy trunks. But however it happened, for a short time he was alone, and you can be sure a man such as he was vulnerable in that situation.

As he rode, the tall oaks crowded in around him. They were so ancient, time appeared to have twisted them out of shape. They loomed and watched, rustling even when the wind was still. The path became very narrow and led at length to a glade, in the centre of which was a grassy mound. The prince thought that the light in that place was unnatural, and a shiver passed through his skin. He smelled magic, even though he had no idea what that was. He noticed that the only birds in the glade were crows, blacker than the night of the moon's dark. Their raw voices seemed to mock him. He noticed that an intoxicating scent rose from the ground, earthy and potent. And it seemed to him, very faintly, that a strange music filled the air, music not of this Earth. He could barely hear it – a distant choir and the tinkle of metal chimes moved by the slightest of breezes. Part of him spoke loudly in his mind: *turn back, turn back*. But another part did not heed these words. He rode into the glade and halted his horse upon the forest lawn. And he waited.

As many of you know, there is another world that exists alongside our own. In all respects, these two worlds are different, yet some would say they are the same. The people of Haven did not speak of the other world: they shunned it. Children in Haven were not told tales to frighten them should they misbehave, so they never feared the darkness. The people of Haven denied this other world existed, in fact, and the strength of their belief was so powerful they were kept safe from its influences.

Others, who lived in different kingdoms, referred to this world as the realm below. To some, it was an underworld, grim and terrible, while to others it was the land of endless summer, where the citizens lived eternal lives, bathed in the light of a sun that was not a sun, but something else.

On this day, when the prince of Haven strayed from the path, the queen of the underworld awoke from a bizarre dream she was having. She stretched upon her canopied bed and rose up from it. She was assailed by a strange feeling that seemed to make tight the very fibres of her being. She too could hear a distant music, and was discomforted by its tone. She felt in her bones that the planets shifted in their positions, and that if she were to venture into the upper world she would see their new pattern in the sky, and this would mean something. So she clad herself in a robe of crimson, and bound her black hair with a rope of inky pearls. She crept like a thief through the halls of her palace, past the king of the underworld as he slept, and came at length to the narrow stair that led to the world above. She came out of the hill in the centre of the glade where Prince Garland sat upon his nervous horse, and she thought to herself, 'what have we here?'

The prince, when he first caught sight of this creature rising from the earth, experienced a shock in his flesh, for she was so *other* to all that he knew. He was unsure whether to be frightened or appalled or disgusted. He recognised her as a witch, even though he didn't really know what that was, for he had never been told tales to frighten him as a boy. He could see that she possessed weird beauty, but this was a beauty he had never seen before, so alien and discomforting. She was nothing like him, he knew, and if he had any sense at all he would put spur to flank and gallop his horse out of the forest in any direction. But when he looked into the woman's black eyes, he saw within them a kindred soul, a heart that beat as his did.

And so they stared at one another for some minutes, she circling the stamping, head-tossing horse, her body stooped over in a predatory crouch, tendrils of her loosely-bound hair brushing the ground. And he gazed down his nose at her, his eyes aflame, still and straight in the saddle and he waited that she might speak. But she didn't, so at length he said, 'Lady, are you lost within the forest?'

The woman looked into his eyes, and he wondered if she did not understand his language, but then she spoke. 'Am I lost? Truly, I don't know. I have just come to this place. It is strange to me.'

'Who are you?' he asked, and she replied,

'I am the queen of another land, far from this world, yet so close. The sky called to me, for it had something to say, so here I am.'

'The sky cannot speak,' said the prince.

'Can it not?' asked the woman.

Prince Garland knew that however he answered that question it would not be with words she'd want to hear.

She laughed at his silence and said, 'Perhaps you are the sign the sky spoke of.'

This announcement troubled the prince greatly, but in a hidden place within him, because he could not imagine what kind of sign this creature might be looking for. There had been no Granny or Nurse in his childhood to whisper to him of the denizens of the other world, so he had no way of knowing what faced him. He was a prince of Haven, untouchable and celebrated. There was nothing to fear. When he spoke, flowers fell from his lips and people sank to their knees before him. When he smiled, clouds moved from the sun. And so he smiled and so he spoke in flowers. 'My lady, if you are really a queen, then you should not be alone in the forest. Come with me to my city and my people will care for you until you know whether or not you are lost.'

The woman raised her eyebrows at him. 'Your city? I cannot go there, sir. The stones of your domain would crumble before me.'

'Those stones have stood for a long time,' said the prince, smiling still. 'I do not think you are a risk to them.'

The woman narrowed her eyes at him. 'I will not go to your city. If you would speak with me, you must do so here.'

'Speak with you?' The prince laughed. 'It is only courteous of me to assist you, that is all.'

'As you wish,' said the woman, 'but now you must go, because the sun sinks beneath the trees and soon the night will come, and that is not your province.'

The prince looked about him and realised that she was right. He thought the time was earlier but already the shadows lay long around him. He felt as if he had conversed with this woman for hours, but of course that was not possible. 'I wish you safety,' he said, 'and that you find your way.'

The woman said nothing to this, so he turned his horse and urged it back along the path, until presently he heard the voices of his friends, who had been looking for him. The sound washed over him like cool clear water and he felt that something was removed from him, something dark, something tainted. He looked back over his shoulder at the forest, where now the shadows clustered like hags, and he thought for a moment he heard that strange music, and a scent came to him, like the essence of the earth.

The ways of enchantment are weird and unfathomable. They come in many forms. The most potent and devastating of witcheries is the natural calamity of love. And sometimes love comes disguised as something else, and sometimes it is wrapped in fear, and other times it comes as a warrior, invincible and merciless, to smash the towers of our very existence. Unbidden, unnoticed, and certainly unwanted, such a warrior crept like a thief into Haven, that city where no thieves roamed.

Prince Garland returned to his parents' palace and put out of his mind the strange encounter in the forest. Perhaps it was unfortunate, during this crucial time, that his betrothed was away from the kingdom, engaged in the polite social activities to which ladies of her station are accustomed. But this meant the prince was in one way alone, as alone as he'd been on the forest path.

That night, as he retired to his chamber, a dire wind came up from the east, bearing with it the scent of earth and the sound of a wolf howling. When the prince went to the window casement, the sky looked purple rather than black, and the stars were fierce. The moon was a thin sickle, sharp enough to cut a man's throat, and the air was cold.

The prince pulled long velvet drapes across the casement. He did this roughly, as if to shut out something terrible. He went to his bed but he could not rest. He felt as if there was something he'd forgotten to do, but he couldn't remember what it was. And all the time the wolves of the wind circled the tower where he tried to sleep. He had never thought of wolves before, but he could imagine them now, white as ghosts, their long paws pacing the swirling air.

When he did sleep, his dreams were frightening, of being awake and trying to sleep. Eventually, the sun called him from these dark visions and he woke truly. A man from a different kingdom might have known by then that something had changed in his life, but Garland lived in Haven, and nothing changed there. So the uncomfortable feeling in his flesh and bones spoke only of illness to him. He wondered whether he should visit the court physician. But then…was something calling to him? He felt in his fibres he was being drawn. Without conscious decision, because he never thought of such things, he found himself at the stables, asking for his horse, and presently he was riding out across the delta. Alone.

He fled like a voiceless prayer into the dark forest of listening trees.

His horse gasped and froth flew from its mouth; its eyes showed white all the way around. Presently, as if guided by unheard voices or unseen hands, horse and rider came to the grassy mound and there, sitting atop it, was the witch queen of the underworld.

'Lady,' gasped the prince. His horse, shuddering, sank to its foreknees and he slipped from its saddle.

'I have thought of you,' said the queen. 'Strangely, I have thought of you.'

The prince strode to her and enfolded her in his arms, which at once felt so right, yet at the same time wrong. He wanted to embrace her, yet squeeze the life from her for making him feel this way. She lay quiescent against him, breathing as a frightened wild animal might, when held dazed against a human breast. The voices of the court, of his betrothed and her ladies, rang distantly in Prince Garland's ears. For a while he heard their laughter and it was tinny and tawdry. What lay against him now in comparison seemed pure and honest. 'You are lost,' he said, 'and I am urged to succour you. Come with me to my father's city.'

'Come into your world?' murmured the queen. Her voice sounded slurred, slightly drunk. 'But I do not know it.'

'We shall be great friends,' said the prince. 'And I shall help you learn.'

'Take me with you,' said the queen.

Behind them, the prince's horse was much recovered, standing once more proud and strong. The prince lifted the witch queen onto his saddle and climbed up behind her. In this, way, with the night of her hair streaming upon the early day, he bore her back to Haven.

Once the royal court laid eyes on her, they believed that the peculiar woman spoke the truth and was of royal bearing. Clearly, her mind was befuddled, and she had somehow lost her way, not just in the physical world but in her mind. She was not mad in a disagreeable way that might have to be hidden and controlled, but distant and confused.

They installed her with the ladies-in-waiting who tended to the queen, the prince's mother. The queen summoned the visitor to her.

'What is your name?' she asked.

'Pavonia Nocta,' replied the witch, a name she made up on the spot, because no being of earthly flesh should know her true name.

'We shall call you Vonny,' declared the queen.

Even the ladies, staring at the dark vision of midnight hair, creamy skin and crimson robes, balked at this homely name. The witch would never be Vonny to those who came to fear her. She was Pava.

In most tales of this nature, you'd expect the prince to fall desperately in love with the witch and want to marry her. Trials might be set for her to prove she was royal. Or she might be bewitched and exiled by rivals to wander the earth, until some kind soul found her and restored her memory or her sight to her – whatever might have been lost. None of these things happened.

Pava spread her poppy skirts about her and sat beside the queen, watching the ladies. Sometimes, she would glance out of the arched windows, where the shadows of flying crows darkened the glass. She appeared bemused, but content. She waited to see what would happen.

Prince Garland, meanwhile, laughed and played with his friends, indulging in all the pursuits considered suitable for young men of his age and station. Naturally, his thoughts wandered occasionally to the strange woman he had brought into the city, but he told himself he was merely concerned for her well-being. One afternoon, he sought her out, to ask how she was faring. She was in the rose garden where there were so many heavily-perfumed blooms that people who walked there could barely breathe. You could make perfume merely by holding a bottle with a bit of oil in it open to the air. The sweetness of Haven, hanging like ropes of silk in the sunlight.

'My lady,' said the prince, bowing. 'Are you well? Are you happy?'

Pava had been walking around the labyrinthine paths, perceiving a pattern there that the inhabitants of Haven did not. 'I am interested,' she replied, crushing a white rose with one hand and bringing its murdered petals to her nose. 'What a strange world this is.'

The prince felt a needle of sorrow make a stitch within him. As he'd suspected, her mind was addled. 'Have you remembered your home?'

Pava frowned. 'I'm unsure it's yet appropriate.' She smiled at him.

He took her hands. 'But are you happy?'

She looked at his hands over hers. 'Oh yes, I'm not sad. There is a lot of light here, isn't there? Doesn't it make you tired?'

The prince felt something give way within his breast as he gazed at her smile, which seemed unbearably innocent, and listened to her mad words. He must protect her.

'What is your name, prince of Haven?' she asked.

'Garland,' he replied, even though he was sure she must already know this fact.

She laughed and raised a hand to reach above him, let the torn petals drift down over his head.

Later, in a salon daubed by sunset, surrounded by women who twittered like little birds, Pava considered the prince, Garland. He was similar to a tree, she decided, not the kinds found in the underworld, those willows with branches like white hair, or the strange growths that were half fungus, half wood. No, he was a summer tree of the upper world, resplendent with bright foliage, the sun caught within his leaves. He would smell of sunlight and his touch would burn. Despite this, she would like to touch him and sensed he felt the same about her, except a mass of twittering birds roosted in his upper branches and he couldn't hear anything sensible or true because of their din.

Pava thought about going home, but then decided to stay a while longer because the upper world and its people intrigued her. Sometimes, when she walked the gardens and terraces of the palace, all the people she passed appeared to be wearing masks, grotesquely smiling masks. Beneath them, these people might have no features at all. Garland too wore a mask, but she suspected that what lay beneath his was something far more beautiful than the stylised, frozen smile he wore. Before she went home, she must look beneath his mask, otherwise she would be forever curious and restless.

One night, she turned into a black cat and slipped like a dark fluid through the palace, up stairs, along corridors, past rooms where people slept and did not dream. She followed her nose, which being a cat's nose at that time was very sensitive. She was drawn to the chamber of the sleeping prince, and realised then that he slept the whole time, even when he thought he was awake. She jumped onto his chest and purred into his face. Experimentally, she sucked in some of his breath to see what it tasted like. Nothing. Still, he looked beautiful, and his mask wasn't there. What lay beneath though was the face of a child, an idiot child who could not dream and was never truly awake. Sadly, she kissed him – sad, because that kiss would wake him and she knew he wouldn't thank her for it.

Garland shifted in his sleep, mumbled a little, uttered a short gasp. Then, making a chewing noise, he rubbed his nose and turned on his side. He began to dream.

Before morning, a crack appeared in the north tower of the palace, but because such things never happened, no one in Haven noticed.

Prince Garland woke late, and felt strange at once. He realised eventually this was because he was grumpy, out of sorts, and he never felt that way. Dimly, he was aware of being very uncomfortable about something, but he didn't know what. Gloomily, he went to eat the breakfast his servants had laid out for him.

After breakfast, he remembered he had dreamed, and the dream had been shocking. The Lady Vonny had come to him in his room and taken off her crimson robe. Beneath it, she wore no petticoats, no underwear. Her skin had been white as the moon but for the black triangle above her thighs, and her dark red mouth, her star-deep eyes. She had done something unspeakable – leapt onto his chest and crouched there, her breasts in his face. And in the dream he had thrown her off, only to lie on top of her, spear her with the ferocity of a hunter bringing down his prey. She'd cried and hissed like a cat.

Now, even the memory of that dream aroused him and made him feel uncertain. His breakfast plate was chipped and the milk in his tea slightly sour.

That day also the Lady Talina came home, she and her maids erupting from white carriages drawn by snowy horses, filling the air with their tweeting laughter. Talina had brought gifts with her for everyone except for the blood, night and snow woman who had come to the palace. Talina had been bred to mate with Prince Garland. There was no other life she could imagine, and it was also unimaginable that he'd want anyone else but her. And yet...

In the cathedral-like throne room, as Talina went to pay her respects to the king and queen, with her betrothed at her side, she noticed the shadow moving slowly behind the columns on the left side of the thrones. A tall woman dressed in a dark red robe, with skin like new cream and eyes and hair like the night. The woman looked at her directly with an expression of curiosity and triumph. At her side, Talina felt Prince Garland flinch, as if someone had stuck something sharp into his side. He put a hand over his breast. The woman amid the columns had paused, standing like a wondrous ghost in the few shadows that were allowed in the palace. Although it seemed that shadows were growing about her.

Who was this creature? Talina, in her relatively short life, had never experienced jealousy, envy, insecurity or fear. Now she felt all of them at once, and her body felt obliged to collapse, since it could only recognise these feelings as the symptoms of illness.

Gazing down upon his fallen betrothed, Prince Garland thought how pale she looked, how small her features were, her brow smooth and slightly glazed, like porcelain. Talina was a little doll, empty inside. She was not exciting like a black flame, like the wind given voice, a creature of blood, night and snow. Then Garland chastised himself for these uncharitable thoughts. This was the woman who would be his loyal companion until he died. He bent to lift her, but by then others were already attending to her.

A part of Garland, a new, untutored but instinctive part, advised him he should take the Lady Pavonia Nocta out of the city and return her to where he'd found her. She represented danger to him, even though he lacked the knowledge to form that idea into words. But despite this resolve, he wanted instead merely to follow the Lady around the palace, watching her from a distance as she wove her dreamy journeys. Where she walked, moss grew deeper into the ancient stones, ivy tumbled down from high balconies like a woman's unbound hair, and the mortar between stones grew damp and friable. Walls became infirm and listed. More cracks appeared. Poppies pushed up between the flagstones. The balmy summer became so hot that crops shrivelled in the fields.

People became irritable and, when they looked at their neighbours, saw reason to find fault and criticise. A man murdered his wife. A wife murdered her husband. One midnight, when the heat was so strong several babies suffocated, two girls threw themselves consecutively from high towers, smashing on the hard flagstones, which splintered beneath the impact. The bodies looked like smashed poppies. That same night a group of young noblemen got into a brawl. One was killed by a sword. Later, another drowned in the Great Canal as he stumbled drunkenly home.

Because events of this nature never happened in Haven, and despite the fact its inhabitants were ill-equipped to perceive darkness, even when it threatened to turn out their lights for ever, inevitably people sought the help of the king and his council. These worthy gentlemen were as perplexed as anybody else, and had no idea what was happening or why. Prince Garland, listening to the debates, could think of only one thing and was surprised no one else appeared to have thought the same: these horrible things had only begun to happen since Pavonia Nocta had lived in the city. But he could not speak his suspicions aloud, because to do so might result in Pavonia Nocta being sent away, and he could not bear the thought of that.

Awake or asleep, he was consumed by thoughts and visions of the dark lady. He could not bear to remain in Talina's presence now, for even the smell of her across a room nauseated him. Cloying, too sweet, somehow rotten. Pavonia by contrast was like a cool stream of dark water to ease his senses that the cauldron of the day tormented. Nightly, she visited him in dreams, although he was too reticent to approach her by day. His nights were riotous orgies of physical pleasure and he woke from them exhausted.

Even the dullest and most unimaginative of people have instincts they cannot control. The citizens of Haven became afraid. Darkness had seeped out of the palace and now wandered the streets at night, streets that were no longer peaceful, where thieves and whores roamed, where spiteful laughter could be heard, and the splash of heavy objects falling into the canals.

'The Lady Pava walks,' people would whisper to one another, and sometimes – sometimes – she would actually be seen, gliding slowly through the night, her dark red gown shedding crimson petals, her long feet unshod, her hair around her like a shawl. Where she walked, cracks appeared in pavements and walls, flags fell limp, flowers died. And other flowers grew up in their place with strange colours: the purple of veins, the red of blood, the blue of dead flesh.

The courtiers, the king's council and the royal family took longer to believe the tales than those who lived in the city about them. When the queen heard the rumours, she pronounced, 'Nonsense, there is a plague! No woman alone can cause that.'

The king called a meeting of the sombre priests from the cathedral and eventually one of them, the youngest of their company, dared to suggest that Pavonia Nocta might be responsible for the calamities befalling the city.

'How can one woman do such a thing?' the kind demanded.

'I have read,' said the young priest, nervously, 'that beyond the world we know there are other worlds. We never see them but sometimes they might... *leak*.'

The king fixed the priest with a frightening stare. 'You are saying Lady Vonny is a *leak*?'

'She is Lady Pava,' said the young priest quietly, 'and yes I am.'

His colleagues tutted and pulled on their beards, but then the oldest of them said, 'In my youth, I heard of such things.' His voice was merely a creak, a sigh, his body curled over like an unborn child's, but for all its thinness his voice carried weight among his peers.

'What shall we do, Brother?' they asked the old priest.

'Say many prayers,' said the old priest, who then fell asleep in his chair.

'I want praying in the cathedral though day and night,' ordered the king. He gestured to his personal guards. 'Bring to me this woman, if that is what she is.'

'Father,' said Prince Garland in a shocked, low voice. 'Please, it cannot be her. She...'

'Quiet!' said the king. 'You brought her here, my son. Perhaps you should be the one to rid the city of her.'

Pava found the city was changing more to her liking. She enjoyed strolling through the summer nights, away from the twitterers at court. She knew that wherever she trod Haven came alive beneath her toes. Some of the inhabitants were more interesting to her now and she would smile at them as she passed, bestow her blessing. Prince Garland, though, she could only reach in dreams. He wore a suit of armour over his real self, crafted generations before, and she could not breach it. Perhaps it was because of that pale, milky scrap he was due to marry. Pava had sent blights to confine Talina to her bed, but her limp influence remained. More often, Pava found herself thinking of home, the dark lord who was her counterpart, the infinite rivers, the endless mountains and the forests shuddering with magic. Was it perhaps time to leave after all? And yet, whenever she thought this, she saw Garland's face, the child inside it, the potential bandaged tight within his heart. Perhaps she should lure him to her home, but she knew this would not work. In her realm, he would melt into a ghost, until he was only a whisper and a sigh. Garland was not robust enough to take the steps down into the dark. This saddened her.

I am bandaged too, she thought, *by an unlikely dream. A future that cannot happen.*

Yet still she could not pull away from Haven and because of this, and the strength of her, the city became ever more like her. She did not consider that the people who ruled might not like this change.

And so, that day when the meeting took place in the cathedral, she was called from her bed in the afternoon. The guards who came to her flinched as they crossed her threshold. The elegant, womanly chambers were now bereft of light. Creepers had fingered in through the windows, the glass shattered. Furnishings had become deepest crimson and indigo and black. White lace upon the cushions was now like dead bracken. Candle wax had dripped into shapes resembling deformed homunculi that clung to the stems of tall candle-pillars, or lolled melting in their bowls. The bed was like a grave, but plush with rotted satin. Pava's maids were now vixen sharp with knowing eyes and pointed fingernails. They laughed at the guards and skittered to the shadows in the corners of the rooms.

'What is it?' Pava asked, rising up from her bed, a perfect vision of blood and night and snow. She raised a hand to silence her maids, who were cheeping and chittering with threat.

'The king demands your presence,' said the bravest of the guards.

Without further words, Pava glided past the guards and through the door so they were forced to run to keep up with her.

Pava knew that a significant moment had come and had no fear of it. She strode to the throne room with plaster falling from the ceilings in her wake. She absorbed the light of torches in the long passages so that darkness prowled behind her.

The entire court was gathered in the throne room where a thousand candles had been lit. Pava could hear croaking coming from the cathedral across the city; the priests' prayers. There was the king and his queen seated on thrones that were now almost too hard and uncomfortable to bear. Beside the king stood Prince Garland, interestingly pale and haunted.

Pava said nothing but stood before this company, intrigued as to what they might say. She noticed then, the young priest in his white habit, standing a short way behind the king's throne, his hands folded into his sleeves. She knew from looking at him that he was braver and more awake than most in Haven, and that he had taken a lamp and gone deep into the lower chambers beneath the cathedral. He had climbed down the damp, twisting stairways so far he'd reached the mildewy libraries that had been hidden away there, long before Haven had grown up above them. In crumbling documents and mouse-chewed books he had found words like 'witch', 'underworld' and 'curse'. He thought he knew her now. She smiled.

'You are accused of treason,' announced the king, pointing at Pava. 'For hundreds of years our city has stood unstained, pure and joyful. Until you came. Until...' And now he got to his feet and his voice thundered out across that vast chamber in a way it never had. '...until you bewitched my son and had him bring you here.'

'He came to fetch me,' Pava said. 'I *did* warn him. I told him bringing me here would break the city.' But there was no note of apology, fear or contrition in her voice. She spoke the simple facts.

'So you confess your crimes?' asked the young priest, stepping forward. He appeared disappointed, but then he had found words such as 'torture' and 'rack' in his researches too.

'Crimes? No,' said Pava. 'I warned him, but he insisted.'

'You could have refused,' said the queen harshly, 'if you knew there was something to warn about.'

Pava shrugged. 'He intrigued me.' She paused for a heartbeat, then said, 'I suppose now I should leave.'

The king and queen appeared confused in the face of Pava's sanguinity. They glanced at one another. And perhaps, in another story, they might simply have banished her from the city, and the buildings would have mended themselves, the people too, and Garland would have married his lacklustre maid, and everything would have gone back to how it was. Only, two things happened.

First, Garland uttered a terrible cry of 'No!'

And this word was a key in the lock of a door behind which was fervour and cruelty.

'Burn the witch!' yelled the young priest. And then everyone was shouting it, but for the king and queen, and Garland, and those of their courtiers who had the most dignity.

Chips of coloured glass fell from the stained glass windows. Three ladies fainted, one after the other, as if struck dead.

'Your grace!' bellowed the priest. 'Execute her! Burn her! Burn the evil from our midst.'

The king opened his mouth, but what he was about to say will never be known, for opening his mouth was enough for the guards and lesser courtiers to surge forward, led by the priest. They lifted Pava among them and ran with her out of the throne room. The quieter courtiers followed them, less hastily.

After this maddened crowd and its bewildered observers had left the chamber, the king and queen sat in shocked silence for some moments. Garland, on his knees, wept beside his father.

'My dear?' said the queen to her husband, in an exhausted voice.

The king merely raised his hands, sighed. No king of Haven had had to deal with such a calamity for thousands of years.

Then Garland leapt to his feet, crying, 'I must save her!' and ran also from the chamber.

Pava could have changed into a raven and flown away, for she knew they meant to burn her, but as she had no fear of fire, decided instead to remain and see what would happen. They carried her to the cathedral square, where all the priests came out like a herd of sheep in their white, woollen habits. Guards restrained her as the crowd searched for wood to burn, a stake to which to bind her. People came running from all over Haven, taking up the cry of 'burn the witch!' They brought with them kindling and lumber, which they threw onto the mounting unlit bonfire.

And then at last Pava was dragged up the pile of wood and tied to the stake. She neither struggled nor protested, merely watched the crows circling the high towers. Already the air smelled of burning. The young priest put torch to wood and quickly flames leapt up greedily. Bells were tolling, people shouting, some weeping.

Pava intended to enjoy the flames, then turn into smoke and go home. She knew she'd no chance of waking Garland now, so must accept defeat. She'd let these bleating sleepwalkers have their spectacle, something to remember her by, for in murdering her they slaughtered any chance of regaining their blithe innocence. A small revenge for their insolence. But then, as the edge of her crimson gown took light, she saw Garland riding fast towards her, his horse pushing through the crowd.

Oh dear, she thought, sighing, as Garland leapt from his horse and began scrabbling up through the burning wood. *He will quite lose his beauty*. His hair and clothes were alight, his hands reaching for her. He'd not make it. Kindly, she leaned away from the wood, extended her body into a long snakelike thing and held out her arms so he could take hold of her wrists.

'Poor boy,' she said to him, for she could see now he was truly awake. 'I can't let them burn you too.' So she blew upon him, blew him backwards onto his horse, to the moment before he'd started climbing. Then, flexing her shoulders she sprouted the wings of a great raven, burst her bonds, rose up with a mighty 'caw!' and flew away.

At once, a rainstorm filled the sky from nowhere, pelting down like spears. Flames hissed and died. People cowered, fell beneath the weight of the water, crawled to safety. Some were crushed in the struggle.

Garland alone remained still, upon his horse, staring at the sky. The rain was his tears, a deluge of them, given to him by her. He felt released.

While thunder crashed and the storm tore into what remained of his city, Garland turned his horse and made for the main gates. Later, some people said they saw him, riding away, and that his horse sprouted wings so he took to the sky, followed her, his witch.

But this didn't happen. Garland merely rode away and found another life, somewhere else, full of texture.

As for the queen of the underworld, she returned to her realm, and in the way of all the best stories lived happily ever after. But sometimes, she'd wake up in the morning, with deep bruises around her wrists, and know he was in pain.

The Farmer's Bride

Back in the 1980s, during my era of soul-destroying office jobs, I discovered an old anthology of poetry. Where? I can't recall. In a charity or junk shop perhaps, or on the book-shelves of a grand-parent's house. The poems in this collection were often strange and otherworldly, and one of them was 'The Farmer's Bride', by Charlotte Mew. This poem captivated me from the first lines. I was drawn in by its fairy-tale music and nuances, its gorgeous imagery.

Many years later, I rediscovered the work of Charlotte Mew and researched her history. Tragically born into the wrong era, (1869), Charlotte – or Lottie as her family called her – does not appear to have had a happy life. Although she acquired the patronage of famous and respected writers – among them Thomas Hardy, Walter De La Mare and Virginia Woolf – she never became as well known for her writing in her life time as her supporters were, even though she had modest success as a writer. And it has to be said, she's hardly known now. She wrote short stories and poems, and was described by one author as 'almost certainly chastely lesbian'. She dressed as a man and kept her hair short. I wondered when I read this – and still do – whether that chasteness was assumed and imposed upon her by the author, because gay people in that era had nothing like the freedoms and respect that their modern counterparts have fought for and acquired.

Charlotte's father died in 1898, leaving his family inadequately provided for, and two of her siblings ended up in mental institutions. Charlotte's writer friends helped her financially, by assisting in securing a Civil List Pension for her, which eased her difficulties with money. Charlotte herself succumbed to deep depression, following the death of her sister from cancer in 1927. She was sent into a nursing home and there eventually committed suicide in 1928, by drinking the cleaning fluid, Lysol. A horrible way to die.

I've always felt deeply moved by Charlotte's sad tale, thinking that if only she'd been born into a later century, her life might've been different. As a tribute to her work, I wrote this story, keeping the title from her poem. As few will have come across this beautifully lyrical piece, I've included it before the tales begins. It can be found in her collection 'The Saturday Market', which is freely available online, being out of copyright.

The Farmer's Bride
A Poem by Charlotte Mew, 1916

Three Summers since I chose a maid,
Too young maybe – but more's to do
At harvest-time than bide and woo.
When us was wed she turned afraid
Of love and me and all things human;
Like the shut of a winter's day.
Her smile went out, and 'twasn't a woman—
More like a little, frightened fay.
One night, in the Fall, she runned away.

"Out 'mong the sheep, her be," they said,
Should properly have been abed;
But sure enough she wasn't there
Lying awake with her wide brown stare.
So over seven-acre field and up-along across the down
We chased her, flying like a hare
Before our lanterns. To Church-Town
All in a shiver and a scare
We caught her, fetched her home at last
And turned the key upon her, fast.

She does the work about the house
As well as most, but like a mouse:
Happy enough to chat and play
With birds and rabbits and such as they,
So long as men-folk stay away.
"Not near, not near!" her eyes beseech
When one of us comes within reach.
The women say that beasts in stall
Look round like children at her call.
I've hardly heard her speak at all.

Shy as a leveret, swift as he,
Straight and slight as a young larch tree,

Sweet as the first wild violets, she,
To her wild self. But what to me?

The short days shorten and the oaks are brown,
The blue smoke rises to the low gray sky,
One leaf in the still air falls slowly down,
A magpie's spotted feathers lie
On the black earth spread white with rime,
The berries redden up to Christmas-time.
What's Christmas-time without there be
Some other in the house than we!

She sleeps up in the attic there
Alone, poor maid. 'Tis but a stair
Betwixt us. Oh, my God! – the down,
The soft young down of her; the brown,
The brown of her – her eyes, her hair, her hair!

The Farmer's Bride

As the Yuletide holly bared its bloody poppets in the lane, she'd been married only a four-month. Thomas Gifford, a gentleman farmer, ten years older than she, had wed her in the simmering high summer, taken her tiny, sun-gilded hand in his among the corn, where the regal poppies had shed their crimson gowns like fragile brides. Her parents had been pleased. It was a good match, and they'd feared their fey Melusine would never catch the eye of a man – she being what she was.

The priest had bound their union in the old grey church hidden by yews. The sun had pressed itself through the high coloured windows, and the blood of Christus had flushed her skin, her pale linen gown. Red: that was the colour she saw most of all in this land of green and earth.

She hardly ever spoke, which was one of the reasons her father had feared for her future. His own mother had sometimes whispered that Melusine, with her fey, faintly inhuman beauty, might be a changeling child, but the old woman had a love of gossip more than any true suspicion, and love had never thrived between her and her daughter-in-law. 'She's no changeling,' Melusine's mother would declare. 'Put the holy cross on her tongue and see the truth of it. She's but a babe, and a little touched. She'll make a good wife for a man.'

True, Melusine was a strong girl, despite appearances, and had a way with the beasts of the field. She would work from sunrise till the twilight. Yet there was a strangeness about her; some affliction must have struck her in the womb. Not simple, no, but a stranger among her kind. Poor little Melusine. She was fair enough and obedient enough not to invite fiercer censure.

At first, as Mistress Gifford, the girl had been resigned to her fate. Thomas was not a cruel man, and she imagined that life with him would be good for her. She tried to be personable, and murmur words appropriate for a wife, but something sealed her tongue in the presence of others, and had always done so. In private, she chattered to the animals, unaware that sometimes others heard her and puzzled about it. In fact, she loved language; to her each word possessed its own magic and wonder. It was not that she did not want to speak to people, but that she could not. Mostly, she had nothing to say to them anyway. Perhaps they did not speak her language.

She had her own room, at the top of a narrow, twisting stair, and each night, she would listen for the creak of the boards which would advise her of her husband's approach. This too she bore in patient silence. She knew the way of the animals, and what must be between a man and a maid. She kept his house for him, and he called her his little mouse. Yet she knew he was disappointed. Perhaps he thought her strangeness would hide a passion. If it did, she did not offer it to him. Before Yule, she ran away.

All her life, she had been haunted. The feeling would come to her in the evenings, in the summer fields, with the shadows of clouds dappling the hills. It was as if the world was a far larger place than it seemed, and something immense and unimaginable would be revealed to her. At these times, the landscape became still, almost unreal. Her lungs would squeeze shut, and the air would shimmer before her scalding eyes. She would have to sit down where she stood, afraid yet full of a strange desire.

Other times, this feeling would come to her in the yard as she worked the pump or fed the chickens. It was as if thunder had boomed over the landscape, and yet the sky was clear. Looking up, she would expect to see tongues of lightning split the clear blue. Only a bird would be wheeling high on the ocean of air. She might hear a piercing cry, and the feeling would crash over her like a wave, like a deluge of rain. Again, she would crouch down, grip hold of whatever solid was near, gasping and drowning.

These episodes she put down to what her mother called her 'difference'. There was something wrong with her. Her mother had advised her to conceal these convulsions, and she always had. They might fade away as she grew older, or had a child of her own. Melusine knew she would not have a child, not with Thomas. The idea felt wrong, and she had learned that when things felt a certain way to her, she was generally correct about them. This too, she kept a secret.

When Melusine was five, the priest had spoken out against Mistress Mathen, a woman of the parish. Living alone, she too had been good with the animals, and also with people. Many a body trod the violet path to her cottage by the lee, and she would offer possets to cure an ague, sweet leaves to press against a burn. Then the Aitken child had been struck with a spasm of the heart and Mistress Mathen had offered up her posy balms. The only outcome had been that the Aitkin cow offered sour milk and its calf was born with two heads. The child had died, writhing. Mistress Mathen was a witch, said the priest with flecks of spit at the corners of his mouth. She must be burned. Melusine's mother had whispered to her daughter in the dark. It was not necessary actually to be a witch to be identified as one and then disposed of. The priest was a good man, but he saw the shadows in everything. 'Go to church regularly, my little flower,' her mother murmured. 'Have your lips shape the words, if not your tongue. Look to Christus and he will protect you.'

Mistress Mathen had died upon a pyre, and the smell of her burning meat had stolen like a curse across the landscape. Even so young, Melusine had decided that day she would never die in such a manner. She would fold in on herself and forget things, and she did.

On the night she saw the angel, four months after her marriage, she knew her strangeness had slipped over into something more terrible. This was no holy creature like the statues with sad faces and drooping wings that stood guard in the church-yard. This was a being of fire and storms, whose eyes were the smoking flames of madness, whose voice was a howl that broke men's hearts. It manifested from the shadows in her high, narrow room in the farmhouse. She awoke from a dream she could not recall and her eyes searched the darkness. Thomas could be heard snoring in his chamber below. She felt afraid – almost – certainly not alone. Then she saw the blue glow in the corner of the room, and the being had stepped forth as if coming through a door. Behind it, if she could but see, there would be another world of light. The angel, however, cast shadows of radiance that eclipsed everything but the immensity of itself. It hissed to her in a language she could not fathom. It raised its right hand and pointed at her heart, all the while silver tongues of fire falling from its lips, its hair. To Melusine's eyes, it was an effulgent creature, yet her heart knew that it was, in reality, black.

She scrabbled her way backwards in the bed, until her body was pressed against the rough head-board. She uttered little grunts of horror, her breath puffing on the cold air. Outside, the stars shone like unwinking eyes, as God beheld her unholy transaction. All her life, when the episodes of strangeness had overtaken her she had sensed a far-off presence in the fields, like a shadow she could not see. Now it was manifest before her in all its dark glory. It had come for her soul, which all these years had been leading a stolen life in the world of men. Thomas knew not what he had married. She would bring a blight upon his house, and the wrath of the Church. What could she do but run?

Thomas, waking from a libidinous dream, stumbled up the stairs to his wife's room, and found the door hanging open. Winter had invaded the room with its cold breath, and a frost had formed over the furniture, the blankets of the bed that lolled onto the floor. She was not lying there awake with her wide brown stare, as he was accustomed to find her. Through the open window, he saw a slight black shadow rippling over his fields and knew that it was she. Something cold, hard and hungry stole into Thomas' heart. He was a good man, but he was a man denied. He sensed the 'otherness' in Melusine and wanted to taste it, yet lacked the knowledge and the words to frame this desire.

'She is out among the sheep,' they told him as he ran out into the yard, pulling on his coat. His people had been awakened by the crashing of the great front door, by the babble of the disturbed hens and the alarmed honking of the geese. She had left chaos in her wake, and a sense of herself like a perfume, lingering on the chill air.

They chased her across the seven acre field, dark and ploughed, and over the spreading downs, where the heather bunched fibrous and unyielding. She flew like a hare before their flaming brands, her feet bare and pale against the crackling, frost-rimed soil. She ran all the way into the village, and here they cornered her in the churchyard. It was old Mag found her, crouched behind a crumbling tomb, her hair hanging over her wild eyes, all in a shiver and a scare. Then, they brought her home, Thomas a silent presence behind the company. He watched his girl-wife struggle in the hold of the women, heard her strange mutterings. What had possessed her? He shuddered. In the house, they dragged her up to her room, closed the window tight, and turned the lock upon her, fast.

Trembling on her bed, Melusine heard them leave the house, saw the yellow lights wink out one by one in the cottages around the fields. She heard Thomas' heavy movements in the kitchen far below, and then the more subtle sounds, of the beetles crawling over the hearth, of the cracking of the last embers in the fire, and finally, his breath, his weeping.

She did not want to be cruel, but now this room filled her with terror. She was marked, and her fate was inescapable. In this colourless world of midnight, even her blood would be black. She leaned her face against the cold window, and whined beneath her breath.

Down the winding road, on the other side of the village, there was a modest castle of three stories. In this place lived Sir Renaud Aquinas, lord of the district. Renaud had inherited his estates at a young age – his father had only died a few months before in a hunting accident, while his mother had succumbed to a mysterious palsy three years previously. Renaud was regarded as a handsome man, yet insular. Books meant more to him than social gatherings. Women might cut their eyes at him to no avail, despite the machinations of local dowagers and matrons, seeking to foist nubile relatives onto the house of Aquinas.

On the night Melusine fled across the fields, Renaud was sitting before a roaring hearth in his hall, drinking mellow foreign liquor with the priest, Father Rathford, the two men having recently completed a game of chess after a sumptuous supper. They had heard the yelping of the dogs as Thomas' company brought Melusine to earth in the nearby church-yard, but paid it little heed. Father Rathford was holding forth on the superstitious nature of the villagers, and Renaud, only half listening, nodded and smiled at appropriate moments. 'I despair of them,' Rathford said. 'They are little more than barbarians.'

'Surely, that is a harsh judgement,' Renaud responded softly, pouring more golden liquor into the priest's goblet. He knew that Rathford wished he'd been given a parish in a more enlightened area, a larger town, perhaps, or somewhere in London.

Rathford laughed. 'It is the wine speaking, my friend, exquisite as always, yet...' he sighed. 'I do not lie. The pagan creed lies in a shallow grave in these parts. It takes little for them to go scrabbling at the mould to dig it up again.'

'You have a hard task,' Renaud said politely.

Father Rathford nodded gravely, and took a sip of liquor, rolling the fiery liquid pleasurably around his mouth. His heavy grey robes still seemed to steam in the heat of the fire. 'I give thanks for enlightened men, such as yourself, milord. It brings me comfort.'

Renaud smiled into his goblet, thinking that perhaps the hospitality of the castle provided greater comfort than mere companionship.

After the priest had gone, red-cheeked and reluctant back to his parsonage, Renaud climbed to the highest room of his castle. The hour was late, yet he felt languid and at peace. In the great hall, his servants snuffed out the candles one by one and the old stones of the walls cooled themselves to sleep. In one of the circular turrets, Renaud had his work-room. It was approached by a precarious, winding stair, where ancient dust, fragments of neglected birds' nest and bat droppings made the climb more perilous. Only one other person apart from Renaud possessed a key to the thick, iron-studded door that garrisoned the bottom of the stair.

The work-room was decorated in a fashion very different to the rest of Renaud's domain. Colourful rugs from Persia hung upon the walls and adorned the floors, and the chair and divan were plump with cushions encrusted with gold embroidery. The air itself smelled perfumed with a scent which partially eclipsed a certain sulphurous aroma. Artefacts gathered by his ancestors from every hidden corner of the world reposed in dusty alcoves or crowded upon sagging shelves. The dying fire-light glimmered off yellow brass and iridescent jewels. This was a Sultan's den.

Renaud lit the tapers and replenished the fire himself. No servant stepped across the threshold here. Although monied, Renaud preferred people to think of him as an astronomer and scholar rather than a rich man of leisure. These pursuits gave ample cover to his true interests. He was a man of secrets, who held court with his enemy, the orthodox Church, in the hall below. Now, he stood before the great desk where a hide-bound book looted from a German monastery lay open, and flexed his fingers against one another. *Soror mystica, my sacred sister, how she eludes me. Must I continue in this? It pains me.* He sighed, and a vapour purled from his lips. In a world where all occult knowledge is feared, and therefore persecuted, a man like Renaud must be circumspect. He had long ago woken to his calling, felt the beat of the Great Work course through the channels of his body.

As a child of eleven, out riding his pony on an autumn morning, he had suddenly experienced an epiphany. The world had bleached of colour before his eyes and when his vision cleared it seemed he was in a different place. He could see the life force pulsing through the earth, sucked up by trees and ferns and forest grass. He could see coloured lights high up in the leafy canopy, the living energy of squirrels and birds. And, most importantly, he felt his own connection with the world around him, with every leaf, and beast, fragment of mould and drop of water. The same energy that gave them life surged through him. A web of shining strands pushed out from his body and made union with other strands coming towards him. He knew the secret of life and it was simply this hidden light. One day, he would control it as he controlled his pony. At once, he rode home and told his father.

If Renaud had expected surprise and acclaim, he was disappointed. His father was pleased, but told his son he had been expecting such an event to occur in any case. 'You have the wyrding way within you, my boy,' he had said, 'as do I, and of course, your mother. You have awakened to one of the great truths of the universe and you shall never sleep again.'

The family of Aquinas were magi, and it seemed always had been. Renaud felt slightly annoyed he hadn't been told this before. His special event seemed somehow lessened. However, once it was clear their son followed in their calling, Renaud's parents set themselves diligently about raising their child to the arcane arts. Their pace was measured, because they felt too swift an advancement would rob the boy of his youth. Unfortunately, their early deaths left him alone too young, vulnerable to older members of their Hermetic Order who might take advantage of his estates, his father's priceless books. The world was no easy place for the philosophers of the hidden spirit, persecuted by the sleeping and awake alike. It was hard to place trust in any but the most simple, ignorant souls, such as Father Rathford, who knew nothing and could comprehend nothing, and was therefore no threat.

I am the King of my domain, Renaud thought, and a freak breeze snaked through the chamber, lifting his dark red hair. He searched for a Queen, canicula, bitch of the moon, his tormentress and Guardian Angel, but found none. He could not advance any further until he had established a link with this primal spark of his being, and no matter what rituals he had recited, what elixirs he had scattered and burned, what desperate entreaties he breathed into the aether, he remained alone. Sometimes, he sensed a far off presence, almost teasing him with its distance, but he could not be sure whether this was an illusion or not. Fortunately, he now had help in his quest, but even that seemed ambiguous.

The pages of the book turned slowly before him. His eyes paused at the words of Leonardo 'It should not be hard for you to stop sometimes and look into the stains of walls, or ashes of a fire, or clouds, or mud, or places in which you may find marvellous ideas.' Dreams and phantasms resided in the instruments of his art arrayed around the book: the mercurial serpent with its winding glass pipe, the Hermetic vessel, in whose womb were visions to be sought more than scripture; the dangerous vessel of the dancing bear, an aspect of the dark mother; the basin of the tortoise and the pelican of circular distillation, representing the bird who pecks its own breast to nourish its young with blood. The instruments were but a reflection of the true work that took place within Renaud's soul and his most recent knowledge had come from the east.

'The hour is late, my friend. Will you begin work now?'

Renaud looked up. His mentor, Kalid, – the only other to possess a key to the tower – sat among the shadows in a high-backed chair near the fire. Renaud could not recall noticing the man as he'd replenished the flames. Kalid could melt in and out of shadows with ease, it seemed. He had taken the place of Renaud's own father, following his mysterious arrival at the castle gate some weeks after the old lord had died. Renaud had been suspicious of this taciturn, hooded man, although Kalid had been quick to assure him, in mellifluous, soothing tones, that he had worked with Renaud's parents, and had in fact trained alongside them somewhere in the Orient. On the exact location of this establishment, Kalid seemed vague. He claimed that Renaud's father had appeared to him in spirit and requested him to assist his orphaned son. He had travelled long, through many dangerous places, but now was ready to begin work. Renaud could not advertise Kalid's presence in the castle, although the servants obviously knew about him, and had doubtlessly talked in the village. Kalid's presence in this land was precarious at best, for he was a Saracen, whose kinsmen had been slaughtered by Soldiers of Christ. Yet in the Order, boundaries of culture and belief did not exist. Kalid was an adept; it was his duty to instruct the needy student.

Renaud had learned much already, but Kalid was a hard, relentless teacher, who seemed never to weary. They worked at night, once the other occupants of the castle were asleep, and on many occasions worked through till dawn. Kalid's instruction varied from endless lectures on occult practice, to the performance of complicated rituals, to the telling of tales.

'Tonight, we shall again walk the world of spirit, and you will call to your anima,' Kalid decided. He was smoking from an absurdly tall water pipe, its stem held lightly between his long, agile fingers.

Renaud sighed. He felt immediately tired. 'Am I being tested, Kalid, or do we have to face an unpleasant reality? Perhaps I shall never find this creature. Perhaps I am blighted in some way.'

There was a rustle, then Kalid was beside him, bending low to whisper in his protégé's ear. 'You must not lose heart, my friend. Who knows what events transpired in your previous lives? Perhaps there are more than the usual barriers to cross. We shall partake of the *vinum nostrum*, and you must look within yourself once more. Enter the shadows of your heart.'

Renaud steeled himself at the thought. He had partaken of the mercurial wine on several occasions. Each time, he had been swamped by dreams of hideous clarity. The angels of the corners had released into his mind the four demons, Azazel, Azael, Mahazael and Samael, along with all their poisonous insects and beasts. This is what Kalid had told him to explain the terrifying sights of death, horror and cruelty which had assailed his psyche. Now, as an awakened adept, it was essential he make contact with his Guardian Angel, his connection with divine source of creation, the higher self. In the beliefs of his kind, this was always of the opposite gender, the lost half of the self, in Renaud's case, his anima. But in searching for her, he could not break through the battalions of demons who wheeled around him on horses of fire that breathed the smoke of brimstone.

'Face the shadow of chaos in all its repugnance,' Kalid had said. 'For within lies the gold of your soul.'

Renaud could not imagine ever finding it. Now, he rubbed his forehead, where an ache had begun. He wanted to work, yet did not. 'The anima resists me. I will not find her.'

'Once the Deluge of the initial chaos recedes, she will be there,' Kalid said. His fingers rubbed together quickly, making a papery sound.

It occurred to Renaud that the Arab enjoyed the effects of the *vinum nostrum* on more than one level. Perhaps, one day, when Renaud himself could control the experience, he would find joy in it too. The elixir was said to be composed of the mercurial waters of the *prima materia* – the virgin's milk, the fountain's vinegar and the water of life – yet Renaud had helped prepare it and knew it comprised the less spiritual ingredients of henbane, belladonna, thorn apple and mandragore, such as witches used in their flying ointments.

Kalid offered to Renaud a pewter goblet, in which the bitter brew shivered sluggishly. The Lord Aquinas raised the philtre to his lips; the cup seemed full of disembodied voices, of disturbing thoughts. Closing his eyes, he drank, and drank again. Presences waited in the corners of the room, and the candles bent their flames to their breath.

A sparkling mist stole across Renaud's vision. He collapsed backwards into a chair, blinking at the ceiling where an astral doorway seemed to churn and writhe. They were waiting for him; he knew it. Already he could hear their gleeful howls and the thunder of their infernal horses' hooves.

Thomas told Melusine she must not run away again. It wasn't safe for a girl, out there in the darkness. Who knows but some strange beast might come out of the forest and take her life? Melusine knew she was safe from any such attack, but bowed her head, with her hair over her eyes. She could not explain about the angel, nor how its presence had filled her with a terror so cold she shivered still in the light of day. As soon as Thomas would let her out of the house, she went down to the church with Old Mag. Here the yews, beaded with blood, dripped dew onto the lichened mulch around their roots. Crows shook their branches, flew rasping into the cold white sky. 'Snow might come,' said Old Mag, lifting a finger to the wind.

Melusine pulled her cloak around her, which did not keep out the chill. The world seemed a drab place that day; too damp, and everything was colourless, but for the poisonous yew berries and the blood of a slaughtered rabbit, whose carcass lay half-devoured upon one of the graves.

Inside the church, Melusine slipped into one of the pews, where the wood was misted with moisture. Her breath was a heavy cloud before her eyes. She clasped her hands and tried to pray, unsure of what thoughts she should form within her mind. It was not an angel of Christus who had come to her; was she welcome now in this House? 'Holy Father, cleanse me of all evil. Protect me...'

The prayer seemed hollow, powerless. Melusine kept her eyes screwed tightly shut, her forehead wrinkled in a frown. She could hear old Mag moving about the church, arranging the holly branches and the late-blooming roses in a vase. But there was someone else here, too. She could sense it. Someone sitting right behind her. She could almost feel their breath, a plume of warmth, reaching out to her through the frigid air. She had not heard the great oak door open, nor foot-steps upon the flagged floor. Whoever sat there...

'Mistress Gifford, young Mistress Gifford, isn't it?'

Melusine's eyes flicked open and there was the stooped dark shape of the priest before her, his small yet piercing eyes fixed upon her like some bird of prey. 'Father...' she managed to whisper.

The priest smiled, although she sensed a predator's edge to the gleam in his eyes. 'I heard you had a bad scare the other night. Ended up here in the churchyard.'

He paused, as if waiting for an answer. Melusine could not speak. Helplessly, she twisted her mouth and rolled her eyes, quite aware of how she must appear to him.

The priest loomed closer. 'What frightened you, my child? What chased you through the night?'

She drew away from him, clouds of breath puffing in between them. She was terrified that he knew what she was, saw her black core. Now, he was trying to urge confession, which would be followed by accusation, pain, even the flame. In her panic, Melusine still had a sense of someone behind her, pressing closer, eager and alert. It was almost as if they wished to speak for her. The priest leaned forward, frowning, perhaps concerned. He must not touch her; if he did she would scream profanities at him, or spew flies. Then was a sound like silver knives clashing, perhaps of laughter, certainly not holy. She was aware of a radiant flash at the corner of her vision, and the metallic clatter of monstrous wings. She carried *it* with her, around her. The priest could not see it, but a certain knowing distaste was creeping into his eyes.

Melusine scrambled from the pew and pushed past the priest. Out,

out, into the winter light, where a murderous coven of crows lifted from the yews, rasping hysterically. The sky was full of wings, moving too slow, too fast. And it was there before her on the path – a tall, shadowy figure, its light closed in against the day, yet still inhuman. Behind her and before her. Was there no escape?

She found herself then out in the meadows, stumbling past the cows in their shaggy winter coats, skidding in their frost-rimed dung. Bare trees clawed the colourless sky and the birds wheeled across it in a shape like a crown. Once the creature touched her, she would be lost. She would belong to it and whatever tenuous hold she had on being a normal girl would disappear for ever. Her grandmother had been right. She was a changeling child, born of evil.

The forest was ahead of her now, its forbidding branches a puzzle of darkness that would either hide her, or simply hold her as a prisoner until the dark angel came for her. She had no choice but to run. The air was becoming opaque around her, and so cold. Stumbling, arms flapping, she hurled herself into the shadows of the naked trees.

Renaud saw the girl from his high window. She ran across the fields along the edge of the forest as if the demons of the abyss rode behind her. Her awkward movement attracted his eye and he was drawn to watch. Did some brutish male pursue her, or was she fleeing from a misdemeanour? High overhead, a tangle of crows lifted and fell in a tattered curtain and the sky was so dense. Then it was full of falling stars and the birds were flickering in and out of reality. The snow had come.

Behind him, Kalid stirred in his chair. 'You are close now, very close.'

There is some fault in me, Renaud thought, ignoring his mentor's remark. *Perhaps I am not destined to follow my parents' work. Perhaps I am both awake and asleep, one foot in each world, never fully in one nor the other.* He blinked at the littering snow, his hand upon the heavy drapes, and saw the diminutive female figure spin and whirl into invisibility as the weather closed around her. She looked like a rag on the wind. For a brief moment, Renaud saw a spiralling column of silver light flicker in the place where he had last seen her, but he could not be sure. The *vinum nostrum* sometimes coloured in the world with strange shapes of the mind. He let the drapes fall.

Father Rathford was present for dinner. 'I have had a day to try the saints!' he informed Renaud as they sat down to partake of a sizzling haunch of beef. A servant heaped steaming scallions onto his platter, while another filled a tankard with foaming ale. 'Agues and complaints, and two deaths in the parish. On top of that, young Gifford's bride taking another strange turn – in the church itself! I'll fancy he'll have trouble with her. She's touched – or worse.' These last two words were delivered with a meaningful scowl. 'She's always had a strange way with her.'

Renaud experienced a tremor, but not on behalf of the unknown woman. Rathford's words seemed strangely portentous. 'And now the snow has come.'

'More deaths in store, no doubt – sickly children, doddering ancients and the like.' Rathford tucked into his meal with relish. 'You look tired, milord.'

Renaud could do no more than barely pick at the meat. In truth, he felt weary to his soul. He shrugged.

'Too much peering,' Rathford announced. 'Bad for the eyes and the brain. Put your books away. You should get out more. I do believe you rarely see another body but myself. Perhaps a comely young wife would bring joy to these halls. Think on it. You'll not be short of offers, I'll wager. A spring wedding, yes...' The priest's eyes took on a dreamy cast.

Fortunately, an interruption curtailed the priest's advice: a heavy knocking at the outer door. It boomed throughout the castle.

'Someone in need!' Rathford declared, wiping grease from his chin.

Fate is at the door, Renaud thought, and his flesh went momentarily hot, then cold. He stood up.

Presently, a servant came into the hall and addressed the priest. 'There's some folk at the gate for you, Father.'

'What, they come here? Disturb our dinner?' Rathford's face had gone pink.

'Another death, perhaps,' Renaud said. He knew it would not be that. 'Show them in,' he told the servant.

Thomas Gifford headed the crew, a landowner faintly known by Renaud. He remembered the priest's earlier words concerning Gifford's wife, and knew this must be no coincidence. After a grovelling apology to the lord and his guest for interrupting their meal, Gifford gave anguished voice to his dilemma. 'She's gone, Father. Not come back this eve. Old Mag took her to the church, but she had a turn and fled into the fields. We have searched, but found only five of Morton's kine stiff and dead in the snow, with no mark of injury. Of her, there's no sign. Father, I am afeared. What must be done?'

They believe she killed the cows, Renaud thought. *It often begins that way, with the death of animals.* Though he had heard little of this story, in his mind he saw the mountain of damning evidence that had been mounting against this unfortunate female. They would all be small things, but together they made a dark picture. He wondered, for a moment, whether she was truly a witch or just some stripling moon-calf, cursed for her inherent difference.

'Thomas, I am aware of your problem,' Rathford said, sighing heavily. 'It occurred to me this very day that all was not well with the child. We must find her, of course, before more ill befalls man or beast.'

'But what is wrong with her?' Gifford asked, his words constricted in his throat. 'Can it be remedied?'

The priest got to his feet. 'I will do all I can. Sometimes evil can be cast out, sometimes not.' He turned to Renaud. 'You must excuse me, milord. This is urgent business.'

'I understand. Of course, this poor maid must be found. I will naturally lend my aid to the venture.'

I should not be going out, he thought, as his steward laced up his stoutest boots, and brought out his heavy winter cloak. *The effects of the nostrum seep back into the brain in the hours of darkness. I should speak to Kalid.* But he had to see this girl. He had thought back to what he'd witnessed from his high window that afternoon, and knew that he'd seen her vanish into the forest. And more besides: the light which had seemed to follow her, an incandescent spirit light, like the anima of a magus.

Outside, the world was hushed and shrouded. Already the snow lay thick upon the meadows, and although the moon was eclipsed by the snow-bearing clouds, the landscape was lit by the ghost-light of the winter blanket. Renaud's hounds leapt before him, yelping like puppies, as gaunt as were-beasts in the unnatural radiance. The priest tramped beside him, muttering. They had broken away from the main band, to skirt the forest that bordered the Aquinas estate. Renaud knew the woods well, having spent most of his days there as a boy. If she was what they believed her to be, perhaps this maiden witch would be drawn to the place where his youthful imaginings had conjured spirits from the trees. His mind had enlivened the life force there, and it would perhaps give succour to the girl.

Renaud glanced back at the castle, before they entered the darkness of the trees. A dim light burned in the turret room; Kalid would be waiting for him. No matter. Privilege of birth had protected him from the zeal of the Church, and it was perhaps his duty to offer aid to this wench, whether she had the way of wyrd or not. If he had been born into peasant stock, perhaps he too would have been hunted across the land, brought to earth, bound and condemned.

Amid the trees, snowflakes hissed down through the canopy. A stag broke cover and thudded away down the brackened path. An omen. Renaud would follow it.

'No night for this,' the priest declared. 'I fancy she'll be frozen to a stone by daybreak. Perhaps we should return...'

His righteous sanctimony was tempered by physical discomfort. He had a hand pressed to his beef-fattened flank. Renaud paused a moment, then said, 'Father, fear not. Return to Aquinas. I will scour this area. If I happen upon the maid, I will bring her to you. If not, perhaps the others will find her.'

The priest looked uncertain. 'I should not leave you to search alone, milord. It is my duty to hunt this blighted soul for the love of Christus and his Eternal Father.'

Renaud laughed sweetly. 'I know this land better than any. And I shall not mention I tramped it alone. Go back, Father, seek the warmth of my hearth. The cold does not discommode me. Please, I insist... If we go any further, you will not be able to find your way back alone in the snow.'

The priest needed no further encouragement. He offered a few perfunctory phrases of apology, then turned his steps back towards the castle.

Renaud watched his figure diminish amid the soft deluge of the weather. Then he dismissed the priest from his mind and began to jog down the forest path, following the spoor of the stag. As the forest claimed him, its spirit connected with his soul. He became one with all the hunters of the past, who understood the ways of the land. His sense of smell sharpened, as did his hearing. On his tongue, he tasted a thousand subtle scents of beast and plant, even the distant taint of human sweat, which told him in which direction the other men were heading. This was not his usual way of working, and perhaps leaned more towards the traditions of other orders, those more attuned to natural magic, but his father had taught him to use whatever skill lay to hand, and in this moment, all the paraphernalia of his Hermetic art would be of no avail. His abilities might lack puissance, because he lacked connection with his anima, but he had a far greater chance than the other men of finding the girl.

Melusine thought she must soon die. She could no longer feel her toes and fingers, and it was becoming more difficult to keep her eyes open. The angel had cornered her in a bower of briars. She had crawled through the thorns seeking a sanctuary and now a shivering radiance hovered at the entrance to the barbed tunnel, perhaps waiting for her to come out, or die. What had she done to invite its presence? She could hear it speaking to her but the language was a mesh of elemental sounds that she could not fathom. It sounded like water running through the forest, the fall of rain, the bustle of leaves in the wind and the call of a stag. Part of her wanted to go to it, for she sensed in some way the angel would make her warm again. But another part was afraid. Emerging from this bower of thorns would be like throwing herself over the edge of a waterfall. And yet, they were coming for her, weren't they – Thomas' men, the priest? She could hear their heavy movements through the forest, their hard voices. She could hear everything, even the progress of the king stag that made its way towards her, followed by a hunter. Her perception shifted to this image – it seemed somehow out of place, unconnected with her own situation. They might be ghosts, she thought, or shades of the forest spirit, enacting timeless rituals of life.

Beyond the naked briars, the angel said her name, 'Melusine.' It was distinct and perfect like a word from a song.

Melusine held her breath. Her head swam with the cacophony around her, men's clumsy feet, the breathing of the forest, the crash of snowflakes against the high branches. She put her burning forehead against her raised knees. How could she be so cold, yet so hot?

'Melusine!'

More urgent now, as loud as the sky, yet quieter than the scamper of voles. This was the end of her life and she had a choice. What would take her? The cold, the hands of men, or the voice of an angel? Slowly, she lifted her head. Her vision boiled with light. The angel was so radiant that all the briars looked like fragile burned sticks before it. She could see it clearly now, a tall figure crouching low, silver hair spilling forward, its eyes like white coals. Its face reminded her of a serpent; long, with slanting eyes. In her mind, she answered its summons. 'Leave me! I don't want to go to hell.'

'There is no hell, but in men's hearts,' it replied. 'Come forth, Melusine. Come unto me. Do not shut your mind to me, for we are one, you and I.'

She knew then, in an instant of blinding clarity, that this brilliance was indeed hers. If she reclaimed it – and she had no doubt it would be reclamation – the strangeness of the world would make sense to her. The feelings she had, the differences she possessed, would plait together into a single, shining whole. She could escape her fate, and if this was the Devil's work, then so be it. She did not want to die here in the chilled dark, nor upon a witch's pyre. She would fall backwards into the arms of Fate and see where she landed.

Movement was difficult because she was so numb, but gradually she uncurled herself and crawled towards the angel. Its hands reached out to her through the taloned branches. When she took that shining hand in hers, she would rise up with renewed strength. She would be reborn. So close now. She could see the clearing beyond the briars, and her head was full of a rushing sound. She lifted one hand, reached out.

A stag crashed through the frozen bracken into the clearing. Even the angel looked round: a magnificent beast, the primal archetype of all stags. Its flanks ran with steaming sweat, its eyes rolled and its regal head bowed with exhaustion, the antlered crown kissing the earth. Behind the stag came the hunter; a man in a long, flapping coat, his hair wild around his shoulders. He could be no mortal man. Melusine was not afraid exactly, but overwhelmed. Without thinking, she scrabbled her way through the final barrier of thorns and threw herself against the angel. The breath left her body. She was engulfed in a feeling that was beyond heat and cold. It was similar to the way she'd felt sometimes when Thomas had come to her bed, and dreams of a far-off presence had eclipsed her husband's physical being. She experienced all this and more. The angel was inside her and she inside it. When she stood up, she would be eight feet tall and shining. The man who pursued the stag was *her* hunter, as much as the angel was her angel. As Mistress Mathen had once said, three herbs apart possess little strength, but grind them together and they become something beyond themselves, much greater.

Renaud stood at the edge of the clearing. He was as the Red Slave approaching the White Woman, the body of the alchemist approaching all that is celestial and pure within his soul. She was queen of the snow, and above the trees, the sun glared alongside the moon, his light devoured by ravens. *I have come home*, Renaud thought, and dropped to one knee. All this time, he had searched for his anima in a goblet of alchemical potions, yet here she was, out in the forest, where first he had sensed her existence. He had been blind, lost. And so had she, attaching herself to some strip of a girl, some pathetic witchling, pursued by all that was gross and impure. The time had come now for them to conjoin. She would take him by the hand and lead him into the realms beyond human thought, where all the arcana of his art would be revealed to him. At last.

She was coming towards him, drifting above the white-starred mulch. He dared to look upon her and was surprised to see she did not seem wholly female, but certainly not male either. His heart yearned for the connection. He stood up to face her, opening his arms to take that light into his body.

Kalid sat alone in the high tower, listening to the sounds far below of the fat priest picking at the remains of his meal. The mage pressed the fingers of one hand against his eyes, muttering words from an ancient hermetic work. 'I Hermes, cause to come out to thee, O Sun, the spirits of thy brethren, the planets, and I make them for thee a crown, the like of which was never seen; and I cause thee and them to be within me, And I will make thy kingdom vigorous.' He had caught glimpses of what would happen in the magic of the *vinum nostrum*. Sometimes, he had wished to speak, to tell Renaud his suspicions, but the journey of a magus to his or her Guardian was personal, and no man or woman should intrude upon its course. He had sensed young Aquinas was somehow fragmented – an hereditary blight perhaps that had sent his parents, despite their knowledge, to early extinction. His mother and father had sought wholeness with each other, but they had been mistaken. Sometimes, the universe caused strange things to happen, and it was not the first time Kalid had been witness to an event such as this.

It was nearly dawn when the door at the bottom of the tower stairs creaked open. Kalid heard the footsteps rising higher towards him. What he saw soon after in the doorway was a drenched creature, the warmth of the castle having melted all the snow upon its hair and cloak. Its face was the embodiment of beseeching, full of bewildered questions. Kalid stood up, his vision dimmed by tears. He gestured to summon it, 'As a shadow continually follows the body of one who walks in the sun, so the rebis, though he appears masculine in form, nevertheless always carries within him his feminine part, hidden in his body.'

The being collapsed into a chair before the fire, blinking at the flames. It was Renaud, yet it was a female, both afraid and confused. Kalid gave it wine and it took the goblet with quivering fingers.

'You have a crown of planets about your head,' said Kalid. 'It is the symbol of the metals and the astrological temperaments. You are the star of perfection. Drink, my friend.'

'What am I?' it whispered hoarsely.

'The rebis is hermaphrodite, the divine marriage of male and female, of the sun and the moon. Your separate physical parts shared, and were conjoined by, a Holy Guardian, and fate smiled kindly upon you, for you were able to find one another so quickly in this life, which can be long.'

The rebis put its head into its hands, letting the goblet fall and smash upon the floor. Indigo wine soaked into the rugs, between the boards of the floor.

'Fear not,' Kalid murmured. 'I shall take you from this place into the east, to the great house of Art where your parents trained in their youth. There, you will learn what you have become and of its potential. You will advance beyond the conflict of opposites. Your advent will be welcomed by your brothers and sisters.' He reached down and pressed a hand upon the red hair of the rebis. Bone white, flawless skin showed at its neck where the hair parted. Its frame was at once delicate and robust. It was the dark hunter and the white hart in one body. Slowly, the rebis raised its head and stared at Kalid with wide eyes.

'I did not realise... did not know. The forest... I should have stayed here... stayed in the church... gone home, stayed home...' It shook his head, as if warring personalities fought to express themselves.

'Be calm, my friend,' murmured Kalid. 'Assimilate your separate parts. You are at one now, and have made contact with the divine spark. It is only forward now.'

Forward yes, but the path was littered with dark stones and twists. Monsters lay concealed there, but also light and knowledge. Kalid sighed. He had been right to come here. He had not realised how much he would be needed.

There were no heirs to Aquinas, and the king gave the lands as a gift to another duke, who in due course took up residence with his family. Thomas Gifford presently took another wife, an older woman who chattered all the time. No sign was ever found of Melusine and Renaud, other than a strange, scorched area in the heart of the forest, circled by the neat spoor of a stag. The locals presumed that Melusine had indeed been a witch and had killed the young lord before spiriting herself away from the district. Father Rathford declared she must be thought of as dead, because she'd been no child of God. Thomas was pitied, though few liked to talk to him about his vanished bride. At night, he would lie beside his warm, ordinary wife and think about the small room at the top of the house. He thought about the way she had slept there all alone. Was there evil in her? There had only ever been a stair betwixt them. Sometimes, he would weep and intense feelings would twist in his heart. In his mind, he spoke the words he would never speak aloud. 'Oh, my God, the down, the soft young down of her, the brown, the brown of her – her eyes, her hair, her hair...'

Fireborn

The surreal landscape for this story came from a friend of mine who visualised it during a meditation. She later discovered this place actually exists – the Fairy Pillars of Love Valley in Cappadocia. I recorded my friend's full experience and, from her descriptions and feelings, created this story. My friend saw the strange old woman in her visualisation, and also the peculiar black-gold liquid.

As for the characters in this tale, they were born with the hot landscape, the weirdness.

You can waste a lot of time being in love with people. Or so said my friend, Maqite, as she lay dying of a broken heart. Perhaps it was her calm resignation which kindled the final, fatal anger inside me. That, or my helplessness, as I watched this woman sink and fade like a sunset before my eyes. Sunset colours: that was Maqite. Even as her skin paled and shrank, her hair was the colour of evening across the shawls of her bed. She handed me a bead necklace, said 'Take it'.

It hung limp from my outstretched hand; limp and so cold, splashing colours over my knees as the light passed through the beads.

'Is there anything I can do for you?' I asked her.

She looked at me long and wonderingly. Perhaps there was.

She could not speak the words, because she doubted whether she should or could, but I saw them in her eyes; flickering glyphs that spoke of an unacceptable hope. She was a good woman, and had suffered much in silence. Now, a shivering candle of resentment burned dim against her goodness.

Some months back, a sashaying, slant-eyed travelling-girl had come to our settlement. Her name was Kamaara. She had surveyed our community and attached herself to Maqite at once. She clearly did not intend to waste her time with anyone who did not sit upon the highest boughs of the community's social tree. Maqite was a woman of status. Her lover ruled our settlement with an inflexible will. Everyone adored him, which I suppose made him despise them.

For a while, Maqite's friendship with Kamaara offended me, for hitherto we had been inseparable. Then, extending her questing awareness further, the interloper used her clever eyes and a basket of exotic promises to lure Maqite's lover into her canopy of indigo folds. Maqite had been devastated. I had been furious, and secretly glad, for hadn't Maqite at first been as bewitched by the stranger as her lover now was? I was shocked too, for the strange, beautiful creature who was Maqite's man had seemed immune to feminine wiles. It had always amazed me he had remained by Maqite's side, but I was relieved he had, for otherwise I might have had to do something about him myself. It was a prospect that filled me with feverish excitement, but also a sense of dread. He was like no one I had ever met; inscrutable as a cat, and just as deadly. Better he remained safe in the arms of my friend.

'Banish her!' I told Maqite, when she finally admitted her suspicions to me about Kamaara.

She shook her head. 'No. It will fade. He is only interested in the dazzle. It is nothing. I should have kept silent.'

I knew she still entertained Kamaara in her canopy, and kept her anger under control. But, despite this outer calm, knowledge of the affair only weakened Maqite. It infuriated me that she would not fight. Now, all the life was draining from her. It was hard for her, so hard that they had brought her to this. Hard for me too, with my black, bound feelings.

I replenished Maqite's incense bowl, and went outside, the beads clutched tight in my hand. Her daughter, Mivien, was playing in the dust. Around me, the awnings and canopies of the settlement looked tired in the late afternoon, flapping listlessly. Maqite's tent was seamed with dust; testament to her inability to shake the fabric recently. Mivien looked up and asked me how her mother was.

'Tired,' I said. It was then I decided I could not let her kill herself. Not for this. As for me, I doubted there was anything to do with this matter that could kill me. I had developed an immunity, sipping the poison continually over the six years I had been a member of the community.

At that precise moment, a shape came out of the heat-haze, wreathed in dust. This phantom pranced to a halt before me; a nervous, over-bred horse, betasselled and steaming. Its rider dismounted, conjuring running, crouching boys who competed with one another to lead the animal to shelter. He stood there, desert-dusted, with only his eyes flaming out from the scarf around his face. Whenever he was near me, I could smell burning.

Mivien leapt up and danced past me, crying 'Dadda!'

Her joy at his advent made me feel nauseous. I began to walk away, towards my own dwelling.

'Pashti.' He said my name. To me, a violation, at that time.

I did not turn but said, 'Yes?'

'How is she?'

I knew he would have picked up the child. I could hear her babbling excitedly. How dare he ask me that? 'She is resting.' I am supposed to bow, to manifest my supplication to this man. He has the power to crush me, exile me, perhaps worse. I should guard my words. Still, he let it rest, and I heard him go into the tent, followed by the low murmur of voices, the sharper remarks of the child, who craved his attention. I wrapped the necklace around my wrist. Maqite would not want me to act, but I had to. There was no choice, come ill or good. I waited until sundown, before I blanketed my pony and rode away.

A woman gives her life to a man. Her expectations of life are, in the main part, modest: shelter for herself and her children, continued support on an emotional level. She is quite prepared to fight her own fights to secure nourishment, and will defend her family more fiercely than any man. Her inner ways are unknown to men, as they should be. Something had attacked Maqite so fundamentally her sense of survival had fled. In her place, I would have struck out, exchanged snarl with snarl, cunning with cunning. The thorn, when it had stabbed my friend, had been poisoned. She now lacked the strength to defend herself. I, possessed of sanity and an ability to concoct strategies, must become *her*, fight this battle for her, as she would if she had the stamina. There must be some way to rekindle her energy, so that the war-flag could be passed back. Ultimately, she must be the one to inflict defeat. I could not do this alone, for I lacked the power of persuasion. She sickened, as if cursed, yet could not look with clear eyes upon the cause of it.

Besides, it was also my battle.

To ride to this place, it is essential to perceive the world in a different way; we ride into a dream reality. Nothing but the most severe need would propel any of us in this direction, between the standing stones of The Hovering and The Backward-Looking. There is no trail to follow as such, just a feeling of intense aversion, a prickling of the skin, a grinding of the joints, which signals a person is heading in the right way. I had to blindfold the pony, but wrapped around his eyes a layer of palm fronds soaked in the juice of the desert violet pod, which brings visions of a pleasant land to human or beast; a place where the hawks hover in flocks: an unusual and impossible image. Thus, I tricked him into trotting towards the unthinkable, but still I dismounted at the place where the red scrub becomes glistening black stones, and tied him to a shrub beside a mud pool, where he could nuzzle the gloop and believe himself supping nectar. If the palm fronds dried out before I could return, he would come to his senses and rid himself of the blindfold, before galloping in terror back to the settlement. I hoped this would not happen, for I had ridden, by then, for two hours.

I walked into the shunned territories. People lived there, we knew that, and they were feared, for they were not like us. It was said they were exiles from a far, high place, where they had grown tall in the rarefied air. I had never seen any of these people, and sometimes doubted their existence, but for the tales that were brought to us, and the garbled, fevered rantings of those who travelled towards them, desperate and numb to fear, seeking answers and favours. The tall people were known by many names, but we called them *Yazatas*, the adorable ones, out of wary respect, for we lived too close to their lands. In the holy books of our people were the commandments which forbade us to build in stone or wood. This rule was said to have come from a Yazata mystic, who had come to our people when we lived in a town of obsidian glass. He had shaken his staff and the town had shattered. Now we lived under fabric and hung charms at the swaying portals to ward off eyes of evil, which were the eyes of a bird, hungry and yellow. The holy books said many things about the Yazatas, although only the seers and scryers had read them all. We knew that the adorable ones understood true sorcery, and that they worshipped the demons of fire. They were known as a dangerous and capricious race, to be avoided. Why then was I walking towards them, when I had laughed at the desperate fools who had gone this way before?

The answer is simple. The Yazatas were powerful, and could proffer solutions to any problem, for those who were brave enough to ask.

I walked down into a valley, following a path scoured, as if by running water in some far-distant time, through the bleached yellow rocks. The crags here were lumpy and twisted, as if wrung by the hands of giants into tortured shapes. That, or they were petrified titans, frozen in anguished poses, shying away from a divine lightning blast, or a vision of ultimate truth. I began to feel uneasy. My teeth ached, and I was sure I could hear sounds that were not there at all.

At last, the path led me out into the open. It was a place that looked as if a god had punched the earth; an uneven oval hole in the rocks that it might take an hour to cross. All around me the stone reared high, while the flat centre of the valley was marked by strange monoliths; twisted red and ochre stone catching the light.

My heart was beating fast. As I approached, I realised that among the bulbous towers of stone there was a village, or rather the stones *were* the village. The nearer I came, the more the scene before me seemed to solidify. Between the dwellings I could see the smoking remains of many fires, dying in wide, shallow pits. The ground beneath my feet changed from yellow dust to black and grey cinders. Each crunching footfall threw up a reek of ashes. The air smelled strongly of smoke, which was acrid as if weeds had been burned. From the sentinel towers, I sensed watching, waiting eyes, although I could see no sign of human life. Only a few skinny dogs were nosing among the embers, and they did not appear to notice me.

For a moment, I halted in the shadows of the towers, and considered turning back. An instinct within me warned I should go no further, that to carry on I risked death or something more damaging. Yet would I be allowed to escape, now that I had come this far?

My flesh tight against my bones, I walked between the silent, watching towers. Daring to look up, I could see that each one comprised layers of rooms – which I presumed were living quarters. Each tower had only one entrance, at ground level, but dull rags flapped before rough-hewn holes that punctuated the towers' height. Strings of tiny bells hung from these openings, chiming thinly in the wind, wound around what looked like long hanks of hair or combed hemp. I sensed a thousand watching eyes, and kept on walking, simply because I was too afraid to stop.

She stood, as if waiting for me, at the edge of the settlement. It seemed to take an age to reach her. Her unnaturally tall, angular body was swathed in dark cloth and she leaned into the wind. When the distance of only two or three strides separated us, I halted and said, 'I have come.' I had no doubt she was expecting me. She wore a ragged shawl of charcoal grey fabric around her head, which she held closed at the neck with a long-fingered, dark brown hand. Tails of grey-black hair whipped around the edges of her shawl. Her face looked very different to those of the ancient desert peoples I had encountered before. The cheek-bones were high, the nose aquiline, giving her a haughty appearance. She seemed to be unthinkably ancient, yet her black eyes were bright, and her skin strangely smooth. Her lips worked in rhythmic chewing, and whatever she had in her mouth exuded a thin stream of black liquid, which ran over her chin. She did not seem concerned about this. I could hear her muttering faintly to herself, but the words meant nothing to me.

'Will you help me?' I asked her. Simply by looking at this strange woman, I understood the danger I was in, and the folly of having come to this place. Still, it was too late to regret that now.

She nodded and bade me follow her, away from the settlement, up into the rocks. A path was cut there, worn smooth beneath the passage of countless feet. My heart beat painfully like the dull throbbing of a bruise. My vision became dark. Above me yawned the entrance to a cave; shocking yellow rock against the lilac sky, framing a core of black. Throwing back my head, I watched the shimmering image of the woman enter into the darkness, but I could not follow. She must have sensed my reticence, for she turned back, looked at me for a few moments, then beckoned for me to come to her. I detected a sense of impatience in her gesture. Wasn't this what I had come for? Why now did I balk at the very threshold of understanding?

Then, I saw his face hanging before my eyes; a mirage of deceit. The image retreated before me, mocking, and I walked after it. Thus, I entered into the dry darkness of the cave. I said aloud, 'He is the most beautiful thing alive.' But the only response was the soft sifting of desert dust, duned by the restless winds, and the threading plash of water. I knew that I had surrendered myself willingly to the caprices of a place of power. The air hummed with it. Deep within my ears rustled the crackle of flames and my nostrils were filled with smoke and the perfume of clear water.

As my eyes opened to the darkness, I could see that the far wall of the cave was curtained by a waterfall, which frothed into a wide, shallow basin. I thought to myself, *'Why, the water is powerful here, yet they worship fire.'*

My guide stood beside the spuming basin. I could see her bare arms now, scored with ancient black tattoos. She was grinning at me still, her jaws working as she chewed. Then she spat onto the sandy floor, expelling a black, greasy wad of something, and wiped her mouth. She spoke to me, but her words were harsh explosions of sound, which I could not understand. Pulling a grimacing face, she gestured towards me, and laughed.

'You know why I am here?' I asked her.

She grinned more widely still, and turned in a whirl of ashen cloth, to duck beneath the waterfall. I did not want to be left alone in this place. Anything could come. Anything could happen. One wrong move and I would be dead. Perhaps that was why she left me there. These thoughts were part of the ritual I had begun when I had made my decision outside Maqite's canopy.

I waited as patiently as I could, although my heart still hammered with the desire to flee. The busy water, the walls themselves, seemed imbued with spiritual presences, none of which felt benign. I began to wonder whether I would escape this place alive and even moved back towards the mouth of the cave. But just as my toes nudged the bar of sunlight across the threshold, I heard a movement behind me. Turning, I saw my guide had returned. In her hands she held what appeared to be a bottle of green glass.

'Come,' she said, the first word she had spoken that I understood.

I hesitated.

'The weak are afraid,' she said, 'and the selfish, and the ignorant. Are you any of these?'

I summoned my courage and went to her. Her hands were awash with viridian light, and at that moment I realised the bottle itself was not green, but filled with a brilliant emerald liquid. She held the vessel out to me. 'This is black gold.'

I wanted to ask why, in that case, it was green, but shrank from doing so. I nodded.

'Do you know what it is?'

I shook my head. 'No, madam.'

She laughed. 'Oh, but I thought this was what you had come for.'

'Perhaps it is,' I answered.

She teased me with the bottle; holding it out to me, then withdrawing it. 'Do you have the right currency to trade with us?'

It occurred to me then that I had brought nothing with me but myself, and I grew cold to think that my body and soul might be currency enough. 'Name your price,' I said, but my teeth had begun to chatter.

The woman narrowed her eyes at me. Still holding my watering gaze, she withdrew the stopper from the bottle and held its lip to her mouth. I watched as her long, brown throat worked, swallowing. My own mouth had become dry. When she withdrew the vessel, her lips glowed vivid green, until she wiped the stuff away with the back of her hand. Her black stare held me, but as I blinked at her, helpless, her eyes filled up with green fire. It was the gaze of a serpent goddess. Her nostrils flared and she took in a great lungful of breath, held it within her, then gasped it out, shuddering. I could sense power pouring from her in invisible flames. She held out the fatal bottle to me, and said, 'Drink, then.'

I took it from her, and the glass was cold against my palms. Serpent light sickened my flesh. A strange aroma curled from the lip of the vessel; acrid and sweet. Sorcery lived within the bottle, a witchery that could be drunk. What would it give me? Knowledge, power? Then I thought of the many costumes of Lady Death, the many masks she wore. One of her gowns was a livid green, and she shook its skirts in the faces of those who craved life.

I shook my head and handed the bottle back to the Yazata woman. 'Thank you, but no.'

She grinned, took the bottle and re-stoppered it. 'You are wise,' she said. 'Come.' She placed a dry hand upon my shoulder and turned me towards the entrance and the brilliant light of the afternoon sun, which scorched the cinder paths of the settlement below. We stood there, upon the lip of rock, looking down upon the towered dwellings.

'You see,' she said, gesturing with the hand that held the bottle, 'that is my home there.'

I followed her gesture with my eyes, but could not discern which bulbous tower she indicated. 'Yes, madam, I see.'

'How many layers can you count?'

I guessed. 'Six?'

She grinned. 'Seven. You cannot count very well. My great great grandmother went to live in that dwelling when it was but a single layer. When her son came of age, he took a wife, and built another layer to live in. My dwelling is on the fifth layer, and my great grandson is already building the eighth.'

'Does no one live at the bottom now, then?' I asked.

'I told you,' she answered. 'My great great grandmother lives there.'

'She must be very old,' I said.

The woman nodded. 'True. She is very old.' She held up the glass bottle. 'This is our elixir, what people come here for. The elixir of life or the potion of death. It depends upon your heart, and your reasons for using it.'

'Longevity,' I said. 'It gives you that.'

'Among other things.' She smiled. 'You are not here looking for a long life.'

I shook my head. 'No.'

She squeezed my shoulder. 'Come then, come back into this sacred place, and tell me of your desires.'

I was reluctant to do so, having hoped our business could have been concluded there and then, but she had still not named a price.

We went to sit beside the bubbling pool, which the Yazata stirred with a long, brown finger. There were flashes of silver beneath the water's surface, which might have been fish or thoughts. The Yazata drew her curving brows together. 'Your heart beats with black blood.'

I squirmed upon the rocky floor. 'There is a man.'

'Of course.'

I pushed back my hair. This was not easy for me. 'He has abused my friend. She loves him and has given him her life, her body, yet he has committed an act of betrayal with another woman, a stranger. Maqite, my friend, is dying because of it. She is a good woman. It is not right that she should suffer. I have come here looking for justice.'

'Ah, death,' said the woman, and turned her bottle of black gold in her hands.

I shivered as I looked at it. 'Yes!' The word came like a flame from my lips. I wanted him dead so badly. I hated him. It was strange that I did not think of Kamaara, who might have been easier to dispose of.

'He cares nothing for the feelings of others. He is as cold as the night-wind, and as cutting. I swear his glance can strip flesh from bone. But he has a cold, cold beauty, and people love him because of it. He has a strong spirit.'

'Born of fire,' interrupted the woman.

I shook my head. 'No, no. Nothingness, that is all.'

She sighed tolerantly. 'We can smell the smoke of his kind, even here, so far from your home. In his veins runs a liquid flame and his thoughts are smoke. If you did not love him so much...'

'I do not!' I interrupted.

She ignored me and continued, 'Or if you did not hurt so much, you would see that he is born of fire.' She lifted the vessel of black gold before her face and looked into it. 'Caught in a bottle, he is, like a captive djinn.'

I looked up into her eyes. The green glow had faded from them a little now; they were a mysterious mossy-black. 'Does it matter that he's born of fire?'

She nodded. 'Of course. It is the most important thing. Perhaps the real reason you are here.'

I closed my eyes, as if being unable to see would prevent me from considering her words. It did not occur to me that she might have some interest of her own in this man, or even wish to influence the outcome of my visit. 'I am here to find a means to dispose of him. I will buy the black gold to kill him, if you would tell me how to use it.'

She put her head on one side. 'You must have heard, of course, that to attempt to use our elixir for the wrong reasons could kill you.'

'I will not drink it,' I said.

'I did not say you would.'

I felt my face grow hot. 'My reasons are right and just. He has abused too many people, and perhaps you are right in saying that I love him, but if I do, I am the victim of his enchantment, and love against my own will. It must end.'

'As you like,' she said, grinning, and stood up. 'First, the price.'

I remained seated, looking up at her. There were no words to say that I could think of.

'You must give a little life for death,' she said. 'That is the price.'

'Life is precious to me.'

'As it should be. We shall take only a sweet drop of it.'

When we came out of the cave, the sky had turned the black of panther hide, lacquered with stars. Now the firepits of the Yazata settlement were alive with brilliant flame, and around each one, a group of people sat. I felt disorientated. Had time passed so quickly? When we had entered the cave, it had been around mid-day.

We paused beside one of the fires. The people scared me. Like my guide, they were dressed in dusty black, and their faces were grey with ashes. Lustrous black eyes shone out at me. All the figures were seated but for one, a mature male. Everyone's attention was centred upon him and he muttered an incomprehensible incantation at the flames. His hair hung down his back and his face was gaunt. I could see his skinny body through the gaps in his loosely hanging robe.

My guide leaned down and put her mouth close to my ear. 'He is our priest, the favoured one of our family. What he forges in flame is neither life nor death, but elemental force. He has kindled armies of the dead for great kings. He has summoned sand storms to choke a man's enemy. He has birthed djinn and deva from the cauldron of fire, and corked them into a bottle. You could buy one to release upon your enemy.'

'No,' I whispered back. 'It must not be that.'

'As you like.' We stood silently as the priest finished his incantation. Women scattered powdered substances into the flames, their long brown arms flashing out like serpents from their dark robes. Sweet, stinging fumes rose like spirits from the flames.

Now my guide stepped forward, pushing me before her. Her long hands curled upon my shoulders like the claws of a vulture. 'Here is one who would buy,' she said. 'She will trade a drop of life's liquor for black gold.'

The priest looked at me then. What I saw within his eyes had no name, but it instilled within me the greatest fear I have ever known. I could not look away from him. He was fierce, with his long, wild hair and his ashen face, and his eyes glowed like polished beryl with the elixir of life. I had no idea how old he was; he could have been eighteen or eight hundred. My mouth and throat had become utterly parched. I wished I could faint, for I was sure I was about to endure something unspeakably terrible.

The priest made an abrupt gesture and another tall, sinuous male figure rose from beside the fire. Reluctantly, with the most gripping terror, I looked at him. He was completely robed; just a suggestion of an ashen face visible beneath his draped hood. Then two exquisite hands snaked out from the folds of cloth and tweaked back the cowl. I realised what stood before me was the most beautiful man I had ever beheld, more beautiful, even, than my hated beloved. It is amazing what the sight of such loveliness can do. I am ashamed to admit it, but my fear abated somewhat. His enormous eyes were lined crudely with charcoal, which also accentuated the hollows of his ashen cheeks. His hair was like the wing-feathers of the black griffin, softly falling over his shoulders. In his lovely gaze resided the knowledge of all the aeons. He held out his strong, slender hands to me and I took them in my own.

At that point, everything around me faded into oblivion. His finely-drawn lips were expressionless, but his eyes smiled at me; flecked with hints of scorn and pity, yet otherwise quite gentle. He pulled me down to sit opposite him beside the fire.

'What must I do?' I asked him, but he merely blinked slowly and shook his head.

He squeezed my hands, and then widened his eyes. A shock coursed through me as if a bolt of lightning had pierced my mind. He held me in his stare like a snake holds the eyes of its prey, and I remembered how dangerous these people were, how unpredictable and how unknown. My body began to shake, and his grip upon my hands grew stronger. My crossed knees hammered against the dusty ground. My throat corded. I could not breathe. I wanted to scream, but could summon no sound from my arid throat. Then, I felt a wrenching inside my head, my heart, my belly. Something tore within me. Through the power of his eyes alone, he sucked part of myself away from me, drew it out through my own startled stare, took it into himself. Then, he thrust away my hands and threw back his head, gasping, his mouth wide in a smile of pleasure and satisfaction.

I exhaled with a groan and slumped forward, my vision spinning. I felt as if I was extremely drunk, to the point of sickness, but my body could not vomit. My flesh was held in the vice of the most excruciating numbness and cramp. I curled up and writhed upon the cindery dirt, tears squeezing between my tightly-clenched eyelids. Was I dying?

Then, I felt hands upon me. Someone dragged my limbs out straight and forced something cold and hard between my teeth. Icy liquid, which burned like fire, ran down my throat. As it hit my stomach, the pain that gripped me melted away. I found myself blinking up at the bright stars.

I knew then: demons were not worshipped in this place. They were created here.My guide, the ancient woman, took me out to the edge of the settlement. 'What will you use my essence for?' I asked her.

'Don't worry,' she answered. 'When the time comes for us to use it, you will not know in any way. It has gone from you. No longer yours.'

I shuddered.

We had reached the shadow of the rock, where my path would lead back to my pony and the world I knew. Strangely, I was reluctant to leave. I looked back at the tall dwellings, black against the stars, and the crimson fires, greedy in their pits. I realised I had seen no children among the Yazatas, but perhaps they could risk breeding only rarely, if their lives were so long. I knew I would never come here again.

The woman withdrew something wrapped in a scrap of hide from her robe, which she pressed into my hands. I felt the hardness of glass between my fingers. 'Use it wisely,' she said. 'It is the intention which counts. Some things are destined to die, others to thrive. Only your heart knows which.'

'Thank you, madam,' I said, and obeying an instinctive impulse, reached out to embrace her. She returned this importunate gesture rather stiffly, then pushed me away to arm's length.

'Make haste,' she said. 'Those born of fire are alert for lone travellers beneath the stars' white flames. Smoke-men and djinn alike.'

I knew she watched me until the path turned a corner and the rocks hid me from view, because I looked back at the last minute, and saw her tall shape standing there, dark against the sand.

I reached the settlement of my people at dawn, my body racked with pain and exhaustion. For a day, I slept, and without dreams. In the evening, the call of the stars woke me and I went to bathe in their icy fire. Had I been changed? I wondered about it. I felt tired yet energetic, melancholic yet hopeful.

The bottle lay where I had cast it beside my cushions that morning. Its verdigris glow filled my canopy with emerald fire. I picked up the bottle and held it to my breast. I closed my eyes and thought about the one I wanted to punish, whom I might never have. Not because of Maqite, or my feelings for her, but because I feared he had no feelings for me. None that I could understand anyway. Born of fire. A desert creature, dry and hard and quick. He had been forged in a fire-pit and contained in a bottle. Someone had released him upon us, this djinn, whose fire was cold and who did not glow with flame, but was smoky, arid and caustic. Kneeling there among my cushions, with the star-fire coming in through the entrance, and the green glow battling with it upon my fevered skin, I accepted certain truths. I was proud and vain and fierce. I would love him until I died, beyond his own death, if necessary.

I walked out into the night. There was music; the chime of bells, the lament of a flute, the shrill warble of a girl's high voice and the beat of drums. I went to Maqite's canopy. It was full of weeping women. Kamaara stood among the curtains, her skin white as death's hand, her eyes dull. I knew she too was expiring, and would vanish by the morning, gone the way she came, a phantom. I did not have to do anything about her. She was irrelevant.

The women kneeling around the bed muttered prayers through their tears. 'Maqite is dying,' they told me, and I requested that they leave us together for a while. This, they were happy to do, because I was her dearest friend. I knelt beside her.

'Pashti, where have you been?' she asked weakly, smiling to see me. 'Would you leave me to depart this world alone?'

I put my right hand behind her head and lifted it, held the unstoppered glass vessel to her lips. 'Drink,' I said.

Her lips quivered. 'What is it, Pashti?'

I swallowed. 'Please, just drink.'

Trusting me, she did so. I saw her eyes fill up with green fire. They blazed out at me, and she laughed. Her upper body reared up from the cushions and she held out her arms to the sky beyond the entrance to her dwelling. It was as if a beloved voice were calling out to her from the stars.

I watched and waited. All of my future hung upon these moments.

Presently, Maqite sank back down to her cushions with a rapturous sigh, and died there, smiling. I had not anticipated the outcome, only trusted my own heart.

I went back out into the night and summoned the women who, obeying custom, began to wail and keen.

I found him out beyond the peaked canopies, alone beside the water of the spring, sitting beneath a leaning tree. He glanced at me, his eyes hard, and I said, 'She is dead.'

He nodded, his hair hanging over his breast. 'It was expected.'

'Don't die from grief yourself, will you!' I threw myself down beside him, and he seemed surprised I had done so. Normally, I ran from him, and would not endure his company or the touch of his eyes.

'You blame me,' he said.

I nodded. 'Yes. And no. Certain of your actions are unforgivable.'

He sighed and leaned against the tree. 'I did not ask to be born,' he said.

It seemed to me an easy statement. I took the bottle from my pocket and tossed it into his lap. He stared at it, the green glow reflected in his eyes. 'What is it?'

'Yazata elixir,' I said. 'I went yesterday to fetch it for Maqite.'

He touched the glass with his artist's fingers and glanced at me. 'You were too late. How... pitiful.'

'Yes.' I stood up.

'You took a great risk.'

'Yes.' I looked down at him. 'Still, why waste it? You drink it instead.'

'I'm not dying.'

'It will give you longevity. I've seen it.'

He laughed, and I turned away painfully from his terrible loveliness. 'Drink with me, then,' he said.

I looked back at him and forced myself to suffer his eyes for a while. 'I don't know what will happen.' I watched him take the stopper from the bottle and drink.

Born of fire. *It will kill him, and I will be glad*, I thought. He blazed before me and it seemed to me as if dark, smoky wisps fled away from his body. Djinn! I must have made an astonished noise, for he frowned at me.

'Well, will you drink or not? I was brave enough to.'

I squatted beside him. 'You are not sad at all, are you?'

He was very still. 'A little,' he admitted, 'but what is a sanctuary to some is a prison to others.'

'Not that much of a prison,' I reminded him scathingly.

'Some people were trapped inside with me. Now I am free.'

He held the bottle out to me, and I drank.

I tipped back my head and swallowed a taste of chalk and velvet in a sauce of flame. I opened my eyes wide and the universe spun before me. Born of fire. We are. Desert creatures; kin to the djinn, to the deva.

I laughed at the spiralling sky.

When I had calmed down, he reached for my hand. I did not look at him, but we both stared out upon the night, thinking of our days to come.

Just His Type

This story was inspired by anecdotes told to me by a writer friend who was active in the Earth Mysteries field. He ran groups, wrote books and organised conventions on the subject. Sometimes, given the nature of his work, he ran into peculiar people. And occasionally, him being a trusting sort of person, some came closely into his life – with consequences no one would have imagined. The subject itself can affect people in unexpected ways, and reveal sides to them they didn't know they had.

The incidents in this story did not happen to my friend, and thankfully he never had a partner like the woman described here, but these things could have happened, if the wind had been blowing the wrong way... And of course, as a writer of peculiar tales, I just had to investigate what the wind might have brought in.

As in some of my other stories, the details of life are relevant only to their time. There are no mobile phones in this story – people had to leave messages on answerphones – and it was written when you could still smoke in restaurants!

The trouble was she was just his type. Sitting at the back of the stuffy pub function room, her eyes fixed upon him, she commanded his attention, apparently without effort. He could tell she was tall, because her head was the highest on the row. Her hands were clasped in her lap and she was dressed in black.

She had come to watch the famous historical investigator and author, Noah Johnson, deliver a lecture. He found he was playing to her alone throughout the evening. He knew the talk, 'Vampires in Myth and History', off by heart, having delivered it countless times before. He updated it constantly, but essentially, it was the same old stuff: colourful but careful. He was selective about what he gave the punters. He knew how to please a mixed crowd.

The regular meetings, 'Enigmas of History', were going well. He ran them once a fortnight in the upstairs room of his local pub, The Gun and Duck, and now had a regular attendance of around fifty people. Sometimes, he had to turn some away. More than fifty and the front row started fainting. He'd started the meetings to augment his writing income, for the periods when funds were slack – a downside of any writer's life. But they were going so well, he had planned more events; outdoors, now that summer was coming. Sarah would have loved all this. But he mustn't think about her now. She was no longer part of his life.

Noah's friend and assistant, Gary, dimmed the lights in preparation for the slide show. Some of the audience were fanning themselves with the handouts Gary's girlfriend, Abby, had placed on every seat prior to the meeting. The windows were open, but did little to improve the air quality in the room.

One by one, the slides slipped across the screen: illustrations copied from ancient texts, photographs Noah had taken himself while investigating in far corners of obscure Eastern European countries. Some of them had been reproduced in Noah's best-selling book, 'The Search for Nosferatu'. The subject no longer captivated him: he'd done that and it was over, but the public were always hungry for more. Noah had moved on to other things and was currently researching his next book, which was concerned with the mythical landscape of the remote Scottish islands, and how the strange ancient structures there might have come to be built.

When the lights came back on, Noah's eyes were drawn immediately to the girl on the back row. He half expected to see that she'd left. That would be just his luck, but no, there she was, sitting straight and demure, gazing at him from beneath downcast lashes, a slight smile on her lips.

He began to answer questions from the audience, but was anxious to keep it short tonight. If people wanted to air their opinions, which most of them did, especially the regulars, they could continue in the bar downstairs. He interrupted a woman as she was speaking. 'Hey, it's too hot up here. Shall we move down?'

Most of them would go home, but the ones who saw themselves as the core of his group would remain until closing time. It was only nine o'clock.

People started rising from their seats, apparently as eager as he was to escape the hot function room. The woman who'd been interrupted looked crestfallen, somewhat confused.

Gary and Abby began clearing up, gathering the dropped leaflets, packing away the slide equipment. 'Good turnout,' Gary said.

'You could hire a bigger place,' Abby suggested. 'You'd still pack it.'

Noah was looking at the crowd shuffling out. He saw that the girl in black had remained in her seat. He smiled at her and she stood up. He went towards her.

'Excuse me, Mr Johnson, would you mind if I asked you something?'

'Of course not,' he said. 'Come down to the bar. We usually stay on for a few drinks.'

'Thank you.'

He put his arm behind her proprietarily to guide her to the door.

'Thanks, Noah!' Abby called behind him. 'We'll just finish off, shall we?'

He grinned back at her and she shook her head in mock disapproval. Abby was used to him and he knew how much he could get away with.

Downstairs, punters insisted on buying Noah drinks, but he bought one for the girl himself. 'I haven't seen you here before,' he said, leaning on the bar.

She pulled a face. Her features were delicate, mobile. 'No, I've only just moved here. It was great to discover this group, especially that it's run by you. I've got all your books.'

He laughed. 'Thanks.' In his mind, he could hear Abby's warning cry of: 'Noah! She's a fan, Okay? For God's sake, be careful.'

The girl brushed strands of dark hair from her eyes. Her well-shaped lips were painted perfectly in a dark purple. Her dress was of black lace and velvet, down to the floor. She was virtually the same height he was. 'I'm Lara, by the way. Lara Hoskins.'

Noah handed her a vodka and tonic. When she took it from him, he saw that her lace cuffs came right down to her fingers. The nails were painted black. 'So, what did you want to ask me?' He was conscious of the eyes of his 'core group' upon him, their resentment at a newcomer monopolising him. Normally, this was the time for Noah to hold court.

'Well, I have to admit it was the subject of the talk tonight that most attracted me,' Lara said. She laughed nervously. 'Not that I wouldn't have come anyway, of course...'

'And?'

'Why don't you talk about the origins of the vampire myth?'

'I do. You heard it.'

She was silent for a moment. 'I think we both know there's more to it than that.'

'Essentially, the myth is European, although there are parallels in Mesopotamian and Judaic mythology.'

'But where do those myths come from?'

'There are recurrent themes in every mythology. People the world over have the same fears, the same desires. There's no reason to think the vampire myth comes from a single root source.'

'But in 'Nosferatu', you implied differently.'

'What are you getting at?' Noah said, grinning. 'Don't tell me you're a vampire searching for your roots!'

A vampire would certainly not colour up the way she did then. 'I have a serious interest in the subject,' she said. 'I'd hoped you'd take me seriously too.'

'Look,' he said. 'If you want the truth, I think people can become obsessed with certain myths, especially the vampire ones. It's dangerous.'

'How?' She looked hungry.

'Any obsession is dangerous. I don't like to encourage it.' He was thinking of Sarah. Her face was before his eyes, sad and despairing.

'What happened?' Lara asked in a low voice. It was as if she knew already.

He could tell her easily. She could be his confessor. 'I knew someone,' he began. Then a hand slapped his back.

'Hey!' It was Abby. 'Don't tell me you haven't got drinks in for us!' She smiled at Lara. 'He treats us like lackeys!'

'Sorry,' Noah said. He turned to attract the attention of the barman.

For the rest of the evening Abby refused to leave Noah's side. He knew why. Abby knew him too well. She was good company and gave no indication to Lara that she was suspicious of her, but Noah was well aware of his friend's feelings.

After last orders, when the group was breaking up, Noah said to Lara, 'There's an event next Sunday. We're going on a tour of local ancient sites, churches, springs and so on. Should be quite a convoy. Would you like to come?'

'Well…' Lara put her empty glass down on the bar. 'Might be

difficult. I don't have transport.'

'I could pick you up,' said Noah.

'Great!' Lara opened her bag and rummaged in it. 'I'll give you my address. What time?'

'Oh, about mid-day.'

'It'll cost a tenner,' said Abby, somewhat darkly.

'Good value,' Lara said, taking the lid off a fountain pen.

Outside, in the car park, Abby started on Noah. 'What are you up to?' she demanded. 'I thought you'd decided to leave punters well alone.'

'What do you mean?' Noah countered, fiddling with his keys.

'I mean that you fancy her. It's obvious. But you've been down this road many times before. You know where it leads.'

'She's just coming to the event,' Noah said. 'What's wrong with that? Lots of other people are going and they're all punters as well.'

Abby folded her arms belligerently across her chest. 'I'm not stupid!'

'Give him a break, will you,' Gary snapped.

Abby was not to be deterred. 'She's a fan, Gary, and she's got her sights set. There's something a bit odd about her. I can just feel it.'

'He's a grown man,' Gary said in a tired voice. 'For Christ's sake, Ab, you sound like his bloody mother.'

'I'm the nearest he has to that,' Abby said, getting into the front passenger seat of Noah's car.

For the next few days, Noah couldn't stop thinking about Lara Hoskins. Abby was wrong to be so suspicious. Of course, he *had* met Sarah at a lecture, long before he'd begun the regular meetings, and perhaps this was why Abby was so scared for him. He'd dated lots of girls since, some of them plucked from the 'Enigmas of History' group, and he was the first to admit that none of them had worked out particularly well, but he was sure this was different. Lara was bright and had an enquiring mind. There were no warning signs. Her hands had been steady on her glass all evening. She'd been open and sociable.

By Sunday morning, he was buzzing with anticipation, and spent more time than usual on his appearance. Lara was probably about ten years younger than him, in her mid-twenties by the look of her, but that didn't matter. He looked young for his age. All his life, women had flocked to him.

When he drew up outside her house, she came through the front door before he'd even turned off the engine. She was dressed in black jeans and T-shirt, with a black hooded fleece tied around her waist, presumably in case it got cold later. Her long dark hair was caught up in a severe pony tail but swished provocatively around her head and shoulders as she ran down the short drive to the road. She was as slim as a boy and looked athletic. Noah's heart turned over. She was gorgeous.

'Hi!' she said breathlessly as she virtually threw herself into the car. She smelled strongly of an oriental yet floral scent.

'Hi,' Noah echoed. 'I like a woman who's ready on time.'

Lara laughed. It was a bright, free sound, devoid of artifice. Of course, she'd been ready for hours.

When they arrived at the meeting point, Noah was pleased to see there was a good turnout – about seven packed cars. Abby was going round collecting money and distributing maps.

At each site they visited, Noah had the group sit down and meditate to see if they could pick up any information from the past, such as what the site might have been used for in ancient times. He never did this at the indoor meetings. This was his select group, with whom he was prepared to try more 'weird stuff', as some referred to it.

During the meditation, Lara saw a great deal of detailed and pertinent imagery.

'I think you're psychic,' Noah told her privately.

'Oh, I know *that*,' she said.

'You couldn't be more perfect,' Noah said.

Lara smiled. 'When can we continue our conversation?'

'Later. How about dinner?'

'Sounds great.'

Noah had to lose Abby and Gary for the evening, which was not easy. He didn't want Abby to know he was taking Lara out, sure that she would insist that she and Gary went with him. Fortunately, they'd brought their own car that day, so at the last site Noah whisked Lara off quickly, virtually without saying goodbye to anybody. He knew he'd have to pay for it later and could anticipate Abby's terse message that would be waiting on his answerphone when he got home. But for the time being, he didn't give a damn. Both he and Lara were giggling as his car skidded away in a cloud of dust and gravel.

'Why do I get the feeling we're playing truant?' Lara asked.

'Sometimes, I want a bit of privacy, that's all,' Noah answered. 'The trouble with these events is that people want it to carry on till all hours. Sometimes, that's fine, but tonight...' He glanced at her and she smiled.

He took her to a Thai restaurant he'd never visited before, secure in the knowledge that none of the group would track him there. The food was rather lacklustre, but it didn't matter, because Lara was sitting opposite him and her smile seemed to enfold him in a hazy golden mist. They were both high on the sense of being secret conspirators. They were high on the potential of what might happen later.

Lara seemed content to listen to Noah talk about his new book, and it wasn't until the coffee arrived that she broached the subject she'd brought up after the meeting last Tuesday. 'Why did you react so badly to my question?'

'I don't think I did. Some things I just steer clear of.'

'So what's the story behind it?' She took a sip of coffee, smiled disarmingly. 'Or is that a secret?'

Noah leaned back in his chair. 'It's no secret. If you become part of the core group – and I'm sure you will – anyone would tell you. Basically, while I was writing 'Nosferatu', I was involved in more than the obvious method of research. The problem came from that.'

Lara put her head to one side. 'What do you mean?'

'You saw what we did today. People are keen on the psychic stuff. On one level, it's harmless, and most people never go beyond that. But on another, it isn't. Sitting outside an old church and trying to visualise images of the past can't hurt anyone, because it's dead and gone, nothing more than a psychic photograph. But other things, well, they're more alive, still around, so to speak.'

Lara laughed, lit a cigarette. 'Are you trying to tell me that you contacted a vampire psychically?'

Noah hesitated for a moment. Part of him didn't want to say more, but Lara's wide eyes were fixed upon him with a bright, intelligent gaze. He felt safe with her. 'I worked with a girl called Sarah. People don't realise this, but a lot of the information in my books comes from what I call 'inspired' sources, from psychics. Most of what

I find out can't be used in a serious book, because it can't be checked out and verified as fact, but it gives me a feel for and understanding of the subject. Sarah was my assistant and also my partner. She was very psychic.'

'*Was*,' Lara said, her chin resting on her hands. Smoke curled around her in slow tendrils. 'That sounds ominous.'

'Let's just say that I was interested in the origin of the vampire myth, just as you are. I'd investigated all the legends of blood-drinking demons, from medieval Europe right back to Sumerian times. Somewhere along the way, the flavour of the subject changed.' He gestured with both hands. 'It's difficult to describe, but the idea of the vampire as unfortunate undead – perhaps a victim of their circumstances – mutated into the idea that the original vampires were very much alive and that their vampirism was by choice, a necessary facet of their belief system.'

Lara nodded enthusiastically. 'That's my thought also.'

'It all seemed very academic to us. We called them the vulture people, a shamanic tribe who indulged in blood drinking and sacrifice. Sarah picked up some interesting stuff that pointed us in the direction of certain ancient sites in Turkey. The imagery she saw could be verified. These places existed and there was archaeological evidence that a shamanic culture had thrived there, one that worshipped vultures. They believed that drinking blood gave them superhuman abilities. Whether that was true or not, we thought that other tribes would probably have regarded them as supernatural, as demons, even, because of their bloodthirsty habits. We believed that there was a diaspora and that factions of this tribe might have moved gradually into Europe, eventually giving rise to the vampire legend.

'Every evening, I'd have Sarah go into a kind of trance, guiding her further and further back into the past, seeking the true story. It seemed we were meant to discover all this, to make the link. The vulture people became more real for us: powerful shamans, who used the rites of blood to change their world. As time went on, Sarah started to get jumpy about it. She said she sensed little dark things that scuttled in the folds of these creatures' vulture wing robes, that they had begun to touch her. She wanted to stop, but I persuaded her otherwise. I thought we were getting close to something that would prove my theory incontrovertibly. We had to continue. But then, one night, Sarah brought something back with her.'

There was a silence, while Lara took a long, meditative draw on her cigarette. Then she said, 'And Sarah couldn't cope?'

Noah pressed the fingers of one hand briefly against his eyes. He could hear her screams even now. 'It was too overwhelming, too *alien*. We always did these sessions by the light of one candle, so we couldn't see much, but it was as if the night just surged into the room. We were surrounded by a presence, not evil exactly, but beyond good and evil. It was amoral, and we were *nothing* to it. Even I could sense it, and I'm no great psychic. In moments, I realised how we'd been playing with something inconceivably huge and beyond us, something immeasurably powerful. We'd pulled at its skirts too insistently and now it had noticed us.'

'What happened?'

'Well, once Sarah started screaming, I just leapt up and put the lights on. If something really had been there, it disappeared.' He finished off the warm lager left in his glass and shook his head. 'Sarah was writhing on the floor. I didn't know what to do. The noises were hideous. In the end, I slapped her. It's what you're supposed to do, isn't it? And she kind of came out of it. But even if the thing had gone, it left a taint behind.'

'Did it kill her?' Lara asked bluntly.

Noah detected a faint note of scorn in her voice. 'No, no. Of course not. Sarah was an experienced psychic, but she was damaged by what she'd felt and seen. It changed her and there was nothing I could do. Nothing. She became paranoid, jealous and afraid. It destroyed us.'

'It wasn't your fault,' Lara said, reaching out to touch one of Noah's hands.

He laughed cynically. 'They all said that, but it's not true. I was so eager to discover the truth, I didn't think about the dangers. I just kept pushing and pushing. After we split up, Sarah lost her job. She just lost it, big time. The last I heard she'd admitted herself to hospital. She dropped all her old friends.'

'It wasn't your fault,' Lara insisted. 'Sarah just wasn't strong enough.'

'She was,' Noah said. '*It* was stronger than both of us.'

'I don't believe that.'

'You weren't there. Even as a writer, I don't have the words to describe how terrible that night was, how real the entity that came to us. This wasn't Christopher Lee in a silk cape, Lara. This wasn't a nice, safe little meditation like all those we did today. This was the most raw and primeval energy; it could snuff you out like that!' He snapped his fingers before her face, but she did not flinch.

'I want it,' she said.

He laughed shakily. 'What?'

'It's what I want. I need to know the truth. I'm not afraid.'

Noah raised his hands and shook his head emphatically. 'No. You don't know what you're asking for. The vampires you're so enamoured of, they're just fashion accessories, a romantic myth. You don't want the truth, believe me.'

'How dare you!' Lara snapped. 'You make me sound like some stupid little girl who's just into looking weird. I'm not enamoured by anything.' She thumped her chest with a closed fist. 'I've lived with this stuff all my life, felt it tugging at the corners of my mind, trying to make itself known to me. Their carrion smell has always been strong to my senses. When I read 'Nosferatu', I thought I'd found someone who would understand, who wouldn't think I was mad.' She put her hands against her head, scraped them through her sleek, confined hair, pulling strands of it free. 'If you really are so against it, why did you put all those coy clues in the book?'

Noah thought she now looked demented, with her hair beginning to fall over her face, a hectic flush along her cheekbones and those wild, wide eyes. But she was breathtakingly beautiful and, in those moments, he could believe she was as strong as she claimed to be. 'You'd better tell me what you mean by saying you've lived with it,' he said.

Lara ducked her head in assent and then summoned a waiter to order more drinks.

'No,' Noah said. 'I'm driving. Let's get the bill. We can talk at my place.'

They were silent in the car on the drive home. Lara sat with her hands folded in her lap, staring through the windscreen. Noah wondered what he was doing. He guessed what would come. In was as inexorable as a tidal wave, and he could already see it massing on the horizon. He could stop it now, take her home.

They passed the turn off that would lead to her road. His hands tightened on the steering wheel. In ten minutes, he was parking the car outside his house.

Inside, Lara wandered around the living-room, touching lightly the ancient artefacts that clustered on every available surface. Sarah had collected most of them, but hadn't wanted to take them with her when she left. She hadn't taken anything, or exercised her rights to have half of the house. She'd just wanted out, to cast off any vestige of her life with Noah, desperate to live in the here and now, in safe mundaneity. But it was denied her. No one else should go to the place where Sarah was. No one.

Noah made coffee in the vast silent kitchen, where modern appliances gleamed on the spotless work surfaces. Sarah had had the kitchen installed, paid for it herself. The cutlery and crockery Noah had used for his lunch still lay in the sink, but generally he kept the house tidy out of respect for her, as if she was still around in an etheric kind of way, and might disapprove of clutter and mess. On the way back to the living room, he took a bottle of brandy and two huge globe glasses from his liquor cupboard and placed them onto the tray next to the cafetiere and mugs.

Lara was curled up in the big leather armchair by the hearth and had lit the log effect gas fire. She had also managed to find the tiny ashtray that Noah kept reluctantly for guests. 'You're so lucky,' she said, as Noah came into the room. 'This place is great. Tons of books and things. How many bedrooms has it got?'

'Five,' Noah answered.

'I'm in the wrong job!' Lara said, laughing. She seemed just like an ordinary girl now, gamine and flirtatious.

Noah set down the tray on the coffee table and set about pouring drinks. 'We got this place for a song,' he said, rather apologetically. 'It was a dump. Sarah did it up.' He looked around the room. 'Worth a bit now, of course, but all I'd need is a couple of bad years and I'd have to sell it. Writing is not the millionaire's game it's made out to be, you know.'

'I'm surprised to hear you say that,' Lara said.

'Most people are. They think we all live like Jackie Collins.'

'No, I meant that you know how to change fate, how to make things happen. Why don't you use it for yourself, so that you don't get any of those "bad years"?'

'You've lost me,' Noah said, pushing a glass of brandy and a coffee across the table towards her. 'I'm a writer, a researcher, not a bloody magician!'

Lara smiled, turning in her fingers a lock of hair that hung beside her face. 'Oh, come on! What about the "weird stuff"?'

'If I knew how to meditate money into existence, I'd be rich. But I don't. I just use the "weird stuff" to delve into the past.'

'But the vulture people knew how to change their world. You said so.'

'Strangely enough, I have no compelling desire to drink blood and murder people.' He was enjoying their exchange, sure that the undercurrent was sexual.

Lara picked up the brandy globe. 'You've contacted them,' she said. 'How many people have done that? If you weren't scared shitless, you could use that energy for yourself.' Slowly, sensuously, she drained her glass.

Noah knelt back on his heels, his hands braced against his thighs. 'I think you are a dangerous young woman,' he said.

'You wouldn't have to kill anybody,' she said, holding out her glass for more brandy. 'I'm sure the smallest of blood sacrifices would do.'

Noah poured out a generous measure of the golden liquor. 'I'm not going back there, Lara. I got burned and sensibly pay attention to what hurts. You don't put your hand in the fire twice.'

'When people have no fear, they can walk across red hot coals,' Lara said. 'I'm scared of madmen with knives, and perverts hiding in alleys. I'm scared of people, because they're shit. But etheric entities don't frighten me. They don't have hands of flesh and blood. They can't fire a gun. The only way they can hurt you is through fear, your own mind. You must know that.'

Noah hesitated. He could feel the conviction pulsing from Lara's body. 'You are a witch,' he said and took a long drink of his brandy. It burned his throat, felt good.

Her eyes were hooded now. 'Take me there, Noah. I'm not afraid to go alone and I won't freak you out by having the screaming heeby jeebies. Just take me there.'

'Why?' he said.

'Because they want you to,' she said. 'I've heard their voices whispering in my dreams since I was a child. I've seen their shadows in the curtains of my bedroom every night. I've felt their carrion breath on my face in the dark. I'm one of them, Noah. Not in this life perhaps, but I *know* them. I want to go home.'

The silence in the room was absolute and the atmosphere had become still and watchful, as if vulture shamans were already gathering round them. It was as if Lara had conjured something into being through the passion of her words. There was no way he could disbelieve her. She looked remarkably sane, but driven. He could not speak.

'I'm not some sick cow who wants to drink blood,' Lara said in a conversational tone. 'I don't have a black bedroom or collect horror films. I don't want to be a vampire in the traditional sense. I just need to know what it is that has been trying to get through to me, that's all.' She smiled. 'God, I must sound mad. What else do I have to say to convince you I'm not?'

He stared at her, wrestling with himself, thinking of Sarah.

'I'm a bloody good psychic,' she said mischievously, cocking her head to the side. 'You can always use one of those, can't you?'

'Then why do you need me? If you're that good, do it yourself.'

'You have the map,' she said. 'You are the guide. It's that simple.' She adopted a mock serious tone. 'I'll look after you, Noah, don't worry. You'll be *perfectly* safe.'

His meditation room was at the back of the house on the second floor, overlooking fields and a small wood. As he'd always done with Sarah, he kept the curtains open and lit a single candle. His heart was beating fast, but not through fear. He was not sure exactly what he felt. As he prepared to light some loose incense, to help conjure the right atmosphere, Lara said, 'Have you got a pin?'

'What?'

'To prick our fingers. We should put our blood into the incense.'

'Lara...'

'*Noah...?*' She was laughing at him.

It took some minutes to find a pin, by which time Lara had consumed another globe of brandy. Noah himself was beginning to feel the effects of the alcohol. Perhaps it was numbing his sense of apprehension. He let Lara prick his thumb and squeeze a bright droplet of blood from the wound, which she shook into the incense. Then she put his thumb into her warm mouth and sucked it. 'Scared?' she said.

'Horrified.'

She pricked her own thumb, but didn't offer to let him taste her blood. It was a slight disappointment.

Lara lay down on the rug before the cold hearth, while Noah sat crossed-legged beside her, and took her gently into a light trance. The words were soporific. His own eyelids began to droop. He led her back through time, made her watch the centuries fall away, until he told her to visualise herself standing at the mouth of a cave amid high, wind-sculpted crags. Beyond the threshold, all was dark.

'This is the Shanidar Cave,' he murmured, 'home of the vulture people. Walk into it.'

He paused, listening to her light breathing. 'Tell me what you see,' he said.

'Darkness,' she replied. Her brow had creased into a frown. 'But I can smell...'

She would say blood, he thought.

'Flowers,' she said faintly. 'Everywhere, flowers. They've placed them over the bones. I see them. So many bones. There are wings...'

'Is anyone there with you?'

'Yes.' Her voice was like that of a child, young and tremulous.

'Do you want to leave?' Noah said. 'You can leave at any time.'

'No. He knows me. He wants to give me something.'

'What?'

'The talking bone...'

'What does he look like?'

Suddenly, Lara gasped, her eyes flew open and she sat bolt upright. Noah reached out to steady her. 'It's okay,' he said.

She turned her head slowly and when she spoke, her voice was deep and rasping. 'Keep me not from her, son of Lamech. Her laughter filled the mountains and bowed the heads of the wild beasts. Shame took her from me. Shame!'

Noah could smell carrion, the reek of her breath.

Abruptly, Lara sighed and fell back gracefully onto the floor.

'Lara,' Noah breathed, leaning over her. 'Lara. Are you all right?'

She laughed and wriggled her body on the rug. 'Oh *yes*.' Without opening her eyes, she reached up for him, dragged him down. When he kissed her, he tasted brandy, the flame of it.

'Thank you,' she murmured, between kisses. 'Thank you.'

Her skin was hot beneath his hand, exuding the last warmth of her perfume. He made love to her where she lay, wondering if she was fully in this world or not. It didn't matter. She was a dream come to life, a woman who could walk alone into the dark and come back laughing and smelling of flowers.

Afterwards, she lay naked beside him, smoking a cigarette. 'What the hell was there to be scared of?' she said. 'Have I brought anything back with me? No. And believe me, I willed it.'

Noah lay on his side, stroking her taut belly. 'What did it – he – look like?'

She grimaced. 'Pretty much how you'd think. At first, he was crouched down, wrapped in this immense cloak of black feathers. It looked like it had been made from the whole wings of a single vulture. I could just see the slits of his eyes peering over the top. He resembled a vulture himself... like a vampire! Although he was crouched down, I could tell he was a giant; magnificent, wise and savage.'

'That's pretty powerful imagery,' Noah said.

'Then he stood up and opened his cloak of wings. Beneath it, he was dressed in animal skins. His body was covered in some kind of paint, but it wasn't blood. There were patterns in it like primitive cave paintings. He did have bones in his hair and wore a necklace of bones. Bird bones, I think. You'll be pleased to know he had pointy teeth. All of them.'

'Filed down?'

'Probably.' She took a fierce draw off her cigarette. 'Oh, I don't know. Maybe I saw what I wanted to see, or was influenced by what you said earlier.'

'What about what he said through you?'

'I don't know. It was as if he'd known me before, obviously. He seemed to know you too, in a way. Lamech was the father of Noah in biblical myth, wasn't he?'

Noah nodded, uncomfortable with the idea that the entity might be aware of him.

'If the whole thing wasn't subjective,' Lara said, 'maybe I lived in his time once. Maybe we were lovers. I certainly felt really horny when I came out of it.'

'He doesn't sound very attractive!'

Lara stubbed out her cigarette and reached for Noah's crotch. 'Oh, but he was! Beautiful, in fact. His eyes were amazing, this deep piercing blue. Christ, I wanted him to possess me. Utterly. It was the archetypal thing.' She laughed huskily. 'I'd have been quite happy for him to sink his teeth into me.'

Noah leaned over and nipped the skin of her throat. 'Come on, let's go to bed. It's getting cold in here.'

They made love several more times. Noah felt euphoric, hardly daring to believe a woman such as this could come into his life. She was full of humour and warmth, serious about her ability yet amusingly irreverent. She was uninhibited, open, mysterious and fey. A witch woman. A priestess.

'Where have you been all my life?' Noah said.

'I bet you say that to all the girls,' she replied, and they giggled like children at the stupid clichés for several minutes.

About four o'clock, Lara said she was tired and turned onto her side in the bed. Noah studied her for some time, drinking in each detail of her smooth contours, the spill of dark hair upon the pillow. He passed his hand in the air above her body, and she squirmed and made a sound of pleasure as if she felt him stroking her aura.

'Beauty,' he whispered. 'Love.' He lay down to sleep, closing his eyes with the after-image of her white flesh burning in his mind.

Waking came with a shock in the grey of predawn twilight.

He was aware at once of cold, and saw that the bed beside him was empty. A terrified pang of loss coursed through him, then he saw her clothes still draped on the pale wicker chair by the window and told himself she had gone to the bathroom, or else to get herself a drink.

He lay on his back and pulled the duvet over his chilled torso. A hiss in the corner of the room made him start.

'Lara?'

He sat up. Most of the room was still in shadow, but he thought he could make out a dark shape hunched in the corner near his clothes rail. 'Lara…'

He reached to turn on the bedside lamp, but the switch did not respond. The bulb must have gone.

Again, a hiss, low and sibilant.

Something moved in the shadows, sidled forward. He saw the eyes clearly first: a deep piercing blue. She was naked and had covered herself in what looked like dark paint, which was possible because there were a few tins left in the garage. Her hair was wild and straw-like, filled with a sticky substance. Her tongue protruded unnaturally from her mouth, like that of the destroyer goddess, Kali. Her teeth could not possibly be pointed. There were no tools in his house she could have used to do that. She hissed and stamped with one foot.

'Lara.'

He got out of bed slowly. This was so different to the time before with Sarah. Lara wasn't screaming. She wasn't raving or weeping.

Her eyes followed him as he skirted the room.

He held out his hands in the universal gesture of peace. 'Lara, wake up. You're dreaming. It's not real. Lara.'

She made a threatening lunge towards him, growled and stamped both feet. He jumped back. It was unreal. He couldn't feel anything, because it was so unreal.

The night had come into the room. Not darkness, but the essence of night, the absence of light. The cold of the Earth before the first dawn rose.

'Lara…'

She came for him then, scuttling with crablike speed across the room. She grabbed him by the shoulders and he felt the sharp prick of her fingernails. She stank of rotten meat and there was a crust around her lips. She was bleeding from the mouth. Her teeth were filed away to ragged points.

What pain she must be in. What pain…

He fought back. This wasn't Lara. This was the darkness he had hidden from for so long. Perhaps it had always been here, lurking in the shadows of his house, in his memories.

She was so strong, like a tigress. She pushed him back onto the bed and straddled him. Her breasts looked heavier than they had been earlier, scored with the marks of her own fingernails. She uttered a shriek and lunged for his neck.

He should be afraid, shouldn't he? This *thing*, this monstrous abomination dredged from the primal soup, was feasting on him, tearing at his flesh, kneading his skin with its claws, sucking the life from him. It stank of Hell. Yet he was aroused by it. He wanted her and she let him do it, her body bucking in frenzy.

And he saw it then, the tunnel into history. The rivers of blood that carried the memories of humanity. *It is within all of us,* he thought. *We have tamed it and dressed it up in a silk suit. We have made it dead. We have contained it in books and films and lascivious dreams. We have contained it in nightmares. But ultimately, it is within us all the time. And it is alive, pulsing, warm and wet, stinking of musk and spoiled meat.*

Lara wasn't stronger than Sarah. The opposite was true. Because Sarah had rejected this. It was what she had seen and felt and had never spoken of. The search for Nosferatu didn't begin in the grave, but in the reptile brain, the primordial remnant of beast within every human mind. It was demonic. It was divine.

In the late morning, with bright sunshine coming into the kitchen, they were politely formal with each other. She said she had badly chipped a tooth falling over in the dark. They didn't talk about how she'd decorated her body. The mess in the kitchen had been cleaned up by the time he had come downstairs and she was freshly showered, smelling of his patchouli body wash. She joked about her loathing of dentists as she carefully drank hot coffee. He made toast, then apologised and offered something softer: scrambled eggs perhaps? She wasn't hungry, she said.

He rubbed his neck. 'Ah well…'

She had to go to work at two. Worked part-time in a local shop. Perhaps she could get an emergency dental appointment before she went in.

He had work to do too. The book would be late to his publishers otherwise. Nice day, though.

Yes, nice day.

At the door, she pecked his cheek in a brief kiss. 'We must do this again,' she said.

'Must we?' Many words hung unspoken between them.

She smiled. She looked very tired and there were purple rings beneath her eyes. 'I think I got what I wanted. Didn't you?'

'Lara…'

'You can call me. Or not,' she said. 'I don't need you now, Noah, but I kind of like you.'

He watched her run down the path to the road. She had rejected a lift. He leaned his forehead on the doorframe. Once your eyes are open, you can never close them. Sarah knew this.

He shouldn't see Lara again. He should attempt to forget all that had occurred. They'd been drunk. She'd broken one tooth, that's all. It had been less than he'd imagined. As if to remind him otherwise, his neck twinged painfully. He felt light-headed, sick, suddenly able to imagine the future, the long, slow, agonising stretch of it, the descent into realms he dared not think about.

He shouldn't see her again. But she was just his type, wasn't she? Just his type.

A Tour of the House

This collection would not feel complete to me without a Wraeththu story in it. As readers of my work will know, Wraeththu propelled me into the life of a writer, and I continue to write about their world many years on. For any readers of this collection who've not encountered Wraeththu before, they are – to cut a long story short – an androgynous race who rose from the ashes that humanity had made of the world. I've written nine novels about them.

However, this particular story, which appeared in the Wraeththu Mythos collection 'Para Imminence: Stories of the Future of Wraeththu' is in some respects based on fact.

Shugborough Hall, a stately home near to my town, was the seat of the Earls of Lichfield; the last in the line to have lived there being Patrick Lichfield, the celebrated photographer. A few years ago, quite some time after his death, his private apartments were opened to the public. This gives a glimpse into the hedonistic life he must have lived in the 60s and 70s, when he counted many rock stars, actors and actresses and other famous creative types among his friends. When I visited these rooms and prowled along the corridors, peering at the photographs on the walls of the bright young things who once used to party at Shugborough, cavorting among the follies and gardens, I felt unaccountably sad. These lives had gone. Those of them who weren't dead were now old, no longer the beautiful creatures of the past. And how grotesque it was that people were wandering through these rooms, where perhaps the unheard echoes of mad parties still reverberated – that long dead youth – now only the province of coach loads of visitors, picking over the remains. I was also somewhat sickened by the fact that the National Trust had seen fit to fill out some of the rooms with furniture from other properties. The theme park wasn't even faithfully real.

In stately homes, the lives once lived there seem far removed from us, lost in history, but at Shugborough, in those particular apartments, the history is very close to us. It makes you realise how fleeting youth and beauty are, how fragile life can be. I left the estate greatly affected by my visit.

In writing a story about the future of Wraeththu, I decided to feature the house We Dwell in Forever, the home of the Varr leader Terzian, which in the story has become the equivalent of a National Trust property. The visitor, Gred, feels as saddened there as I was at Shugborough. I wrote the piece only a few days after my visit. However, this is a story, and of course in stories the past might come back.

The house had not been lived in for over a decade, yet somehow, even as a museum or a place of learning, it still retained an ambience of homeliness. We Dwell in Forever. But the hara who had so named the house were long gone.

Gred stood in the doorway, shaking the rain from his umbrella, water dripping from the tendrils of his long dark hair that hung over, or were stuck to, his face. A har standing beside the reception desk indicated his umbrella should be placed in a stand with several others. Water pooled on the cream marble floor. Outside the sky was blue-grey with summer storm, while the foliage of the soaring ancient trees was acid green against it. Within the house, the double-doors of highly-polished oak stood open to the day, but the hallway was dark, smelling of rain and trodden grass.

Other visitors were clustered around the desk, looking at informational guideleafs. A soft-voiced guide, dressed in a uniform of moss green tunic and loose trousers, was gathering a group of hara together, ready for the next tour of the house. Gred decided grudgingly to join them. He had travelled far on this pilgrimage. He had wanted to visit for so long. Part of him resented having to share the experience with so many others. But he was just a tourist, like them. There would be no special privileges.

The tour would begin in five minutes. Gred closed his eyes briefly, a ghost at the edge of the crowd. He thought about the feet that had walked these marble tiles, that had descended the sweeping stairs ahead. He thought of the tragedies and romances of history, wrapped up in legend.

'We shall start with the lower west wing,' the guide said.

The group turned as one towards a corridor that led off to the left and followed the guide, who moved slowly, allowing everyhar to absorb the surroundings, examine the fittings, the pictures on the walls, the atmosphere itself.

'The house was built in the style of the type of country mansion found in ancient Alba Sulh,' said the guide. 'During the human era, this estate was undoubtedly occupied by a moneyed family attempting to emulate the lives of Sulhian gentry.'

A soft ripple of laughter spread through the group.

The guide smiled indulgently at the follies of the past. He paused before a painting. 'The hara who came to inhabit this house during the Upheaval were susceptible to the same impulses. Here, for example, is a portrait of our tribe founder, Terzian, with his horse and dogs. In style, it resembles the antique paintings of high-ranking humans that would have been found in all the large houses of ancient times, especially in

Alba Sulh. There are many pictures within the house in this style. Useful for us because they tell us much about the hara who lived here.'

The artist had captured a day very similar to today, Gred thought. Early summer, searing green foliage, a purple sky gravid with storms. Terzian, young and proud, his yellow hair a shock of corn against the bark of an old oak. His horse; whites of its eyes showing, yet standing calm. At Terzian's feet lay the hounds, looking up at him, tongues lolling. This was a har who had built a tribe, slaughtered thousands, human and hara alike. Long dead, but living in a picture. Gred wondered if the portrait had hung in the house following Terzian's death or whether it had been very recently brought out from storage, unwrapped from dusty cloth, simply for the benefit of tourists.

'Do any of the family still occupy any of the rooms?' somehar asked.

The guide shook his head. 'No. Although the family have only recently donated this property to the Megalithican Heritage Trust, no Parasilians have occupied it for at least eighty years. Until about ten years ago, it was used as a centre for the Galhean Arts Brotherhood, who lacked the funds or resources – or indeed inclination – for proper upkeep. The family did little to maintain their ancestral home. We still have much restoration work to do.'

'Why did they leave?' Gred asked.

'Marlet har Parasiel had a new house built for the family following his chesna-bond to Ambel har Unneah. Some say he was plagued by ghosts...'

Again, a ripple of laughter.

The guide made a languid gesture with one hand. 'In fact he thought it time for the family to move away from the past and the looming shadows of those who had come before. Megalithica had changed, as had Galhea. History, especially of the volatile kind associated with the early Parasilians, should remain in a museum. This is what the house has become.'

Madness, Gred thought. *How could anyhar leave this place, its ghosts, its histories? Somehar having no imagination or no heart.*

The guide was gazing at Gred speculatively. 'It is rather like reading a novel,' he said. 'The stories are romances, probably less than half true. Nohar wants to live in a story. The new house is very beautiful. Parts of it are open to viewing twice a year.' His smile had become somewhat tighter. 'Now, shall we continue? To our left is the family sitting room.'

Most of it was roped off to protect the elderly carpets and furniture. A small area was provided for everyhar to crowd into. There was a smell of ancient dust, perhaps caught in the heavy drapes at the windows, which were tall and with wide sills, where hara might once have sat to gaze out at the gardens, the long driveway, lined by poplars, which wound towards the town. There was also a green smell; a whiff of pine. In the fireplace, long unused, was a vase, filled with a glorious display of evergreens: several species of ivy twined around sprays of fir branches and sprigs of holly. The guide indicated this. 'The foliage display you see was a tradition upheld by the family in remembrance of tiahaar Cobweb, who was Terzian's consort in the early days of the house and subsequently lived here for nearly three centuries. We have reinstated this tradition.'

'Why is it in the fireplace?' somehar asked. 'Did they burn it as a tradition too?'

Yet more laughter.

The guide was grinning now. 'No, it originally stood upon a side table between two of the windows. When we took over the place, there was still a fragmenting old display there that had perhaps remained from the days of family occupation.'

'Did you keep it?' Gred asked.

'The display is replaced regularly,' the guide replied. He sniffed dismissively. 'Members of the family who were in residence would meet here in the evenings. It was sometimes used to entertain guests known well to the Parasilians. An informal room.'

Two large unyielding sofas, several stiff padded chairs; all looked uncomfortable and far from informal to Gred. 'Are these the original furnishings?' he asked.

The guide shook his head. 'Unfortunately, the original furnishings that remained were beyond repair. The items you see here are our attempt to recreate the room as it once was. They came from another house we care for.' He rubbed his hands together. 'Come, we have the dining-room and the main reception salon further along this corridor.'

As the group moved on, Gred lingered a moment, gazing back into the room. Here, Cobweb had sat upon the floor before the fire, perhaps sketching in one of his notebooks. Many of those remained. One was on display in the museum in Immanion, held open at a page, under glass. You couldn't touch it. Gred held out his hand to the air of the room. It was all still here, just a little.

'Tiahaar?' The guide was calling him.

'Excuse me,' Gred said. He caught up with the rest.

In fact, there was very little left of the original appointments. Megalithican Heritage had filled the rooms with furniture that belonged elsewhere, to other lives. What was the point of trying to emulate the past when the pieces were merely mismatched impositions? Empty rooms would have been better or even the rotting remains of what the Trust had found when the house had opened its doors to them and let them in. Cobweb might have approved of the Galhean Arts Brotherhood. No doubt they had made a mess, not cared at all about maintaining an image of the past. They had just lived here.

The original mahogany dining table remained, although the guide complained it had to be covered with a cloth, since the GAB had used it as a cutting table for various projects and had ruined the surface irreparably. The guide talked about what a magnificent piece it had once been. Gred wondered why the Trust hadn't replaced it. He nearly said so, but held his tongue. Places were set for diners as the Trust assumed they would have been. Multiple sets of cutlery, several different glasses for several different wines. Delicate, gilt-edged crockery.

Gred could only think of gloves left on the table, and books, some pencils, a few feathers and stones from the garden that harlings had brought in to show the family. Crumbs on the table cloth, knives smeared with butter laid across plain white plates. Cold cups of coffee, half drunk. This was what he'd always imagined when he'd heard stories of the past; he had always felt he'd 'seen' beyond the dry facts into these colourful lost lives. He was quite sure the Parasilians would never have eaten off the polished table, except when distinguished visitors were present. Most of the time, it would have been swathed in rough white linen. Gred thought of shoes kicked off beneath the chairs. Mud traipsed in from the stable yard. He thought of laughter. Sullen silences. An argument. A reunion. Simmering lust. A sharp-tined fork plunged into a hand. He knew that story, how Tigron Calanthe, long before he became Tigron, when he was still mad, had stabbed Terzian with a fork in this room. The Varrs had sheltered Cal when he'd needed sanctuary. In their way, they had helped save him. News had come to this room also, as the family had sat to eat breakfast or dinner. Gred could visualise the door flying open, somehar rushing in with something to say. Sometimes something bad.

In the reception room, with its views of the terrace where urns still stood, resplendent with ferns, the guide talked about how the Parasilians had entertained there. 'Terzian initiated the custom for all the seasonal festivals to be celebrated here at the house. Hara from Galhea were invited, and festivities were held outdoors so that everyhar from the local community could be accommodated. Within the house, high-ranking hara, their friends and family, plus members of Terzian's militia, would gather in this room. The family maintained this tradition until they moved to their new residence. The Galhean Arts Brotherhood, of course, did not continue it.'

'Do the family still hold these festivities in their new home?' somehar asked.

'The house is open twice a year for viewing,' the guide repeated. 'Those times coincide with a couple of festivals and there is some entertainment provided in the grounds during the evening. I believe there is a guideleaf about it in the entrance hall.'

'I suppose all the famous hara of the early days of Wraeththu came here at some point,' somehar else said. 'Would Tigron Pellaz have been in this room?'

The guide nodded. 'Undoubtedly. He visited the family before he became Tigron, and thereafter remained a constant friend, especially to tiahaar Cobweb, who was often an advisor to him.'

Gred smiled to himself. So few words to describe such a huge history. *'Visited the family before he was Tigron...'* This idiot had no idea. Gred gazed about the room from beyond the tasselled ropes that kept everyhar away from where events had actually happened. He closed his eyes and inhaled. This room would always be redolent of Natalia, the winter festival. The flames would have been ferocious in the imposing fireplace. The sideboard to the left of the room would have been heaped with traditional, seasonal fare. The air would have been heavy with the scents of mulled wine and sheh. And among the guests, a thousand embers of feeling.

It was true that the Aralisians, the ruling dynasty of Immanion, had often spent Natalia here, especially so in the later years of Pellaz's reign. Galhea had become the capital of Megalithica eventually, the small agricultural town expanding into the metropolis it was today. In those days, the house had been on the edge of the town. Now its hill was surrounded by roads and parks and suburbs. The Parasilians and the Aralisians, separated by an ocean, remained close allies if not close friends. Yet the magic had somehow seeped away from that famous alliance. The characters who played the stage today were not the towering, vibrant creatures of history, who had shaped early Wraeththu, who had bled for it.

The guide broke into Gred's thoughts. 'You are a student of history?' he asked, somewhat archly. He must have noticed Gred's absorption in the house.

'In an amateur fashion,' Gred replied.

'You are from Almagabra?' Was that a slight note of accusation? Gred's accent coupled with his olive skin must have given him away.

Gred smiled, inclined his head. 'Yes, I am. As you can imagine, Galhea holds great interest for my harakin. It is a large part of our heritage, or shall I say our *combined* heritage, since, for Parsics, this area is also of great significance.' That sounded too pompous.

The guide had narrowed his eyes. 'You are Gelaming, then.'

Gred was tempted to lie. 'That is my tribe, yes.'

'Then naturally this area holds racial memories for you,' the guide said dryly. 'The Gelaming concentrated their efforts in Galhea, especially after the death of Terzian.'

'I thought that Imbrilim was their centre, to the south,' Gred said. 'The Varrs, then later the Parasilians, always maintained control of Galhea.' So far, the term Varr had not been mentioned in the tour speech.

'Superficially, yes,' the guide replied. He perhaps became aware how the tour group was starting to feel uncomfortable and smiled brightly, raised his voice. 'The history of this area is colourful, but again much of the detail has been embellished over time. Shall we move on?'

The group visited Terzian's private office, a small room now empty but for a desk and chair. The guide did not speak about how some of the greatest decisions of Megalithican history had been made in this room, nor that it had been Terzian's son Swift's office for a great deal longer than it had been his father's. The guide did mention that the desk and chair were original, though.

From there, the group moved on to the domestic quarters, the kitchens and laundry. These had been reconstructed and filled with copper pans and other antique-looking artefacts. Wax vegetables and fruit were placed neatly on the table.

While the guide spoke about the day to day running of the house and what tasks the staff had engaged in, Gred stared at the table. It too was original. He tried to think of festival times, when the kitchens had been busy and fragrant with cooking, but all he could see in his mind's eye was a time of panic and fear. The attack on Galhea by the Teraghast tribe was fairly well-documented, and Gred had read all he could find on the subject. Now, he could only visualise the body of Ithiel har Varr laid out on this table, his throat cut. He'd been killed in the town when the Teraghasts had attacked it, all those centuries ago. Hara had brought him here, the house's defender. It had been a time when grim decisions had been made. Swift had been absent then, dealing with the aggressors further afield. Gred visualised Cobweb, Swift's hostling, alone and frightened, having to rally his hara round him in the face of limitless threat. This house had died for a while after those times, when the Teraghasts had sacked it, and the family had been forced to flee into temporary exile.

Some of the Parasilians had remained Varrs at heart, Gred had no doubt. He could not think of a figure like Ithiel, such a prime if quiet mover in the early days, Terzian's right-hand har, becoming Parasilian in anything but name. They could call their tribe something else to hide the past, but it had never left them, not really. Perhaps that was another reason why Marlet had built his new domain, on the other side of the town, far beyond the river, surrounded by trees. This hill could not be seen from there.

There were no roped-off areas in the kitchens and the tour group was free to walk through the rooms and touch things. Two hara brought refreshments on a tray – the traditional local sheh liqueur and hot tea for those who preferred it. Gred took a glass of sheh. He smelled it but didn't drink it. He wandered from room to room. Part of him wanted to weep, another part simply wanted to sneak off like a harling and explore the rest of the house on his own. The guide, no doubt, would notice.

Once the refreshments had been consumed, the tour continued. Now the group was taken upstairs to view the bedrooms. To Gred this seemed slightly voyeuristic. However, the reality of what he saw banished that feeling. The rooms looked twee, too tidy, and again furnished with items from other houses. Cobweb's chamber held no feeling of him, and neither did Terzian's. The group was shown the bedroom used by Swift before he came of age, and the quarters of Tyson and Azriel, other sons of the house. Strange how so many hara had lived in these rooms since those times, yet they were still referred to as belonging to their original occupants. Gred thought of later Parasilian harlings lying awake at night, besieged by history. It must have lived on here. It must have haunted the place. In many ways.

'The attics were only opened up and refurbished following the siege of Galhea,' the guide said, as he led the group towards the narrow staircase that led to the upper story. 'When the family returned to Galhea, they found the house had been badly damaged. Tiahaar Cobweb had parts of the attic converted into a studio, as he was something of an artist. He also commissioned a new apartment for himself up here.'

Is it going to be mentioned he made a chesna-bond with an Aralisian, Snake har Aralis, Pellaz's own brother in fact?

'Tiahaar Swift, who was by then Master of Galhea, took over the east wing on the first floor with his immediate family.'

No, didn't think so...

Gred felt cheated of the experience he'd wanted, but for that he'd have had to be alone. Two great Wraeththu dynasties had combined in this house. Battles of many kinds had been fought and won, or fought and lost. But the years had not nurtured the alliance of the two houses. Now they were only the most distant of relatives and there was an undeniable distaste of the Gelaming branch on this side of the ocean. It was reflected within the entire tribe, hence the guide's frostiness upon discovering Gred's origins. No mention was made of the Aralisians who had once called Forever home: most importantly Cal, then Snake and his son Moon, who had formed a chesna-bond with Tyson har Parasiel. To Gred, it felt as if these hara had been erased from the house's history, undoubtedly because of being Aralisian. In part, perhaps the Gelaming's reputation as relentless conquerors was deserved. But that had been only the start. If it hadn't been for that great alliance, perhaps the world would be a different place now, and not a better one. The guide had alluded many times to history being rewritten with a romantic slant, but it seemed clear that in Galhea it had been rewritten in more than one way.

The guide led the group back downstairs; the tour was over. He told everyhar about the restaurant in the converted stables, and where maps could be found for those who wished to explore the gardens.

But there was one final sight to be shown before the group left the house. This was a reception room off the entrance hall, somewhat unprepossessing and allegedly used rarely by the family at any time in its history. The guide said that Terzian and Swift might have met lesser dignitaries in this room or received messengers. But it was famous now for only one reason and that was because a portrait of Cobweb hung over the fireplace. Why it had been placed here, in this unloved corner, Gred couldn't guess. Perhaps once it had lived in another room.

The tour group expressed an audible gasp when they saw it, perhaps even those who'd seen it before.

'Yes, it is magnificent, and strangely bewitching,' said the guide. 'It was commissioned by Tiahaar Swift when his hostling was one hundred years old.'

The portrait was of a willowy har with pale luminous skin and abundant black hair, dressed in flowing garments of pale green. He was depicted sitting upon a stone wall in a dark and secluded corner of the gardens. He seemed to shine from the picture, his deep brown gaze at once melancholy and whimsical.

'Is it... embellished, do you think?' somehar asked. 'I mean, was he really that... arresting?'

'There are other pictures,' the guide replied. 'I think we can safely say that tiahaar Cobweb was indeed as beautiful as the legends say.'

Gred went to the restaurant and ate a late lunch of very good cold roast chicken and salad. He drank one large glass of the local sparkling wine, made from 'flowers of the field' as the menu said. He sat alone, his mind strangely empty. Outside, the sky had cleared a little and the wet stones of the courtyard beyond the window of the restaurant gleamed and sparkled in sunlight. Gred had picked up a map of the gardens. He was savouring the moment before he began the last part of his tour, this time thankfully without company.

First he visited the lake with its blanket of water lily pads and cuffs of yellow orris. A mass of huge orange and silver fish haunted the banks, expectant of food from the tourists. To Gred they looked like entrails, squirming and tangled as they were. He had nothing to throw to them. The sun was hot now, although dark clouds still roamed the distant sky. A shimmer of steam rose from the lawn as Gred walked barefoot across it, his sandals dangling from one hand. The umbrella was a nuisance, awkward and damp beneath an arm. He walked around the lake towards a folly of tumbled stones. Here, evergreens scented the air. Gred put his sandals back on. The stones were rough beneath his feet, sometimes sharp. He was surrounded by 'presence'; he could put no word to it other than that. If he concentrated hard enough, could he summon the past to him like moving pictures? He wanted to know everything about the hara who had lived here in the distant past, but most of the details were lost. He felt Wraeththu had a tendency to tidy away their history, embarrassed by their early heritage, tainted as it had been by the humanity that had lingered in the harish psyche.

He saw the summerhouse as shards of whiteness through the trees. No other tourists had come to this spot as yet, perhaps most still engrossed in leisurely meals at the restaurant. The summerhouse was round, its wood painted ivory. Within was a central pool with a fountain. Water spattered onto the stone bench that surrounded it. Gred sat down and closed his eyes, listening to the music of the water. His heart felt swollen with love. *I was born into the wrong time*, he thought. He yearned for the passions of the past. At thirty-five years old, very young by harish standards, he felt momentarily ancient, displaced in time. He sighed, opened his eyes, and found that somehar was sitting next to him. He physically jumped and uttered a smothered cry.

'Excuse me, I startled you,' said the har beside him. This har was dressed in clothes of dark green, perhaps an employee of the Trust, since his garb resembled their uniform. He had very long black hair, covering him like a shawl. He did not turn to face Gred, which seemed a little odd.

'It's fine,' Gred said. 'I was lost in my thoughts, didn't hear anyhar come in here.'

'It has always been a place for meditation – of one kind or another.' The har laughed softly.

'I've been on the tour,' Gred said. 'I was hoping for more history.'

Now the har turned to face him and Gred's chest contracted. For a moment, he could not draw breath. That face. Those eyes. 'You are... you are Parasilian?'

The har nodded. 'Yes. I expect the family resemblance is obvious.

As is yours, of course.'

'Er... mine?'

'Aralisian, yes?' Again the har laughed. He reached out and touched Gred's arm briefly. 'Don't worry. I won't tell a living soul.'

Gred risked a smile although he was feeling light-headed now, disorientated. 'That is probably for the best. Do you work here?'

'No, I just watch them.'

The har must be quite old, Gred decided. He had a translucent quality to him, which was often seen in older hara: the slow fading to spirit. But the resemblance to hara like Cobweb and Swift was shocking. Gred hadn't expected that. His mind was a maelstrom. He should use this moment to ask for information and stories, but his tongue was a stone in his mouth. He felt shaken in a peculiar way.

'I'm glad you came back,' said the har.

'I... this is the first time I've been here.'

'That's not what I meant. You should visit the family. I can tell you haven't.'

'They moved from here,' Gred said. He felt that was reason enough to explain why he hadn't visited them.

'Forever is a leaky old place,' said the har. 'Don't think too badly of Marlet. I try not to. Anyway, the Meglets probably look after the place far better than we ever did.'

'Meglets!' Gred laughed. His unease was fading. 'It's such a pity they've rammed the rooms full of things that don't belong here, though. I would have preferred emptiness to that.'

'Well, they have to earn enough funds to maintain the place. Most visitors want a theme park, not reality. Marlet and Ambel took most of the furniture with them to Murmur Heights. You'll see more to your taste there, I'm sure. And they *will* talk to you, if that's what you want.' The har touched Gred's arm briefly again. 'Perhaps it's time for old alliances to be rekindled.'

'I wonder why they ever faded. I sometimes think it might be because hara are embarrassed about the past, don't want to be reminded of it.'

'It's not just that,' said the har. 'Things happened over the years. Petty arguments. Differences of opinion. The Parasilians didn't want Immanion to have its fingers in the Megalithican pie. And by that time, all the original players were gone. Emotional attachments were gone.

But I do think Marlet would be open to patching things up a little. Times change.'

'Yes. Thank you.' Gred paused. 'Perhaps I could go to the Heights with *you*?' He wondered if that was too presumptuous.

The har studied him for a second. 'I stay here mostly,' he said. 'You don't need me to guide you. Just say I sent you.'

'Who... sent me?' Gred asked.

'They'll know.' The har stood up. 'It will rain soon. You'd better set off.' These words were clearly a dismissal.

Gred also got to his feet. 'I will. Thank you. It was... very interesting to meet you.'

The har inclined his head. 'Pleasure to meet you too.' He walked to the door and out into the green light.

Gred couldn't follow. He was rooted to the spot. Then the rain came and he was released. Outside, he opened his umbrella and fled back to the house.

Gred took a float car to Murmur Heights. He wasn't sure if this was really the right thing to do or what kind of welcome he might expect. But the strange har in the summer house had affected him deeply. He kept trying to dismiss the thought he'd met a ghost, but it nagged at him seductively.

There were guards at the gates to the Heights, to whom Gred presented his identification. The guards appraised him warily. Aralisians on Galhean soil again? They did not obstruct him unnecessarily, however. It seemed there was little fear in this land of hara who might wish the family ill.

The front door to the Heights was opened by a har in a green uniform of flowing garments, much like the uniform of the Trust employees and the har he'd met in the summerhouse. Rather stiffly, Gred told this har who he was and that he hoped that the family would not mind that he'd come to visit.

'Come in,' said the har. 'This is a surprise. I'll tell tiahaar Ambel at once. Tiahaar Marlet is not at home.' He gestured for Gred to come into the hall. It was indeed a beautiful house, full of light. 'Allow me to take your coat and umbrella.'

Gred shrugged off his coat and handed the items over.

'Thank you. Please sit here. I won't keep you waiting long.'

Gred sat down on the chair indicated to him. He felt slightly breathless.

Presently, a tall mature har, with a plait of chestnut hair hanging heavily over one shoulder, and an open, good-natured face, came into the hall. He was dressed in loose tunic and trousers of a colour to match his hair. 'Hello. I'm Ambel har Parasiel. I believe you are a relative, if somewhat distant!'

Gred stood up, bowed his head. 'Yes, tiahaar. Thank you for receiving me. I am Gred har Aralis.'

The har waved an arm at Gred. 'Hush. No need for formalities. What brings you to our home?'

He gestured for Gred to follow him, and Gred noticed how similar this house was in layout to Forever. They would turn left and presently come to the family sitting room, and they did.

'I've always been interested in the history of our two families,' Gred explained. 'And then I had the time for a protracted holiday and thought I'd come over here. I went to Forever today.'

'Fascinating place, isn't it?' Ambel said. He indicated Gred should sit down on one of the sagging old sofas, which embraced him like loving arms. 'I've ordered tea for us. It won't be long.'

'Forever is a wonderful house,' Gred said. 'But then, so is this one.'

Ambel looked around him. 'Yes... In some ways we were sad to leave Forever, but it is a... *heavy* place. We both thought it was better for the younger generations to have a new home, somewhere lighter and not so damn haunted.' He laughed.

'Really haunted?'

'But of course. What can you expect? It was never *our* house, Gred. Not really. It belonged, and still belongs, to the hara who created our tribe and who shaped early Wraeththu. It's right that the house is now for everyhar. It's their history.'

'I felt there wasn't enough of it there.'

'Well, there's so *much* of it, and the Trust don't like to dwell on the melodrama, as they see it. We have plenty of old pieces here that we brought from the house, if you want to see them. Marlet will be back soon. He can show you his collections. But I warn you; it can be boring after a couple of hours!'

'Thanks. I'd like that, and I *won't* be bored.'

'You must stay here, of course. Have you booked into a hotel in town?'

'Not yet, no. That's kind of you.'

'Kind?' Again Ambel laughed. 'Don't be ridiculous! We'll want the gossip from Immanion too. There is a lot to talk about.' He paused. 'Marlet was only recently thinking of contacting Sahaan, you know. We wondered if overtures would be welcome.'

Gred grimaced. 'If you contact anyhar, make it Tulsel. Sahaan is not the most affable of hara. Tulsel is. He's my high-father.'

'Well now we've contacted you, so we're halfway there,' Ambel said. 'What a fortunate coincidence!'

'Somehar... somehar told me to come here. He told me to say he'd sent me. One of your relatives. I met him at Forever.'

Ambel frowned slightly. 'Oh, who was that? I can't think of anyhar who'd be over there today.'

'He didn't give me his name, but he was an older har. He looked very Parasilian, if you know what I mean. It sounds mad, but I did wonder if he was a ghost, to be honest.'

Ambel drew in his breath, rolled his eyes. 'I see. Why am I not surprised?' He shook his head. 'He's a stubborn old beast. He won't leave, you know. His rooms here are barely touched.'

'You mean it's somehar who still lives at Forever? The tour guide said all the family had left.'

Ambel paused a moment. 'Technically, we did. The har you met is not a ghost, but he might as well be. It was Cobweb.'

Gred couldn't speak for a moment, and yet he had known all along really. 'That's impossible. Surely?'

'He won't leave this world, Gred. He should, but he won't. Don't ask me why. Everyhar else has gone to wherever they go. He's not like us. He's not wholly *here*. He doesn't really have to 'live' anywhere.'

'But nohar lives that long. Do they?'

Ambel shrugged. 'As I said, he's not quite *with* us. It's not something we talk about with outsiders. As far as everyhar else is concerned, Cobweb faded nearly a century ago. He keeps himself to himself most of the time. But he would have seen Pellaz in you, no doubt, so decided to communicate.'

'Does the Trust know he's still... *haunting* the place?'

'Not officially, no. Marlet has told him he shouldn't hang around there during the tourist season, but I suspect that the Trust secretly likes the idea of ghosts. The visitors would no doubt relish it. I expect Cobweb does manifest from time to time when the mischief takes him.'

'Does he ever come here?'

'Sometimes, usually just to make me jump. I'll be in the house or the gardens then suddenly he's there beside me, criticising whatever I'm doing, or complaining about the Trust, or demanding I make him a meal. He doesn't have to eat much, but occasionally enjoys the experience of good food. I sometimes think he's still around because he's just too stubborn and awkward to move on. He's not sad, though, and that's the important thing. If he's happy, he can do as he likes, in my opinion.'

'This is hard to take in,' Gred said.

'Understandable,' Ambel said airily. 'We're just used to him. I realise it must be rather a shock. Which is no doubt what Cobweb intended. I'd be grateful if you didn't talk about this too much. We don't want to attract attention to Cobweb. He's persistent but in some ways fragile.'

'Of course. I'll be discreet.' Gred smiled. 'I'd give anything to be able to talk to him properly, though.'

'Who knows? He might comply. He might not. I can't predict. Ah, here is Zaya with our tea. You've met our housekeeper, of course.'

The har who'd let Gred into the house had appeared with a tray.

'Do join us, Zaya,' Ambel said. 'Gred has had a Cobweb experience over at Forever.'

Zaya pulled a humorous face. 'Oh dear. Nothing too alarming, I hope.'

'Not at all,' Gred replied. 'I want to say... without sounding too sentimental... that I'm really glad I've been welcomed here. I wasn't sure what to expect.'

'I suspect this wariness has maintained the distance between our kin long after any stupid arguments in the past were long forgotten,' Ambel said. 'I'm also glad you came, or that Cobweb interfered enough to send you to us.'

When Marlet came home, he was not alone, and suddenly the Heights was filled with noise. Hara and dogs spilled into the room where Gred still sat with Ambel. Introductions were made; a list of names and a sea of faces Gred could not remember. Hounds jumped up at him, eager to lick his face. He felt slightly overwhelmed, but he'd never been good with crowds. Marlet was something of a throwback to the Terzian strain, as he lacked the fey dark appearance of Cobweb's type, being fair of hair, tanned of skin; a har of the outdoors. While he was ostensibly ruler of Galhea, the post was mainly ceremonial; day to day government of the Megalithican tribes was the domain of the Hundred Fires, the name for the ruling council of the country. Marlet was a land custodian, more at home in the fields than in any chamber of government. That was clear.

Marlet was more restrained than Ambel had been in his greeting of Gred. He wasn't hostile, or even impolite, but the reticence was plain to see. Gred didn't feel he should make too much effort to break that down. This might appear artificial. Marlet must take him as he was.

'Is it your duty as envoy of Immanion to meet with us?' Marlet asked.

'No,' Gred replied. 'Nohar knows I'm here. I didn't want to be burdened with any diplomatic tasks. I just wanted to be here in Galhea, see for myself.'

'You are discontent,' Marlet decided. 'You seek solace in the past.'

Gred uttered a wordless protest, but Marlet held up a hand.

'No matter. You're welcome here. I hope you find what you're looking for.'

Dinner was a raucous affair, with multiple family members and their harlings and pets stuffed into the dining-room. The food was excellent but the din soon made Gred's head ache. Everyhar had to shout to make himself heard, cats jumped on the table, and were only occasionally brushed off it when they became too unashamed about stealing food, harlings squabbled and eventually ended up running around the room, yelling at one another. To Gred, it was like a madhouse. His own family were restrained and courteous. Harlings sat quietly at the occasional big family gathering. Animals would not be allowed in the room. Now, Gred faced a barrage of questions from the Parasilians, some of them quite presumptuous, who apparently found the Aralisians pompous and easy to mock. His own questions, the ones he ached to ask, lodged in his throat. He couldn't bring himself to ask them.

Eventually, Gred pleaded exhaustion and asked permission to retire. It occurred to him that the Parasilians were in actual fact very like how he'd imagined their ancestors to be; informal and numerous. He recalled the fantasies he'd had earlier in the dining-room at Forever. Reality was something different.

Ambel escorted Gred to the room that had been made ready for him. 'I can see the family have tired you out,' he said. 'They mean well, but they are rather draining, I know.'

Gred smiled. 'A little, although I envy you as well. I have nothing like that. I live alone mostly, keep away from the family. They are not as intimate with one another as yours are.'

Ambel eyed him speculatively. 'Don't feel you have to join in with all family gatherings while you're here. You're free to come and go as you please. Zaya will see to your meals if you prefer to be alone. Just let him know.'

'Then I would be a poor guest. Forgive me, I'm simply not used to this kind of life.'

Ambel put a hand on his arm. 'Sleep well and sleep long. I usually take my breakfast late, in the orchid house. You are welcome to join me there. Around 10. Just ask a member of staff where to find me.'

Gred inclined his head. 'Thank you.' He opened to door to his room, was about to step inside.

'This room...' Ambel said, rather suddenly.

Gred paused. 'Yes?'

'As you'll no doubt have noticed, the Heights was constructed to the same design as Forever. You will be sleeping in Cobweb's room, the one he originally had. Well... its copy.'

Gred nodded. 'Thanks... Perhaps I can dream more here than if I stayed in that travesty of a room back at Forever.'

'Indeed you might,' Ambel said. 'Goodnight, harakin.'

Alone inside the room, Gred sighed and leaned back against the door. A lamp glowed dimly on a table beside the low bed, which was spread with a beautiful embroidered coverlet of dark green and cream that depicted a tangle of birds and trees. An oil burner on a chest beneath the window released a gentle scent of jasmine. Fresh fruit had been left for him in a green glass bowl, along with cordials and a pitcher of water. Gred mixed himself a drink from an essence of 'flowers of the field', most likely the same that were used to make the wine he'd drunk earlier. He gazed out of the window at the gardens. A wind had come up, making the trees dance. Everything was utterly dark close to; in the distance were the dim lights of the town like snakes of fire.

His drink consumed, Gred took off his sandals and went to lie on the bed fully-clothed. He knew Ambel had put him in this room for a specific reason.

How do you tell when a ghost enters your space? Does the air go cold, condense, and an unreasonable feeling of terror shingle the skin? Or is it more subtle than that, a simple awareness you are not alone, and that the presence with you is 'other'?

After maybe twenty minutes of staring at the wall, thinking of not much at all – perhaps in readiness his mind was clear – Gred saw a shadow by the door, which resolved itself into a shape that walked towards him. He sat upright on the bed, hands braced against the coverlet. Was he afraid now? He didn't know.

'They will have told you, of course,' Cobweb said. 'May I sit down?' He didn't wait for a reply but seated himself graciously at the end of the bed. He seemed to waver like a mist, more like a ghost now that Gred was sure he was not.

Cobweb folded his arms and regarded the speechless Gred. 'Such a sad soul,' he said. 'What are you searching for here?'

'Meaning,' Gred replied awkwardly.

'Ah, I can't give you that. Life is such a strange, cruel thing, isn't it? I look back on mine and it's as if it happened to another har, or was a book I read. I don't know when things changed and I found myself in the other half of life. I can't remember it happening. When I was in the first one, I thought nothing would ever change, and then I would die, but it's not like that. The life of youth is another world to the one I live in now. It dies but you are not dead, you're just this older har and the past has gone, along with many of the hara you loved, even though they might still live. You wake up one day and realise most things you took for granted have disappeared or been done with. You are somehar else. But you can remember so well...' He sighed, then smiled with great warmth. 'I should not be here to heap you with melancholia. In truth, I feel no grief, only an astounded wistfulness. But that is not how you feel, is it?'

I have been given a chance, Gred thought, *so rare and brief; I must make the most of it. Every second will count.* 'No... I feel... lost.' He shook his head. Couldn't he put it better than that? Words eluded him.

251

Cobweb waited patiently. Gred felt the har trusted the words would come. And so they did. 'When I look at the world, in Immanion, everything seems so... *bleached*. It doesn't feel real to me. I don't think any other har feels the way I do. We live in a prosperous country, we have peace, we have art, we have exploration, we have learning. If there is darkness in the world, it is far from our door.'

'That is what we worked for all those generations ago,' Cobweb said softly. 'It didn't come easily, I assure you. There were dark ages.'

'I know and that is why I yearn for those days, those hara,' Gred said. 'In peace have we become somehow less? Is it only conflict that drives a har to passion and greatness?'

'Perhaps so,' Cobweb said, 'but perhaps also you are an anachronism. All those hara in Immanion – and indeed around us here now – are content in the world that was made for them. They do the things they were supposed to do – the pioneering frontier is within. Or they explore the Otherlanes and beyond, seeking the mysteries of the multiverse. That's not so bad a life, free from war.'

'No, most hara would say it is the perfect life.'

Cobweb reached out and squeezed one of Gred's feet. 'But not for you, poor harling. I would be a liar if I said those early days weren't cauldrons of great passion, daring and courage, even though we lived in blood and terror many times. Love was an anvil on which our hearts were forged. All that was human within us was a bonfire, raging always. And that is perhaps what is lost to me now.' He frowned. 'What a quandary. I wonder why I'm still here, but there is no call for me to the ancient graveyard and beyond. Even though my loved ones wait for me there, and will wait for me forever, this world is still my home. I would not say I am here by choice, but then I have no great yearning to leave it either. And it is your home also, Gred har Aralis. So what is to be done with you?'

Gred laughed weakly. 'I would not presume for you to sort *that* quandary out!'

Cobweb pursed his lips, thought for a moment. 'The hara who are not already in bed will still be sitting round the dining table. It won't be hard for us to sneak out unseen. Well... for *you* to do so. I go where I please, seen or not. I'll clear a space for us. Come.' He stood up.

'Where?'

'Where do you think? Silly harling. We'll go to the house.'

Cobweb took Gred to the stable yard, again a copy of Forever's. True to his word he had 'cleared a space' for they ran into no family or members of staff. 'This is so typical of us now,' Cobweb said, as he led the way. 'These float car things stabled alongside our horses. We still use horses, although some hara with the gift can fold through an Otherlane in the blink of an eye. I regard these inconsistencies with affection.'

'Car or horse?' Gred asked. 'Or will you fold us there?'

'I was never a great lanes traveller,' Cobweb replied, 'despite being the grateful recipient of many other gifts. I *think* myself to where I want to go most of the time, but could never take anyhar with me. And I do appreciate speed and comfort. We'll take a car tonight.'

It seemed incongruous to Gred, if not utterly bizarre, for Cobweb, this being of myth, to take the driving seat and competently pilot one of the Parasilians' sleek grey float cars out into the night. He steered it above the trees, where the stars were watchful sparks. He left the lamps unlit and the roof open, so they wafted through the darkness as if on a magical carpet.

'This seems absurd to me,' Gred said. 'I would never have imagined you driving a float car.'

'Whyever not? The energy that vitalises them is the pure source, made from hara themselves. That to me is magic. Also, a car is less likely to have a funny turn and throw you into a ditch. Ah, here we are.'

Cobweb landed the car softly on one of the lawns at the back of Forever. There appeared to be no security at the house. There were no lights to be seen.

'They just lock up at night and leave this place unguarded?' Gred asked.

Cobweb chuckled. 'Galhea, for all its pretensions to grandeur, is still a country village at heart. Everything is safe here.' He sighed, gazed up at the house, which glowed pale in the starlight. 'I am still deeply in love with the old place. Perhaps it is the house more than anything that tethers me to this world.'

Gred ducked a formal bow. 'Then, tiahaar, it would please me greatly if you would conduct a tour of the house – this time a proper one.'

Cobweb inclined his head. 'Of course.' He offered his elbow for

Gred to link with. 'Come.'

They entered the house through a window-door that led into the old family sitting-room. It was ostensibly locked but the mechanism was so old a gentle shove made it give way. Now Gred was on the other side of the ropes that earlier had fenced the room from him. It made him feel spectral, somehow.

Cobweb lit a candle, and Shadetide shadows danced across the walls.

'I don't know how you can bear it,' Gred blurted, 'coming here now, it not being your home.'

'I had to get used to many things or go entirely mad,' Cobweb replied. 'The time for tears is done. At least I have the choice over which memories to revisit, and I choose to remember all that is good. Forever deserves no less.'

'Are there ghosts here other than you?'

Cobweb laughed. 'Me, a ghost? Ha!' He patted Gred's shoulder. 'Well, there are quite a few. They are simply memories, the house dreaming, or thinking aloud, as it were. There are no chained souls here, Gred, only thoughts.'

'You must miss everyhar, though. It seems cruel you are left alone.'

Cobweb said nothing. He was prowling round the room, examining the appointments and ornaments, few of which could have once belonged to him.

'I mean,' Gred continued awkwardly, 'I know you have family – lots of it – but it can't be the same, surely? I don't wish to pry but...'

'These are the things that eat at you, I know,' Cobweb said. 'You want more than ghosts, don't you? You want to be able to slip through a chink of time and find yourself back here, hundreds of years ago.'

'Yes. If I am honest, yes.' Gred paused. 'If you are honest, isn't that what you would want too?'

Cobweb considered. 'My hara call to me,' he said. 'Quite often. Snake, Swift, Tyson, all of them. But it is as if I say back to them, "wait a minute, I'm not quite done". I don't feel any urgency to join them because they are always there, and at the same time, always with me. Time means nothing in the realm they call home now. Perhaps they are sitting waiting for me to join them for dinner, and then, when I do join them they'll have waited only five minutes, even though centuries have passed in this world. I'm not alone, Gred. I don't feel that way. All I lack is physical closeness, and after all this time that is not something I crave or need in order to survive. Not in this world at least.' He smiled wistfully, perhaps thinking of his chesnari who waited for him somewhere "other". 'But would I go back?' He was silent for a moment. 'No. Because now I can relive all that is good, and there was much that was bad. There are certain things I would never want to live through again, nor would I want those I love to relive them.'

Gred frowned, nodded. 'Yes, I can understand that.'

'You would not enjoy them either,' Cobweb said. 'Early Wraeththu were savage, Gred. You would be shocked, terrified even. When Cal, your ancestor, lived here, he was ravaged, ruined – in his mind. He came back to us, some time after his first visit with Pell, believing that Pell was dead. He had killed the har he thought partly responsible on the way to us, in the most gruesome way imaginable. He murdered one of the greatest hienamas our kind has ever known, the har who was one of the first of all incepted Wraeththu.'

Cobweb stared at Gred, who felt his shock must show plainly on his face.

Then Cobweb nodded, as if satisfied by what he saw. 'Cal was a husk for a long time and suffered greatly to overcome all that he was. Many early hara were tormented like that. They had seen, and lived through, so much that was terrible, unspeakable. And the ruin wasn't always confined to the mind or spirit. When I first met Snake he was horribly disfigured, one half of his body crippled.'

Now Cobweb paused, perhaps reflecting on that time, and Gred found he was able to speak, somewhat inadequately, he felt. 'I'm sorry... I didn't know. It was wrong of me to assume...'

Cobweb shook his head. 'Some things you will not have been told or read. To you, I expect Pellaz's famous consort Calanthe is remembered only as a wise and mighty ruler.'

Gred grimaced. 'Not entirely, although obviously there is a lot I don't know.'

'Much,' Cobweb agreed. 'This room...' He turned in a slow circle, hands on hips. 'Here I loved. Here I saw harlings grow. Here I spent priceless moments with friends and those I loved. It is a good room. Here I remember Snake, whole again, cured by what we found in the deepest mysteries of aruna together. That is a beautiful memory. But if we were to go Terzian's office, you would feel death sentences hanging over you. If I showed it to you as it really was, you would smell blood... carrion... You might even see it, some of it.'

'Did you... did you love Terzian?' Gred asked.

Cobweb appeared to pull himself in, become somewhat more reserved. 'Of course. He was a great and powerful har. Whether I would have loved him if he'd been only a farmer or something is another matter. I am not blind to realities. I was drawn to powerful hara, as many are.'

'But you were one of them too.'

'Not initially. Those around me contributed greatly to who I became, not least your ancestor, Pellaz. We were alike in some ways. He too came from humble beginnings, but it was right he became all he was. Anything else would have been a waste.'

'I never met him,' Gred said, somewhat bitterly.

'Yes, well, he was impatient to get away,' Cobweb said. 'This world and the hara in it often annoyed him, and it got worse over time. This world *does* age you, Gred. It makes your physical being grow thin; it's just part of what this realm is, even if you're a har who can live for centuries, perhaps even millennia. But what's inside us never fades or grows feeble. Some choose to fade away over time until they are blown like gauze into another life. Pellaz wouldn't wait for that. He wanted somewhere else, so off into the Otherlanes he went. Others close to him chose to join him at the time. They were done here, so they sought a new world. Perhaps that was his way of "going back", only it was starting anew.'

'I was never told that,' Gred said. 'They never tell us that. They say that Pellaz and his kin faded. They went to a mountain and were taken to what is beyond.'

Cobweb snorted derisively. 'How biblical! I suppose they don't really know what happened or it's what they want to believe. Perhaps Pellaz did go to a mountain to open a gate. I can't remember. All I'll say is this: if he was standing here now, he'd call you insane for the things you desire. He'd say, "get out of this realm, young har. If it bores you, there are limitless exciting places to discover".'

'Is that it? I'm just bored of my life?'

Cobweb shrugged. 'Only you can answer that. I'm not sure if you're capable of withstanding true danger and excitement, but if you are, the

Otherlanes and its realms are where they lie. But if you go there, and I mean truly go deep and explore, you might not be able to return. And then you might regret your decision, lost in an alien environment where you would never feel at home. Pellaz had outgrown his home; it was different for him. You are young, full of fancies and desires and yearnings. You have a lot of living yet to do in this world.'

'Perhaps... perhaps I should look for Pellaz,' Gred suggested.

'Not yet,' Cobweb answered shortly. 'If a harling leaves the nursery before it's ready, reality will rapidly cause its demise.'

'I don't feel that young,' Gred said. 'In fact, quite the opposite. I suppose every har is young in comparison to you, though. I understand your impatience with us.'

'It's not impatience,' Cobweb said. 'Anyway, did we come here to have this conversation or to explore?'

'Both, I think.'

'Then let's explore now.'

Cobweb led Gred through every room in the house. The stories he told were not of conflict, courageous deeds, terror or destruction. He spoke of small amusing things, such as silly words Swift had spoken as a harling, various awkward romantic affairs that had taken place, arguments that had ended in humiliation or farce. They had come to one of the bathrooms on the second floor. 'Tyson was terrible as a young har,' Cobweb said. 'He would push the harish system to its limit. I remember once a distinguished Gelaming visitor found him unconscious on this bathroom floor with his trousers round his ankles. It took some time for the har to push open the door since Tyson was lying behind it. Tyson's excuse was that he'd been meditating and had gone on some strange travel vision. In reality, he was just blind drunk and had fallen off the toilet.'

Gred laughed. 'You're not doing a very good job of persuading me the past is not a good place to visit. I wish I'd known all those hara.'

'They're just stories,' Cobweb said. 'Make your own.'

'In Immanion?' Gred asked incredulously.

'Even in Immanion there must be hara you'd want to know. It's just finding them.'

'With my face, that's difficult. I carry the baggage of the Aralisian dynasty. Few hara beyond Phaonica's Mount are at ease with me.'

'Then go somewhere else. Be somehar else. The world isn't exactly small.' Cobweb sighed. 'You've only looked at a very small part of it, haven't you?' He shook his head. 'By all the dehara, this takes me back! I might as well be lecturing Pellaz again when he was having one of his *episodes*.'

'Perhaps that was why I was drawn here.'

'I'm beginning to think that was likely,' Cobweb said dryly.

They had come to the threshold of Terzian's bedroom. Cobweb had left it until last. Even all the rooms on higher stories of the house had been explored first. 'So much drama lingers in here,' Cobweb said. 'Really, most of it is embarrassing now. We were so self-obsessed.'

'Tell me a drama.'

Cobweb rubbed a hand over his face. 'Oh, I'd rather not. Not one of my personal ones, at least. But Terzian died here, in that bed. It's the original.'

Gred approached it.

'Lie on it,' Cobweb said. 'Pearls were delivered there, a har died, many loved.'

Gred laughed shakily. 'Now history frightens me a little.'

'You see? You know your skin will crawl if you lie on that bed. My skin crawls in this room too. It's one of the bad places. Swift tried to live in it for a while. He soon saw sense.'

There was a silence. Then Gred said, 'Thank you for all this, Cobweb. I really appreciate it.'

'My pleasure. I sometimes like to indulge myself and tell the old stories. The family have heard them a hundred times, so are a poor audience nowadays. There are a couple of the harlings I quite like. They seek me out all the time, and now and again I'll let them find me. It doesn't pay to lose my mystery and be too available. They love it, anyway.'

'I wish I was one of those harlings.'

Cobweb stepped forward and embraced Gred. 'But my dear thing, you are!'

The tour was over. Cobweb and Gred went back to the sitting-room, where Cobweb extinguished the candle, now burned to a stub (a ghostly story for tomorrow's visitors?), and they went outside. Cobweb pressed the window door shut and the tired old mechanism clicked back into place.

'I will never forget this night,' Gred said.

Cobweb took hold of Gred's arm again. 'But it's not over,' he said. 'How about we return to the Heights and assault Marlet's collection of rare sheh vintages? I have many more stories to tell and now, quite frankly, they are bursting to be let out.'

'I'd like nothing better,' Gred said.

They talked until morning, when the staff began to appear in the kitchen to prepare breakfast. Cobweb and Gred were still seated at the kitchen table, with two empty bottles of sheh before them. Gred felt happily, woozily drunk. But not tired. The staff did not seem surprised to see Cobweb there but had perhaps been trained by Ambel not to register surprise in such circumstances. This was still Cobweb's home, if only his "other" home. A har discreetly made coffee and placed it before them.

'You should sleep,' Cobweb said.

'But then you'll be gone, and it will be over,' Gred replied.

'Never that,' Cobweb said. 'Have your adventures, Gred. Find hara you like. Fall in love. Take aruna with a har who makes you feel as if the act was created solely for you and him. Go into wildernesses. Find mysteries. Then come here to tell me of them.'

'You'll let me find you?'

'You'll have to wait and see, won't you?'

Gred slept for three hours and then sought out Ambel in the orchid house. Beyond the arched windows, the day was clear.

'I heard you had a sleepless night,' Ambel said, indicating Gred should take a seat beside him at the wrought iron table. 'It isn't often the staff come across Cobweb in the house.'

'You knew he would come to me,' Gred said.

Ambel shrugged. 'Strongly suspected. He *is* difficult to predict. But I can see that in some ways he has inspired you. You feel a lot lighter to me today.'

Gred nodded, grinned. 'It was an unforgettable experience.'

'And did he help you choose a path?'

'I think it was more like he told me to make my own map. I'll have to think about it.'

'Cobweb once told me that he and Pellaz would argue fiercely sometimes. Pellaz didn't always like the advice Cobweb gave him. But invariably, he took it.' Ambel handed Gred a glass of tea. 'Well, enough of the past. I hope you will stay here for a while with us, and then when you return to Immanion we can initiate greater contact between our families. That, I personally believe, is one of the paths to go on your map.'

Gred paused. 'I think…' he said eventually, 'that the hara in my country have changed far more than those I've found here. I don't mean it to sound rude, but in some ways being here *is* like stepping back in time. You might be disappointed by my harakin. They seem to me to be dour and dull in comparison.'

Ambel laughed delightedly. 'Perhaps they need some shaking up! Pellaz and his kin were never dour or dull, I *do* know that.' He reached out to take one of Gred's hands. 'And also, young har, bear in mind that the hara of Phaonica's Mount are not the entire population of Almagabra. I think you've been locked in your rooms for too long! Never mind braving the daylight enough to come here. Perhaps there are places for you to explore closer to home.'

Gred pressed Ambel's fingers, held onto his hand; an intimate gesture he could not remember doing even with his own hostling. 'Cobweb said the same.'

'You see?' Ambel released Gred's hand. 'Now, breakfast. Then you can delve into Marlet's collections. I'm afraid it's been mentioned we should have a dinner gathering while you are here, so hara from Galhea can meet you. Is that acceptable?'

'Yes, it's the first step, I suppose.'

'Good. You never know what might come of it.'

As Ambel set about preparing a plate of food for Gred from the various dishes available, Gred stared out of the window at the sky. Overnight, his life had changed completely. It was like shedding a skin or perhaps even emerging from a pearl. He felt, for perhaps the first time in his life, a sense of excitement, as if events and experiences – and hara – were gathering unseen amid clouds around him. They were not dark clouds, merely a shifting mist that concealed what was to come. He would walk into that gladly.

When the Angels Came

Hopefully, most of you reading this collection will be familiar with some of my work, and might even know that my novel, 'Burying the Shadow', is my reinvention of the vampire myth, influenced strongly by legends, from all over the world, of fallen angels.

The following fragments were written while I was researching 'Burying the Shadow', and were inspired by the stories of fallen angels gleaned from Enochian mythology (from the ancient text 'The Book of Enoch'), Milton's 'Paradise Lost' and ancient Sumerian legends. I had a vague idea that one day I might turn the short accounts into a novella, but once I got into the flow of writing Shadow, these fragments became a forgotten file on my PC, and were only rediscovered some years ago as I was browsing through my story notes.

A version of these fragments appeared in a chapbook to accompany my Guest of Honour appearance at the Birmingham SF convention, Novacon, in 1992.

I've always been fascinated by the idea of superior beings arriving – or appearing – among human communities in ancient times to impart knowledge; a possible real event that inspired the legends of angels, gods and all manner of other semi-divine beings. The Sumerian legends, as extravagantly and somewhat over-enthusiastically interpreted by Zecharia Sitchin in his book, 'The Twelfth Planet', held a particular interest for me as I was researching. Although the book suffers dramatically from Von Danikenism, (Sitchin's ideas require a certain suspension of disbelief concerning alien visitors), he explores many of the ancient legends in depth, describing the apparently all too human in-fighting, scandals and power struggles of the gods, as they sought to colonise a new world. As a book on mythology, rather than a possible para-history, 'The Twelfth Planet' was a great inspiration. As in the Judaeo-Christian legends, used by Milton for 'Paradise Lost', there were elements among the divine community that resented the authority of their superiors and sought to seize power of their own. While bemused human beings evolved from mere beasts of burden into intelligent creatures in their own right, the gods stampeded back and forth around them across the land, (in space rockets, Sitchin would have us believe!), quarrelling and destroying each other as their temperaments and rather hysterical politics saw fit.

In Enochian mythology, I found the rebels appeared to have a more altruistic motive for their rebellion; they desired to give humankind knowledge that the gods, (or God), kept jealously for themselves. The angelic teachers imparted to humanity information about magic, science and medicine. Their punishment for this crime was eternal damnation and torture. The Enochian angels were forced to watch all the children they had created with mortal women die.

The fragments that follow are first person narratives that describe what happens 'when *the angels came'. I suppose they could be part of a prequel to 'Burying the Shadow'. The fragments are raw, unpolished, but I resisted the urge to work on them further. As they stand, they capture (for me) the voices of the characters as they relate the events, the actual moment of narration.*

On the Marsh

These people, where did they come from? I heard talk they fell out of a low pass cloud, the kind with the bloody-brown fringes. Possible? Maybe. All I know is they strange as people can be. How do I know that? Well, you see this? Yes, you can touch it… One of them gave it to me. What is it? You tell me. Feels weird, doesn't it? Yes, it does get warm. What? Oh, they call it a show-stone. I want it to show me things, but I don't know how. It's too late now…

No, don't go. You talk to me. You talk to me, because I was the first to see. You want to know, don't you?

I was out in the marsh, digging up mud lizards, when it happened. It was a misty day, shapes all around, but not spirits singing. I headed out early because Ma wanted the lizards quick. We ate the tails, but the rest went to the barter ground, out on the flat fields where the old trees are. I was poking around with my spike, waiting for the squish and squeak, which meant I'd spiked a lizard, when my gut started to tell me something. I remember standing up, and noticing how quiet it had got. Nothing marshy moved at all. It was like everything was holding its breath; critters, water, mud and air. I got a feeling I was being belly-stalked by something bad, and all I had was a lizard spike. Some protection! I hunkered down in the tussocks and kept my lizard spike ready, thinking that maybe I was going to die. Weird things can happen on the marsh, but we don't talk about them much.

Then I saw a darkness in the mist. It looked like a man. *Was* a man, to my eyes. 'Stranger,' I said, standing up. We did not fear other men in those times. He did not say anything, and I was wondering whether he was lost. Very tall. I couldn't see much because of the mist, but I knew he was watching me. 'You looking for something?' I said. He didn't move. I was starting to feel uneasy. Maybe he was sick, so I began to leap the tussocks to get to him. That's when he disappeared. I swear it. Just vanished. So weird. I went home pretty quick after that.

The First Witch

She had terrible green eyes, you know; terrible. Her hair was the colour of wet blood, arterial blood, from somewhere deep anyhow, and she wore those clothes that were like moss. We were scared of her, but interested. Know what I mean? She'd lived alone all her life up on the Cloudy Steeps, for as long as anyone can remember. When we heard the spirits singing to turn the world golden, she just spat at the grass and called it mud. On misty days, if you squinted up the Steeps, it seemed that tall figures were standing motionless around her shack. Later, we found out that the strangers had gone to talk with her – long before they talked to anyone else around here, but then she was strange herself, like she knew something we didn't, so perhaps she was just 'the one' for them.

Me and the other kids used to go up to her shack once in a while. She'd shout insults at us through the door rags, and then bring out a jug of that thick ale she brewed and a pipe of skerry moss to pass the time. She'd sit on a big round boulder outside her door, sit like a boy with her knees up, with her fierce hair, the pipe in her mouth.

'You killed anything yet, sonny?' she'd say and then flash her eyes like it was a joke.

I was aching for the day when I could say yes to that question, but some part of me knew it would never come.

Her hands were amazing, the fingers just a little too long and always seamed with moss juice. These hands, they would just hang there between her knees as she talked and sometimes the fingers would twitch as if they were waiting for something to grab at. Our kin never used to talk about us going up there – the girls never came – but we guessed the women were afraid of her. That is, they were afraid until they *had* to go visit her and then it was time to muffle up in a cloak, bend into the mist, and just melt away from the village. No, the women never talk about her, not even now.

The Late Caller

My story is this. There was a wind outside, like a beast howling. It was night-time, very cold. Fire burning in the cottage, the smell of burning peat and oatcakes. I was burning my legs, so close to the fire. My back was chilled. I was listening to the sounds outside, sounds like furious hands pulling at the planks across the windows. I could hear my mother and my aunt chewing in their sleep on the platform at the back of the cottage. My place was always next to the fire. I had a pallet there. I never slept on the hair-filled couch, because things lived in the stuffing that made me itch. I didn't want to move, burning up my legs so close to the fire.

It was unusual for someone to come a-knocking so late, but not totally unlikely. My aunt waves hands over the dying, so she was sometimes needed at odd hours. I hoped whoever it was would just go away, and didn't get up at first, but they kept on knocking, so I knew it had to be serious.

The wind came in like a hungry dog and I said, 'Don't just stand there!'

Then he came in.

I didn't know him, never seen him before. He was so tall I thought he had to be foreign, or something. I wondered what he wanted. Had he come for my aunt? He had a long black cloak on, and a wide-brimmed hat, both of which looked wet through, although I couldn't see him too well. He walked past me to the fire, and put one hand on the hot bricks of the wall.

'What do you want?' I asked him. We didn't get too many foreigners coming to us, and when they did, it was generally to the barter grounds.

'Shelter,' he answered. Just that. His voice sounded strange, but the request did not. It was a wild night outside.

'We've not much room. No beds.'

He turned and looked at me, taking off his hat, smiling. 'Doesn't matter.' When his hat came off, all this hair tumbled down around his face. A stranger's face; none like it around here, highly boned and pale. His hair was the colour of veins in salty rock, dark, but like sunlight was trapped there.

'Who are you? Why are you here?' I wondered whether he had knocked upon other door and been sent away, although that was unlikely.

'My name is Gadreel,' he said. 'As to why I'm here...' He shrugged and looked around the cottage. I suppose he was wondering about the answer to that himself.

'You've come to trade?'

He looked at me keenly, just for a moment too long, and then said,

'Yes. Trade. Something like that.' He took off his cloak and underneath it he was dressed in grey. The cloth too was wet. Only his hair was dry.

'A storm outside?' I asked him.

He glanced at the shuttered windows. 'Yes.' The question had been pointless, of course.

I went and dragged my blanket out from under the couch. 'You can use this,' I said. 'Put your clothes by the fire.'

As he undressed himself, I went into the cold room to fetch some milk. I would heat it in a pan for him. When I went back into the room, he was sitting in my mother's chair beside the hearth, the blanket wrapped round his waist. His body was thin, but so long, if you can understand that. I had never seen anyone so tall. It looked very odd. The room was small around him.

'Are you alone here?' he asked me.

I shook my head. 'No. My mother and her sister are asleep up there.'

'Yet you are still awake.'

'The knocking woke me,' I said.

'Then I disturbed you. Sorry, but I find the weather uncomfortable here.'

'Where you come from?'

'Came down from the High Place. I had to find shelter. There was light beneath your door.'

I poured the milk into a bowl for him. 'Drink this,' I said. He looked at the bowl uncertainly and then took it from my hands. He sniffed the liquid within and put his tongue into it. Then, he drank. 'From the breast,' he said.

'Milk from a goat,' I replied.

Perhaps he was mad.

I told him he could share my warmth beside the fire and he stretched out beside me. I turned my back on him, curling into the blanket. It was lucky it was so big, but even so, I think his feet were left uncovered. I tried to sleep, but all night I lay awake there, feeling his body tremble beside me.

In the morning my mother and aunt were surprised to find this big man in our cottage. I told them his name, and my mother gave him hers. Such is the custom. 'What have you to trade?' she asked him.

Gadreel smiled his strange smile and tapped his head. 'This,' he said.

My mother laughed. 'Your head? Your hair?'

'No. My knowledge.'

My mother laughed again, her eyes sliding towards mine. She too thought him a little mad. 'And what knowledge is this?'

'One part of a great whole,' he said. 'Others of my family will come after me. They will give you wonderful things.'

'And the price?' This was my aunt, hanging over the edge of the sleeping platform like a great bat.

Gadreel looked up at her. 'Less than the gift,' he said. 'To you.'

He came with me when I went to feed the goats. Other people were about, and I felt proud to have him there. He was tall and good to look at, and no-one but me knew who he was. The storm had passed, but the ground was cold and muddy.

'Take me to the hills,' Gadreel said. 'There.' He pointed at the green slopes, at the place where the trees were, on top.

'That is where we worship,' I said.

'Take me there.'

We climbed the damp, slippery slopes, me tugging at the grass with my hands. At the top, we sat down at the edge of the tree circle to catch our breath, and I said, 'I don't think we have use for your knowledge, Gadreel, whatever it is.'

He looked down at me and raised an eyebrow. 'Oh, you think not?'

I shook my head. 'No, but it doesn't matter.'

'You are wrong.'

'Then tell me the knowledge, so I can find out.'

'My knowledge is of the bitter and the sweet,' he said.

I frowned. 'Taste.'

'No. Not that.'

'Then what?'

He sighed and wrapped his cloak around his knees. 'It is too soon to demonstrate.'

'How can you say that? You could die before you told us.'

'How?'

'That tree behind could fall on you. The ground could shake and grab you. Anything. Tell me.'

'You are very innocent here. Like animals,' he said.

266

'Animals don't build houses,' I said.

'Animals don't have love either. You have shuttered hearts, like animals.'

I did not understand what he said.

'You have been kept in ignorance,' he said. 'Too long. And it is not innocence any more, but stagnation. There are things you must know, to progress, to evolve, to become great...'

When he said these things, it was like the sun coming down to Earth. It made me feel that something indescribable but wonderful was about to happen, but I still didn't understand. Then, he did a very strange thing. He stretched out one hand and touched my face, ran his thumb down my cheek and pinched the flesh of my jaw.

'Why did you do that?' I asked him.

'Because I wanted to. Hold out your hand.'

I did so, wondered what he would do next. He took hold of my fingers and traced a pattern on the palm. It was like being tickled by leaves.

'What does this make you think of?' he asked.

I told him.

Then he ran a finger up the inside of my arm. I could feel it in my shoulder-blade. It was very peculiar.

'You must learn to touch one another,' he said.

'What for?'

He shook his head and dropped my hand, grinning to himself.

Something about his amusement annoyed me, so I pushed my hands against his face. He went very still. I could feel the muscles twisting, the outline of bone. He did not look at me, but kept staring, straight ahead. I kept my hands there until my arms began to ache. Why should we touch one another? What's to be gained from it?

'I could fall upon you like the sky,' he said.

The Watching

These people, they are not men. Something else, but wearing the skins of men, the eyes of men, their hands. We took to collecting the sound of them in our flesh, the aorisms of power, without substance yet entirely substance; an unexplored integrity of sound. In this waveforms of kelestic symmetry, we felt the remote passing into the definite. We saw the wings of change form within the ichor of their sound; a thick smoke, sweet upon the tongue, curling into unimagined shapes that suggested surrender, ecstasy, pain, renewal.

These people, they are not men. We learned their names: Semyaza, Kasday, Azazel, Salamiel, Penemue. These are the ancient names of their native land. In this place, on this Earth of now reality, the names are different, but the old cadences can still be uttered, chanted; they will still vitalise the call.

We stand together in the wildest places of the earth, and form a forest of hands against the sky, stretching up, reaching for what is ours to take and yet never to attain. Our bodies begin to pulsate to a subliminal rhythm and we feel the imminence of contained energy, soon to be released. We dilate our throats to the air and resonate the ancient names.

We convoke them, and they come to use, these people who are not men...

Forever Remain... A Myth

'...the angels showed me, and from them I heard everything, and from them I understood as I saw, but not for this generation, but for a remote one which is to come...'

The Book of Enoch

This is the last time you'll look out there, see that cityscape, take in the hot, breathing smell of the city, feel this flesh on your bones, too hot to wear, too damning to discard. Last time. There are dreams in the clouded glass; not the silvered mirror, the harlot's tool, but the glass in your hand, the nepenthe-draught. Too much to recall. The bitter and the sweet. Swallow it all; a searing cataract of forgetfulness. Think you can lose it all? The doing, the watching, the words that were heard? Too late. Done now, and the inevitable approaches. There is only one escape. Discard the knowledge. Hide. Tomorrow, wake reborn. And the memories will sleep in the dark. Watching. Waiting. For the touch. For the summoning. To come through once more.

About the Author

Storm is the creator of the Wraeththu Mythos, the first trilogy of which was published in the 1980s. However, the influences and inspirations for the Wraeththu world go much further back than that, and continue into the future as she plans more stories for it.

Her other full length works cross genres from science fiction, to dark fantasy, to epic fantasy, to slipstream. She has written over thirty books, including full length novels, novellas, short story collections and non-fiction titles. She had also written nearly a hundred short stories, across genres.

Storm is the founder of Immanion Press, created initially to publish her out-of-print back catalogue, but which evolved into the thriving venture it is today. Her interests include magic and spirituality, Reiki, movies, music and MMOs. Among her many occupations, most of which are unpaid, she runs a Reiki school and a guild called Equilibrium on the EU servers of World of Warcraft. She lives in the Midlands of the UK.

Through the Night Gardens

A Transmedia Project by Storm Constantine

https://throughthenightgardens.wordpress.com/

'Through the Night Gardens' is a new transmedia project by fantasy writer, Storm Constantine.

The chapters of the story will appear as 'episodes' on a new blog, (address above), which are free to read. Each will have an accompanying landscape – created using the 'dimension' building feature from the online role-playing game, Rift – which can be visited and explored in the free-to-play game, should readers wish to do so. Screenshots from the landscapes will also appear within the story chapters.

This project brings a new dimension to storytelling. An audio book and accompanying videos are also being planned, with the chapters of the story eventually being published – with new characters and sub plots – as a full length novel in printed form and eBook.

The first chapter, 'The House on the Red Cliffs', was published in December 2015, with an additional five chapters to follow. Full information, and the story itself, can be found on the blog.

In association with Immanion Press
http://www.immanion-press.com

Also From NewCon Press:

Orcs: Tales of Maras Dantia – Stan Nicholls

The final word in the author's international best-selling Orcs series. Join Stryke, Haskeer, Coilla and the rest of the Wolverines – the toughest, meanest mercenary band around – as they embark on their most dangerous missions yet. The book also features an Orcish interview with the author conducted by the late David Gemmell, and an excised opening chapter from the novel *Weapons of Magical Destruction*. Both are published here for the first time.

Azanian Bridges – Nick Wood

"I read *Bridges* with much pleasure… Chilling and fascinating." – *Ursula K. Le Guin*
In a modern day South Africa where Apartheid still holds sway, Sibusiso Mchunu, a young amaZulu man, finds himself the unwitting focus of momentous events when he comes into possession of a secret that may just offer hope to his entire people. Pursued by the ANC on one side and Special Branch agents on the other, Sibusiso has little choice but to run.
"This is a gut-puncher of a novel; original, brilliantly written, and a page-turner of note." – *Sarah Lotz*

The 1000 Year Reich – Ian Watson

Ian Watson, author of the very first novels in the Warhammer 40K universe, makes a long-anticipated return to military SF with "In Golden Armour", one of three original stories in this fabulous new collection from the man who wrote the screen story to *AI: Artificial Intelligence* for Stanley Kubrick (later filmed by Steven Spielberg). Eighteen stories that vary from action-packed to thought-provoking, from humorous to chilling: Ian Watson at his best.

Lightning Source UK Ltd.
Milton Keynes UK
UKHW041320201118
332651UK00001B/293/P